# FORTUNE

A NOVEL

# FORTUNE

## ELLEN WON STEIL

LAKE UNION
PUBLISHING

Text copyright © 2023 by Ellen Won Steil
All rights reserved.

Published by Lake Union Publishing, Seattle

www.apub.com

Amazon, the Amazon logo, and Lake Union Publishing are trademarks of Amazon.com, Inc., or its affiliates.

ISBN-13: 9781662512100 (paperback)
ISBN-13: 9781662512117 (digital)

Front cover design by Olga Grlic
Back cover design by Ray Lundgren
Cover image: © gyn9037 / Shutterstock; © H Art / Shutterstock;
© Cultura/Ryan Benyi Photography / Getty; © Cédric VT / Unsplash

Printed in the United States of America

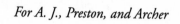

*For A. J., Preston, and Archer*

# PROLOGUE

Mrs. Edie Parker placed the key against the lock.

Her hand shook, the metallic-gold tip scraping the jagged outline of the slot, a maze of negative space separating her from the contents of the safe-deposit box, its putrid-green color making her mouth water. She wasn't sure if it was from apprehension or her crazed appetite to see what her husband had left behind.

A locked box.

Could mean so many things.

A love letter filled with all the words that should have been said. A cherished childhood memento, stowed away for a moment like this. And then there were those items, the ones that rattled one to the core. Terra firma no more, crumbling everything but questions into oblivion.

She steadied her hand, biting her lip with effort until she noticed her sleeve. Her cream suit jacket's sleeve covered in dried rusty blood.

Her husband's blood.

Was it just this morning she had been the one driving? How was that even possible? She could still taste that deep sip of her dark roast. The taste of what life had been before the accident.

She remembered glancing at her husband in the passenger seat. He was nodding off, as he usually did midmorning. Was he getting that old?

She'd checked her own face in the rearview mirror. A few lines here and there like creases in tissue paper, but nothing spectacular. She wasn't like other women, digging their heels in the ground and scorching the earth with refusal. She couldn't wait for it, to achieve the status of becoming the spectacular—spectacularly old.

She was already old. Just the "plain" kind.

"Jonathan." Her voice was gentle.

A raised peppered eyebrow was his response.

"We're almost there—Johnny."

When he opened his eyes, Mr. Jonathan Parker looked youthful for a brief moment as he rubbed them and stretched. He surveyed the cornfields whipping by. The midwestern late-summer wind hot in one fashion and then swirling with cool relief the next.

"Ribbon-cutting ceremonies are for yuppies."

"Ridiculous. We're not young. And we don't live in the city."

"That's right. So let's turn around, shall we?"

He winked. She smothered a smile.

"You worked on this wind farm deal for six months straight with no sleep. We had to postpone our trip to the Maldives, and you want to skip it?"

"Sure. Sure." He put his hands behind his head and leaned back. There it was again, the boyish charm still clinging to the old man's shape. Edie felt the outline around her heart swell a little.

"Mr. Jonathan Parker, of Parker Inc., skips out on his own wind farm's opening day. What will they say?" she taunted.

"They'll say he's a rich old prick."

She laughed and let her head tilt back, taking her eyes off the road for a split second. The car swerved slightly, and she gripped the wheel. It wasn't enough. The car skidded and then fishtailed, sailing into the right edge of the two-lane county highway. Gravel skidded under the tires and ground unforgivingly into its treads.

She slammed on the brakes. They lurched. A cloud of brownish-red dust enveloped the vintage Aston Martin.

"Christ," Jonathan muttered.

Her cup of dark roast had tilted in its cupholder. She slid it back in place.

"Slight mishap."

"Let's not make it a big one." His tone had gone from sarcastic to murky in less than ten words.

"Let's." She reached over and took another long sip before reversing and rejoining the highway.

Jonathan began to rub the back of his neck. Then the top of his head and over his mouth as he looked out again. He seemed to be searching between the rows of the cornfields, each dark slit a slight glimpse into his head.

"Johnny."

"Yes'm."

"Since we've been married for forty-seven years, we have earned the ability to cut through the bull crap. You've got something to tell me."

He peered deeper into the fields, the seat belt cutting into his neck.

"I've known for months."

"Edie."

"Now, what is it?"

"So dark out there," he muttered.

"Johnny?"

A Mack truck hauling granite honked and passed them. Edie jumped. She could see its red-orange bed go by out of the corner of her eye, a mountain of gray rubble and rocks in the back.

"Out where?"

He turned and looked at her. "In here." His eyes were suddenly round and glowing as he looked past her. She followed his gaze and saw it.

A softball-size orb, made up of jagged mineral edges. Millions of years had gone into forming this geological sailing mass before it went through the windshield.

The back of the granite truck disappeared in a cloud of dust.

She heard glass crackle. Not *shatter*, as she would later describe it to the responding officer. Like ice splitting on a frozen pond.

She recalled apologizing over and over to the EMT about the blood on her cream suit, wondering out loud why she had chosen such a color. When she realized none of the blood was her own, she began to ask where Jonathan was. But no one would answer.

No one would look her in the eye.

Later, at the hospital, she was discharged without a scratch. The nurse placed a plastic bag of his personal effects in her hand. His worn leather wallet. Rolex. Cracked phone. But it was the key that caught her eye.

A metal key no more than two inches long. The numbers 202 etched into its round head.

It wasn't a key to a door—it was too small. A safe or safe-deposit box was more likely. She held up the key between her thumb and forefinger, a sudden urge to demand answers from it overwhelming her. Nothing about this morning made any sense. The rational part of her knew there would never be a good-enough reason for why it had happened. But yet . . . all she wanted was for one more word from Johnny. One more gesture. One last touch from him.

The need for it consumed her entire body.

She didn't hear the nurse asking her if she wanted to speak with the hospital liaison about arrangements. The only sounds breaking through were the clicks of her heels against the speckled vinyl floor as she clutched the key in her hand, the edges cutting into her skin.

The Rosemary Hills Credit Union was closing as she knocked on the door. The branch manager appeared behind the glass, looking stunned to see *her* there.

"How can I help you . . . Mrs. Parker?"

She simply held up the key.

The box was presented to her, smaller than she had anticipated. She was left alone; the unforgiving fluorescent lights of the bank vault flickered and dimmed.

She inserted the key. Each notch she could feel click into place as she slid inward. When she heard it unlock, she felt bile creep onto the back of her tongue and slip away. Closing her eyes, she lifted the top and flipped it over. Her chin fell toward her chest, and she felt it pulsating.

She let her eyes look.

The box was empty. With one exception: a single photo positioned facedown. It looked as though it had been recklessly cut out—an asymmetrical rectangle. Like a shape that had fallen out of a Picasso painting. She didn't touch it, afraid to disturb its very presence, instead studying it from where she stood.

The words *Baby Ava?* were written on the shiny white backing, the question mark looping up her throat as it caught a small guttural sound. And then there were the names. Three names scrawled like a list of grocery items:

*Cleo Song*
*Alexandra Collins*
*Jemma Slater*

She reached in and turned the photo over.

The image assaulted her eyes, climbing up and jerking around any decent thought she'd ever had. Her jaw tightened, her skin stretching over the bone as she gripped the sides of the metal box. She blinked up into the flickering lights, her mouth pinched shut.

# CHAPTER 1

*September 17, 2022: Lottery drawing*

White picnic tables dotted the clearing in Avalon Park, where just two weeks earlier it had been occupied by a full-on Labor Day carnival revel. Each bright table a clean marker going against the grain of the grass. A geometric ensemble meant for the people of Rosemary Hills to gather at on this most momentous of nights.

Tonight, a winner would be crowned.

Bulbous yellow lights were strewn along the trees, somehow romanticizing the increasingly tense atmosphere. No one was jumping around in celebration. The crowd's energy had the same feel as a congregation. Low, polite murmurs before the preacher began the service.

A podium had even been set up. Necks strained to see if anything else had been placed upon it. The news crews had arrived well before noon. Police had blockaded them a good hundred feet behind the last row of picnic tables. Reporters cleared their throats and conducted strange vocal exercises—who knew when they would be covering something this big again?

It was homecoming night, but most of the high schoolers had forgone going to dinner before the dance. *This* was far more interesting than fumbling through a mediocre forty-dollar meal, trying to make conversation with their dates.

Yet somehow . . . somehow something so physically small yielded such command over them all.

Tiny clusters. Tiny clusters of cells, made up of microscopic chains that contained the power to produce big results.

*Big truths.*

By 6:45, the park was packed, a sea of an entire town ready to finally meet its maker. The rest of the town was dark and unoccupied—the site of the DNA lottery drawing was the beckoning light shining brightly, a nucleus calling out for all to join.

Three women sat huddled together near the last row, their pasts tying their hands behind their backs as they looked on with quiet urgency.

*Just get through tonight. Get through tonight.*

On the other side of it, the lives they had worked so hard to build could continue on.

A glass box containing thousands of names on white papers was wheeled out to the center of the podium. The mayor cleared her throat and excitedly began to spin them around, turning the handle with tauntingly deliberate circles.

But she was interrupted, her expression falling from jubilant to stunned as the chief of police whispered in her ear.

Her mouth met the microphone: "We have a match. A DNA match."

———

https://DNAlottery/tracker.com
Date: September 1, 2022
Number of Entries: 861
Days Until Drawing: 16

*If you are interested in participating in the Rosemary Hills DNA lottery, please fill out the intake form below. A representative will reach out to you within 1–2 business days. Remember: you must be 18 years or older and provide proof of residency within the last 20 years.

Comments:

"What a waste of money . . . you'd think they would find a better way to utilize it. Like help with child hunger in America. 12 million children in America go hungry each year!"

—Susan H.

"Spare us the bleeding hearts, Susan H.! I'll take the money. LOL."

—J. Golding

"How does this work exactly? I let some bureaucrat take spit out of my mouth with a Q-tip and then I have a chance to be a billionaire?"

—Riley M.

"Why would she want to do this? What's in it for her? Anyone else care more about that?"

—Justine Q.

"So . . . does anyone think this is wrong? Like is it even legal?"

—Marianne T.

"Does anyone else think this is about Baby Ava?"

—Anonymous

# CHAPTER 2
## CLEO

*August 29, 2022*

Cleo Song immediately regretted letting the woman with the ugly hat switch rows with her. The droning of the plane's engine, coupled with the sounds of flushing and the constant opening and shutting of the bathroom door, plus the sweet, unsavory smell mixture of cleaner and unmentionables, created a cloud of remorse in her head.

"Do you mind?" the woman had asked. It hadn't really been a question, now that she thought about it.

She had just finished settling her six-year-old son, Rockwell, into his seat, his blue-and-neon-orange headphones on, iPad ready to go with his favorite movie. She could recite *Trolls* by heart now.

"Mind?"

Rockwell glanced up as the woman hovered in the aisle, probably having caught sight of the hat. A straw panama lined with leopard print, adorned with a silk floral scarf. Cleo instinctively placed her hand on his soft head.

"I have such a fear of flying, dear. And I just know that if I sit in that last row, it will be the last of my nerves."

The woman took her hat off and began to fan herself.

*Dear.* She couldn't have been that much older than her. But Cleo found herself being agreeable, engaging in the autopilot role of "nice

Asian lady." Where would she be in this world if she didn't have the approval of the woman in the ugly hat?

"*Thank* you," the woman said as Cleo shuffled Rockwell out of their row and into the rigid seats of the very last one. Missing armrest. No reclining seats.

It was going to be a long flight. Even if it was only from Chicago to Des Moines.

Rockwell nudged her gently. "Mommy? Can I watch it now?"

"Yes—yes, sweetheart." She placed the headphones back over his ears and swept his light-brown hair out of his eyes. He would need a haircut this week, before school started. She wondered if he even realized the finality of their trip. To him it was probably just another visit to his grandmother.

But it wouldn't be *just* that.

Who was she to judge? It hadn't even hit her until they were getting their tickets. The kiosk had frozen when she'd hurriedly tried to retrieve them. She was already antsy when they trudged through the long line and finally reached the airline's counter.

"Cleo Song?" the agent had asked.

"Walk—I mean . . . yes. Song."

The agent looked down at her passport.

"I haven't had that changed yet. But here. This is my updated driver's license." She slid it across the counter, her face stoic in the picture.

"And this is your . . . ?" The agent peered down at Rockwell.

"Son. Rockwell. Rockwell Walker."

It was the first time she had said it out loud. Her son now had a different last name from hers. She hadn't expected this to cause the back of her eyes to sting. It had been her choice, after all, to change her name. To change where they lived.

To change everything.

The plane had taken off, and a flight attendant handed her a cocktail napkin.

"Something to drink?"

"Fresca, please." She pointed to Rockwell. "He's fine." She reached into her bag and pulled out an apple juice box, along with her phone. Once she got her Fresca, she took a drink and slid in her earbuds. First she dealt with a couple of emails and a text message from her mother asking when they would be arriving, and then she read a handful of articles on people.com. Her cup was almost empty, so she chewed on a few pieces of ice.

She was about to close the browser when she refreshed the screen to find a new headline: Widow of Parker Inc. Founder Announces DNA Lottery.

Parker Inc. Cleo was familiar with the name. Not because it was the equivalent of the Apple brand in the energy world, but because it came from her hometown of Rosemary Hills, Iowa. Everyone there knew of Jonathan Parker. She wasn't aware he had passed, as the last month had been especially . . . busy. She opened the story to find a *Today Show* video link at the top and played it. The volume was so loud she looked around to make sure she hadn't disturbed nearby passengers, even with her earbuds in.

Hoda Kotb's pleasant face beamed with energy as she read the latest story.

"After the sudden death of Parker Inc. founder Jonathan Parker, his surviving wife, Edie Parker, made a surprising announcement early this morning. It was almost a month ago that Jonathan died in a freak auto accident involving a free-falling rock from a passing truck. Well, less than two hours ago, Edie announced Parker Inc. would be funding a DNA lottery. Now, just what is this DNA lottery? Here in the studio with us to explain is NBC News correspondent Jo Ling Kent."

"Thank you, Hoda. As bizarre as it may sound, this DNA lottery is happening. According to Mrs. Parker's statement released by her attorney, voluntary DNA submissions can be made in exchange for a ticket, which is then eligible for a drawing. What does the winner receive? One million shares of Parker Inc. stock. Now, with the value of Parker Inc. stock at forty-six dollars a share . . . well, you do the math. That's right.

A value of forty-six million dollars. Although there are some stipulations. Only those with proof of residency in Rosemary Hills, Iowa, can participate. And half of the winnings must be given to a charity—of the winner's choosing, of course."

Hoda smiled and shook her head slightly.

"Wow. Forty-six million dollars for your DNA? If I were waking up in Rosemary Hills this morning, I would be pinching myself. How exactly does one give a DNA submission?"

Jo Ling Kent looked down at her notes at their round table and then back up, not missing a beat. "We did ask Mrs. Parker's team about that, and DNA will be collected through a cheek swab or blood sample."

"And why exclusive to Rosemary Hills, Iowa, residents?"

"Nothing conclusive on that yet, Hoda. What we do know is that both Jonathan and Edie have ties to Rosemary Hills. Their primary residence is on the outskirts of this Des Moines area suburb, and they do own a significant amount of land."

"Has Mrs. Parker said *why* she is doing this?"

"Her attorney says the statement is all they are revealing for now. But with people left with so many questions about this unprecedented lottery, we are definitely hoping to find out more."

"That's for sure. Here to discuss the legal implications of such a DNA lottery is NBC legal correspondent . . ."

*No . . . it can't be about that.*

Cleo's phone slid out of her hand and dropped down the side of her seat. Rockwell poked her arm.

*Can it? And what if it is . . . what if the truth is finally coming out?*

"Do you know if Grandma Ji-Yeon will have dinner waiting for us?" She pulled her earbuds out, her fingers suddenly numb and thick. *We did the unthinkable . . .*

"Mommy?"

She turned her chin down at his placid face, his expression furrowed. "I'm not sure, Rocky sweetie. Maybe. I would think so."

"Good." He seemed utterly satisfied with this news and returned to his movie.

She retrieved her phone, gripped it forcefully, and tapped it a few times against the armrest. The flight attendant returned, instructing everyone to prepare for landing.

*Landing? Didn't we just take off?*

# CHAPTER 3

## EDIE

*August 29, 2022*

"Edie, the governor wants to speak with you."

"Tell her I'm busy."

"This is the third time she has asked for you."

Edie's steely silence and rapid head turn toward her attorney was answer enough. Robin Khaled had been the Parkers' attorney for the last two decades. She had dealt mainly with Jonathan over the years. But now, with Edie in charge, she seemed to tread lightly.

"The meeting is about to start here soon. Can I bring you anything?"

"I can manage, Robin."

"Coffee? Tea?"

"I don't need you to be my housekeeper. My diligent attorney will do." Edie stood up and brushed off the top of her navy skirt. She went to the tray set out by Belinda (her actual housekeeper) and poured herself a glass of water.

"Who all's coming?"

Robin shifted on the oversize leather ottoman toward Edie. "Ambrose and Lennox."

"Both of them?"

"Yes."

"This would be the first time all of us have convened."

She nodded.

The meeting was to take place in the Green Room. One of the largest rooms in the Parker home, it boasted a vaulted cathedral ceiling, bookcases lining the entire north and south walls, imported stone flooring from Belgium, and a towering Carrera fireplace, which was the focal point upon entry. Jonathan never liked to flaunt their wealth too much outside their home—well, homes. But within the privacy of their four walls, all bets were off.

And Edie now lived in it alone.

Minus some of the staff she'd kept such as Belinda, the house felt hollow. She was beginning to wonder how much longer she could roam the halls—every nook and cranny contained some memory of Johnny. Shortly after the accident, she'd discovered a Nutter Butter wrapper that had fallen under his desk. They had been his go-to snack when he was elbow deep in work.

She'd felt her throat tighten up before throwing it away. She had yet to cry. Not even the funeral (which had been kept very small and private) had drawn up tears. There had been too many questions and tasks to deal with after the accident. News outlets had dived in like vultures, wanting to get her take on the random tragedy of Jonathan Parker, the first glimpse or snapshot of the billionaire widow. She was angry at first, more than anything. Angry that Johnny was gone and furious that anyone would try to profit from this.

And then there were the board members.

To her they were a singular voice that streamed in from a conference room in New York City every few days. "Checking in" on her—or really, keeping their grasp on her. The moment the news had gotten out about the accident, Parker Inc. stock plummeted. Points were everything to these fools. It was amazing how different Johnny's philosophy on business had been compared to theirs. Perhaps that was why they had gone into complete alarm over it all.

Johnny *was* Parker Inc.

"You do understand what this means, Edie?"

Eight blurry faces had zeroed in on her, each one framed in their video conference. She recalled never feeling more alone than right then.

"Of course," she'd answered.

There was a ninth face missing. One she had grown accustomed to loathing. Someone considered to be almost *essential* to Parker Inc., as Johnny had been. At least that was how Johnny had deemed it. Perhaps more important than she ever felt comfortable with. A constant shadow to her husband, always lingering like a rope that never untethered. Johnny had kept a specific "roster" over the years of those he could count on. But it was this particular player whom he trusted most above all the others.

"Does anyone know the whereabouts of Mr. Oliver?" one of the faces asked.

"Kane?" she corrected with a broken informality.

"Yes . . . Mr. Kane Oliver."

Hearing his name made her shoulders stiffen. She wished she had severed him from her husband's life years ago . . . when she'd had the chance. If only she had gone with her instincts. But at times he had been a steady confidant to Johnny. Maybe that was why Johnny believed Parker Inc. needed him. Maybe that was why she chose to ignore Kane Oliver all this time.

"He is indisposed at the moment," another board member announced.

*Indisposed . . . of course.*

"Well, he is needed immediately. This is a crisis."

More talk among blurry faces meandered in and out of her ears.

She had hung up when it was all over and gone straight outside, Belinda calling after her, but she ignored her faint pleas.

Rosemary Hill's chief of police, Soren Lennox, was the first to enter the Green Room now. He was slight in stature—without his uniform, one would guess him to be something innocuous as a bait-shop owner, not the head of a police department. He had the most shrewlike face

Edie had ever seen. But he had always been loyal and a good friend to Johnny.

"Edie," he said, taking off his hat.

"Please. No sympathy. Not from you. I've had all I can take."

"Holding up okay?"

"I'm fine," she said, bobbing her head robotically. "You know Robin." She gestured toward the seat by the fireplace.

Robin stood up and shook hands with Chief Lennox just as Liam Ambrose entered.

"Apologies for being a little late," he said. His red hair seemed to light up even more with the glow of the fire.

"No need. Please sit. I would like this meeting to be a quick one." She took the seat nearest the fire.

"Soren, this is Liam Ambrose. Jonathan's private investigator of many years."

The two men exchanged modest pleasantries.

"I'm sure there's a reason we've never met," Chief Lennox said gruffly.

Ambrose shrugged. "Jonathan could be very . . . self-contained about certain things."

Edie closed her eyes for longer than a blink. She turned to Robin. "Well?"

Robin sat up straighter. "Thank you for joining us, Chief Lennox and Mr. Ambrose. I . . . we"—she motioned to Edie—"thought it best if we all got together, in light of Edie's recent announcement this morning."

Chief Lennox twirled his hat around in his hands. "I've got to cut to the chase here, Edie. What is this all about?"

Edie looked over to Ambrose before taking a deep breath. "Perhaps Ambrose could enlighten you more?"

"Yes, Ambrose. *Please* do," he said in a stony tone.

Ambrose placed his fingertips together and leaned forward. "As I'm sure you could guess, Chief Lennox, this is more than just a giveaway of stocks, if that's what you even want to call it. This is closing in on some unfinished business."

"Unfinished business?" Chief Lennox looked bewildered.

"Yes. There was a certain . . . matter that Jonathan seemed to want resolved. And now that he's gone, Edie here is trying to finish that."

"And how is this DNA lottery going to accomplish that?" Chief Lennox protested. "You know this thing was only just announced and it's already getting out of hand. Our office has been inundated with calls and emails all day. People lining up, asking to get their cheeks swabbed or arms poked. Some people are even bringing in Dixie cups of their spit. What are my officers supposed to do with this?"

Edie stood up and went to one of the wall-size windows overlooking the east field. "Where there's fortune, there are fools," she whispered.

"Huh?"

"Nothing. Something someone used to say." She rubbed her arms and turned back to the gathering by the fireplace. "Ambrose—please continue."

"I'm sure you're familiar with DNA databases, Chief Lennox? I don't have to—or want to—school you on something you already know about."

Chief Lennox sniffed. "Of course I know about that."

"Well then, you may have heard how asking for communities to provide—*willingly* provide—DNA samples has helped solve some of the most unsolvable crimes in recent years."

"You may have to *enlighten* me more on that, Ambrose."

He leaned in closer. "The Golden State Killer. Notorious for dozens of rapes and murders in California over decades. Eluded authorities until they finally were able to nab him a few years ago. Do you know how they were able to do that?"

Chief Lennox crossed his arms and leaned back.

"A DNA search very similar to the one Edie has set forth—minus the pot of gold at the end. These samplings, in addition to existing databases, can narrow in on a suspect. Think about it. AncestryDNA,

23andMe? Millions of Americans are eagerly and freely giving their DNA already."

"So you're saying—" He stopped and cleared his throat.

"Yes, Chief. We're trying to solve a crime."

The room went still.

"And you think this will really work?"

Ambrose nodded once. "Theoretically. The idea of gathering DNA samples is nothing completely novel. Truro, Massachusetts, almost two decades ago—police tried it to find the person responsible for stabbing a forty-six-year-old mother to death."

"Well, damn," Chief Lennox said quietly. He raised his eyebrows. "Does Mr. Oliver know about this?"

Edie shifted her gaze to Robin.

Robin placed her hand up with her pen poised in the air. "Kane Oliver is not involved in this. More importantly, there are legal implications to consider. While we are asking for completely voluntary samplings, there are those who argue this is still an infringement of civil rights."

"How so? If you want to give your saliva freely?" Ambrose asked.

"The idea behind it is that the omission of a sampling inadvertently makes someone look guilty."

"Well then, does that idea even have standing? Say, in a court of law?"

"That's always the question," Robin replied with a delicate smirk.

Chief Lennox pivoted to Edie. "So that's why you brought me in on this, isn't it?"

Edie couldn't help but smile. Johnny had been right all these years—Lennox was no dummy.

"We would like your cooperation in assisting Edie with this matter. We know there will be backlash, controversy. The media has already swooped down on this, bringing in legal experts on talk show segments, and social media has of course gone viral with its sentiments. Not to mention the local media attention."

"My cooperation?"

Robin stared at him blankly. "Yes. Your cooperation would mean backing by the Rosemary Hills Police Department."

His eyes began to narrow; his hat twisted in his hand.

Edie paced toward him from her spot by the window. "Johnny counted on you for matters in the past, Soren. There's no need to pretend in front of me or any of the others here."

His head raised up sharply.

"And I believe it went both ways, if I remember correctly."

He nodded faintly, locking eyes with her for a second before looking away, the skin by his eyes seeming to tighten.

———

The meeting ended shortly after 8:00 p.m. Belinda escorted the three visitors away as Edie remained by the fire.

She twirled the emerald pendant around her neck. Johnny had given it to her shortly after their wedding day, when he had next to nothing in the bank. She had worn it proudly, couldn't care less that it was a peon of a jewel size.

It was when Johnny made his first million that she had gifted him in return—the same type of stone but embedded in a thick gold ring. She made him promise never to take the ring off.

"That's ridiculous, Edie. Of course it has to come off sometime," he'd complained after the novelty and romance of the moment had worn off.

"No, it doesn't. Now promise."

He had rolled his eyes and laughed. "I won't promise. But I won't take it off either," he had said and then kissed her forehead.

The Green Room was silent, minus the wind that had picked up and bayed through the halls like in some Charlotte Brontë novel. Only Edie was no romantic heroine. She was simply a woman who had loved her husband deeply. A man she knew every fiber and marrow of.

Or at least she thought she had.

*Baby Ava. Baby Ava. Baby Ava.*

She shut the doors to the Green Room.

Clutching her hand to her chest, she leaned against the wall and slid down. She had been keeping "such a brave face" for so long, holding her breath underwater. Until she couldn't take it any longer, coming up for air to let all her anguish out.

She could hear and see it all over again.

The crackling glass, sudden and sharp like a high-pitched squeal.

The first blood she noticed was on her coffee cup. Mixing with the spilled dark roast, the blood and coffee circled together like water and oil.

It was the quiet that scared her.

She looked over and saw the rock lodged in where her husband's face used to be. Bits of bone fragment and cartilage popped out like confetti, scattered across the windshield into some grotesque painting.

She shook her head fiercely, shaking the image out of her mind as she slapped her hand over her mouth. The hot air sucked in and out as she stifled piercing cries.

# CHAPTER 4

---

## ALEX

*August 29, 2022*

Alex Mitchell was a damn good divorce attorney.

She knew this not as a boastful or arrogant thought but as a fact. She liked facts and stuck to them. She had a nearly perfect record when it came to representing her clients—or it would've been perfect if it hadn't been for that bitch of a judge who'd had a grudge against her ever since her second year of law school. Her name was synonymous with "divorce" in Rosemary Hills. If you wanted it done right, you called Alex. Fact.

She was in the middle of one of the most expensive and lucrative divorce negotiations of her career, involving the owner of a popular sporting goods franchise and the town mayor, a real estate mogul. Fact.

Yet all she could think about in that moment was how her mother would react if she didn't respond to her text within the next five minutes.

Her mother still held that *Don't mess with me, young lady* air over her, even though Alex was thirty-five.

"The accrued interest on that mutual fund should clearly be characterized as marital property . . ."

Why aren't you texting back, Alexandra? We are meeting for lunch.

"Alex?"

**Do not be late.**

"Counselor?"

She turned her phone over and grimaced. "We both know that's utter bullshit."

"Are you serious?"

"*Counselor*," she added.

Griffin Alvarez hid a smile. They had sparred for years—respectfully—but he had learned when she began to get feisty that he'd better watch out.

"Maybe we should move on from the mutual fund."

"Great," Alex answered and hit him back with a vaudeville smile of her own.

She lightly touched her client's wrist to reassure her. Mrs. Janet Vogel (known as "Vogel the Mogul" around town) was not only Rosemary Hills's first female mayor but also owned practically half the commercial real estate in the Des Moines metro area. Alex admired her as a businesswoman and because she'd had the gumption to kick her husband to the curb after Mr. Vogel's salacious dealings with her barely-of-age niece. Many women in Rosemary Hills would have looked the other way before considering divorce because of the still-lingering and utterly outdated stigma of being "a woman on her own." It was as though a rain cloud from the 1950s hovered over them all.

Her mother would have disagreed with Mrs. Vogel's decision.

"We both know Mrs. Vogel came into the marriage with significant assets. It was, in fact, she who lent Mr. Vogel a significant amount of money to start his sporting goods franchise. The fact is she accrued most of her real estate property and assets long before the marriage."

"Yes. But Mr. Vogel helped manage said properties."

She smiled. "Mr. Vogel's name is not on any of the titles or deeds of these properties. And such management was actually done quite poorly."

Griffin shifted in his seat. "Poorly? By what standards?"

"By the standards of not screwing the property managers."

"Adultery is not a factor in this issue."

"Yes, but actual ownership of the asset is. And such conduct certainly doesn't show that."

"A judge would think otherwise, Alex."

"We could do that. Yes. If trial is what you want, I'm ready to go tomorrow if necessary."

Mr. Vogel looked stricken by this idea. Griffin cleared his throat roughly.

"Let's resume after lunch then?"

———

Alex hurriedly parked her car in front of Fig & Olive, the upscale lunch spot her mother had chosen. She was about to climb out but then swung her face in front of the rearview mirror for a quick makeup and hair check. Better to spend two minutes fixing it than hear her mother lament over any flaw for twenty. She shook her hands in her honey-brown hair and gave her lips a smear of coral-tinted balm. She looked at the time.

*Dammit.*

Maud Collins waited for no one.

Which was why it was no surprise to Alex that she found her mother starting to rise from her seat at the table, like some demigoddess ascending from her throne.

"I'm sorry, Mother. I came as fast as I could."

Maud was silent. This was never a good thing.

"Please, sit back down."

She descended back into her chair stiffly. The mini white crystal chandeliers, robin's-egg-blue linen tables, and sleek white decor did her mother no favors in making her appear any less bitchy.

"Did you wait long?" Alex took a sip of ice water and gave the approaching server a quick hand signal under her chin. The server wisely detoured.

Maud removed the cloth napkin from her plate and gently placed it on her lap. "Not too long," she finally uttered, the tone of her voice on the velvety side. Always low and cool, as Alex liked to think of it.

"Should we order?"

"Not yet. Violet is coming. She's finishing up her voice lesson."

Alex felt her neck tighten. Her temples pulsated.

"I didn't realize she was back from summer camp," she said softly.

There was hardly a time it seemed Violet wasn't away at some camp or another, not to mention the private boarding school she went off to each year.

Maud's mouth tensed.

"Music camp. Not summer camp. She didn't spend the summer splashing in some *E. coli*–infested lake. She is *very* advanced now in Chopin."

The mere mention of Chopin gave Alex a tension headache and had her recalling the hours she'd spent sitting stiffly on the dark-brown Baldwin piano bench, her bottom completely numb from staying there so long. Until she had perfected a piece, she was not allowed to move from that position.

There were more consequences than the silent chill from Maud.

She tried hard to forget those.

"Enough about camp." Maud tucked her chin-length jet-blue-black hair behind her ears, her pearl earrings shining like some sort of spotlight. "Did you see the news this morning, Alexandra?"

Alex scanned the menu. She was sick of beet salad. Her mother ordered that every time they came here. *If beets could kill.*

"The news?" Maud prodded, mouth moving into a tight line.

"I didn't have time. I thought I told you, this case is insanity. I was up most of the night preparing for today's negotiation. We should probably order—I have to get back soon."

Maud dipped her hand in her red leather handbag and came out with her phone in one fluid motion.

"Here. Have a look then." She slid the phone across the table to Alex like a Vegas blackjack dealer handing out cards.

Alex scrolled through the brightly lit screen. Her temples were now engaging in a full-on war with her blood vessels. Each word of the news article brought them closer to bursting.

*This can't be happening . . . why now?*

Her throat went dry. The clinking of silverware in the dining room sounded far off, as if she were hearing it all from the outside.

*Keep it together, Alexandra.*

She took another sip of water and focused on setting the glass back down as steadily as possible.

*Maybe it's nothing. Maybe you're assuming all too much.*

"This is the biggest news to ever hit Rosemary Hills. Why didn't you text me earlier?" Alex asked quietly.

Maud shrugged with an eye roll. "I figured you're an attorney. You probably read the news."

"Mother . . ."

"Interesting, though, isn't it? I can't imagine participating in something so garish."

"Well, do we know—"

"I will tell you what we know. We know Mrs. Edie Parker has lost her husband, one of the richest men in America. She has now lost her mind. We know she's engaging in some public stunt, and now our town will have to deal with the publicity and aftermath. It will be a circus, is what this will be."

Maud looked the menu up and then down. "I'm getting the beet salad."

*Christ.*

The server came back and took their orders. Alex settled on the cauliflower soup and green tea. A strong coffee probably would have suited her—better yet, a large glass of pinot noir. She observed Maud cautiously as they ate in relative silence. Each small piece of beet, cut like a piece of steak, slipped in between Maud's lips with precision.

*Focus. Focus on what you can control . . . focus on work.*

Alex took a few spoonfuls of soup before texting her assistant, Hattie.

**Have the depositions ready and in the exact order I color-coded. Don't mess this up.**

She trusted Hattie. The fact that she let Hattie do anything for her meant there was extreme trust. But even that trust came with instructions.

No one could do what Alex did.

No one lived every day the way she could. *That* she was certain of. It was one of the facts she carried around on her chest and not her sleeve.

"Violet," Maud crooned. "You're very late, honey. Take the chair next to your sister."

Her younger sister. Her *baby* sister. She would be eighteen soon. It was often difficult for Alex to look at her. She was the opposite of Alex. There was a lithe way she carried her arms, her entire carriage. Undisturbed. Like a cherub of tranquility and wonder at the way the world worked through deep, deep rose-colored glasses. She was a virgin, not just in the traditional sense but in being unscathed by the barbs of life—even those from Maud. Alex got the sense that even when this naivete was broken someday, Violet would come out the other side untouched.

That gave Alex comfort.

She tersely nodded and started to say hello to her, but Violet would not have that. She slid her arms around her neck and gave her a kiss next to her ear. Alex felt her neck tighten again.

"Sissy. I missed you! How's the case coming along?"

Violet threw herself back in the chair as Maud sniffed. She grabbed a piece of cranberry bread from the basket and took a large bite.

"Mmmm. These are still warm. You have to try this, Alex!"

Alex shook her head. "I need to be heading back."

Violet's light dimmed the slightest bit. But she bounced back, slapping the arms of her chair.

"Can you believe what they're saying about that DNA lottery? I'm sure you've heard about it—"

Maud put her hand on Violet's wrist. "Yes. And we don't need to talk about it anymore. It's pure nonsense."

"That much money? And there's only, like, what . . . a few thousand of us in Rosemary Hills?"

"Sixty thousand," Alex corrected. "Not counting previous residents." She took a sip of her tea and handed her credit card to the server.

"That's not even the best part! Everyone is already saying this is about Baby Ava."

*Baby Ava . . . it's starting already.*

"Enough," said Maud.

"Why would she even care about that? Some dead—"

"Quiet, Violet."

Violet stopped and stared back at Maud. She wasn't afraid to keep looking. Alex had so many moments just like this growing up. But for Alex, there was no recourse other than to look away each time. She had never dared to have any sort of standing with this woman.

By far the biggest difference between her and Violet.

Maud gave a compulsory smile. "You haven't ordered yet, Violet. Why don't you take a look at the menu?"

The three women sat hushed.

# CHAPTER 5

---

## JEMMA

*August 29, 2022*

"Don't tell me," Jemma said.

"Yes. Another one." Peter rolled his eyes.

"Could they be any more obvious?"

She sighed as he slid a memorandum in her hands.

"Why . . . why? *Why* do they care what I wear to senate hearings?"

She would be the first to admit she wasn't the most conservative of dressers. She had breasts and a tight ass and was proud of it. Everything that needed to be covered was covered—wasn't that all that mattered?

"Perhaps a quarter inch of cleavage was just too much this time." Peter chuckled.

"Peeeter! This isn't funny," she whined, shaking her shoulders a little.

She was a coin of a woman. One second a graceful, intelligent state senator, the next a whining adolescent who could rival her daughter.

District Sixteen was the toughest state senate seat to run for—notorious for being high profile, high pressure, and high gossip. Yet Jemma Danowski had hung on to it for the last four years.

And she had every intention of doing more than just hanging on for the next four.

She had ridden the storm of controversy that had slammed her from day one. Was it the state budget cuts on public education funding?

The lack of response to low-income families during the summer floods in Polk County two years ago? Her voting record?

No. Far more imperative issues like her hair color; her supposed "youth" in the state senate, overrun with older white gentlemen; her parenting style to her teenage daughter; her remarriage; and oh, of course, the vagina between her legs.

Even Peter, her office admin, was a controversy. To Jemma, Peter was the smartest fresh-out-of-undergrad intern she had ever worked with. His wit was sharper than knives, and his ability to think two steps ahead always astounded her—he had to have some continuous game of chess running in his head. He was warm and generous, funny as hell to share a few margaritas with after work. And he identified as nonbinary.

Her office had received hate mail and death threats for a month—until Jemma released a public statement saying she was ready and willing to fully prosecute. The hate mail dwindled, but the haze of ignorance remained.

"Ignore it. Waste of energy, remember?"

Peter winked with one of his jade-colored eyes and retreated back to his desk.

She sank into her chair and threw the paper into the recycling bin.

"I hate that you're right," she scoffed. "And I hate that your lashes are *still* prettier than mine, even after I got lash extensions!" she called after him.

Her phone rang. "Jemma Danowski speaking." Her tone switched back to professional.

"Mom."

Her shoulders relaxed and tensed at the same time. "Poppy, what is it? I'm still working."

"You said my new track leggings would be here by this afternoon. They're not."

"Well then, maybe they'll arrive tomorrow instead."

"But I need them!" Poppy yelped with desperation.

"You have three other pairs."

"Mom. This. Is. Serious."

"Poppy—if you are so concerned about this latest major catastrophe in your life, I suggest you reach out to Jeff Bezos himself. Now, I will be home in an hour."

"You suck!"

*Beep, beep, beep.*

"Poppy . . . ," Jemma hissed under her breath.

She dragged the phone in her hand across the desk. Whatever happened to the little girl with red ribbons in her hair who blew her kisses and put bandages on Mommy's ouchies?

Fifteen years is what happened.

*It's a girl!* the ultrasound tech had said excitedly. Naturally she would say it with enthusiasm. Had it been a lizard, she would have announced, *It's a lizard!* just the same.

Jemma had been twenty years old, a junior at the University of Minnesota studying political science, when she saw those two pink lines. Owen, her boyfriend at the time (then fiancé, then husband, now ex-husband), took it surprisingly well. They never should have married, but it was what "all parties involved" thought best. Those parties included both sets of their parents.

*Oh, a girl!* she had replied, trying to match the excitement. But on the inside she wasn't sure how she felt. Disappointment at first, mixed with a rush of terror. What would a girl think of her? Would she be good enough? What had she done that would ever impress her—be anything to look up to? She wasn't ready to be a mother to anyone, let alone a girl.

As the white exam-table paper crinkled and rode up her bottom, she vowed then and there to herself—to her baby, to God (even though she grew up a fair-weather Lutheran)—that she *would* be enough. And they would *never* be one of those mother-daughter duos who bickered and argued over rubbish.

She was sure God was laughing somewhere at her. At least about the fighting part.

After years of Jemma being a preschool teacher, she and Owen had looked at each other one day and decided enough was enough. It had to have been the simplest divorce of all time. Poppy was thankfully young enough where she seemed to adjust well. And Henry was just an infant. She became a single mom of two kids and found herself at square one. She finished her undergrad, snatched a job at a PR firm in Des Moines, and then met Finch.

Finch—a proud geek who got in on digital marketing early—had built a successful SEO company shortly after they married. Poppy was ten at the time and easily clung on to Finch. They moved to Rosemary Hills, and Jemma moved on to the state senate.

And then Poppy decided to get her period.

"Peter!" Jemma called out as she tossed some files and her laptop in her bag. "I'm heading home!"

She was about to throw her phone in when a text message popped up. It was from Finch.

**Did you hear anything from Dr. S yet?**

Even through the glow of his electronic words, she could sense his poking optimism—which only aggravated her already-annoyed mood brought on by Poppy. She started to text something snarky back but then thought better of it.

Snarkiness wasn't going to bring on good news from the doctor.

*God knows we need it.*

# THE STORY OF BABY AVA

**September 2013**

They named her Baby Avalon. The police did, or perhaps it was the media. Nonetheless, she was found near Avalon Park and had a name, which over time was shortened to Baby Ava. Tiny bones wrapped in a tartan scarf. Six to nine years ago—that's what forensics had come back with.

*No evidence of trauma.*

A rarity for anyone on this earth. To leave with no trauma suffered. Not a scratch on the body, ego, or dreams. Maybe that tiny body was lucky in that way.

Hundreds gathered in Rosemary Hills for the memorial service. It was the kind of thing people left their homes for, out of a mixture of curiosity, boredom, and a need for something meaningful. *Yes, I was there. I was there to send off that poor soul, because who else would?*

The jogger who found her—because it was always a jogger—was on a run with his dog that fall morning. Avalon Park was known for its thick woods and trails weaving in and around the river, frequented by many citizens of Rosemary Hills. The authorities would later say it was astonishing how long it took for the body to be discovered, considering this fact.

As the story usually goes, the dog (a retriever mix) took off from the owner and began to dig at the bottom of a tree. The tree's roots were almost exposed from the high waters and abnormal erosions of the last two summers.

Baby Ava was ready to make her appearance.

Her discovery left a pin in the hearts of Rosemary Hills. A prick that would grow deeper and bleed heavier the longer her story remained unsolved. For who could leave such an innocent soul like that? Such purity—the untouchable had been touched in the worst way possible.

She represented those who had suffered loss. Those who had been injured and forgotten. Those who remained lost and begged to be discovered. Even though she had left this earth without suffering, her ending deserved justice.

Her evidence box in the storage room of the Rosemary Hills Police Department was scanty at best. The scarf was sealed up in a bag, along with DNA samples from the remains. A few files held interviews, including the jogger's and the responding officer's.

But there was no one else to turn to for answers. It was as though Baby Ava had appeared out of nowhere. A conjuring for this town to obsess over.

And obsess people did.

Years passed with no new leads. Nothing to add to that roomy box. Just the occasional local news story highlighting the anniversary of her discovery.

And every year on that same September day, all windows in Rosemary Hills lit a solitary candle in her memory.

She was not just an abandoned baby. She was the child of a town that desperately needed answers. It was *their* child who had been lost. *Their* hearts that had been broken.

And she would be redeemed.

# CHAPTER 6

---

## EDIE

*Ten days after the accident: August 11, 2022*

She had waited after opening the lockbox before telling anyone.

She was still in her nightgown when she called Ambrose. He arrived to find her sitting on the cushioned bench at the foot of her bed, feet tucked under, chin on her knees.

"Edie? Everything okay?" He seemed alarmed by her unkempt appearance. She was a woman who never presented herself with anything less casual than khaki pants and a blouse. Yet here she was just out of bed.

She tilted her face up to him, shadows under her eyes. "I need to show you something, Ambrose. And I need you to not react."

He nodded with professionalism.

She held the photo out, her actions mechanical as she placed it in his hands.

Ambrose cleared his throat, flipping the photo and then back again. He put his hands together, rubbing the top of them over his mouth. She thought she caught a look of alarm in his eyes . . . or perhaps fear as he shifted them back to her.

"What the hell, Edie?"

She sat back down on the bench. Her shoulders slumped forward.

"So you knew nothing of this?" she demanded.

He looked at her incredulously. "What?"

"Johnny never mentioned the safe-deposit box? What was . . . in it."

"Edie, no. Never."

She studied him further. He was the only one left. The only one left to share this with. Yes, Johnny had trusted him explicitly. But could she?

He seemed to sense her uncertainty and stepped closer.

"If this was something I knew about, I would have shared it with you already. Believe me."

She suddenly felt too weary to question it anymore and nodded.

"We need to solve this case," she said in a low voice.

He stopped to take her request in, his eyes widening and then shutting briefly. "Edie . . . I don't understand—I mean, why?"

"Because it's what Johnny wanted."

"Wanted? How can you be so sure? Yes, it's written down with a question mark—"

"I gathered that much," she snipped.

He held the photo up to the light and then down again. "Edie, he kept this secret. I don't think he would have wanted you to find out about it, let alone act on it."

She pressed her lips together firmly. "Maybe. Or maybe he knew I would eventually find out. We knew everything about each other, Ambrose. Everything."

Ambrose shook his head. "If you take this on, it would be like stepping right into where he was. Do you really want to go there?"

"Yes." She straightened out the fabric of her nightgown and smoothed her hair.

"And gain what from it?"

"I'm not looking to gain anything, Ambrose. Frankly, I don't need your permission."

He took a step back, reminded of his place. "Right. I know that, Edie. But Johnny would want me looking out for you."

The lack of sleep may have softened her. "I know."

"This is a nearly twenty-year-old case, Edie. There's a *reason* it's still unsolved."

"If anyone can help me, Ambrose, it's you."

"Appealing to my vanities won't help."

She shrugged. "My husband wanted to solve this case."

"Why? Why do you think he cared?"

Edie's eyes seemed to come alive. "That is the million-dollar question."

He looked back at the photo in his hands for another moment before finally nodding. "I'll need time to figure something out."

She took the photo back before placing her hand on his arm. "And Ambrose? The three names. Cleo, Alex, Jemma. Find out everything you can about them. *Everything.*"

---

**Eighteen years ago**

Homecoming night was not for the weak.

The hours of preparation often created too much anticipation. Too much expectation for one meager night. The gym was a bubble of hot gas that grew with each dance, each awkward glance, and each rejected heart. And then there were always the lucky few who were granted some sort of meeting of the minds—a slow dance that would keep those hungry hormones fed for a month or two at the most. These were all legitimate worries, of course.

For three girls—three young women—this was not the night to have those worries. How they wished for those. Instead, they had been thrust into something that would never be washed from their minds.

They sat in the truck as one of them tried hard to contain her screaming.

Blood seeped down the middle seat. They didn't have time to get a towel.

Where they were going, no one could ever know. This was their secret. This was what bound them.

This was the night that silenced them.

# CHAPTER 7
## CLEO

**August 29, 2022**

The Volkswagen rental smelled faintly of cigarette smoke and fast food. Cleo struggled with the booster seat, Rockwell kicking the ground impatiently behind her.

"Mommy, how long until we get to see Grandma Ji-Yeon?"

"Not long, baby," she said through gritted teeth, wriggling the seat. *Michael always handled car seats.*

She aggressively clicked the seat belt into place as if to snap away any further thoughts like that. *It's done.*

Six months ago, she was Mrs. Cleo Da-Eun Walker. Wife of the good Dr. Michael Walker. Sought-after dermatologist in Chicagoland with his own practice on Michigan Avenue. They had a condo near his office and a remodeled Tudor-style home in the suburbs of Glencoe. Rockwell was the apple of his eye, or so she thought. She got to stay at home and dote on him. There was little to complain about.

She met Michael on the last day of classes sophomore year at Northwestern. Never Mikey, Mike, or Mickey. Always Michael. He had a reputation for "yellow fever" on campus, but she ignored it. She would be different. The sex was great, although he dominated most of the time. After Rockwell was born, it became average to nonexistent.

Her life became the classic fairy tale of the nursing new mother: unwashed hair, breast milk–stained camis, bags under the eyes that would shame raccoons, and the personality of a rock—a known side effect of zero sleep. But for a while, Michael had such eyes for Rockwell he barely noticed.

How could he not?

Rockwell, with the light-gray eyes and head full of thick hair. One dimpled cheek.

Hardly cried, and that first smile sent them into orbit. She could still see the image of Michael in the nursing chair even through the haze of a late-night feeding. Holding his little body against his chest like a football, small baby-animal-like coos from Rockwell. Soft singing from Michael. She'd never even heard him hum before then.

Eventually, Michael found someone else to sing for. His office manager, Linda Tang.

Cleo wanted to blame it all on that. It was easy to point the finger at his inability to keep his dick in his pants. She knew it had happened before.

But she had become complacent. A party to the crime. She found herself trying even harder to please him. And the more she did this, the more sickened she felt. He may have sniffed out the smell of desperation on her.

He was the one to file, a week after Valentine's Day.

She was surprised when he agreed to let her take Rockwell to Iowa. And then suddenly she wondered if the images she had of him with Rockwell were even real. He had been a good father in the beginning. But it wasn't to last. Babies never stay babies forever. The older Rockwell got, the less interest Michael seemed to have.

She could kill him for it.

Her phone chimed. Her mother asking again about their arrival.

The drive from Des Moines International Airport to Rosemary Hills would take twenty minutes. Longer if there was traffic. She placed her hands on the steering wheel and let out a big whoosh of air. It was happening. She was returning after all this time.

Why, of all the places her mother could have chosen to settle down, had she picked Rosemary Hills, Iowa?

"Because it's the best. Good for children," her mother had explained when Cleo had questioned this major parental decision at the age of four. *Yes. Only the best.*

Her mother had emigrated from South Korea while she was still pregnant with Cleo, her brother Ronnie barely two. Their father had abandoned them, and as far as she understood, according to her mother, that made him good as dead. She gave birth to Cleo in California before making her way on to Rosemary Hills, gritting her way to owning a small flower shop before selling it a few years ago.

She didn't want to complain or sound ungrateful. Her mother had done everything for her and Ronnie to give them a good life, leaving them wanting for very little growing up.

Still. It hadn't been the easiest being Cleo Song in whitewashed Rosemary Hills.

Kids were less forgiving about being different two decades ago. She always felt she had missed the right generation to grow up in. Today's youth celebrated differences. To blend in was mundane and avoided.

But that was all Cleo tried to do back then.

The first Halloween she could recall brought on that initial "sting." The stings were nothing major on their own. But collectively, they began to injure her—bloat her with resentment. Her two friends in first grade at the time—Ellie and McKaela—joyously announced their costume choice at recess.

"We're going to be Mary-Kate and Ashley Olsen!" Ellie exclaimed.

"Twins! Because we look like twins," explained McKaela—despite one having straight brown hair and the other curly auburn hair.

Cleo tried to hide her disappointment. She had thought maybe they would be three witches together. "Twins? That's only two. Maybe we could be triplets?"

"That wouldn't work, silly!" McKaela squealed.

"Why not?"

Ellie stared back at Cleo as if it were obvious. "Because . . . you know."

She had felt her cheeks burn in embarrassment. It should have been anger or any surge of emotion that would cause her to retort, to *defy* this logic. But somehow her own nervous system betrayed her from the start and trained her to be embarrassed.

Her friends went trick-or-treating as the Olsen twins, and she trailed along in a witch costume.

"Look, Mommy!" Rocky shouted from the back of the car.

There it was. The **WELCOME TO ROSEMARY HILLS, IOWA!** sign covered in pale-pink roses and green border trim. Population 61,000. Where the niceties were all intentional and the unpleasantries, well, of course, accidental.

Back in 2004, every teenage girl had the requisite SUV parked in her driveway, the symbol of middle-class royalty. The rows and cul-de-sacs of dream homes, newly built from five approved models—each one a version of brick with ecru siding. Three-car garages and basketball hoops in the driveways. The streets were named after flowers: Dahlia Lane, Aster Circle, Lily Avenue, and don't forget Rose Street. Where homecoming weekend was just as important as Christmas—maybe even more.

She relived it all as she drove past the sign and sailed into the veil of her youth. Suddenly it was like a drop cloth had fallen on her and she couldn't see anymore, her mindset being pulled back to another time, hot plastic warping and bending.

It was homecoming night all over again, eighteen years ago. The smell of teenage perspiration and the echoes of high-pitched chattering came back to her. She could still hear those first sounds through the noise. The truck screeching to a halt.

Pain in the air—so profuse she thought the three of them would choke on it. The release of it taking her breath away.

And then that first cry.

The small cry that made her cover her ears, their curves pulled in like pink shells.

# CHAPTER 8

## ALEX

*August 29, 2022*

There should never be any surprises before, during, or after dinner in the Mitchell house. That was Alex's rule. Each week, a chart was laid out on the scheduling board that corresponded to the matching one she was sure to put on her husband's phone.

"She's six, Alex. *Six*," her husband, Davis, often protested.

"Yes, and what does that have to do with being organized? Is there some age at which children suddenly need to learn that skill? No. It starts now."

Davis would roll his eyes and scoff.

*Fight. Fight back with me, Davis. At least there would be some sign you cared . . . an urge of some sort.*

She and Davis never fought. Their conversations were far too muted and below the surface to summon any sort of argument. The waves between them had long ago settled into a placid pond—no storm could drag over it to change that.

He was an accountant. She was a lawyer. They had a smart, well-mannered daughter. Two plus two should always equal four. Didn't it?

"Sasha. Are you finished with your homework?"

Her daughter bounced into the kitchen. "Yes, but what are we having for dinner?"

"You know where to find that, Sasha," she answered, pointing to the chart.

It was Monday. And Mondays were always salmon on top of brown rice and asparagus. Alex closed her eyes and knew exactly how the rest of the evening would pan out. At 6:00, Sasha would eat sitting up straight, napkin in lap. She would finish at least two-thirds of her plate and all her milk because she knew better than to leave the table otherwise. Davis would ask how excited she was about school starting. They would both clear the table while Alex did the dishes. At 6:45, Davis would help Sasha get ready for bed. Alex would draw the bath, and they would both tuck her in for a story. By 7:15, Sasha would be well settled in bed. Davis and Alex would go their separate ways outside Sasha's bedroom door, splitting apart like string cheese, Davis to work out in their basement gym, Alex to the study.

When she opened her eyes, she was sitting in the study chair. The reliability of the evening soothed her, and she took a sip of her wine.

Maud had been that way with her father. Two soldiers throughout the day, marching along until the end, when their line would separate, one turning one direction, the other continuing straight. Until one of them kept going—her father.

She barely knew what it was like to have a father.

He left when she was young, and she sometimes wondered if he hadn't, what kind of mother that would have made Maud. Would she, too, have marched in a different direction . . . ?

She opened her laptop and began to work on a brief—only to wander into her browser and read more about the DNA lottery.

Her heart quickened with each news link, with each post. A rabbit hole of searches—YouTube videos on Parker Inc. Comments on Twitter, Facebook, and Instagram speculating what the "crazy widow" was up to.

And then the latest story about Baby Ava.

A trending CNN feature on Rosemary Hills. An image of Avalon Park next to the title: "Could DNA Lottery Solve Baby Ava Case?"

Up until then, her world had been steady and rhythmic today, the beat synchronized with her hard-set plan. It always did—it was her lifeline to staying afloat.

But it wasn't enough this time.

Because something from the past had resurfaced. Ugly and cracking the earth from below as it rumbled to get out. Eager to break through and take hold of her.

*Nothing has happened . . . not yet, anyway. Don't get ahead of yourself.*

Her hands shook despite her feigned reassurances. She looked down at them as their involuntary tremor almost appeared to be some strange dance move. A blur of confusion and vibrations.

*But what if it all gets out? What if . . .*

She clamped her racing thoughts together, cutting them off—pressing so hard she was sure her bones would bend.

# CHAPTER 9

## Jemma

*August 29, 2022*

"H! H is for Henry!"

"H!"

Jemma's chest relaxed at the squeals of giggles. She held her baby boy in her arms and wished—as most mothers do—he would stay that way forever. He wasn't quite "baby" status anymore, being four. But the sweetness still lingered like the last notes of a sad sonata.

Henry squirmed out of her grasp and reached for his favorite book, *The Very Hungry Caterpillar*. He traced the rainbow-colored cover with his index finger.

"Hungry, hungry."

"Is Henry hungry?"

"Yes!" He jerked up and down once and flashed all his teeth.

"Does Henry like spaghetti?"

"Yes!"

"Okay, my baby. You play in your room and be good. Mommy will come get you when it's ready. Want me to get out your train set for you?"

"No!"

"No, thank you."

Henry smiled with all his teeth again. "Thank you."

She went to the kitchen and started boiling the noodles. There was frozen leftover sauce somewhere in the freezer—she was sure of it. Half the freezer's contents were on the counter by the time Poppy entered.

"Spaghetti? Again? Really, Mom? Have you not heard of Paleo?" Jemma's face was red from straining inside the freezer.

"Well, hello, *Poppy.*"

"What's with the attitude?" Poppy asked, placing a hand on her hip. She shot back a look of her own. "Don't hang up on me again like you did earlier. I mean it."

"It wasn't a hang-up. I was just ending the conversation before it escalated. Isn't that what you say?"

"No—I have never said that. And it's rude and completely inconsiderate—ahh!" She held the Tupperware with the frozen meat sauce victoriously in her hand. "I found it!"

She was alone in her triumph. Poppy had already found her way onto one of the kitchen island's wicker stools. She looked down at her phone and giggled. Jemma couldn't help but notice how much she was starting to look like her ex. Wavy hair that didn't quite meet the standard of being curly—it had grown down to her waist this summer. The same turned-up nose and crinkle when she laughed. A recipe for adorableness, with a dash of freckles and two dolloped brown doe eyes. Those little-girl charms somehow endured. But she had started to inherit Jemma's Marilyn figure. Every time she noticed it—a flip of her hair or a shirt that she was starting to outgrow—her insides felt like they were trying to escape up and out of her esophagus.

"Am I even allowed to ask?" She shook the frozen sauce into a pot.

"Ask what?" Poppy looked up, instantly suspicious.

"What was so funny?"

Poppy's cheeks went pink. "Nothing . . . it's no—no one." Another trait she shared with Jemma's ex—a terrible liar.

"Say, Mom. You heard about that lottery, right? That DNA thing?"

Jemma paused in the middle of adding seasoning. The steam from the boiling noodles made her sweat. "Yes. And what do you think about it?"

She felt her words come out carefully, as if each one were a toe dipping the water, testing the temperature, careful not to make any waves.

Poppy's voice echoed in her ears.

She herself had read about it as soon as she got to the office, Peter rushing to her desk and bitching right away that he had never been a Rosemary Hills resident—how his cheap parents had chosen to live in Normandale instead. On any other day, she would have laughed at his banter.

But today . . . today she felt the walls caving in on her.

*Mr. Jonathan Parker . . . widow creating DNA lottery . . . windfall for Rosemary Hills residents.*

She kept reading the words again and again.

*The baby . . . they've already started talking about the baby . . .*

"Mom? Are you even listening?" Poppy jutted her chin out with annoyance.

"Yes. Uh, you were saying . . ."

The water began to boil over. She cursed and turned down the burner.

"What's with you today?"

She heard the front door open before she could answer.

"Damn—what smells so great?" Finch asked. His dark-coffee-colored arms reached out for Jemma, and she immediately went to him.

They'd been married for five years, but the sight of her second husband still gave Jemma that tingly sensation. If Poppy knew the thoughts Jemma normally had about her stepfather, her appetite for dinner would cease to exist. But right now—right now *all* she wanted was to embrace him and pretend she was safe from it all.

She felt relief as he held her, giving her enough to get through making dinner.

"Do I need to leave?" Poppy groaned.

"What? No hug for Papa Finch?" He feigned disappointment and tilted his head.

She relented and got up to give him a quick hug.

"Good day or bad day, little mama?"

"How about a plus minus one?"

He ruffled the top of her head and went to the deep farmhouse sink to wash up.

The one somewhat stress-free zone in Jemma's life was Finch and Poppy's relationship. There was an ease about Finch; just his presence was a dose of Valium—soothing Dalai Lama dynamism. He could calm Poppy down without even trying. Never quick to anger, a natural cheerleader of life.

Although lately it had been tested—and not by Poppy.

They finished dinner with little incident, Poppy retreating to her room as soon as the last dish had been put in the dishwasher.

Finch came up behind Jemma, rubbing her shoulders. She went slack and turned to bury her face in his chest.

"You all right?"

*No. But I'm going to keep pretending.*

"Yes. When am I not?" She laughed immediately at her own answer.

"Is today the day?"

*Of course . . . let's not forget the other life-altering worry in my life.*

She puckered her lips inward. "Yup. Today would be that day."

"Let's not wait around like last time. Do something fun instead."

"Oh? You want to play Twister or Jenga while we wait to find out if we lost another twenty grand?"

He mocked disbelief with a huge smile. "Who doesn't do that?"

She placed her hand on his face and tried not to cry. She had cried enough tears—a person was allowed only so many, right?

They were on round three of the game. Or was it technically round 3.5, since the second round they'd had to pause and restart due to the cyst they'd found in her right ovary?

She had gotten pregnant so easily with Henry and Poppy. But when it came to conceiving with Finch, the first year had produced nada. Her doctor told her it was nothing to be too concerned about. Nonetheless, into the second year of trying, she'd insisted on testing.

There was nothing medically wrong with either of them. What was it the doctor had called them?

*Perfectly reproductively compatible.*

She didn't believe the results, so they looked into two more specialists. This time the test results were even more promising—they should have had ten babies by then. But whatever was on paper was not translating to real life.

They were referred to the top IVF clinic in Des Moines.

Her midsection had permanent bruising and needle marks. The pretesting, the blood panels, the injections, the massive bloating, the excruciating egg retrievals, the embryo transfer—all for naught. She didn't mind the physical pain. She was willing to endure even more, if that was what it took.

But it was the disappointment in Finch's eyes each time that made a light inside her dim more and more. If anyone deserved to be a father, it was Finch Danowski. She was convinced it was her fault.

Her flaws—her past. They were punishing her, and thereby punishing him.

*Innocent bystander.*

And now they were down to one viable embryo. They had transferred the embryo a little over a week ago. Dr. Stork (the irony was too much—she sometimes wondered if he'd had his name legally changed) decided to wait a little longer this time before the blood test.

"Let's *really* make sure we're ready to check for the levels."

He hadn't called yesterday. Today was it.

Another day of playing the game.

Her phone lit up.

## THE STORY OF EDIE AND JOHNNY

She was the girl in the green peasant dress. He spotted her smoking a cigarette with her girlfriends in the corner booth. She had great posture and a smile that didn't seem forced. He had come alone to the bar that night after his roommate bailed on him when a better prospect turned up involving a tight miniskirt and white knee-high boots.

It was the 1970s, and she was barely out of college. Unsure what to do next, she was considering auditioning to become a stewardess. He already knew what his future held; he just needed to make sure she was there with him.

Edie still had that dress. It hung in her closet, always the first item on the right.

Johnny had not been terribly smooth in asking her out that night. She wasn't sure if he was mad at her or just mad, but she said yes to a drink later the next evening.

She wore the same dress, and he ordered the same drink that he would the rest of his life. Whiskey on the rocks with a squeeze of lemon. She actually wasn't much of a drinker and preferred smoking.

"You're not going to have a drink?" he had asked.

"I'm good," she replied, taking a drag of her Salem menthol.

"Those will crystallize your lungs, you know."

"So I've heard." She flicked a piece of ash off her upper lip.

He took a long sip from his glass. "Listen. I'm not trying to tell you what to do. I'm not the type of man to tell a woman what to do. But

I know that I'm going to marry you someday. And I'd like you to live alongside me for a while." He plucked the cigarette from her fingers and put it out in the red plastic ashtray.

It was the most romantic thing anyone had said or done in front of her.

She slept with him that night. She could still feel the way his hands dug into her arms that first time. It made her feel wanted—as though she held all the power.

They were married shortly after that. Proper church wedding in Rosemary Hills, Iowa. Johnny's father owned a hog farm in the area. He grew up motherless, as she'd passed away right after giving birth. He would often claim to Edie that his father always blamed him for it.

After the ceremony, Johnny whispered in her ear, "Tolerate me, promise?"

She had smiled and whispered back, "I promise."

There was no honeymoon. It was straight to work for Johnny.

Edie was the only wife in his small circle of friends who worked at the time. Johnny never protested. He was engrossed night and day with his first business venture. She worked days at an accounting firm and nights as a nanny for a local family with two children. She didn't mind watching other people's children. She truly liked kids—their complete honesty and lack of frivolity she embraced. She just never wanted to watch any of her own. Edie had made that clear to Johnny from the beginning.

"I'm not like other women. I don't want to have babies. That's the way it is. And if you aren't okay with that, well—now is the time to say so."

He never questioned her decision or asked for a reason. Why should there be a reason? It was simply what she wanted for her life.

And getting pregnant wasn't it.

When she accidentally got pregnant a few years later, she had an abortion. When it happened again when she was almost forty, she had her tubes tied. Johnny said nothing, seemingly unmarred by all of it.

When Johnny's father passed of lung cancer, he sold the hog farm. One of the few times she saw him close to tears. Not over his father's passing but selling the farm. Years later, he bought it back and then some—taking over almost every adjacent farm.

Their first home together was a two-room apartment above the laundromat in town. She could make supper and have a conversation with him while he took a shower. They weren't entirely poor, but they didn't have much. But those days of working long hours and coming home to meet for meals were some of the happiest for Edie.

Johnny's first business involved a fleet of semitrucks. When that took off, he bought two more smaller transportation companies based in Minnesota and merged them all together. He quickly built a reputation for his hard work, but also shrewd business sense. He could not care less what people thought about him.

He wasn't going to stop there.

They moved out of their apartment and into a little brick house on the west side of Rosemary Hills. His interests began to move from transportation to wind energy—acres of flatland in Iowa meant opportunity. Edie, in the meantime, quit her accounting and nanny jobs to help out with the books.

They were a team, Edie and Johnny. It didn't matter how hard the work was, how long the hours were. How late they would finally get home. Edie would often joke they should save money and live in the office. Sometimes they would end up sleeping there, Johnny at his desk and Edie on the pullout couch.

She wished she had savored it. The grind and the weary hours with only the two of them. That was when he'd needed her the most.

"You still tolerate me, Edie?" he'd ask, half-asleep at his desk at two in the morning.

"I promise," she would reply as she took off his reading glasses and draped him with a blanket.

Then the economy sailed upward in the eighties. Business was more than booming for the Parkers. When he first formed Parker Energy, she knew things were never going to be the same. She watched as he poised his pen above the business-formation agreement. This was it—they had better hold on to their seats.

The late eighties were a blur of travel. Acquisition of a gas company in Utah. A visit to an oil field in Albania. A monthlong trip overseas to Beijing. Piece by piece, brick by brick, they added on to their growing energy conglomerate. But there was never time for just Edie and Johnny anymore. There was always a third party in the room vying for as much of Johnny's attention as Edie had previously been granted.

It was probably why she detested the board members. Each of them was another of these third-party leeches.

Only *she* knew how Johnny thought and acted. How the wheels actually turned in his head.

That was until Kane Oliver stepped into their lives.

She carried with her the suspicion even to this day that their meeting was not happenstance. A paranoia that infested her wariness of him.

It was Johnny who'd suggested they go to Salerno for their anniversary in '89. He had heard from some of the board members how beautiful the seaside Italian town was, a postcard of colorful stucco buildings and tiled roofs against an inlet of shimmering aqua. She remembered the third morning of their trip so vividly, as she lay on the beach in her white suit, with Johnny offering to get her another drink. It was nearing lunchtime when she began to worry and considered looking for him, but he returned to their spot.

Except with someone else in tow.

She shaded her eyes to look up at the tall figure who cast over her with boldness. She could smell his oaky aftershave and made no effort to suppress her nose from wrinkling.

"This must be the lovely Edie. Johnny has talked so much about you," he said, extending his hand, the ring on his index finger glinting in the Mediterranean sunshine.

"Oh . . . has he?" she answered, giving Johnny a peculiar glance.

Johnny motioned toward him with a sweeping arm.

"This is Kane Oliver. I ran into him at the bar. Another midwesterner. Iowa, in fact—would you believe it? We got to talking about how we both got into our businesses."

He was handsome but not in the conventional way—his nose was slightly too large for his face, but it was his upper lip, which seemed to curl when he smiled, that dripped with charisma even she couldn't deny. His flinty-ice eyes were sharp with intellect, the smooth way he talked making it hard to disengage from him.

She immediately disliked him.

But Johnny remained intrigued. Kane, too, was self-made, coming from nothing, and perhaps it was because of all the other board members he could never really relate to, never quite *fit* with, that he actually listened to *this* one.

They spent practically the rest of their vacation together, the three of them, with Edie feeling like the third wheel. Kane recommended all the restaurants, having been to Salerno twice before, and told them they had to see Positano before they left—Johnny was already taking in his advice, with each suggestion, each morsel, each instruction further persuading him.

"You must try the fresh-caught octopus—it's like no other."

"I won't let you leave the Amalfi Coast without tasting a lemon right off the tree."

"Say, Johnny . . . have you considered expanding your wind energy division?"

When they returned to the States, Kane didn't waste any time. He met with Johnny for drinks in Des Moines to discuss "further business." Edie was not invited as the third wheel this time.

He was a souvenir they had brought home, but only Edie seemed to realize it was one who was becoming a fixture in their own living room. Eventually, Kane was brought on as a consultant, then vice president, then board member.

It was Kane who prodded Johnny into pumping up the acquisitions. Urging him to think bigger, to never stop and rest on his laurels.

By the time Parker Inc. was incorporated in the early 1990s, Edie and Jonathan Parker were worth an estimated $600 million.

"Isn't it enough?" she had asked.

"What's enough, really?"

She urged Johnny to take a breather and settle down in one place for more than a month. She wanted them to have roots, to finally exhale. They began to build their home.

While they also had a ranch house in Telluride, a penthouse condo in New York City, beachfront property in Malibu, and a home under construction in Vancouver, "Rosemary House" (Edie's nickname for it) surpassed them all. The acres upon acres of land gave them free range to conjure up whatever they fantasized. A team of three architects created one of the most admired homes in the Midwest, photographed by renowned architecture and home magazines. But Johnny—leaning on the advice of Kane to be more discreet—refused any more than that.

"A quick interview—over the phone."

"Forget it, Edie. I don't want people to see me as garish."

"Honey, this is garish as all *hell*," she had told him.

Rosemary House contained ten bedrooms, six bathrooms, an indoor pool and sauna, an outdoor pool, two gourmet kitchens, a game room, a theater, a full indoor gym, two studies (one of them the Green Room), a tennis court, a bowling alley, and an immaculate garage that housed Johnny's favorite vintage cars from his collection. This was merely the structural part of the property. The acres of land hosted a garden, a fountain, a barn house for their horses, and a storm shelter, complete with a fully stocked emergency setup.

Kane effortlessly slipped in as a "frequent guest" of Rosemary House. A quick drive from Des Moines to visit Johnny in person over whatever latest fire he had managed to put out for Parker Inc., which would almost always turn into an invitation to dinner.

Edie would smile her way through them as Kane looked across the table at her.

"This is a lovely spread, Edie."

"You can thank Belinda," she would answer.

Was it genuine appreciation in his eyes? Or was it triumph? A gloat for having taken the seat next to her husband?

Dinner would lead to drinks in the Green Room. She would excuse herself but always heard them during those evenings, raucous laughter and conversation streaming in and out of the halls.

"Fraternity hour," Edie would mock to herself with contempt.

Johnny eventually set up a local headquarters in downtown Rosemary Hills, even giving Kane an office, much to Edie's dismay. It did little to slow him down, and Edie wondered how they were as busy as ever. She tried not to complain. Tried not to be the nagging, salty wife.

When she looked back at their marriage, it was mostly a smoothly drawn line. Not perfect but certainly on the even side.

Of course, there were exceptions.

Like blips on a polygraph test. Lines that skid upward and then back down with rapid intensity. Why bother dwelling on them? The life they had together was extraordinary—a course forged together that some people wouldn't even bother dreaming of.

But the blips existed, as they do in any marriage. Ink spots that spread out and bled.

He had been settled at the Rosemary Hills office for some time, their life easing into a comfortable routine. Kane's visits were not as frequent as they used to be, and she found they had more time for just *them*. Edie and Johnny.

It came abruptly, like a frost overtaking a harvest-ready field over-night. It was as though something had disturbed him . . . troubled him. He became quieter . . . short tempered at times. Snapping at her and Belinda in the evenings over the smallest things. Things he wouldn't have wasted breath on before.

"What is this? You know I don't like veal."

"Don't change the channel twenty flippin' times, Edie. Pick something."

She chalked it up to boredom and suggested they take a trip. But nothing seemed to appeal to him.

He was a man who had tasted it all. Wealth tasted grittier than either of them had expected.

"Johnny . . . what is it? Something is clearly bothering you," she'd finally asked.

"It's nothing . . . nothing, Edie," he answered.

But the look in his eyes read anything but *nothing*.

And then one evening she awoke to a noise. Quiet at first—until it crawled inside to stir her. She had been in a deep sleep, having taken an Ambien. A figure stumbled in the dark toward the bathroom, the light triangled out to her face.

"Johnny?" She felt like a child, making sure the monsters were gone, the blanket pulled up to her chin.

The bathroom door closed and water ran.

"Johnny?" she asked again.

He flung the bathroom door open, and it bashed against the wall, no doubt leaving a scuff mark. His hair was matted like a lost mutt, skin ruddy and eyes bloodshot. He faltered forward toward the bed and got within a few inches of her face. She immediately smelled the cloyingly hay-like odor of whiskey, coupled with an aftershave she disdained as much as the man who wore it.

"Mr. Oliver," she snapped.

Her initial reaction was more anger and annoyance than anything else. She drew the covers up higher.

"This is ridiculous. Why are you in here?"

"Oh, come on, Edie. All these years? You can call me Kane."

"Mr. Oliver, I believe you are drunk," she said.

She began to feel alarmed, maybe even fearful. She wanted to scream at him to leave. Yet her defenses made her calm . . . formal.

"Edie . . ." Hot stale breath puffed toward her.

"Please leave this instant, Mr. Oliver. And where is my husband. I am sure—"

She hastily sat up as he fumbled toward her on the bed.

"Edie . . . don't you ever wonder?"

He leaned in close to her face.

"Wonder?" she asked, her voice quiet.

"What it's all for? What makes it worth it."

His mouth moved against her ear.

She wasn't sure what troubled her more. His drunken presence in her bedroom . . . or the fact that she didn't mind his mouth against her ear.

"Get. Out," she said coldly.

He smiled once and then retreated, stumbling off the bed and leaving the room as she sat frozen, shaking—wanting the last moment to be a nightmare that had never happened.

# CHAPTER 10

## CLEO

*September 1, 2022*

Cleo drove down the dirt country road, rocks drumming against the sides of her doors. *Pop, pop, clunk!* She looked down at her phone to make sure the address was right.

*In eight hundred feet, turn right.*

"Right? Right where?" She tossed her phone onto the passenger seat in frustration. If there was a house around here, it would eventually show up. The area west of Rosemary Hills was nothing but dusty country roads and soybean fields.

She had hoped the morning would be more promising. The last few days at her mother's home had not been.

By the morning after her and Rocky's arrival, her mother was already showing her disapproval. Tucked under her breakfast plate of sliced melon and scrambled eggs was the local newspaper, the job section circled in marker.

At least the marker was blue instead of an aggressive red. That much she'd give her mother.

Rocky sat down excitedly. "Oh, oh! French toast and powdered sugar!"

"Mom. The job section in the newspaper? Nobody uses this anymore." She picked up the paper and slid it to the other side of the kitchen table. "I have *this*." She held up her phone.

Ji-Yeon shook her head as she sat down next to Rocky and cupped her coffee carefully in her hands. "You alone now, Cleo."

"Alone? I have Rocky."

"Yeah! She has me!" Rocky exclaimed through a bite of french toast.

"Eh, eh. Chew first." Cleo pushed his plate closer to him.

"I never thought you and Michael end up like this. Never, never. Not in million years in my life I think my daughter end up like this."

Ji-Yeon took a long draw from her coffee mug and then whispered in Korean as she twirled the gold band on her index finger with worry. It was the one she had managed to save and bring over from South Korea.

Cleo eyed the nervous twisting and tried not to sigh. There was no point in arguing with her mother. It wouldn't change the fact that disappointment dripped on everything in the kitchen, including Rocky's syrup.

The most annoying phone jingle Cleo had ever heard blared from her mother's phone. It was a cross between "Baby Shark" and the Macarena—synthesized chiming and ringing at top volume.

"Oh. Ronnie—ya!"

Ronnie's tan, chiseled face appeared on her screen. Ji-Yeon turned so everyone around the table could see him before answering excitedly.

"Omma!"

"Ronnie. Look! Rocky. It's your uncle Ronnie!"

Rocky smiled cheesily and went back to his breakfast.

Ronnie had not been back to Rosemary Hills for years. He had better things to do as a sought-after international patent attorney. Amsterdam one month, Hong Kong the next. His fiancée was one of those Instagram influencers who spent her days taking the most asinine and posed pictures of herself in whatever scenic city they were in. Most of her pictures involved her putting food slowly in her mouth. Cleo often wondered how much of this food she actually ingested. Sailor was her name, but of course her handle was something ridiculous like @SailorMoonGirl.

"How's Sailor Moon?" Cleo popped her head into the frame.

"Shorty!"

"I'm not that short anymore."

"Mom said you were coming home soon. I didn't realize this soon."

"Yeah, well . . . here I am."

"Sorry to hear about Michael."

"You don't have to be sorry."

She turned the phone back toward her mother, who chattered away in Korean. She was so animated when anything involved Ronnie.

Golden boy Ronnie. Cleo was happy and proud of him. She really was. He had always been a good older brother. She didn't discredit any of that.

But suddenly, being back home was magnifying how low the bar Cleo had set for herself was.

The next day, the posting had shown up as a notification from her job-matching app. Whoever had posted the position had liked whatever was in her LinkedIn profile—which wasn't much. Yes, she had a decent college background. But experience since then? In addition to "Mommy to Rocky," she'd held a few temp positions at various publications in Chicago. But nothing that impressive.

The posting was simple:

> Looking for reliable individual to read to an immobile in-home patient. Ability to work odd hours and have open availability. Pay is hourly. Inquire at the following email address.

She could certainly stand reading to someone for a few hours. Anything to get out of the house. Rocky would be in school shortly.

She inquired via email as requested. By the end of the day, a woman named Patricia had called her. She explained she was the in-home nurse and would be hiring "on behalf of her employer." Patricia gave her an address and told her to drive over the next morning around ten.

Cleo cursed a few times as she continued on the country road. A dark front rolled in, and she began to get nervous when it started forming a wall cloud. She turned the car radio on to keep her ears open for any tornado warnings in the area. A mile and a half later, she rolled up a hill and finally saw the house.

The farmhouse was quite striking. All white with a black metal roof and oak accents. The home had clearly been renovated for a modern look—the front door was a midnight blue. She parked in the long driveway. The air smelled of rain mixed with cow dung. A picturesque red barn in the distance explained that part.

She rang the doorbell, and a woman immediately answered.

"You must be Ms. Song?"

"Cleo. Yes. Cleo Song."

The woman opened the door wider to usher her in.

"You're Patricia?"

"Yes. I spoke with you on the phone."

Patricia wore light-blue scrubs and a lavender cardigan. She was rail thin, with fluffy bangs and a tightly wound bun.

"Can I get you anything to drink, Cleo?"

"I'm okay, thank you."

The foyer had deep, rich cedarwood floors. The entire wall to the left was covered in shiplap. A stone fireplace crackled with a real wood fire; the mantel was adorned with a giant longhorn skull.

"Should we have a seat in the living room then?"

She followed Patricia toward the mantel. The deep holes in the skull's head seemed to stare at her as she sat in a cognac leather chair.

"As I said over the phone, I'm the in-home nurse. I work at the Rosemary Hills Hospital on weekends and shifts when needed. But I'm mainly here as caretaker. I'm hiring on behalf of the patient I work for."

She seemed nervous, as if she realized she was talking too much. She swallowed and then forced a smile.

"Do you have any experience working as a caretaker?"

Cleo shook her head. "No. But I do have a son, if that counts."

"It really isn't about caretaking. The job is very simple. You would read for an hour. Likely a few times a week. But the days and times would vary. Is that something that could work for your schedule?"

"Yes, I think so…I mean I recently moved back to town. I don't have much going on at the moment."

Patricia clasped her hands on her lap, fiddling with her ring. "We need someone who is reliable. Even tempered. You seem like a fairly calm person. And most importantly, someone who can be discreet."

Cleo's eyebrows furrowed briefly. "Discreet?"

"My patient is not someone who will be communicating much."

"That's okay, I'm not much of a talker," she said gazing downward.

"I mean at all."

"What?" Cleo looked up abruptly.

"With the exception of reading out loud, there will be no talking." Patricia locked eyes with her. "Nothing at all," she repeated.

*Oh.*

"My patient prefers not to be bothered."

*Hmm, this could be interesting.*

Patricia examined her. This was the part where others probably left the interview. The demands were strange. But the oddities of the situation actually attracted Cleo. She liked the unusual—as if they were always meant for one another.

"Is that something you are comfortable with?"

*What do you have to lose? You have no other options right now.*

Cleo shrugged. "Why not?"

She looked taken back—startled even. "Great . . . that's great. I'll need to do a background check first, of course. But would you be willing to start almost immediately?"

"Sure—I mean yes. Do I get to know her name? His name?"

"No. You will walk in the room. There will be a book preselected on the table. Simply sit in the chair next to the table and read. I will come get you when the session is over. Any questions?"

Cleo shook her head.

"Good. Then you can start tomorrow."

———

On the drive home, Cleo's stomach gnawed at her. She hadn't really eaten much for breakfast, only the banana she'd grabbed as she rushed out to the driveway before her mother could ask her more questions before the job interview.

As she made her way back into town, she approached Whittner's, a coffee shop high schoolers would frequent back in her day. She hadn't set foot in there in years. The last time was probably when she brought Michael home to meet her mother. It had been the only time, actually. He had been polite but made some comment about how he "preferred the city."

*Snob.*

She parked in front of Whittner's and wondered if they still had the mini cinnamon rolls packed with extra brown sugar.

The coffee shop was nearly deserted at midmorning on a weekday. One woman ordered in front of her. She stepped up when it was her turn. The girl manning the register looked completely over her shift already, her green apron barely on. She said nothing to Cleo. No greeting, no hello. Just a dead stare.

"Small black coffee, please. Whatever medium roast you have."

The girl entered a few things on her tablet and looked back up, engaged as ever.

"And two mini cinnamon rolls."

"We're out." She scratched her chin.

"Oh." Cleo began to reach for her credit card. She paused. "Any chance you'll be making more . . . please?"

The girl stared back with more intensity. "Yeah. But you'd have to wait."

"Okay . . . how long?"

"A long time."

She nodded and began to hand her card over. Inconveniencing anyone had not been part of her making. She was the kind of woman who always vigorously brushed and flossed before the dentist. "Right. Sorry."

The girl smirked in triumph.

She felt a trigger being pulled. The corners of the girl's mouth going up set off a rip cord in Cleo's head. This girl was probably half her age. Why did she care if she stepped on her toes? Why was she apologizing, for that matter?

She was sick of apologizing. She was sick of hearing *women* apologizing.

*No, I'm not sorry. I am saying sorry to nothing.*

Heat spread through her ears—she wasn't sure if it was embarrassment or anger, but it didn't matter.

She had cashed out all her sorrys.

She yanked back her hand. "You know what? On second thought, I can wait."

The girl's lips formed into the size of a small mouse turd.

Cleo thrust her card forward. "What's the total on that then?"

Twenty minutes later, Cleo sat at the table in the front window. She licked a sticky mess of cinnamon and brown sugar off her thumb. She almost started laughing with utter satisfaction. Too bad she didn't have anyone to toast to with her coffee.

"You're going to need a wet wipe after eating those," a deep voice said.

She saw black boots. Her eyes traveled up to the makings of a police uniform. The silver placard tag read HART.

"How many years has it been, Cleo Song?"

She didn't recognize him at first. The police officer standing above her was built, a slight scruff on his face peppered with a little gray.

The last time she'd seen him, he was a boy. "Young man" was probably stretching it, even for sophomore year in high school. He'd been much scrawnier, with longer hair. Ironically, he'd also donned all black back then—but in baggy pants and a hooded sweatshirt.

In elementary school, the golden-haired boy had been obsessed with soccer. She still remembered meeting him on a winter day in second grade. The teacher wasted no time in partnering the class into "reading buddies" that morning. When it came her turn to be assigned, she looked up to see a lanky boy with one front tooth missing. He had a scar that ran from the left-side corner of his mouth down under his chin that spread as he grinned at her. She would later learn it was from a dog bite.

He immediately pointed at the Princess Toadstool sticker on her sweater. Ronnie had let her take one from his Super Mario collection.

"Princess Toadstool," he said.

She nodded shyly, opening the book they were supposed to be reading.

"Did you know she was originally named Princess Peach?" he said, leaning closer to examine it.

"Huh?"

"Play any *Super Mario 64*?"

She remembered blushing. "Sort of."

"Yeah?"

"My brother Ronnie makes me play with him."

"Any good?"

She shrugged and turned back to the book with a smirk.

"That means you're pretty good!" he said excitedly.

There was something about the boy with the scar—a comforting kindness that made her feel braver than usual.

"There's a secret slide," she whispered.

"Secret slide?" His eyes went wide with curiosity.

"Yes. Princess Toadstool's secret slide . . . it's a secret level."

"Wow," he uttered, clearly impressed.

She felt her cheeks go red again.

"Princess Peach's secret slide," he said, nodding and smiling at her.

That smile greeted her throughout elementary school. She always assumed he was simply like that with everyone. What made her think she was special in receiving it?

And then, somewhere between the angst of eighth grade and puberty, he decided he wasn't the golden-child athlete. He grew out his hair, listened to Sonic Youth, Blink-182, and Nirvana, and wore dark long-sleeved clothes, even in the summer.

But he still remained kind.

She stared up at the officer for what felt like a few seconds too long.

"Will?" she asked. "Will Hart?"

"I was afraid you didn't know who I was. And then I'd have to pretend to just be a friendly neighborhood cop."

He smiled, showing the scar was still there, slightly faded.

She had always liked that scar.

"You look . . . I'm so sorry. You look different."

"The punk emo kid? Hard to pull off at thirty-four. But you? Exactly the same."

Her cheeks felt heated. "I'm not sure if that's good or bad."

He tapped the coffee cup in his hand. "It's good."

*Did he remember the past like she did? Sometimes she wondered if it had all just been on her side.*

"Are you visiting your mother?"

She bit her lip slightly with embarrassment. "No. Living with her. I moved back with my son."

"You have a son?"

"Uh-huh. He's six."

"Oh, so you're married." He looked down at her hand.

"Divorced. You?"

"Never been."

"Married?"

"Either."

She reached up to her mouth, suddenly aware there was a good chance she had a glob of dried brown goop on her face.

He laughed. "Don't worry. I would have told you."

Will Hart. She would be lying if she said the name had not popped up in her head now and then. Only because she thought her time in Rosemary Hills had already been served.

"You're sticking around then. Does that mean you're going to go to the Labor Day parade?"

She nodded slowly, still trying to get through the thick hail of memories falling down on her unexpectedly. "My son, Rocky, has never been."

"Great! I'll be in the parade. Official duty." He chuckled. "Give me a wave?"

"Sure."

Her eyes followed him as he left the shop.

*I tried that night. I really did. But I still wonder if you did too.*

# CHAPTER 11

## JEMMA

*September 1, 2022*

"No night-light?"

"No. I'm a big boy." Henry shook his head emphatically as he clutched his favorite stuffed animal, a worn cream rabbit named Rarebit. His light wavy locks fell over his forehead, and she swept them back and smoothed his hair.

"Okay, Henry. No night-light then." She stooped to switch the sailboat light off.

He looked down contently at Rarebit, gave him a tighter squeeze, and then gazed up at her with large, pooling eyes.

"Do you want me to stay with you awhile longer, sweetie?"

"Yes." And then that smile spread across his face that made Jemma melt—her heart complete butter. There was nothing sweeter to her than the sound of his tiny voice. He reached out and gently tapped her arm as she knelt next to his bedside. He was no longer considered a toddler, but he still loved his afternoon-nap ritual.

There was something about a little boy and a mother's love that didn't compare to any other kind. At least for Jemma. It began the moment she'd first smelled that newborn skin—intoxicating, sweet, and alluring, his soft woolly head nestled under her chin. She felt her heart had never been whole until that first cradle of his little body. Her baby boy forever etched in every fiber of her body. She had just met him, but she would always know him. He had taken up residence in her chest cavity, and she gladly made room for him—wholly ready and willing to sacrifice anything for him.

Her baby boy.

If she closed her eyes, she could recount hundreds of memories, all tucked away like snapshots in a scrapbook. She could pull them out and look at them one by one with such nostalgia and longing. Each day of his life, a Henry was presented to her. And that Henry disappeared forever once night fell, his eyelids closed to the world. Because the one who woke up would replace the Henry she had loved the day before. It was a death in a way—an odd kind. She would look at Henry and think back to the four-month-old Henry, all rolls and chubby layers of glorious baby fat. The recollection was so sweet and so blissful that she felt herself well up. And yet that Henry was gone.

Motherhood was the ultimate bittersweet fruit.

"Mommy, why do you always leave me?"

She felt a catch in her throat, something between a lump and a laugh. "Leave you, Henry? I'm not leaving you. I'm just letting you take your nap."

He shook his head. "That's not it. It's more than that."

"How so?"

"When you leave, it's different. I can't explain it."

Jemma leaned down and kissed him on each cheek. "I will never leave you, Henry. Never."

He still looked a bit unsure but settled for the time being. She loved how she could see him thinking, the decisions being made right in front of her with every flicker of his eyebrow and twitch of his mouth.

"Okay, Mommy. But . . . promise?"

"I promise."

Their nap and bedtime rituals were so important to both Henry and Jemma. Not because every parenting book Jemma had ever read demanded *routine, routine, routine. Did we mention yet? Stick to a routine!* But it had become essential for them. That period of time where it was just Jemma and Henry. No one else dared to interrupt them or partake in this mother-son duo's before-sleep ritual. It was a little bubble that encased them as they talked in low voices, Henry reaching up to play with her hair—the soft touch of her little boy's fingers and sweet kisses—his arms wrapping around her neck.

For Jemma, it was always the best part of her day.

She'd needed it more than ever lately. A battery recharge after an especially rough last few days. If it were up to her, she would have spent them holding Henry and soaking in his comforting embraces.

The news had not been good.

"We got the results back," Dr. Stork had said right away. The one good thing about him: he never wasted phone calls with small talk. He had been working with IVF patients long enough. He knew that did nothing to help.

"Are we knocked up, Doc?" Finch had asked half jokingly, half hopefully.

*I wish he hadn't.*

He made it worse—so much worse.

"I'm sorry. The levels do not indicate a pregnancy at this time. I'm afraid it could very well be that this embryo did not implant. We can try testing again one more time in a few days, to be sure. However, the likelihood of viability . . ."

*Implant. Levels. Viability.*

She stopped listening after that. Her heart, which had been racing up until the word "sorry," immediately slowed down to a steady pulse—maybe a little too slow. What does it mean when your body handles extreme disappointment so readily?

Finch glanced at her and took over the phone, nodding and taking in every word intently.

She shuffled to the kitchen and immediately poured herself a glass of wine. She could hear Finch finishing the call and hanging up.

She was polishing off her first glass and pouring her second when Finch walked into the kitchen.

"Wait—what are you doing, sweetie? Dr. Stork said there's a small chance with another test. He says we should remain hopeful with another egg retrieval, and with the last one going so well, there's no reason this time—"

"Finch. You don't need to do this." She took another sip and wiped at her upper lip.

"Do what?"

"Make everything okay."

He scrunched his face up in disbelief and then scoffed. "That's a bad thing?"

"No. It's not a bad thing. It's just a Finch thing to try to make it all okay. When *really?* It's not, honey. Nothing is okay right now. Let it breathe for once." She felt her voice catch, and she turned away.

*No more tears. Not another one, remember?*

His face softened. "C'mon, baby. You don't have to be like this. I'm just as upset as you. But I choose not to let it take over."

"Oh, it has taken over. Trust me. Every spare moment I have during the day to even *think* is taken up entirely by this—this nightmare we continue to stay in."

He lowered his head. It never stopped amusing Jemma to see such a big, robust man look so much like a lost puppy. But it wasn't enough to bring out a smile—not this time. She was in too far with the disappointment and wine.

This time it had cut deeply—a flesh wound she didn't think would ever stop bleeding. She was worried that if she kept going, the damage would be irreparable. But mostly she worried that Finch had no idea how much pain he was in for. A bear completely blissful and unaware that, this entire time, he had been caged in a zoo.

"Have you even stopped to think about the fact that it was our last embryo?"

"Are you saying . . . you don't want to do this anymore?" His voice was shaky.

"No. But I want you to really think about if things go south again. What then?"

"Then we keep trying—"

"Definition of insanity, Finch!" She didn't mean to explode. Yet it came out of her like a fist punching through a paper bag.

Finch placed both hands on the counter and stuck his head between them. He stayed there for a moment and then raised his head up.

"Okay, baby. I didn't realize insanity to you is being hopeful."

"Fine." She raised her arms up and slapped them against her sides in exasperation. "Bad choice of words. Here's a better one. 'Masochistic.' You happy?"

"Who said anything about happy? Of course I'm upset. It tears me up that I can't give you a baby. I don't have to explain that to you because you know me. But there's no sense in completely losing your shit at this point, Jemma. We've come this far. What's a little more?"

*What's a little more.*

She pinched her mouth shut to prevent another explosion from exiting.

Finch stepped toward her and slid his hands over her shoulders.

"Come here," he said softly.

She fell into his arms and did everything she could to stifle her crying.

———

Jemma opened the front door to find Peter standing there smiling, a bottle of rosé in one hand and a bag of Cheeto Puffs in the other.

"You know I don't drink and do politics."

"Since when?"

"Gimme."

She snatched the bag and ripped it open, popping one in her mouth.

"Bad day?"

"Bad week."

"When is everyone else coming?"

Peter set the rosé on the counter. "Any minute."

She pointed to his feet, covered in white-and-gray snakeskin booties. "Are those . . . are those mine?"

He pretended to be shocked. "What? Are you accusing me of taking from that fabulous closet of yours? Psssh."

"I've been looking for those. Hmm." She turned to the cabinet to gather four glasses and a tray.

Fifteen minutes later, she sat in the home office. To her right sat Peter with perfect posture. Directly in front of her was campaign manager Stevie. Stevie had stuck with Jemma ever since they'd met at a gay bar in downtown Des Moines. Stevie had hit on her, unaware of the fact that Jemma was straight. They immediately hit it off. Stevie had actually been the one to encourage her to run for the state senate.

And then there was Kyle—the most straitlaced-looking publicist one could ever imagine. Jemma never really knew his age, as he was one of those men who would probably look around forty his entire life. He wore square rimless glasses and a perfectly tailored suit, no matter what the occasion, including a Cheetos and rosé campaign meeting.

"All right. What's on the agenda?" She popped another Cheeto in her mouth.

Stevie handed her a folder. "Latest poll numbers. They look solid. You're leading in almost all of them. But let's not forget, you're the incumbent—people tend to go with what they know until those ads really start hitting home. It's still too early. The home stretch will be right before Halloween. But all in all? Solid as of now."

She shuffled through the papers. "I like to hear good news first. You know me. Okay . . . what's the bad?"

Kyle opened his laptop. "The usual commentary by Sylvia Motts. She's quoted in the *Des Moines Register* saying, 'Jemma Danowski's record this past year has especially demonstrated her lack of ability and forethought to lead on many major issues, including the recent vote on the school budget cuts.' And then she went on to attack your clothes in a very passive-aggressive yet slightly comical way. Do you want me to read that?"

Jemma shook her head as she took a sip from her glass. Sylvia Motts was the staunch conservative running against her, both inside and outside politics. The woman could be the love child of Joni Ernst and Phyllis Schlafly.

"What else, Kyle?"

He cleared his throat. "We've been getting a lot of emails and phone calls about the DNA lottery, wanting your comments. Some people are even demanding you shut it down."

She raised an eyebrow and stared down at her glass. Suddenly it was hard to move.

*Why can't this go away?*

More time must have passed than she realized, because she looked up to find the three of them gawking at her.

"Jemma?" Kyle asked hesitantly, the reflection in his lenses blinking at her.

She took a shaky breath and answered in her best authoritative, take-charge voice. "I don't see why that would be a relevant campaign issue. Stevie?"

"Not particularly. But it wouldn't hurt to give a statement if asked by one of the local outlets."

"All right. Let's have something ready in case."

Kyle nodded and immediately began to type on his laptop.

———

Once her motley crew had left, Jemma took the half-empty bag of Cheetos up to her room. She sprawled on her bed, a sleepy glow drawing over her from both the rosé and the exhaustion of the last few days. She and Finch were doing . . . okay. They seemed to be playing a dance of "I'm going to stay out of your way." Which was probably more draining than just going at it.

Soft giggles drifted in from Poppy's room—rhythmic titters and then high-pitched laughter. They would grow stronger and then come back down to hushed snickers.

The wave of teenage emotion was strong in that one.

She remembered how hard she was on her own mother growing up—the harsh thoughts she had about her. Thinking she knew better—that one day *she* would do better than the little they had. How typically "teen" of her. Her mother working long hours at more than one job, struggling to make ends meet, while all she had to worry about was what boy she would talk to that night.

She used to take the phone, its long yellow extension cord dragging down the hallway into her bedroom, laughing at the nothing comments of boys who would all flirt with her in class the next day.

Getting boys to notice her in high school was never a challenge. In fact, high school wasn't a challenge for Jemma at all. It was a rolling high from girls wanting to be just like her—bending over backward to get her approval. Boys stumbling over each other to be the one to get *Jemma Slater* to look in his direction. Even teachers—sensing the hierarchy she had in the food chain of high schoolers—would give her preferential treatment. Ah yes. This one was the queen of the pride. She never asked for all of it. It simply tumbled into her lap.

Until it didn't.

The first kisses had led to the first fondling of her breasts. The next time, she found her bra was taken off. And then she couldn't stop the tidal wave that followed. Because who would she be if she didn't behave like the prom queen she was?

The heavy petting and breathing wasn't enough for the boys. One boy in particular.

And the magical ride that had gone round and round slowed down. She couldn't get off this one.

# CHAPTER 12

## EDIE

*September 2, 2022*

Ambrose arrived at Rosemary House in the late afternoon, tablet tucked under his arm as they settled themselves in Edie's office.

"As you know, all three women currently reside in Rosemary Hills. They grew up here as well. They have married names, or *had*, I should say—one of them is divorced."

He opened their pictures—headshots that appeared to be for profiles on Facebook or Instagram. She leaned forward and searched their faces, hoping for some sort of secondary recognition, an answer to the question pulsating in her forehead every morning as soon as she woke up.

*Who are they, Johnny?*

"A profile was created for each of them. If you select their photo, it will take you to the full report." Ambrose turned the screen toward Edie.

"And their ages?" she asked, sitting back in her desk chair.

"Midthirties. Cleo Song is thirty-four, Alexandra Mitchell thirty-five, and Jemma Danowski thirty-six. All Rosemary Hills High School graduates, a class in between each of them."

"So that would place all of them in high school at the time of Baby Ava's death."

"Hypothetically, yes. So far, the forensics information I dug up has the infant's death estimated at around seventeen to eighteen years ago.

Even with improvements in technology, forensics still hasn't pinpointed an exact timeline."

"Unfortunate," Edie murmured. "Anything else yet on our own investigation?"

"I've assembled a team. Chief Lennox wasn't thrilled when I asked him for access to the forensics data. To be honest, he's kind of being a pain in the ass about it."

"I'll talk to him," she said briskly as she scrolled through the report on each woman. She paused at one section.

"A politician?"

"Up for state senate reelection this year. She's somewhat of a controversy, it seems."

"A lawyer. And the third one is unemployed?"

"Yes."

Edie's eyes ate up each line of information from the profiles, scanning voraciously, hungry for more. "Can I keep this?" she asked.

Ambrose hesitated. "If it's just for a while. I can get you hard copies of everything."

She pried her eyes away from the screen long enough to look up at him. It occurred to her right then: he was a man who knew so much about her husband, these women, and even her, but she knew so very little about him.

"Ambrose."

"Yes?"

"Did Johnny ever say anything to you about Mr. Oliver?"

He tilted his head. "Say anything?"

"Yes. You know how much he trusted him. Probably more than you."

He shrugged. If he was bothered by this statement, he chose not to show it. "I'm sure there were matters Kane Oliver was privy to that I wasn't."

"And Johnny never confided in you about anything—anything he may have wanted to keep from Mr. Oliver?"

"No," he answered without any deliberation.

She surveyed his expression. He was likely a very good poker player, his affect emotionless and plain. He had learned to lie in his profession—and was a very good liar at that.

"Edie?" He shifted his feet.

"What is it?"

"Have you considered what Johnny would have wanted? I mean *really* considered."

"Meaning?"

"That perhaps this DNA lottery, the whole search, is the opposite of it all. He did lock that photo away—"

"I knew my husband better than anyone else. And that includes you," she cut in icily.

"Yes," he said quietly.

"I think I'm good here. You can see your way out, please," she said, dismissing him and turning back to the profiles.

She remained at her desk until well past dinner. Belinda left with an untouched tray of food. When it was near midnight, Edie finally called it a night, slipping into the hallway and down to the Green Room.

She found her way in front of Johnny's portrait. She raised a glass to his expressionless face and then took a sip of whiskey, gritting her teeth. The alcohol practically burned her tongue.

"To you, Mr. Parker," she said quietly, taking another drink.

His eyes in the portrait—the glossy oil paint—seemed to move right back to her.

*What was it that troubled you?*

Something hot started to rise up from her core. A bubbling up of searing liquid. She spat the whiskey back into the glass. She coughed and then spat again with anger, wiping her mouth with the back of her hand. The sudden rage violently took over her as her hand shakily gripped the glass.

*You could have told me, Johnny.*

The more she looked at his face, the more she felt the resentment slipping out of every pore in her body. She held the glass up, aiming, but put it back down. She would not resort to such actions.

She fell to the floor, head tucked down. She couldn't look at it any longer.

*Why? Why did you have to leave me, Johnny?*

———

He ordered the monkfish. Even though she advised him the za'atar seasoning would be too strong.

"You don't have the palate for that, Johnny. I can see it already," Edie had warned.

It was a month or so before the accident when Edie suggested they go to New York City for the weekend. Johnny had been burning the midnight oil, ensuring the success of the wind farm deal that was opening shortly. His irritability was starting to creep up, mirroring the humidity building in the Iowa summer. They flew on a Cessna out of Des Moines on a Friday afternoon. She had made reservations at Le Bernardin, a favorite of Johnny's. They were such regulars that Éric Ripert kept a special table for them in the back that tended to be discreet.

"I've had it before, Edie."

"No, you haven't."

"The white fish with the crust."

"That was something different. That was the—" She put her hands up in surrender. "Fine, fine. But I still think you should have gotten the black bass."

The evening had begun with their usual banter.

She was right. He ended up hating the monkfish, and the server quickly fired up the rack of lamb to replace it. She smothered the smugness building up from her throat—he was already getting aggravated, cutting into the lamb harshly and taking each bite with a look to the side, avoiding eye contact.

"Why don't you get your drink, Johnny?" she suggested lightly.

The whiskey helped. He grew jollier with each sip, laughing at some of the stories she brought up of their first trip to New York City, when there were no smartphones, and finding someplace to eat or stay meant using the yellow pages.

"Do you remember that awful motel in Tribeca?"

"Off Franklin Street?"

"Yes." Johnny pointed a finger at her. "That's the one. So different back then. We were starving because our flight came in so late."

"The pork and shiitake shumais."

"Ohhh. I'd kill for one of those right now, Edie. I really would. I wonder if that place is still open."

They shared a smile, and he reached across the table, taking her hand and then squeezing it.

"Edie."

He seemed shy.

"Yes?" she asked with curiosity.

"Do you ever . . . I mean, do you wonder what it would have been like with more than just us?"

She took a sip of champagne, half laughing into the flute. "You mean if we had children?"

He shrugged, dismissing it quickly. "Ah. It must be the whiskey talking." He looked down at his empty glass. "Speaking of." He motioned for their server but froze.

"Another one already?" she bantered.

The lines around his mouth dipped slightly, but he said nothing.

"Johnny?"

She turned to his line of sight.

Kane Oliver strode in their direction. He whispered something to the hostess, who smiled at him as if they were old friends, then waved toward their table. He wore a dark cobalt-blue suit tailored within its last inch. He had more silver in his hair these days. But his self-assured smile was brasher than ever.

"Ahh, my favorite couple," he said with arms out to them.

Johnny smiled courteously. "Kane."

"I heard you were also dining here, and I had to stop by and say hello."

"What—what brings you to New York?"

Kane laughed. "Didn't you hear?"

Johnny looked down at his empty glass again, shaking the ice before searching for one last sip. "Hear what?"

Kane placed his hands on his chest. "You're looking at the new owner of a penthouse suite in Tribeca."

"Congratulations," Johnny said flatly.

"Yes, congrats," Edie mirrored quietly.

She looked up at Kane, who seemed to be studying Johnny.

The silence lasted a few seconds, but it felt like a weight pulling them down.

"Excuse me for a moment," Johnny said, leaving the table briskly. His tone was civil and his movements even keeled as he buttoned his suit jacket. Johnny was never one to be impolite.

She lowered her eyes and cleared her throat.

It was just her and Kane.

She wasn't sure he even remembered the last time they had been alone in a room . . . she had never told Johnny about Kane's behavior from that night. She never saw the point in it—like drawing water from a dried-out well.

"Well. Either he had to take a piss or he's over the lamb," Kane finally said, picking up a bone from the plate to examine before setting it down.

"I don't think it's either of those," Edie replied firmly.

"Oh, Edie. Don't tell me you're still cross with me," he said.

"I'm sorry?" She straightened up in her chair.

"You don't think I forgot all about that night . . . do you?"

She felt her chest tighten. "I don't know what night you're referring to." In her head, her voice came out strong. But she knew he could hear the wavering—the teetering. The cowardice and shame she felt.

"Oh . . . but I think you do," he said, leaning in closer.

He drew a finger against her shoulder, touching the exposed part of her olive cap-sleeved dress as if it were a single dot to mark.

She jerked away and looked up with relief to see Johnny returning to the table.

He didn't make any indication he was sitting down. Instead, he stood by her place at the table and took her hand. "Well, we were about to head out. Good running into you, Kane."

She barely had a chance to say good evening herself before they made their way to the front of the restaurant. She looked over her shoulder to catch a glimpse of Kane. He hadn't moved, instead standing at their table with his hands in his pockets.

Watching them . . . watching her.

# CHAPTER 13

## ALEX

*September 3, 2022*

"If you prefer, we can go somewhere more private," Alex said quietly.

Whittner's was starting to fill up with patrons looking for their afternoon caffeine pick-me-up.

The final divorce decree lay in front of her client.

A stack of white papers that would seem to erase the last fifteen years of Mayor Janet Vogel's life. Janet stared at it, looking almost afraid to touch it. Her hand hovered and then traced the three yellow tabs indicating where she would make the divorce—the one she had claimed to want so badly for the last year—a reality.

Alex had been a divorce attorney for almost ten years at this point. But no matter who the client, or how long or tumultuous the marriage— rich or poor, gay or straight—this was the part where the finality of it all came at them like a brick wall. All the back-and-forth negotiations, depositions, financial disclosures, even squabbling had come down to this single stack of papers. There was no going back.

"No. Here is fine. It doesn't really matter where I do it," Janet finally answered.

She picked up the pen and held it next to the first yellow pull tab.

"Janet. I want you to listen to me. It really is okay if you need a minute."

Alex could be the fiercest, most unforgiving negotiator, but when it came to her clients, she was the gentle mother to a lamb.

"I guess . . . I didn't realize—"

"Checking on you ladies to see if you needed anything else?" A chipper coffee shop employee stood by with a tray of half-empty mugs and a plate dusted in crumbs.

"No. We need a minute," Alex snapped and glared back.

His grin dissolved like a cube of sugar in hot water, and he swiftly moved on.

Alex nodded encouragingly to Janet. "Go on. You were saying?"

Janet clicked the pen a few times. "I didn't realize this was going to be so . . . so difficult. I thought I would sign laughing."

"It's okay to feel that way. It's been a long year. You're going to be overwhelmed. But I don't want you to feel pressure."

"I don't. But I expected to feel, I don't know—happy? I mean, I thought I'd relive the anger I felt toward Greg. After all I did for him. What I thought was for us? He threw it away. And it's been a constant rage against him ever since I found out he was sleeping around—with my niece for God's sake. This unrelenting, permeating . . . rage."

She paused to shake her head, and then her face dropped.

"Now that it's here in front of me, I don't feel that anymore. I wish it could be the way it was before. You know?"

Alex nodded. "I know."

But she *didn't* know. It was her job to not only take care of her clients in every legal way but also to help them believe they were making the right choice.

In the end, though, there really was no right choice.

"Janet? Do you think living in the past is going to help?"

She sighed and flipped through the papers. "Will this?" Her shoulders sagged. A successful businesswoman and town mayor had been reduced to an unsure, weepy mess. The sight of it all irritated Alex. She wanted to reach across the table and shake her back to her senses. But she was irritated by something else.

What had she said?

*Rage. Permeating rage.*

When had she and Davis ever felt that for each other? That fine line between pure unadulterated passion and loathing. Anything on the emotional scale above annoyance was completely foreign to their marriage. But wasn't it good they had no conflict?

Or was it like a marriage having no pulse? DOA.

*Focus, Alex, focus.*

She took a deep breath and placed her hands on the table. "Janet. You got everything you wanted. All the businesses. Most of the properties. Greg is going to have to start over. This is exactly what we discussed when you first came to me. He's the one who's going to have to face a different life every day. This is what you requested. *This* is what you wanted."

Janet buried her face in her hands. "It is. It *is*. I asked for this."

"Yes."

She watched as her client signed the biggest divorce settlement of her entire career. Three signatures. *Check, check, check!*

"Congratulations: you are officially divorced."

Janet sighed and looked into her empty mug. "I think I need more coffee."

Alex winked. "I think we can do better than that."

———

After sharing a cocktail with Janet just shy of noon, Alex hurried home to get ready for the Labor Day weekend parade. Hardly anyone missed it in Rosemary Hills. Labor Day weekend was the biggest town holiday of the year before everyone got hectic with school and charged toward Thanksgiving at warp speed.

Sasha bounced into the kitchen as Alex started loading the cooler with sparkling waters and sodas, each one carefully placed in neat rows and stacked seamlessly.

"Nala's dad bought fireworks."

"Hmm. That's nice for Nala—I guess." She shook a brown grocery bag open and prudently placed chip bags and plastic plates in an organized fashion.

"She said I could come over after the parade."

"As long as that's okay with Nala's mommy and daddy."

Should she put the napkins in the bottom of the bag? Or would it be better to layer them on top with the plastic utensils?

"It is. And she said we could set off fireworks right away."

"Oh, okay—wait. She said what?" Alex slammed the cooler shut.

"Start fireworks."

"Absolutely not, Sasha. That is way too dangerous for a little girl."

"You said I could go over!"

"Not if that's what you are going over for."

"Then you lied to me."

Alex felt her face flush. "Sasha Hannah Mitchell, you know that isn't true. I said you could go over to Nala's house. I did not say you could play with fireworks!"

Sasha's face scrunched up.

*Here we go. The salient signs of a tantrum.*

She released a fake wail, followed by crying.

Davis appeared as he buttoned up a midnight-blue polo. He smoothed his already neatly combed hair as he brought in a waft of cologne. "What happened?"

Alex put her hand up. "Nothing."

Sasha sat down hard on the kitchen floor and cried harder.

"Doesn't look like nothing. Sasha, what's wrong, honey?"

"Davis . . . don't. She's having a tantrum. Don't give her an audience. Remember, we talked about this?"

He ignored her. "Please tell Daddy what's wrong."

"Mommy . . . wonletme . . . meanfireworks!" Sasha blubbered. He picked her up and patted her back.

"Great." Alex threw her arms in the air.

He narrowed his eyes. "What is your problem, Alex? You know she's not one of your divorce clients."

"Of course I know that. Do you even want to know why she's upset? She wants to play with fireworks. So please—go ahead and indulge that."

It was the closest thing to an argument they'd had in months. She secretly relished it. It was as though signs of life were breathing between them.

Davis looked taken aback. "Fireworks? Well . . ." He placed Sasha back down. "Sasha, honey. Mommy is right. You're too young for that."

She had settled down by this point. He took the opportunity to distract her. "How about a cupcake before the parade?"

"So now you're rewarding her for that?"

"Let's drop it, Alex." Davis turned to the refrigerator, completely dismissing her.

He came back around with one of the red velvet cupcakes Alex had stayed up baking the night before and handed it to Sasha.

"That's not on her food list today."

Davis whirled around and placed his face close to Alex's. "Enough already, Alex. We're not robots."

He grabbed his keys from the counter.

"You're not going to the parade with us?"

"I thought I told you already. I have to finish up some work at the office. I'll meet you both at the carnival." He knelt down. "Sasha—give me a kiss and hug. I'll see you later. You enjoy your cupcake, sweetie."

It wasn't until Alex heard the car start in the garage that she moved again. She looked over at the kitchen table, where Sasha was quietly enjoying her cupcake. The garage door shut, bringing her further back in motion. She had been choosing to ignore it for the last few months. The random work projects. Claiming he had "told her already," a ridiculous notion because she would never forget something like that. The sudden need to look good. He never wore polos on weekends, let alone cologne.

And he never missed the parade.

Was she paranoid? His actions were on the subtle side. Tiny pebbles that hardly made waves. She had been a divorce attorney long enough to know that it wasn't ever some grand gesture that led to a discovery.

*Wait, what discovery?* She almost laughed out loud. She had been knee deep in her work for too long. Davis was far too practical, conventional to even consider something like that . . .

And then there was the comment.

*We're not robots.*

Was he right? Was it all too much?

Maud had been *too much*, the overbearing force in the household growing up—her father a much smaller figure. They were the David and Goliath of married couples. She had tried so hard, so very hard to be anything but even a shadow of Maud.

Yet here she was. Facing a sick, twisted parallel of mother-daughter mirroring. And she wanted out of their miming game.

*No, I am nothing like Maud. Sasha has it easy compared to that.*

Although admittedly, Sasha was presented with the similar highly structured, rigid upbringing Alex had been subjected to. She reluctantly recognized she had her daughter in a hold that some would say was a bit too strong. But she came from a place of complete love and devotion—a need to protect her. Her objective was to make sure Sasha felt none of the pain that she had as a little girl.

"Pain." That wasn't a strong enough word.

Pain. The night her father left.

It was the last time she would see him. Her father had come back for his things right as they had begun to eat dinner. Maud sat silently at the dinner table, a single glance at Alex, daring her to even try to get up and greet him.

"You did this, you know," he'd said.

"Did I?" Maud mocked.

"Yes."

Her voice may have been pure anger. But as she stared down at her plate and reached for her water glass, her hand shook weakly.

"Daddy?"

He knelt next to Alex, hand still on his suitcase. She wanted so badly to throw her chair back and cling to his neck—hang on like an ornament and follow him out the door. But she sat as still as possible, head down, eyes cast slightly to the side to catch a glimpse of him.

"Alex . . . I'm going to go away for a while. But I promise—"

He stopped, clenched his fist, and turned to glare at Maud. Whatever he was about to promise, he knew he wouldn't be able to keep.

"Alexandra, return to your plate," she ordered.

"She's not a dog, you know. She's a little girl."

Maud tilted her head and smiled tightly, knife and fork poised gracefully in her hands. "Yes, and you're leaving her."

There was no sign of him for months. A year later she received a birthday card—a pink bunny with glitter. But that was the last she ever heard from him. It was like he faded away and had never been part of her life at all. An imaginary friend she had conjured up and released years ago.

After her father was gone, she had felt so very exposed to the elements of Maud. There was no one else in the house to soften the inelastic hand she ruled with.

Her mother was a woman always in survival mode. Hands up, ready to guard against the next throw of disappointment or upheaval. Doing it all with a stiff and righteous front, an iceberg ready to cause damage.

But she seemed to crave something else.

Underneath all the harshness, there was a woman who needed to be wanted. Desired, just like any other woman. Except with her husband gone, she had a daughter to care for—alone.

Her mother hadn't worked in years. She didn't waste much time, soon getting a job at a drugstore. Alex was often alone while her mother worked overnight shifts. She would hear her come home early in the morning, the keys hitting the bowl on the counter as she lay in bed unable to return to sleep.

She wasn't sure if she was ever able to truly relax around Maud. Her mere presence put her on edge, waiting for the next move that would displease her.

For most little girls, Easter morning was a time of excitement. Alex had dreaded it. Easter service meant a pretty dress. A pretty dress meant it had to be kept immaculate. Maud had bought her a peach dress, a satin sash, and black Mary Janes. She had tried with every ounce of energy to stay clean in that dress. She sat quietly in the living room while she waited for Maud to finish up.

But there was that loose tooth.

It kept snagging at her gumline. The more she tickled it with her tongue, the more the jagged edge would cut into her mouth. And then she felt a slight tear . . . blood trickled down her chin. She frantically grabbed at her face.

It was too late. A single drop of blood met her collar.

Maud came in and noticed it immediately. Her eyes flashed, and she roughly picked Alex up by the arm and dragged her into the bathroom.

"Look at this. Is this what good little girls do?" She pointed to the blood spot and took a washcloth, scrubbing fiercely.

"It's not coming out . . . Alexandra!" She stopped herself. Instead, she tilted Alex's head back.

"Open."

"Mother . . ."

"Open!"

She obeyed. With one wrenching jolt, Maud placed two fingers on the tooth and ripped it out. Alex cried from the pain. Blood splattered down her dress front.

She wore a plain navy dress to Easter service, her mouth swollen and full as if stuffed with cotton balls. She was around Sasha's age.

Maud came to her room that night. She apologized in her own way. Smoothed her hair a few times and then told her it was for her own good.

"Someday you'll understand, Alex. Mother is just trying to make you strong."

She had nodded dutifully. Her mouth did feel better without the loose tooth.

"Your father always thought I was too harsh on you. Do you think so, Alex?"

She shook her head and quietly mouthed, "No."

"I thought so," she replied as she pulled the white quilt comforter up higher over Alex. "You know . . . my father left, too, when I was young. It was very hard on my mother and me. She didn't—handle it as well. Being abandoned and cast aside like that . . ."

She straightened her hands and looked down at them.

Alex tilted her chin up and out from the comforter. "You never talk about her."

"Who?"

"Your mother."

Maud had stared back, her mouth open to say something else. But she moved her head away and patted the sides of the comforter before folding the top of it down in one even line.

"Time for bed, dear Alex." She reached her hand up, poised to touch Alex's cheek. She withdrew and reached for the lamp instead, turning it off.

She sensed in the darkness her mother's urge for it to be quiet. For her daughter to be silent and still, nonexistent in the night.

# CHAPTER 14

*September 3, 2022*

Rosemary Hills's Labor Day Parade was held promptly at 5:00 p.m. the first Saturday of September each year. Rain or shine, the parade went on—one year a tornado watch was issued, and not a single eyebrow was raised when most of the town remained in their parade-watching postures. Tradition trumped change in every sense of the word on this day.

Every shop, restaurant, and business was closed. Signs flipped over on Friday night in anticipation for the next day's celebrations. Anyone who needed groceries or a last-minute shopping trip on parade day was almost certainly "not from around here."

When asked if the parade would be canceled, given the controversial DNA lottery recently set forth and the risk of protesters, Mayor Janet Vogel was quoted saying, "Over my dead divorcée body."

The entire afternoon prior to the parade down Rosemary Street was filled to the brim with pie-eating contests, three-legged races, the crowning of Miss Rosemary Hills, and, of course, the opening of the carnival that graced the town with its presence each year. A wide and long clearing near Avalon Park was the setting for the carnival—where the smell of kettle corn, fried dough, and cotton candy and the shrieks of children on rickety rides all converged into one giant declaration that the town's Labor Day festivities had begun.

The dragging humidity of August had somehow dissipated on this day, giving room to unusual high winds and dry air. The tall switchgrass in the field danced with each wave of coolness that seemed to be calling for summer to make way for fall. A bundle of balloons came loose at one of the carnival booths, a sudden burst of colors outlined against the sky.

—

# CLEO

Cleo's eyes followed a red balloon as it brushed right above her head and then sailed higher and higher. She held her hand up over her brow and didn't look away until it was a tiny speck, dissolving into nonexistence.

She smiled down at Rocky, who was awestruck by the lights and sounds of the carnival. His gray eyes scanned the sights with laser focus, as though he didn't want to miss a single whirl of a ride or throw of a ball in a rip-off game for cheap stuffed animals. He'd started to lead her to a fried Oreo stand when she noticed the time on her watch.

"Rocky, sweetie. It's time to head to the parade."

He looked up at her with pleading eyes. She felt extreme guilt lately. Way beyond the normal, everyday "mom guilt" that plagued her regardless. Hers was the kind that flew off the meter. With Michael being absent, she felt this constant need to please Rocky—somehow making up for it all. But the rational part of her brain (if *that* even existed these days) knew that no matter how many fried Oreos on a stick she let him eat or rides she let him go on, it would not replace what they had left behind in Chicago.

*Damn you, Michael.*

That same thought would pierce through each time she yielded to another one of Rocky's requests. She repeated it again as she handed Rocky the mess of a dough ball on a stick that reeked of a nauseatingly sweet and oily aroma.

The parade was just about to start as she found her mother waving at them from her lawn chair. Ji-Yeon made it a yearly tradition to camp out in a prime location a good three hours before the parade began. This year, she had brought along two additional lawn chairs. Even as early as lunchtime, it wasn't unusual for the front rows to already be filled or "claimed." The claiming had gotten so out of hand last year that Mayor Vogel had to issue a "no more than four" chair-claiming ordinance.

"Hurry, hurry!" Ji-Yeon called at them, waving Rocky into her arms. She held him close to her chest as the blares of the fire engines cut through the hum of the crowd. Each side of Rosemary Street was packed with people among a montage of coolers, lawn chairs, and blankets.

"Here we go!" Cleo shouted excitedly over the noise.

The high school marching band set forth with drums and cymbals proclaiming the beginning of the parade, followed by a fleet of fire trucks. Firemen threw what looked like sheets of candy to the children.

"Mommy?" Rocky looked at Cleo for permission. She nodded and handed him a grocery bag to fill with the giant Tootsie Rolls and rainbows of Dum Dums that had already rolled by his sneakers.

The ginormous "rose" float passed next. It was one of the highlights of the parade, the rose in a different form each year. This year, the rose was a vast papier-mâché island for Miss Rosemary Hills and her court to sit upon.

"Is that a princess?" Rocky asked.

Cleo had to stifle a snort. "Kind of."

The Knights of Columbus, Lions Club, and Shriners floats were next. Most of the town's men over sixty waved lightly at the crowd.

*Where are the women's clubs?* she thought. *Some things never change.*

A long line of Little League, soccer, and other sports teams made up the middle of the parade. Parents called out to their kids, and each one grinned cheesily back—their moment to shine.

Rocky's grocery bag was now bulging and ready to rip from all the candy he had collected. She was in the middle of asking her mother if she had another bag when the Rosemary Hills Police Department float sailed by—a large semi hauling a flatbed of police officers, many flinging buckets of candy into the air.

She felt sixteen again. Frozen, awkward, and unsure of whether to even look for Will. Would it be obvious if she waved? Did he even remember their run-in at the coffee shop? She considered turning around and pretending to be busy. But wouldn't that look rude and immature?

And then she spotted him before she could make a decision. He sat on the back end of the flatbed and flashed her a huge grin as he chucked an overflowing bucket of candy right in Rocky's direction. Rocky squealed with excitement.

"Thank you!" he called after him.

Will waved back.

Cleo thought her face was going to burn off from the rush of red.

"Who was that?" Ji-Yeon asked in Korean as she scooped up a few mini candy bars into Rocky's stash. The police department's float was the last one, and the avenue was suddenly clear.

She didn't have time to answer.

Across the street she saw her. Clapping and cheering for the police department. Next to her, a little girl jumping up and down with excitement. She looked about Rocky's age. Her hair was longer than it had been in high school. She wore conservative periwinkle bermudas and a sleeveless white collared shirt. Her head turned in Cleo's direction, and her clapping slowed down until her hands remained clasped.

Alex stared back at Cleo, her mouth in a half grimace, half smile that quickly thawed into a straight line. Her arm started to raise as if she was attempting a wave, but it fell limp.

Parade-watchers quickly began to fill the street, as though the pavement were swallowing them all up. Heads bobbed up and down, masking the face from the past. Cleo strained to see it again.

But by the time the crowd cleared for a few seconds, the woman and her daughter were gone.

———

As promised, Cleo returned to the carnival with Rocky, while her mother camped nearby with their lawn chairs to rest. Cleo handed him twenty dollars and told him he could play games worth that much, and that would be it.

*We'll see,* Rocky's smirk seemed to say.

He played ring toss a few times and then fished in a pool of rubber ducks to win a goldfish. By then the twenty was almost gone.

"I'm thirsty," he announced, holding the water-filled bag up to his face, his nose nearly poking the goldfish.

Cleo quickly looked around and spotted a lemonade and smoothie stand. She stood in line holding on to Rocky and felt a tap on her arm.

"Sweetie, we have to wait in line. I know you're thirsty."

"Sweetie? I guess I'll take that."

She twirled around, startled to see Will standing behind her. No longer in his uniform, his sudden casual civilian look was especially striking.

"Oh, I thought you were . . ." She looked over at Rocky.

"Your son? Hi there." He held his hand out to Rocky.

"Hey! You're the one who threw all the candy!"

"I did. I hope you got enough."

Suddenly shy, Rocky put his arm around Cleo's waist and drew himself in.

"It's okay, Rocky. This is Mommy's friend, Will. He's a police officer."

"So nice to meet you," said Will, politely peering down at him.

Rocky popped out from hiding. "Hello."

"That's better," Cleo said and then tucked him under her arm.

Will gave a friendly laugh.

"What's so funny?"

"I just . . . life is so strange. The last time I saw you, you were probably sixteen, wearing boot-cut jeans, and here you are—a mom."

She shrugged apologetically. "It's been a while."

"It looks good on you. Being a mom."

The line started to move ahead. "You here by yourself?" She looked behind him.

"Yeah. Kind of. Some of the buddies on the force are here, but to be brutally honest, I really came to get something fried on a stick."

She laughed. "I'm pretty sure that's something you can accomplish tonight."

Rocky wiggled with impatience as they waited in line. A teenage boy wearing a pink hat and apron stuck his head out. "Next!"

"Listen. I'd love to run into you again at Whittner's. Do you think you might be there this week?"

Will leaned forward slightly with a shy expression.

Cleo felt her face on fire for the second time that day. Rocky yanked at her shirt. "Mommy!" She patted his shoulder a few times.

"Oh. Yes. I'm sure—sure, I'll be there . . . okay, sweetie. What kind do you want?"

"I'll see you around then," Will said. He gave Rocky another smile and wink.

*God, he really does look good.*

She swiftly paid for a strawberry lemonade and whisked Rocky away.

"Bye, police officer man!" he shouted.

———

# ALEX

"Are you listening, Mommy?"

Alex felt the bottom of her shorts being tugged on. For a moment she forgot where she was. Her daughter's face appeared to be underwater, her mouth moving in slow, shape-shifting drawls. The clamor of the parade crowd dispersing seared through her ears, jolting her back to attention.

It had happened so quickly.

One second she was helping Sasha open a package of grape Nerds, and the next she looked up to see Cleo Song standing across the street. A ghost tugged at the root of something planted so deep inside her that she almost gripped her midsection in response. The face across the street was more inquisitive than threatening, yet the pounding in her chest and head grew louder. She looked down again at Sasha, her voice still mute.

"Can I? Please, Mommy?"

"What's that?"

"Mommy!"

Her exasperation finally broke through to Alex.

"Sorry, Sasha. What is it that you want?"

"Go ride the kiddie train with Nala? And when is Daddy getting here?"

She looked up again and searched the cluster of faces that had replaced the ones from before. Cleo was gone. Had she imagined it?

"So . . . can I?"

Nala and her mother looked on with a mix of anticipation and confusion, the curly-haired girl clinging to her mother's arm.

"Oh. Yes. As long as it's okay with Nala's mom."

They agreed to meet at the ticket booth in a half hour. Her sudden child-free state magnified the fact that Davis was still not there. Alex sent him a text.

**Where are you? The parade is over and Sasha is asking for you.**

She stood by a popcorn vendor and waited a few minutes, but no response. She started to call him but pulled her hand down to her side. *I'm not going to hound him. He would be here if he wanted.*

She decided to head to the ticket booth early. As she waited, the distractions of Sasha and Davis dissipated and were replaced with Cleo's placid face. Her hands began to tremble. When was the last time she ate? Did she even have breakfast? She stepped up to the nearest food vendor and shakily handed over a five-dollar bill for a corn dog. The first bite released steam into her mouth. She jolted her head back and cursed.

"Language, Sissy!"

Violet, who suddenly appeared out of nowhere, gave a silvery laugh and blew on the end of the corn dog. The ends of her hair swept over Alex's wrist as she brought her head back up.

"There. Now take a bite."

Alex silently and slowly complied. "What are you doing here?" she asked after finishing chewing.

Violet shook her hair back and dusted her hands on her cutoffs.

"What do you mean? The whole town is here! I'm with some friends." She nodded to the left. A group of teenagers in a circular formation looked down at their phones, heads bowed in unison.

"Mother let you out of the house in that?" Alex pointed her corn dog stick at Violet's shorts.

She thought back to how severe Maud had been about her clothing at this age, how constricting it was. How Violet had been spared from the same enforcement. And from other inflictions . . .

"Not everyone can pull off bermudas like you," Violet teased and then gave another carefree giggle.

Alex's midsection tightened again. She brushed crumbs off her mouth and began to walk away.

"I need to get going. Sasha is waiting for me."

"Really? Wait. One ride with me. Please?" Violet placed her hand on Alex's shoulder.

"I can't. I told her friend's mother I would—"

"Oh, c'mon, Sissy! We've never gone on a ride together," she pleaded.

"I don't think so. I need to get to my daughter."

Her abdomen suddenly felt as if it were being wrung out to dry. The skin around her throat felt tight.

Violet persisted and latched on to her arm. "She'll be fine. C'mon, Sissy. Just one quick one. I think the Tilt-A-Whirl is right over—"

"No. I said no, Violet," Alex replied coldly and then dropped her arm down. "And stop calling me that."

She didn't look over her shoulder as she walked away. She didn't have to. The confused, roaming eyes of Violet were already firmly in her memory.

———

## JEMMA

The parade had worn out the rest of Jemma's clan. She decided to spare them the campaign meet and greets at the carnival and went solo.

Her outfit seemed to raise a few eyebrows. She swore she heard an elderly woman say "No decency" in a hushed voice.

She had texted a photo of herself to Peter earlier that morning with the caption **Too much?**

Peter's response? **Never.**

And that was why she kept him on her payroll. Why couldn't a woman in her midthirties wear a red body-con dress for some Labor Day weekend festivities? It wasn't *that* low cut. And the red wasn't fire-engine red. It was more of a maroon.

She made her way through the crowd, being stopped every few food booths or stands for a picture or to talk about how nice the weather was. In Iowa, you talked about the weather, goddammit.

"Senator Danowski! I plan on voting for you!"

"Shame what that Motts lady keeps saying about you."

"Can I get a selfie with you? My husband just loves you."

"What are your thoughts on that DNA lottery thing?"

By the time she'd reached the outer edge of the carnival, she was ready to call it a night. She made a right at the Pronto Pups truck and stepped out toward the beginning of the park's tree line. She could see the sign for Avalon Park, the white block letters illuminated by the carnival lights.

*So this is where they found you . . . this is where it all goes back to.*

She must have been staring at it for a while before the banging of a metal food truck door startled her.

Her feet suddenly hurt, the high wedge sandals obviously a mistake. She went around behind the food trucks to avoid the crowd. She was starting to feel tired, and the thought of putting Henry to bed made her pick up the pace. As she got closer to the carnival entrance, she noticed a little girl chasing a boy in what seemed to be an animated game of tag. She smiled—the girl reminded her a little of Poppy. Poppy from ten years ago, a girl who would giggle with delight at a sparkler on a night like tonight.

The little girl ran to her mother.

*Alex.*

She stopped midstride. Her eyes went from Alex to the little boy, who ran to a woman with dark hair that cascaded down her shoulders.

*Cleo.*

The three women halted as if time had stopped. They searched each other's faces for the same recognition, a game of reflection. A circus fun house full of warped mirrors bringing back the past, each taking turns to draw the others in, a cautious reception.

Jemma was the first to break the silence. "How long has it been?"

Alex crossed her arms and rubbed them as if suddenly cold. "Eighteen years?"

"That long?"

She had likely spotted Alex in more recent years in town, always from a distance—silently passing but never really acknowledging each other. Never stopping for even a brief exchange, pretending the other didn't exist out of sheer survival. What would they have even said?

"Well, it's good to see you both," Cleo said softly. The little boy smacked her behind.

"Got you, you're it!"

"Rocky . . ."

The three women laughed in relief. The beauty of children—bringing adults to their senses at the most somber of times. Even if a reprieve for only a brief moment.

"Your son?" Jemma asked.

Cleo nodded proudly.

"I didn't know you were in town."

"I just moved back."

Alex stepped closer. "I don't mean to be the rude one here. But I'm going to cut right to it. You both have obviously heard."

"The lottery?" Jemma pulled the edge of her dress down.

The word hung heavy in the air.

Cleo glanced at Rocky. "Maybe we should . . ."

"Another time?" suggested Jemma.

Before any of them could respond, they had to shield their eyes. Headlights blared on them, creating a glaring spotlight. The lights dimmed to reveal a long black Lincoln Town Car, blending into the night. The passenger door opened, and an attractive woman wearing a pantsuit stepped out. She looked first toward Alex.

"Are you Alexandra Mitchell?"

"Yes," Alex replied in an annoyed tone.

"And Cleo Song? Jemma Danowski?"

Cleo looked over at Jemma with confusion.

"How do you know—"

"I'm Robin Khaled. The attorney for Mrs. Edie Parker."

"And?" Jemma demanded, her hands on both hips.

"Please come with me. She would like to see all three of you."

# CHAPTER 15

## CLEO

*September 3, 2022*

Cleo shielded her eyes and brought Rocky in closer. The bright head-lights seemed to isolate them from the rest of the carnival crowd, casting a bubble around them.

The three women looked back at the attorney as if she'd come there to abduct them. She took a step back, perhaps to ease their trepidation.

Alex immediately lashed out.

"I'm an attorney as well, and why would we even consider getting in that car? What authority do you have? And I didn't quite catch your name?"

"Robin Khaled. I work for Edie Parker."

"Well, Robin, if Edie Parker wants to see me, she can come to my house."

"I'm afraid that isn't possible."

"Then I guess we're done here," she said sharply and then gripped Sasha's hand.

Cleo felt a sudden instinct of urgency.

*This can't be ignored.*

She swayed toward Alex to stop her but hesitated.

*It could be our only chance to get answers.*

She stepped forward. "Wait." She held her hand under her nose for a moment as if to collect herself. "What exactly is it that Edie Parker wants from us?"

"I'm not able to tell you that," answered Robin evenly.

"Of course you aren't," Alex sneered.

Robin kept her cool. "If you want more information, you will have to talk to Mrs. Parker herself."

Jemma moved in front of Cleo and Alex as if to guard them.

"And if we don't?"

"I can only say this: you don't want to cross Edie Parker."

"Is that a threat?" Jemma's eyes flashed.

"No. I'm only trying to help you." Robin opened the back seat door and then returned to her place in the front of the car. She held the door open with her right hand.

"Talk to her. If you don't like what she has to say, you are of course able to walk out at any time." She waved her hand. "Freely."

"Where would we be going?" Cleo asked.

"Rosemary House."

Everyone in town knew of Rosemary House. It was like an exclusive painting in a museum—admired at a distance but never touched. No one was allowed beyond the private gate and stone walls built around the perimeter.

Cleo turned to Jemma and Alex. "Let's just . . . see what she has to say. If we don't, this will only linger over our heads."

Jemma twisted her mouth to the side with consideration. "She's right, you know."

Alex remained unconvinced, her jawline set hard. "What's there to gain by going?"

As stubborn as Alex was presenting herself, Cleo caught a glimmer of something else in her voice. A twinge of uncertainty or—panic maybe.

"You know if we don't, you'll go home and you won't be able to stop thinking about it."

Alex gave the slightest of nods. She shot a hard look back at Robin. "I'll have to arrange for someone to watch my daughter. The children aren't going in that house—*that* I'm not budging on."

"My mother can watch them," Cleo offered. "This won't take long, will it?"

"I don't think so," Robin replied from the car.

Cleo lowered her voice to a more soothing tone. "She can watch Rocky and Sasha. And we can come right back here after and then all go home."

She saw Alex's shoulders relax a notch. After careful instructions and handoff of the kids to a concerned-looking Ji-Yeon, the three women entered the back of the spacious town car.

The ride to Rosemary House was in absolute silence. Every creak of a seat cushion, clearing of the throat was magnified in what seemed like a tomb of a vehicle. Down the main county highway it went first and then took a sudden right onto a rural road. In the dusk it was hard to see where they were. Ten miles later, the car took a sharp turn and the darkness cleared. Bright floodlights exposed an expansive wrought iron gate.

The driver pulled up to the main entrance, in front of dark-red double doors that were twice the height of standard ones. Robin exited the car and opened the door for the women. They filed out and then into the house. The entryway was brightly lit, the Calacatta flooring reflecting with such shine that Cleo almost felt bad stepping on it. She followed Jemma, with Alex trailing behind.

Alex stood stationary in the doorway as if her legs had locked. She seemed out of breath, her right hand clutching her lower left arm.

"Alex?" Cleo paused as she looked over her shoulder. "Hold on."

Jemma stopped her charging stride. "What's wrong?"

"Are you all right?"

"I'm fine. I just didn't think—" Alex's voice trailed off. She blinked hard and seemed to snap out of whatever trance she was in. "I'm fine. Let's get this over with." Her snappy tone had returned.

Robin led them farther down the hall to another set of double doors.

"This is the Green Room. Please make yourselves comfortable. Mrs. Parker will be with you shortly." She opened the doors and gestured in as if she were the maître d' leading them to their table. "Belinda?"

A petite woman in an all-black shift dress brought over a tray of coffee and a carafe of water. She appeared to be older but moved with swiftness and precision.

"Can I bring you ladies anything else? Tea?"

The three of them glanced at each other for answers as they sat in large armchairs by the fireplace.

Taking their collective reserved state as an answer, Belinda retreated. Cleo's eyes roamed over the room. It was a lot to take in at once—the Green Room had the makings of a museum's library. Wall-to-wall bookcases. The ceiling so high it was practically a rotunda. Each wall housed a large framed portrait—surely custom oil paintings that must have cost a fortune. One depicted the front of Rosemary House, the second Edie Parker sitting in a grassy field, the third a landscape of the rolling hills that flanked the estate, and the last—Mr. Jonathan Parker himself. The background obscure, he was painted from the waist up, arms rigidly at his sides.

Cleo studied that painting in particular as it was directly in her eyesight. He hadn't been an especially handsome man—in fact, he'd have a forgettable face if it wasn't for the fact he was a famed billionaire. The painting was likely commissioned when he was younger, with only a few streaks of gray in his hair. She spotted a bright-green jeweled ring on his right hand, practically in a closed fist, the gold paint of the band shining bright.

She returned her attention to the other women. No one touched the tray or cups.

And so they waited.

A few minutes in, Jemma had opened her mouth to speak when the doors opened.

"Apologies if I kept you waiting," a smooth voice said to them.

In the entryway stood a regal-looking woman. She wasn't large in stature, but her presence was a big one. Dressed in a cream jacket and skirt, she appeared to play the part of a politician's wife. Her cola-brown hair was cut evenly right at her neckline. Her glass-like cornflower-blue eyes shone with intelligence. She may have just hit seventy, but she made it appear so uncomplicated.

Each step she took toward them made her more of the teacher and the three grown women before her little girls shrinking into their seats, unsure of this new authority in the classroom.

"I'm Edie Parker."

"We know," Jemma said with a dash of haughtiness.

Cleo shot her a warning look.

The corners of Edie's mouth raised faintly. "I'm not going to pretend like you wouldn't. I'd be surprised if you didn't. Feigning modesty is something I don't have time for."

She took a chair next to Alex, who stiffened subtly.

"The problem is I do not know any of you." Edie's eyes remained closed a millisecond too long when she blinked, giving her the appearance of someone talking through water.

There was no rushing this woman.

"Maybe you can tell us why you brought us here then," said Cleo.

"Yes . . . well. I would like to thank you for coming, first off." There was such politeness in her mannerisms. Her tone. Every turn of her head and every look reeked of civility.

But the politeness did not create ease in Cleo, or seemingly in the other women. It only turned up the volume on their trepidation.

"I want to assure you that this does not come with a pretense of forcefulness. It makes it even better that you came here on your own."

"'On your own' might not be the right words," said Jemma.

"Perhaps. But you are here, aren't you?" Edie gave a small laugh.

Alex broke in abruptly. "Yes. Clearly. And we don't plan on staying long. So . . . if you wouldn't mind . . ." She turned and looked Edie straight in the eye—she had woken up from whatever lull she had fallen into.

"Directness. Always admirable. Yes. I will get to the point." Edie's long fingers gripped the arms of her chair and then released. "I can't imagine you haven't already thought this is about the DNA lottery set forth? Let's not pretend you thought otherwise. Yes. It is. But there is more."

"Wait—how did you know where to find us? The three of us haven't seen each other in years, and then suddenly your attorney appears?" Cleo asked.

"Would it bother you if I didn't have an answer for that?"

"Yes."

"I'm afraid we will have to leave it at that." Edie brushed Cleo's concern aside like a gnat. She clearly was used to saying what she wanted, when she wanted. "Now, where was I? The point of you all coming here . . . there has been much speculation over why I would do something so outlandish so soon after my husband's death. Giving away shares of the company, one he and I sweat blood and tears over to build, is not something I take lightly. There is a deeper purpose to the DNA lottery."

"You're trying to solve that case," said Jemma.

Edie didn't seem surprised. "Yes. The whole town already has guessed such. The Baby Ava case that has gone unsolved in Rosemary Hills for the past eighteen years. I've heard of it over the years, just like I'm sure the three of you have."

"So this is to help solve an eighteen-year-old case?"

"Not entirely," Edie replied. She stood up and put her hand in her jacket pocket. "This is about my husband. In the days after his sudden death, it was discovered he had . . . an interest."

"Interest," Alex uttered so faintly only Cleo caught it.

"With the Baby Ava case. He wanted to solve it. Identify the poor infant by identifying the perpetrator. In this case, the mother. It was a quest he had. And I have every intention of fulfilling that quest."

"Again, what does that have to do with us?" Alex demanded.

Edie pulled her hand out and laid a piece of paper on the circular oak table centered among them all.

"Recognize the names?"

The three women leaned in. There it was—written unmistakably were their maiden names.

Jemma shrugged. "So what? Our names on paper?"

Edie's eyes brightened as she sat back down. "These three names were found written on a piece of evidence. Evidence found in my husband's possessions."

"And what exactly is this 'piece of evidence'?" Alex asked.

Edie shook her head. "I can't disclose that. Not even the authorities know about it." Her jaw set tightly. "But I do know this. There is only one explanation—the three of you are somehow linked to the Baby Ava case."

Alex scoffed. "This means nothing. Anyone could have written our names and placed it with his things. I can't believe you brought us all this way for this." She stood up and looked at Cleo and Jemma. "Ready?"

Edie disregarded her and pushed on. "I would ask kindly—very kindly—that you simply cooperate." Her head turned slowly to Alex, like a dying record on a turntable. "If this is as ridiculous as you seem to think, then submitting DNA samples freely will be no problem."

Their collective silent response echoed loudly in the chambers of the Green Room.

"Do any of you have a problem with submitting?" She eyed each of them, searching their faces for any sort of trigger.

But none of the women would answer. None of them willing to crack.

For one second she seemed to falter from the quiet. She pressed on and spoke with no remorse.

"The offer still stands to freely submit a DNA sample. The condition, though, is that it must be all three of you."

"Condition?" Cleo asked with a raised brow.

"I'm not one to wait around. But I'm also very fair. I am giving you three the choice to submit your DNA samples on your own volition by the lottery-drawing date. If any of you do not, then I will have no choice but to submit this evidence to the authorities."

She rose from her seat as if a timer had been set off. "And then whatever my husband found will no longer be just three names."

# CHAPTER 16

They were dropped off at the same spot they were picked up. The anticipation in the air was either for the fireworks about to start or the decision weighing on their minds. Alex ran forward quickly to grab Sasha and held her close to her chest. She looked at the other women through Sasha's hair, the fierce look of a mother needing the arms of her child. Rocky reached out for Cleo's hand as Ji-Yeon studied her daughter with a perplexed expression.

On the return ride, they had spoken little. The shock and panic dropped on them had rendered them speechless, left with racing thoughts of just how much they had to lose. Eighteen years—eighteen years of what each of them had managed to build since that night was now on the brink of crumbling away.

Only Jemma was able to utter that they should wait. Think things over. They would meet again soon.

The first of the fireworks burst up into the sky. A brilliant red and then flashing white. The children were open-mouthed, eyes round with wonder.

Whatever momentum they'd had in life was now slowed down, their bodies coated in liquid metal. They were forced to answer the beckoning from the past reaching out with urgency—when they were neither girls nor women.

No one was safe from the widow's request. No one was immune from that night.

———

# JEMMA

*Friday, homecoming weekend: Eighteen years ago*

Jemma refused to go to Travis Turner's party. She'd been exhausted lately, and the thought of cramming herself between six other people on a couch, waving away weed fumes and watching everyone get wasted, did not sound like a good time.

"What's wrong with you? It's our last Friday before homecoming. And you don't want to go to Travis's party?" Ashley asked by their locker after fourth period.

"I'm sick of the same thing every weekend. Don't you want to chill for once?"

Ashley laughed sarcastically. "Chill?"

"Yes. Stay *in*. Maybe watch a movie? C'mon, it would be fun. We can have Shaina over too. Only if she promises to stop being a bitch for two seconds."

They both laughed.

"Jem, seriously, though. This is senior year!"

Ashley looked at her pleadingly. She was a good friend. The kind who hadn't tried to steal her boyfriends and probably didn't talk behind her back *that* often.

"I guess," she began. "If Eric doesn't go."

"Ugh, Eric. All he wants to do is boink you. You can just see it in his face all day."

"Ashley!" Jemma slammed her locker shut.

"Oh, stop acting like you're a prude. I heard you two through the hotel wall after winter formal last year."

Her face reddened.

"Sorry," Ashley said quickly.

She had entered senior year one of the most popular girls at Rosemary Hills High School, without a boyfriend and, more significantly—without Eric Housley. There were rumors of cheating. Eric wanting to move on to bigger and better things. But only Jemma and Ashley knew the real reason they had broken up . . .

*Is this your first time? What's wrong?*

The party was almost exactly as Jemma had predicted. A crowded basement of overly horny seniors, all trying to puff their chests to get attention. Ashley—on the other hand—was not wasting time, flirting with Ronnie Song shamelessly and whispering into his ear. Jemma felt a twinge of jealousy. By then, she was ready to go home.

"Ashley . . . Ashley!" She tugged on her sleeve.

"What?" she asked, giggling as she put her arm around Ronnie.

"Let's go."

"Seriously? No, bitch. I'm staying!" She kissed Ronnie on the cheek and reached for his beer.

"Oh, so it's going to be like that, huh?" Ronnie joked, trying to take it back. He looked up at Jemma and grinned. "How are you tonight, Jemma?"

She smiled—Ronnie always had that effect on her. "I—I just get sick of this scene. Don't you?"

"Yeah . . . I know what you mean," he managed to reply before Ashley put the bottle of beer to his mouth, laughing as if it were the funniest thing to happen this century.

Jemma put her hands up.

*What am I doing here?*

She made her way to the bottom of the basement stairway. The thuds of someone beginning to descend them shook under her feet.

Eric towered three steps above her. He was alone. And he didn't smile.

"Hey," he said.

She tugged at her peasant blouse. "I was just leaving," she said quietly.

He looked at her as if she were something to be feared. "Okay . . . cool then."

She stood motionless as he passed her. She could hear Eric make his way down the rest of the way, the steps creaking even over the Good Charlotte music blasting from Travis's basement computer speakers. Loud whoops and "Yeah, it's Eric!" reverberated up to her, and she ran up the rest of the stairs to silence it.

She didn't go home right away. Sleep hadn't come easily to her lately. She made a stop at the old second-run movie theater on Hyacinth Street, where you could pay five bucks for a movie and popcorn. She quietly gave the ticket-booth worker a five and took her popcorn in the theater to see *Minority Report*. It was the 1:30 a.m. showing. She'd already seen this with Shaina, but there was no harm in watching Tom Cruise and Colin Farrell fight crime in the future twice, right?

When she woke up, the credits were rolling. She drove around after, since her brief nap would likely make it harder to return to sleep. It was almost 5:00 a.m. when she pulled into the driveway.

The refrigerator hummed as she came in through the side door. Her mother wasn't the kind of mom she had to "sneak around." She knew her daughter likely partied and probably had drunk at this point. Her motto had always been "Just promise to call me," whatever that meant.

As she sat at the kitchen table, all she wanted to do was sleep until the dance. She wasn't even sure she wanted to go. It was going to be her, Ashley, and Shaina. When it was evident Jemma did not want to get a homecoming date, the two had naturally followed suit.

Her mother came in, hurriedly putting on earrings and looking for her purse.

"The coffee table," Jemma informed her.

"Oh, right. Thanks, sweetie," she said as she poured herself coffee. "I'm doing a double weekend shift at the salon. I don't know if I'll be back before you go to the dance."

"It's fine, Mama." She sat back in her chair and picked at a crack in the table.

"You sure?"

"Really, I get it. Plus, it's just me, Ashley, and Shaina."

"I still don't know why you aren't going with a boy. I mean, look at you!" She gave a flourished hand gesture. Her mother may have been mostly absent, but she constantly gave her daughter compliments on her looks when she had the chance.

*Looks* are what had gotten her mother to where she was, after all.

A status quo of dreams. Rushing from shift to shift, barely keeping their utilities on, spending her free time at the casino in a cloud of smoke, all while donning long painted chipped nails, hair teased in the same style as it was in the '80s, with a raspy voice. She was the state fair queen in high school, and it seemed the wheels of life had rolled away from her ever since.

Jemma refused to repeat family history. She was going to be more than an aged, smoke-damaged beauty. She was going to will it if she had to. She was going to go where her mother never would. She sat on this thought every day, hands underneath her, brewing in hopes she shared with no one.

"Mama . . ."

"Just saying!" She held up both hands as if guilty. "And—I picked up your dress from the cleaners for you. Surprise!"

"Oh . . . Mama. You didn't have to do that."

A part of her felt warmth and a twinge of guilt. Despite everything, she knew her mother worked the long hours for them both—doing the best that she knew how.

Her mother grabbed her purse and kissed her on the cheek. "Bye, baby. Have fun!"

She was gone before Jemma could utter another word.

She opened the fridge, found nothing appealing, and went to her bedroom. On her door hung the dress, covered in a clear dry cleaning bag. She had found it on the clearance rack; a makeup stain on the neckline had gotten her an extra 15 percent off. She put a hand inside and ran it up and down the turquoise fabric, admiring its shine and smoothness.

———

# ALEX

"You need to run through the adagio section one more time," Maud ordered from her seat on the living room couch. On Saturday mornings, she read while Alex practiced piano.

"I didn't make a mistake."

"No. But you didn't play it with the slowness adagio requires."

"I played slow."

"You played lazily. There is a difference. Now again."

Alex wanted to pound her fist into the keys. But her hands seemed to be trained better than the rest of her and continued to play. When she finished, her mother nodded approvingly and stood up. She went to the coat closet and came back with a maroon dress. It was off the shoulder and A-line. Sequins lined the empire waist.

"I hope you like the one I picked out for you," she said excitedly.

It was rare to find her in anything close to an enthusiastic state. Alex tried to match it and walked over from the piano bench. She picked up the dress and held it against her.

"I love it," she feigned.

"Really?"

"Yes."

"Oh, Alexandra. You are going to look so beautiful." She embraced her awkwardly as Alex felt her hands clutch the hanger tightly.

She had done something she never had before. It had abruptly come out of her—a primal instinct to please or maybe protect, she wasn't sure.

She had lied to Maud.

"All right, enough. We'll wrinkle it," Maud said with sharpness. "When is he coming over to pick you up?"

It was *her* fault, really. If she hadn't badgered her with all the questions. Accused her of deliberately trying to make her unhappy.

A week ago was when she'd uttered her big fat lie.

"Alexandra, it is important to do normal teenage girl activities," her mother had said after hanging up the phone.

Her guidance counselor, Mrs. Oppman, had called . . . again. Asking to meet with Maud about Alex's "sullen and depressive state at school."

She didn't understand this guidance counselor's need to ride her ass. She did everything she was supposed to. Was always on time for classes. She did her homework. Showed up where she was supposed to. Always asked for the bathroom pass. But for some reason, Mrs. Oppman had decided to zero in on Alex and make her just-bearable high school existence unbearable.

"What is it you do at school that draws such attention like this?" Maud had demanded, banging open the kitchen drawers while looking for a roasting pan.

"Nothing," she answered quietly.

"Nothing?" she scoffed and then threw open the refrigerator, yanked out a chuck roast, and dumped it in the pan. Alex could smell the iron gaminess from the bloody meat.

Maud's voice dropped low. "I thought we discussed this. You shouldn't be bringing such attention to yourself."

"I'm not."

"This phone call is clear evidence that you are. What are you trying to do to me, Alexandra? Huh?"

"I'm sorry," she answered weakly.

Alex's apology only made the fury and frustration steaming up in her mother's face worsen. As though her trying to make amends were an insult.

"I have a date to homecoming," she practically vomited.

"You . . . what?" Maud said, her mouth opening.

"Yes. A date. He's a boy in my third-period chemistry class. He asked me yesterday. I thought I told you?"

*Lie. Lie. Lie.*

"That's ridiculous. How would I forget that? Anyhow, this is—great news. What's his name?"

"My date?"

"Yes. Your date," she pushed impatiently.

"Thomas." She spat the name out like it was a grisly piece of meat.

Maud's face relaxed. "Well, I can't wait to meet him. I have to say, Alexandra, I'm relieved you're finally coming to your senses."

*You're going to get in trouble!*

The dance was now hours away. She handed the dress back to Maud, who carefully placed it back in the closet.

*Shit, shit, shit.*

———

# CLEO

Cleo's eyes flew open. It was still early; there was barely any light out.

Tonight, she was meeting Will.

She heard Ronnie sneaking back into his room—the squeak of his bedroom door and then the creeping few steps to his bed. She went out into the hallway, saw that her mother's bedroom door was shut, and crept into Ronnie's.

He was facedown on his bed. The room stank faintly of cigarette smoke.

"You know I can smell it on you," she said.

"Cleo—go back to bed." His voice was muffled in his pillow.

"Do you really think Mom doesn't know?"

"Do you *really* think I care right now? Go."

She ignored him and sat on the edge of the bed. "How was it?"

He turned his head, one eye peering out at her, the rest of his face smushed.

"It was all right."

"Did you hook up with a bunch of those skanks in your grade?"

"Cleo . . . ," he groaned.

She fiddled with a loose string on the comforter. "Did you see Austin Blakesly there?"

"Who?"

"Austin Blakesly. He's in my class."

Ronnie breathed hard into the pillow. "Sophomores don't go to these parties. Not at Travis's."

"Oh."

"Why? Crush or something, Shorty?"

"No—just seeing who all was there."

His one eye looked out at her again and seemed to laugh at her.

Austin was considered the "hot guy" in her class, if one were to be given such a title. And for some reason, Austin had been staring at her in trigonometry this entire week. At first she thought he was staring at Olivia Lockman, whose tube tops were getting shorter and shorter each day. But then she got the nerve to glance back on Tuesday, and sure enough, he was staring at her. Smiled and then looked back at his desk.

*Why would he be looking at you? Guys like him don't go for girls like you.*

But she couldn't help but still wonder over it.

She glanced down toward the floor and spotted the oversize navy hooded zip-up she had been searching for the last week.

"Jerk! That's my sweatshirt."

Ronnie turned to his side. "What? Are you sure?"

"Are you kidding me? Yes. I've been looking for it . . . it's actually—"

She stopped herself to avoid further teasing.

He grabbed at his temples and sank back into his pillow. "You know what? I don't even really care. Just get out of my room," he moaned.

She rolled her eyes and snatched the hoodie. After pulling it on, she zipped it up all the way and threw the hood over her head.

It wasn't any hoodie. It was the hoodie Will had lent her two weeks ago.

She had been "cold" in class, and he, without skipping a beat, had handed her his sweatshirt. It was the first time a boy had done anything like that for her. The soft fabric had felt warm, and she had felt a tingle go up her arms.

Still—she struggled to accept the idea that maybe, *maybe* he wasn't "just being nice." That it wasn't just his nature and had nothing to do with her.

Will had always been so polite.

Always a respectful *hi*, but that was it. Freshman year, he would float past her in the hallways, the boy who wore all black and kept to himself. They didn't have any classes together until second semester last year. She was secretly pleased to see him when she entered Mrs. Quinlan's classroom that first day of Art 101.

They didn't sit next to each other. Not at first. Small glances (on her part anyway) now and then, curious as to how he had gone from golden boy to practically emo kid in one summer.

On the third day of class, Mrs. Quinlan announced they would be taking their single-vanishing-point drawings out into the hallways.

"Spread out. Take extra charcoal with you," she instructed.

It was by no coincidence they decided to each take a spot near the central stairs. Cleo was hesitant at first. Would he find it annoying?

"Our first high school class together," Will said as he adjusted his drawing paper under the oversize clipboard.

"Huh?" she asked, despite knowing very well what he was talking about.

"I haven't had a class with you yet, Cleo Song."

"Oh, right." She sat cross-legged and lined up her ruler. The soft gray lead glided across the metal edge, creating a satisfying horizon. She continued to draw, focusing hard on not putting all her energy into Will sitting so close to her. She wasn't nervous.

And that was what enthralled her.

"I thought I saw you over winter break," said Will suddenly. He shaded in part of a brick wall. His eyebrows lowered in concentration and then broke free when he looked up at her.

"Oh . . . where?"

"You were with your mom, I think."

"Oh, right. My mom has that flower shop. We were unloading poinsettias, probably."

"Those big red leafy plants?"

"Yes. Everyone wants them for the holidays."

"Then it was you. I'm pretty sure I saw those."

She nodded and kept drawing. With anyone else, she would have stayed quiet. But there was such a comfort around him. As if a silk blanket were being pulled over her face and easing her into a sense of security.

"I've got to ask," she heard herself say.

"Uh-oh," he replied.

She put her charcoal down. "What's up with the all black?"

He gave a half grin. She stared at his scar. He didn't seem to care.

"I mean, you used to be this well-groomed soccer kid. And then—"

"I wasn't?"

"Yes," she said turning farther.

"Exactly."

"Exactly . . . so you planned all this?"

He spun on the floor, his legs still crossed. By now they were facing each other, their knees almost touching.

"No. It wasn't planned. But I realized I didn't want to go down a road that I could see every single curve in."

"Okay—so it was out of sheer boredom?"

"I wasn't bored. I didn't want to live something I had already lived in my head. So I changed it. Drew a new route, as my dad says."

Cleo tilted her head. "Will. You are weird."

"Cleo. Thank you."

He smiled in a way that made her stomach flip.

"Princess Peach's secret slide," he said, shaking his head.

She laughed incredulously. "You remember that?"

"Of course," he answered earnestly.

Sixth-period Art 101. Cleo's salvage each weekday. Fifty minutes of Will time, as she liked to call it. When she wasn't in class, she was thinking about what they would talk about next time. What odd fact Will would share and they would laugh over. How near each other they would sit on the floor. It seemed each class, they would inch closer and closer together, her drawing on her belly, while he sat hunched over, cross-legged. An energy buzzed between them, a rare familiarity that was so hard to ever find in another person. The bell would ring, and whatever bubble they had created would burst between them. She would wonder if she had imagined their whole conversation as they snapped up and back into the flurry of the school day.

The last day of Art 101 came and went. There was nothing different about that period. They handed in their final art projects. Mrs. Quinlan let them leave class early.

And that was it.

She watched the summer breeze by, willing it to be fall again. Hopeful for another sixth-period Art 101.

https://DNAlottery/tracker.com
Date: September 7, 2022
Number of Entries: 11,067
Days Until Drawing: 10

*The Rosemary Hills Police Department would like to issue a reminder that Rosemary House is private property. Protesters and anyone trespassing on the grounds of the property will be prosecuted.

Comments:

"This can't be legal. We are all being forced into giving our DNA, our blood, our bodies! Why aren't our liberties being protected here?"

—Sheila O.

"Edie Parker is a crazy old bitch. Screw her! I'm not giving my spit or blood even for millions of dollars."

—R. Cummings

"Gave my sample last week. Stood in line for an hour just to prove residency. The process is slow. Don't waste your time."

—Tasha L.

"Tasha L., you just want to increase your chances, LOL!"

—Henry P.

"Did anyone see the protesters lined up outside Rosemary House two days ago? Crazy shit going on in this town. I'm undecided on whether to give my DNA. It would be nice to win that money. And to help solve that Baby Ava case. May she RIP . . ."

—Jillian A.

"Why the hell does Parker Inc. or Edie Parker care about the Baby Ava case?"

—Anonymous

"Technically I think it's completely legal. No one is forcing you to drive down to the station and give your DNA. If you do, you do. If you don't, you don't. Right?"

—B. Halloran

"Today is the anniversary of Baby Ava. Light a candle, everyone."

—J. Higgins

# CHAPTER 17

## CLEO

*September 7, 2022*

Cleo was thankful for the distraction of a new job. The last few reading sessions with the patient had been quiet and uneventful—for the most part. There was always a lingering sense of something off about the whole situation . . .

She was running a little late this morning. Usually she left for the farmhouse by eight thirty, but Rocky had insisted on reading two books before getting ready for the day.

Ji-Yeon was already in the kitchen, bustling around making coffee and toast.

"Eat something," she ordered her daughter.

"Mom, I'm running late."

"Eat," she said, shoving a plate of avocado toast across the counter.

Cleo restrained herself from rolling her eyes. *Ronnie* would probably sit down and eat for their mother. She gave the tiniest of sighs and sat at the counter, biting the toast quickly.

"Job good?" Ji-Yeon asked.

"It's okay. You do know this is temporary, right? Something to do until I find something better."

"Mmm," her mother murmured, looking away.

Cleo sighed internally this time and wiped avocado from the corner of her mouth.

"It's just you in the house? No one else?" Her mother looked slightly concerned as she poured coffee.

"No. There's the patient. And the nurse. I told you, remember?"

"Maybe." Ji-Yeon took a slow sip and switched to Korean. "What happened the night of the carnival? You never told me where you went, who that woman was?"

Cleo felt all the air suck in down her throat—suffocating. She had been doing okay this morning. So far, she had been able to ignore the jabbing thoughts of panic. Like knives that would descend on her head, hovering over her, ready to attack her mind and make it *go there*.

Where it was hard to climb out of. A hole that had formed over the last few days—Edie Parker standing over her with the shovel.

*Should I just give in? But what will happen if it all comes out? What would happen to Rocky?*

She avoided eye contact with her mother. "She was a lawyer. She just had some questions for us. Nothing to worry about."

"Are you in trouble, Cleo?" she asked bluntly.

*Trouble . . . how could I ever explain the kind of trouble I'm facing?*

She shook her head and then looked at the kitchen clock. "Thanks, Mom, but I'm going to be late. This was good, though," she said, then gave her mother a quick hug and hurried out the front door.

The white wind turbines lined up in the distance looked like giant spinning beasts, their blades whipping through the air. The sheer number of them in a stance together against the surrounding farmland. Unstoppable yet unmovable.

Cleo flew past them on the highway. She had always found the turbines to be soothing—a symbol of home and the countryside.

She was a few minutes late by the time she pulled into the farmhouse driveway. Patricia answered the door looking slightly irritated, her lips pressed together. She led Cleo immediately upstairs.

"Did you have trouble getting here?" Her tone was polite, but there was an underlying passive-aggressive accusation in there somewhere.

"No. The drive was fine," Cleo answered carefully.

"Those protesters lately have been causing roadblocks and traffic. And those ridiculous news crews camping out—I really can't wait for that lottery to be over," she huffed.

*You have no idea.*

Patricia paused outside the room. "I left the book on the side table with a glass of water. Would you care for anything else?"

Cleo shook her head.

"The patient is waiting. I think thirty minutes of reading, then a fifteen-minute break, followed by another thirty-minute session should do for today." She looked down at her watch. "I have to go to the pharmacy in town. Can you manage okay while I'm out?"

"Yes."

"I will see you later then."

She left Cleo to open the door and let herself in.

The patient's room faced east. The oversize windows brought in clear and bright morning light with a view of the brilliant-green cornfield. White linen curtains a few inches too long hung on the edges. An indigo-quilted adjustable hospital bed was placed to the left, and to the right, a small round table with Cleo's water and the book selection for the day.

There it was—that chill of silence. Something clung to the molecules in that room, a continually distressed state. As if a scream were trapped somewhere within those four walls that could never quite find its way out.

The first day she'd entered, she wasn't sure if she should introduce herself. Patricia had been explicit from the get-go.

"You are to walk in, pick up the book, sit down in the chair, and read," she had instructed, her tone somewhere between stern and insistent.

"I shouldn't introduce myself?"

"That is up to you. You can say an introduction at the most and stop at that . . . and I don't mean to alarm you. But there are security cameras set up in every corner of the room. I will be monitoring now and then from downstairs."

*Security? Security for who?*

"Okay." Cleo had nodded, trying to be agreeable.

She'd walked in the room mechanically, barely looking up before sitting in the chair. She could see a figure slumped over in an electronic wheelchair, dark wool blanket draped around the shoulders and a knit cap over the head. The patient did not move once.

The quiet in the room made her feel completely alone yet under the observation of a microscope.

She opened the book set out, *No Country for Old Men*, by Cormac McCarthy, and began to read aloud the first lines.

The patient still did not move. Cleo looked up at the corners of the room to find a small lens in each one. She continued to read. Her throat felt dry after twenty minutes, but she was too afraid to look up again or even reach for the water. When Patricia came in to announce the end of the session, she quickly got up and left.

Her second day, she glanced up a few times. The patient was angled more to the right that morning, revealing a faint outline of a cheekbone. But the shadows cast from the sun made it difficult to see much else. She tilted her head up toward one of the cameras—she had paused in reading and half expected Patricia to jump through the lens, ordering her to continue.

Today, she felt a slight familiarity—enough where her heart didn't race entering the room. As she began to read, she suddenly stopped.

"Hello. I'm Cleo. I've read to you a couple times."

The patient remained unmoved as ever, perhaps staring off into the cornfield, time slipping between each row.

"I thought I should introduce myself since we aren't complete strangers . . . at least my voice isn't."

She looked up at the camera. The shimmer of the minuscule lens glared back at her.

*Why is she keeping cameras on me? Is she trying to protect me? Or is it to make sure I don't leave . . .*

"Anyway . . . I hope I'm doing a good job—I try not to read too fast."

The blanket shifted. She was sure she saw a shoulder move. She blinked a few times to make sure her vision wasn't blurred.

"If—if I'm reading too slow, you can let me know. Just nod."

The patient remained motionless.

"Right. Well—I'm guessing you want me to keep reading."

She opened the book to where they had left off and read. The words spilled over her tongue, a dryness developing as the minutes went by.

"Cormac McCarthy fan, huh? I think I've only seen the movies."

She paused to drink some water when she heard Patricia enter the house downstairs.

Another small blanket shift.

Footsteps climbed rapidly up the stairs.

"Did you want something different? I could ask for something else."

The door burst open. "What exactly do you think you're doing?" Patricia demanded.

Cleo stood up as if she had been caught—but caught doing what exactly?

"I—I didn't think it was a problem to introduce myself. This is my third day with the patient, and, well—it seemed strange not to do that at least."

"I thought I was very clear with you. No talking to my patient," she said in a raised voice.

*My patient.*

Patricia's eyes went wide with irritation.

"I'm sorry," Cleo said, shaking her head slightly. "But what harm do you think saying my name would do exactly?"

"That is not the point," she said, exaggerating each word. "The point is that this is how I conduct the care of this particular patient. Do you understand me?"

Cleo opened her mouth to protest but stopped herself. She couldn't blow this job—it was the only thing she had going that was entirely of her own.

"Yes. I understand."

Patricia looked over at the patient and then grimly over to Cleo. "That's all for today then." She stood to the side to let her through the door.

As she stepped out, Cleo looked over her shoulder. And there it was. The feeblest of movements.

The patient's hand pushed out of the blanket, a finger tapping the arm of the chair three times.

———

On the drive back, Cleo passed the police station. The midmorning protesters were all lined up right outside on the sidewalk. Signs with American flags and the words MY BLOOD, MY BODY, WE DON'T WANT YOUR MONEY, and READ THE CONSTITUTION! bobbed up and down like horses on a carousel. A faint chant floated in through her sealed car-door windows. "Uphold our rights!" She slowed her car down to avoid a few of them crossing the street.

The station wasn't far from Whittner's.

*What the hell . . . I could use something to distract my mind.*

She pulled in and went inside. A familiar face looked surprised and pleased to see her.

"You showed up."

"I did." She held her purse in front of her timidly, as if it was some sort of buffer.

Will stood up from his table by the window. "Can I get you anything?"

"Just a black coffee, please."

She watched him go up to the counter. He must have been off duty, as he was sans uniform this morning. It was still hard for her to believe this rugged man was Will Hart.

"So you decided to become a cop," she said as he came back with her coffee.

"You say that like it's a bad thing."

"No—I didn't mean it like that," she said, slightly flustered.

"Still apologetic, huh, Cleo?" He grinned, and his scar stretched with it.

She shrugged, disarmed by the memory of his smile that hadn't changed. And with it, abandoned her shield of über-politeness, as if it were a hat tossed on the ground. It was funny to her. All these years, and it was like they were in sixth-period art class again. A comfort between them emerged as if time had never passed.

That was what made Will so different.

"I thought you wanted to be a marine biologist. Wait—archaeologist?" she asked as he took his seat.

"I think it depended on the week." His eyes crinkled with amusement. She liked seeing the lines in his face—signs he had lived both well and hard.

She held her cup up to her lips. "Did you end up finishing high school in . . . was it Wisconsin?"

He grimaced. "Yeah, that was fun. It was a pretty lonely two years."

Sophomore year. It was the last time she could remember seeing Will. Over winter break his parents divorced, and just like that, he was uprooted and moved away with his mother.

"And after?"

"I left town like everyone else. Got my undergrad and then sat on it. What's an English major going to do? Should have listened to my mom. She told me to be an accountant."

Cleo's face went soft. "I was sorry to hear about her."

His eyebrows raised. "You knew?"

"Facebook. Not ashamed to admit it."

*More eye crinkles.*

"Yeah. She fought for a while there. My dad didn't take it too well. Even though he and my mom had been split for so long, he must have still really cared about her. Rough few years after that. He's at the memory-care home in Ely."

"Oh, Will . . ."

"You don't need to say you're sorry. He's actually doing pretty well. I go and see him as much as I can."

There was brief melancholy in his eyes before he cleared his throat. "And your mother? I still see her every now and then around town."

Cleo nodded. "Yeah. She's retired. And I'm living with her."

"Right. How's that going so far?" Will asked, raising his cup. "And Rocky? He is such a cute kid."

"Thanks." She beamed proudly. "Rocky is doing great, all things considered. He asks about his dad a lot, but . . . he's in Chicago."

"Not really in the picture?"

She shook her head.

"But what about you?" His chin tilted once.

"Me?" She glanced up, surprised.

"Yeah."

She sighed, lowering her shoulders. "Doing my best. Truthfully, it's like being sixteen all over again. You should see my mom and me battling over just breakfast."

Will laughed heartily.

"Is it strange?" she asked gazing over at him.

"What is?" His dark blue eyes seemed to shine with intrigue.

Cleo leaned in over her coffee cup. "Being around it all constantly. Reminders of the past. Those 'foolhardy' younger years."

*I know it has been for me . . . all too much, really.*

He rested back and draped an arm over the chair next to him. "I guess I don't find myself dwelling on that. So much has happened since."

"Since?"

His face grew more serious. "I mean—do you ever wonder what could have been?"

Her chest felt tighter, heart rate starting to pick up. Was he really going there?

"Cleo."

"Mmm. Yes?"

"You know what I'm talking about . . . right?"

His eyes were so damn sincere. She wasn't imagining this, right?

*Yes. Yes, I think about it. I've probably thought about it every day, but I just haven't admitted it to myself.*

This wasn't the time to be polite Cleo. Well-meaning, don't-step-on-anyone's-toes Cleo. Glossing over it, pretending she had made it all up in her head. He had felt it, too, or he wouldn't be sitting here in front of her. This was the time to say it. Speak up and tell him. She wasn't that same girl anymore.

*This is your chance. You can say it.*

She took a breath, finally ready. Finally having the courage.

A new male patron entered the coffee shop. Her chest tightened again, but not in a good way.

Will matched the path of Cleo's gaze.

"Will Hart?" the man said. He wasn't overweight, but everything about him was puffy and red. As if he had spent too many mornings regretting that extra beer the previous night.

He peered at him and then pointed.

"Austin, right?"

"Yes. Austin Blakesly."

The man approached their table with his arms crossed.

"I'm in town for Labor Day weekend. Visiting folks with my wife and kids. We're staying for the week. How you been?"

"Good. Good." Will seemed like a man acting out of mere politeness. Cleo turned her head away. He looked at her with confused eyes and then back at the man. "You remember Cleo, right?"

The man smiled widely. "Of course. Good to see you, Cleo." He held his hand out. She took it on sheer autopilot.

She had felt that hand on her before.

*You know you want it, Cleo. You looking at me in class all the time with those chinky eyes of yours.*

She felt the hot hands again—practically burning the skin on her arms and wrists.

"You all right, Cleo?"

*Don't pretend to not like it.*

"Cleo?"

# CHAPTER 18

## JEMMA

*September 7, 2022*

"Poppy, I'm only going to ask you one more time. Put your phone away," Jemma hissed into her ear.

She turned back to the front of the library, forcing a smile and hoping her voice had not been as loud as the frustration boiling inside her.

"I told you I didn't want to go to this," Poppy whispered loudly, slouching in her seat. "Why would I want to listen to a speaker about climate change?" She put her hand up and let it slap loudly on her thigh.

"And I told you I didn't care. You need to do something other than sit in your room with your phone. That's all you do."

"That is *not* true."

"I'm not arguing with you here, Poppy." She smiled hard, looking straight ahead.

Peter, sitting in the row behind them, popped his head in between their seats. "I hate to be the bearer of bad news. But ladies, you are being a little loud."

"Thank you for that," Jemma replied, rolling her eyes.

He smirked and returned to his seat.

"You see, Poppy? You're causing a scene."

"Me? I'm not the one freaking out over a phone."

The audience in the library started clapping. A few in the front stood up. Jemma had to admit that this month's Wednesday-night speaker at the Rosemary Hills's Public Library had not been the most riveting. But it was important she show up—especially when the speaker discussed important issues like climate change.

An issue she couldn't discuss right then because she hadn't been listening at all.

Poppy was not entirely to blame. There were other things taking over her thoughts. Like Finch having to give her fertility shots tonight. Like whether he'd given Henry a proper dinner.

Like being forced to provide her DNA on a deadline.

In the last few days, she had gone from complete denial to moments of paralyzing fear. She had always been good at pushing things aside in her head—dealing with things on her terms, a skill acquired over the years to guard herself. But *this*. This was a problem she couldn't make go away.

This time there was too much at stake.

*What if it wasn't like how I remembered?*

She made her way through the crowd, shaking hands and greeting people, all while Poppy straggled along, head hunched down over her phone.

*Why am I questioning it? My memory of it all . . .*

Poppy bumped into an elderly couple near the exit doors, oblivious to anything but the glowing screen, a smile sneaking in over her lips.

*Who the hell is my daughter talking to?*

By the time they got to the car, her jaw set tight as she reminded Peter to pick her up tomorrow morning at seven sharp, she was ready to explode.

"Poppy. We need to have a serious chat here." She slammed her car door.

"Mom! I'm over this," Poppy whined, climbing into the back and choosing the farthest possible seat from her.

Jemma groaned with exasperation. "I am sick of looking over at you and seeing your head practically inside your screen all the time."

She put her seat belt on harshly, virtually stabbing the buckle into the clip. "Who is it that you're constantly texting with, anyway?"

"What?"

"Yes. You heard me. *Who?*"

"That's ridiculous."

"Who?"

"You sound like a fucking owl."

"Watch your mouth!"

"As if *you* don't swear all the time."

"That's because I'm in politics!"

She peeled through the parking lot.

"Jesus Christ, Mom! Can you slow down?" Poppy shrieked.

Jemma paused, exhaling out before saying another word.

"I don't understand why you need to be in constant communication with one person. What could possibly be that urgent?"

She could see Poppy in the rearview mirror, eyes bugged out in annoyance. Mocking her by looping her index finger by her head.

"Mom. First of all, it's not just one person. And second of all, why are you so nutso about this?"

She turned onto the main street downtown. Her steering a little less erratic, she took a breath.

"I want to make sure you're using your time wisely. Your grades are not what they used to be."

"Okay . . . sorry I'm not getting straight As anymore. Big deal."

Jemma thumped the steering wheel. "Poppy! Yes. It is a big deal. If you keep this up, I *will* take that phone away."

She knew what it meant to ignore something as a "big deal" all too well. She had chosen to ignore such a thing in high school. She wasn't a stupid girl back then. She knew better. Yet it didn't matter. And the price had been too costly.

She wasn't going to let the same thing happen to her daughter. Not her Poppy.

"Can you please listen to me, Poppy? For once?" She deliberately lowered her voice two octaves.

Poppy became quiet in the back.

"Maybe I'm going a little overboard. But I want to know who my daughter is talking to all the time."

"All right," Poppy said.

"All right . . . ?" Jemma shook her head exaggeratedly. "All right what?"

"Can we drop this? Seriously!" she pleaded.

"Poppy. Don't do this to me. I would just like a little acknowledgment. I have the big campaign event in Des Moines tomorrow morning. And this is the last thing I need."

They had reached the house. She parked the car in the driveway, Poppy throwing the door open before the car had even stopped all the way and then running inside. Jemma didn't go in after her. Instead, she stayed in the car, knowing Finch would calm her down. Blowing out slowly, her mouth forming a small circle, she tried to compose herself.

She waited ten minutes before going in.

"She in her room?" she asked Finch, throwing the keys on the counter.

"Yes. Give her some time, Jemma. I think she's pretty upset."

She ran her hands through her hair in agitation. "She spends hours on that phone, Finch. Hours. And I'm pretty sure it's the same person. I recognize those giggles. Those giggles are only over one thing."

"Yeah?"

"A boy. I know this. Because I was once a teenage girl."

"So what? So she's talking with a boy."

"There's something . . . obsessive about this. Something off."

"How do you know that?"

"I can just *tell*." She collapsed in a kitchen chair and buried her forehead in her hand.

Finch sighed nervously.

"What?" She looked up.

"I hate to bring this up, but—"

"Shot night. I know."

He pulled a chair next to her. "Are you sure you're up for this? It's okay if you aren't, baby. I don't want to pressure you." He put his hand on her shoulder and rubbed it soothingly.

"No—I still want this."

"You do?"

"Yes."

He brought her in closer, cradling her with both arms.

"It hasn't been easy. Actually, it's been hell. But I'm here. Always. And if that decision means I stand somewhere else with you, that's okay."

"Finch. Really. Let's do this," she said, turning pointedly to look at him.

"Okay. But let's ease into it. How about some tea to relax first?"

She took his hand and kissed it. "Why are you so good to me?"

He raised his eyebrows. "Sometimes I ask that question myself."

They laughed.

———

She began to sob later when Finch injected her. He had done this so many times before that it didn't even hurt very much anymore—the injection site was practically numb at this point. She apologized the entire time. Not for crying. Not for throwing him into the lion's den with Poppy. It was for things she wasn't sure she was sorry for.

As quickly as she'd started up, she stopped. Finch asked her what was wrong as she indignantly wiped her face with tissues. She insisted it was "all fine" and retreated to her study. He left her alone, the television on for a little while. She reviewed her speech for tomorrow, her eyes growing heavy with each line.

*God, let's hope this doesn't put people to sleep tomorrow.*

She eventually fell asleep in front of her laptop, head tilted back in her chair. When she awoke, a blanket was wrapped around her shoulders.

The house was quiet as she finally made her way upstairs. She cracked open Poppy's door. Her daughter was curled up in the fetal position—her go-to ever since she was a baby—hair spread out over her pillow. She heard soft breathing and closed the door. She peeked into Henry's room next. He was usually a deep sleeper, so she was surprised to see him sit up, rubbing his eyes and looking toward her at the burst of light.

"Mommy?"

His call drew her in. Immediately she was at his side and knelt to hold him.

"Sorry, baby. Mommy didn't mean to wake you," she said tenderly into his ear.

He smelled slightly of sweat and baby lotion. She breathed it in as he placed his head on her cheek and nuzzled sleepily.

*You remember it all—right? We did the right thing—you did the right thing. It happened just as you remember it.*

Her phone vibrated in her pocket. It was a text from Peter and Stevie with more last-minute details on the campaign event tomorrow.

*But can you trust it? Can you leave it all to that? Everything depends on it.*

She responded quickly and then held Henry closer. He was starting to go back to sleep, his lips slightly pursed and eyelids fluttering.

Instinct took over . . . the smell of her child took over.

Her hand reached down again. Swiftly her fingers found the two contacts she needed: Cleo and Alex. She typed in a message and then let her phone drop onto the bed.

She pulled Henry in closer, the curve of his cheek nestled so perfectly on her chest.

# CHAPTER 19

## ALEX

*September 7, 2022*

This kind of scene was not for Alex.

She was not the kind of woman who sat in her car. In front of a restaurant. Waiting to see if her husband was having an affair or not. This wasn't her.

Yet here she was: 1:20 on a Wednesday afternoon. She should be working on a brief for her latest client. After word had spread about the success with Mayor Vogel's case, her caseload was getting so big that she was going to need to hire another paralegal soon.

The lunch rush was over at Fig & Olive. The same place Maud preferred dining. It seemed fitting Maud and Davis would pick the same place.

*What are you doing? Seriously . . . drive away.*

When she returned from the carnival with Sasha on Saturday night, he wasn't home yet. She was beaten up from the events of the evening, like someone had set the timer on a bomb in her head. And somewhere, Edie Parker was holding the detonator. She must have seemed troubled, as even Sasha sensed it. She didn't protest once as she was getting ready for bed.

She was left alone with the quiet of the kitchen, making her thoughts louder and louder until the fear took over. The worst kind of fear, the kind that constricted her throat and left her breathless. She snatched a wineglass from the cabinet and poured.

By the time the garage door opened, Alex was two glasses into a bottle of shiraz.

Davis looked neutral at the sight of his wife.

"How was work?" she asked, swiveling on the kitchen stool toward him.

He scratched his head. "Look. It was a long night. I'm really sorry I didn't make it to the carnival, okay?"

*Oh . . . you had a long night? I think I can raise you on that one.*

She swung her head up. "Do you want to know what happened to me tonight, Davis?"

He shrugged and shook his head. "What?"

"Do you even care what happened to me? What happened to your *wife*?"

"Please. I'm begging you, Alex . . . I don't want to get into it."

"We never get into it, Davis."

He ignored the bait. "How was the parade? Did Sasha have a good time?"

"Mm-hmm," she said, her voice muffled behind her glass.

"Lots of candy?"

"Oh, there was candy." She stretched her legs out and then flexed her toes. "So, Davis, tell me. What kind of work does an accountant do on a Saturday? In *this* town . . . on Labor Day weekend?"

He pinched the spot between his eyes and then shot her a stern look.

"Alex, I'm exhausted. A new associate made some mistakes, and as always, I had to do the cleanup work. This isn't the first time, and you know it."

"Why so dressed up?"

She nearly cringed at the accusation in her voice.

"Because I don't want to go into the office looking like a scrub. Even if it is the weekend."

"Well, you look nice."

"Thank you?" He seemed confused by her comment.

"I can't tell you that you look nice?"

Davis sighed. "I don't know why you're doing this, or what's wrong with you—but I'm going to bed."

She let him go to bed—at least that was what she told herself while she finished what was left in her glass. This was the most scintillating conversation they'd probably had in the last few years of their marriage. How could two human beings be side by side so consistently, yet only muster conversations about whether they needed more coffee filters? They had spent countless minutes, hours, and days together. How many times had they stood next to each other, brushing their teeth, the slow hum of their electronic toothbrushes in unison? The silent breakfasts minus the inserted comments to Sasha to "sit up straight" or "finish your milk." The wasted hours being so close to someone else yet so far removed.

She knew Davis. She had to know him—one doesn't spend this much time with another person without *really* knowing them. If they played a couple's game on how well you know your spouse, she would win with flying colors.

Davis was an Eagle Scout. He lost his first tooth playing basketball.

Davis grew up in Minnesota. But was a big Bears fan.

He liked going to the movies. But only if they went an hour early to get good seats.

His preferred position in bed was with her on top. He loved kissing her breasts.

He was a good father to Sasha.

Davis ate sunflower seeds at work. He was always coming home with shells stuck in his pocket. Little black bits in the wash that drove Alex crazy.

Davis could be very vain. He scrutinized his face in the mirror every night, plucking out any gray hairs.

He tended to stay away from gossip—something she always found admirable.

He texted about work quite a bit. Frequently. Actually, constantly.

She knew the code to unlock his phone. She'd unlocked it Labor Day evening.

*Davis has secrets.*

Alex didn't know why she was still stunned. There was a reason she'd snooped and looked in his phone. He was playing outside in the backyard with Sasha, her squeals piercing as he picked her up and then tickled her. It made the discovery even more unsettling.

Unnamed contact. Just a number. The conversation went like this:

Unknown: Are we set for 1:30 Wednesday?

Davis: You bet.

Unknown: Fig & Olive, just like you suggested?

Davis: I am so ready to do this with you.

Unknown: Don't be nervous. She still doesn't know right?

Davis: No.

She dropped the phone as if it were a scorching piece of coal. It clattered on the counter and then onto the kitchen floor, screen facedown.

"Shit." She picked it up and rubbed the screen. No cracks or scratches.

The sound of Sasha's laughs drew closer. She set the phone back where it was on the counter. Davis came in, asking if she was ready to grill the burgers. She nodded and handed him the plate of raw patties.

Wednesday morning, Alex made Davis's favorite breakfast—a Denver omelet with extra ham. She slid a fresh cup of coffee toward him.

"Wow. Alex. This looks amazing. What's the occasion?"

She smiled over her mug and shrugged. "We had so many random leftovers in the fridge from Labor Day weekend. I didn't want to see it go to waste."

He took a bite and then offered one to Sasha, who shook her head in disdain. "Yucky. Peppers."

"Sasha," Alex warned.

"I mean—no, thank you."

"Well, thank you, Mommy," said Davis, digging in for more.

*Eat up, Davis.*

He was halfway finished when she dropped the line. "I have a pretty open lunch hour today. What do you say we meet for lunch?"

He stopped chewing.

"Today?"

"Yes."

"I'm not too sure, Alex." He looked down at his plate. "I have a lot of meetings today. They could run long. You know how it's been."

"So you're already tied up for lunch, huh?" she asked, staring at him.

He raised another bite to his mouth. "I'll have to eat at my desk probably. Sorry. But good idea."

She watched him quickly eat the rest of his omelet. "No worries. I probably should buckle down more myself."

"Mommy? I'm done," Sasha announced, pushing her empty bowl of oatmeal toward her.

Davis left with Sasha to drop her off at school. The dirty breakfast plates and bowls only rubbed in his lies even more. She hostilely cleared and washed the dishes, putting the kitchen back to complete order, and left for the office.

She must have been extra snippy, as Hattie looked relieved when she'd announced she was going out for lunch.

The parking lot of Fig & Olive was starting to thin out now. She pondered moving her car elsewhere but then determined she wouldn't get a good view of Davis.

*I should call him. Make him squirm.*

She tilted her neck back into the headrest and closed her eyes. This wasn't for her. The jealous, obsessive-wife role. What was she jealous of? Some desperate woman who had the same taste in lunch food as her mother? She felt a wave of nausea and then sympathy for all those women she had represented. She had judged them. *How could you let it get like that? Where your husband wants to move on from you? To someone else? You should have taken care of it. You should have had it under control.*

She thought she did.

Maud thought she did.

She had to have been eight, a little older than Sasha now, but she knew enough as she watched Maud in the car. But for her mother, it was a game of cat and mouse at night, not in broad daylight.

Alex had wanted to go to bed. She was tired. Daddy hadn't come home for dinner, so Maud had made her practice an extra hour of piano. As soon as she'd finished the last note of her sonata, Maud grabbed her by the arm, threw her coat at her, and dragged her to the car.

"Where are we going?"

"Be quiet, Alexandra."

They drove in silence until she pulled in front of Marta's, a steak house that had since converted into a Japanese bistro. Alex looked over at Maud, her hands still positioned perfectly on the steering wheel. Her usually straight back was hunched over—urgently waiting for something.

"What are we doing here?" she dared to ask.

Maud reached over and placed a hand over her mouth. "You are only to watch."

An hour passed, Maud barely moving from her perch. Alex felt her eyes growing heavy.

She could barely keep them open. Headlights alerted her as her father's car pulled in. He parked and was idle for a while. She heard a woman's laugh. Her father exited the vehicle and came around to open the door for a woman. She had "parts" that Maud didn't have. Her mother was all angles—a geometry problem waiting to be solved. This woman was none of that. Wave after wave in her body swayed along as she took her father's hand and went into Marta's. Her father bent his head down to kiss her neck. His hand moved across the small of her back and then up under her neck. They both bent forward, laughing again as he whispered in her ear. The intimacy of this shared moment between their melded bodies was palpable.

Alex felt the need to call out "Daddy!" But that was impossible. To do so would have betrayed Maud. She noticed her hands first. The knuckles rising up, her fingertips scratching at the steering wheel. The skin around her neck had grown taut, veins rising through the surface. Her eyes, glassy and shiny. A single breath would have knocked out the liquid that had filled them. But she only stared on at her husband.

When they disappeared into the restaurant, she said nothing. They returned home.

A month later, her father was out of the house. It was the end of their family of three. An end to having a father.

And the beginning of being alone with Maud.

Maud spent the first week in bed. It was unsettling to Alex. She had never seen her in a state like this—unwashed hair, no makeup, and the same nightgown day after day. Alex went on with making herself meals and going to school, cleaning up after herself obsessively. There was no trace she even existed—she covered up her tracks. She never knew when Maud would come down.

And then one evening, her mother called her into her room.

"Alexandra!" she shouted.

She raced upstairs, afraid to make her wait even a second. Maud turned to her as she put a ruby earring on. Makeup had been fully applied to her face, her hair was tidily coiffed, and a freshly pressed skirt hugged her thighs. It was the first time in days she had gotten ready.

"I'm going out tonight. Wash your face."

She obeyed right away.

"Get into bed."

She did so deftly and moments later heard the car start and pull away. Silence would follow, as it would for many nights.

Maud would be gone. Some nights she spent working at the drugstore, a single mother providing for her daughter. But then there were those *other* nights—the nights she would be finding what Alex called to herself "friends."

She permitted two versions of her mother.

During the day, Maud would be commanding and rigid: nothing in her world was ever improper, a woman who held her nose up with a heightened sense of propriety. But at night—on those evenings out with red lipstick and a smile, she was different. Her giggles floating up the stairs and into Alex's bedroom. A higher pitch she had no idea could come from her mother.

Eventually, Maud's friends started coming upstairs. Alex would shut her eyes, tight, trying to ignore it all. But she was still a child, after all. She couldn't help herself one night, when she crept down the hall to see for herself—see who was making her mother act in such a strange way.

She peered through the crack in the doorway. Her mother and another man were in an embrace, their mouths over each other. Maud sharply turned her head away, her eyes piercing through Alex. Alex had fled as fast as her legs could carry her, breathing heavy with the sheets over her head. What was it that she'd seen in her mother's eyes?

Annoyance? Anger? No, it was something else, something deeper and harder to shake.

Shame.

The next morning, she anticipated that her mother would lash out at her for the indiscretion. But she was calm. Even—cheery. She left that night for an overnight shift at the pharmacy but returned early.

Alex pretended to be asleep as she heard her approaching footsteps.

Maud stared at her, reached out once, and then recoiled. She knelt by her bedside and whispered in her ear, "It's just you and me now, darling. And I'm going to make it easier for you." She pulled something out of her pocket and held it out in her hand.

The first glint of the needle made Alex let out a small yelp.

"This won't hurt. I promise."

She slid the shiny needle into her neck and out again quickly—a puncture of good night and pleasant dreams. The tingling sensations flooded throughout Alex's small body. Coursing through each vessel, she imagined a tiny version of herself flying inside her.

Maud had kept her word. There was no pain. Instead, a rushing of numbness. A joyous spread of nothingness that started at the top of her head and made its way down, surging through with vitality. Bursts of euphoria in her veins, followed by a stillness she had never known. The only part of her she was able to move was her eyes. Drifting up and down and then closing.

"That's my girl. Now . . . nothing will disturb you at night. And you will disturb nothing."

*I can handle this. If this is all she wants, I can handle this.*

Weeks went by of Maud putting Alex to bed. Then months, then years.

*This isn't that bad. You actually like this. You can rely on this.*

She really was okay. It was just a bit of stillness at night. She could use a bit of that—who couldn't?

*Good night, Mother.*

*Good night, good night. I am nothing like you.*

She had told herself that—over and over at night. She was nothing like her mother. She would *be* nothing like her mother.

But today she was Maud. Sitting and waiting for her cheating husband to arrive.

She observed a couple going in, likely in their twenties, giggling over something they were looking at on the girl's phone.

*What is it you want to see?*

Davis walked in front of the car. She instinctively ducked down. She put the car in reverse and drove away. She didn't want to see.

Not now. Not like this.

# CHAPTER 20

## CLEO

*Homecoming day: Eighteen years ago*

"Ronnie, I need a favor."

Muffled grunts.

"Ronnie."

One feeble arm movement.

"Hey, drunkie. Wake up!"

"I'm not drunk . . . well, anymore."

"Mom made me come in here to make sure you were okay. She thinks you're sick . . . well, you kind of are."

Cleo prodded Ronnie with her foot, swinging her leg up in one full circle.

"Why are you back in here again?" he grumbled.

"It's been four hours. It's lunchtime, and you're not doing a very good job of being the favorite child."

"Ugh. Cleo. You have got to stop that. I'm not the favorite."

"Oh, really? Then why was I sent in here to check on 'my poor Ronnie-ya,' hmm?"

He finally sat up, rubbing his face so hard Cleo thought he was going to take off some skin with it.

"I brought you a Gatorade." She shook the bottle as a peace offering.

"Now we're onto something." He eagerly retrieved it from her and gulped down three-quarters of the orange liquid. He swiped at his mouth. "Ahhh. I feel like I can think again."

"Yeah. Great." She rolled her eyes. "So about that favor."

"Go on."

"Can I get a ride with you tonight?"

"Ride to where?"

"Homecoming."

Ronnie stood up and hiked his shorts. "*You* want to go? I didn't think you had a date."

"Geez, thanks."

"I didn't mean it like that."

She felt a rush of embarrassment. Even her own brother thought she was a loser.

He rubbed his head. "Cleo. You're too sensitive. I'm just surprised, okay? But seriously, why do you want to go?"

"I'm meeting some friends."

"Then why not get a ride with them?"

"I'd rather ride with you."

He grabbed a shirt from the floor and pulled it over his head. "Fine. But this doesn't mean I'm hanging out with you at the dance. The second we get there, you're on your own."

"Fine."

They both perked their ears suddenly like Dobermans. Their mom was calling them from down in the kitchen. Ronnie made a detour at the bathroom to splash some cold water on his face, while Cleo went downstairs.

The kitchen smelled of spices and seafood broth. Her mother stood by the stove, hovering over a large black stone pot. Red bubbling liquid frothed up as she put in a spoon to do a taste check. Satisfied, she nodded at Cleo.

"Where is everyone? It's time for lunch."

A few moments later, they all sat down together. Soon *dubu-jjigae*. One of Cleo's favorites. It was soft tofu in a spicy seafood broth, with layers of seafood and a cracked egg on top. Her mother generously poured some over everyone's bowl of rice.

They ate quietly at first until her mother spoke up.

"Ronnie going to dance tonight?"

"Yeah," he mumbled between bites.

"With who?"

"Nobody. Just going to meet friends."

"No date?"

"Omma . . ."

"Okay, okay." She hushed him.

He waved his spoon across the table.

"Cleo is going, too, you know. I'm giving her a ride."

Their mother seemed to ignore this at first and took Ronnie's bowl. "Here, eat more." She ladled more of the stew into his bowl and looked over at Cleo.

"Cleo. You too young to go."

"What?" She swallowed the bite in her mouth hard.

"Yes. Too young."

"I don't believe this," she protested. "You're always telling me to be more like Ronnie. So here I am—going to the dance like Ronnie."

"That's not same—" their mother started.

"I'm going. I don't care what anyone says. Right, Ronnie?"

He shrugged and kept digging into his lunch—the hot Korean food clearly more of a priority than sticking up for his little sister.

"Thanks for the help, Ron," Cleo hissed. She pushed her chair back and ran upstairs.

She sat at her desk and rocked back in the chair, her knees propping her up. Her hand reached out to shake the mouse, and the chair rocked forward. The screen came to life, and she signed on to Instant Messenger. After ten minutes, she felt a sudden thrill run through her when he signed on. An instant message window popped up.

WillEat4Free: What's up?

CleoS110: My mom.

WillEat4Free: Uh-oh.

CleoS110: She thinks I'm too young to go tonight. I don't get it.

WillEat4Free: Oh.

CleoS110: Yup.

WillEat4Free: So does that mean you're not?

WillEat4 Free: I mean going?

CleoS110: I don't know. Ronnie said he would let me ride with him.

CleoS110: But it's not a sure thing now.

WillEat4Free: Okay . . . I'm confused, Cleo.

She paused to think over a response. He wanted her to still go, it seemed. Or maybe he didn't really care? She typed out a few different responses, the click, click of the backspace followed by typing and then more backspaces.

CleoS110: I'll figure it out.

WillEat4Free: Cool. See you then.

CleoS110: Okay. Cool.

WillEat4Free: Sorry. I gtg. Got a few things to take care of.

He signed off, and the air went completely out of her body. They were still meeting, it seemed. But did it really mean anything? He had to go so abruptly. Maybe he really did have things to do. Or maybe he was wondering why he was meeting her.

*Maybe get a grip, Cleo.*

———

## JEMMA

Shaina and Ashley plugged in their curling irons simultaneously like Siamese cats, prepping their hair with a smog of hair spray and then turning to Jemma, who sat sullenly on her bed.

"What's wrong with you?" Shaina twirled a strand of Jemma's hair and lay next to her. The remnants of the hair spray cloud made Jemma cough.

"You're so quiet lately. Ashley said you didn't want to go out last night. Not to mention you don't seem to care what you're wearing." She gave her a good dose of elevator eyes. Jemma looked down at her leggings and oversize sweatshirt.

"Wow, thanks, Shaina."

"Really. What's wrong?" Ashley probed more gently.

Jemma hugged a pillow. "I don't see the point in going. All I'm going to do is spend hours getting ready and then spend hours avoiding Eric. I don't want to see him."

"But you'll have us."

"Yeah, right. The second we get there, you're going to make a beeline for Ronnie Song. Who you practically *threw* yourself at last night, Ash."

She smiled widely and then tossed her head back, giggling. "I did, didn't I?" She pulled the pillow out from under Jemma's arms. "C'mon. Get your dress on. I'll curl your hair."

She bounced from the bed to the door, then slid the wire hanger off the top. "Cute baby doll dress! When did you switch from the red spaghetti strap one?"

The dress was a shimmery stiff taffeta—aqua in color with a sweetheart neckline. The empire waist started right below Jemma's breasts, a cascading flow of fabric. She took the dress from Ashley and went into the bathroom. She pulled it on and came back out, waving her hands up and down.

"Eh?"

Shaina giggled. "Oh my gosh, Jemma."

"What?"

"Your boobs are spilling out!"

She turned to Ashley. "Are they?"

Ashley gave her a look of disbelief. "You're seriously asking me? One sneeze and I feel like one will come out and attack me."

A peel of laughter followed. Jemma couldn't help but smile.

"You see? This will be fun," Shaina assured her.

"Last homecoming. Ever. You're never going to forget tonight."

Jemma turned to her bedroom mirror. She patted the skirt down and looked to the side.

She'd worn a dress almost just like this to winter formal last year. That one was less stiff.

Eric had had a few beers that night. Buzzed, but not wasted or an embarrassment of slurs and stumbling. It was the perfect night. Dinner at the Italian restaurant that had opened downtown. Her mother had even slipped her a twenty, after winning a few bucks at the casino. She'd danced to every song and jumped up and down with Shaina and Ashley, spinning around while looking up into the lights with promise. And then Eric revealed his "surprise."

*"I got a room for us."*

Ashley started to comb her hair, taking sections and curling pieces.

*"Everyone's expecting us to. You don't have to if you don't want to, but . . . I mean, everyone will just assume."* She'd spotted a crack in the ceiling as she nodded to him.

The heat of the iron came close to the nape of her neck.

*She was panting hard when he lay on top of her like a wooden plank. The crack in the hotel ceiling widened. She kept nodding.*

"Do you want an updo? Maybe a cute little side ponytail?"

*She suddenly couldn't breathe. She pushed him off when it was over.*

*"I thought you'd done this before. Everyone did . . . why didn't you tell me?"*

"Jemma?"

*"I'm not what everyone thinks."*

*"Why are you crying? Seriously. What's wrong?"*

"I'll curl it first, and then you can tell me what you want."

*"What if I end up . . . just like her. What if this is the best it gets?"*

*"Who? What are you talking about, Jemma?"*

She looked in the mirror at Ashley, who was in deep concentration on the back of her hair. Shaina was on her bed, putting on mascara with such precision.

*"It's not like we did anything wrong."*

———

## ALEX

Maud knocked on the bathroom door.

"Alexandra, I expect you to wash your hair until it's absolutely clean. I've left a fresh robe for you on the hook."

She shut it, and Alex collapsed to the floor of the tub. Her crying was silent, her tears mixing in with the shower water.

She never let Maud see her cry.

This was their song and dance—Maud lashing out and then pretending nothing had happened. As if less than ten minutes ago, she hadn't made Alex feel panic ripping through her body. Blood growing hot as her mother screamed in her face.

By the afternoon, her mother had begun to pepper her with questions.

"You need to start getting ready. Won't Thomas be here soon?"

"He's not coming here. We're meeting in front of the school," she answered as steadily as possible.

Maud's mouth shrank with disapproval. "Don't be ridiculous. Dates don't meet you at the dance. They come pick you up. What kind of boy is this that you're going with?"

She tried to shrug it off. "It's what everyone does these days. No big deal."

"Alexandra, this is your first date. I will call this boy myself if he doesn't come pick you up. Now call him and tell him you'll be ready by six thirty."

The panic started to rise up from her gut. *Keep calm. She still doesn't have to know.*

"Mother, seriously. I'm just going to meet him. Are you going to help me get ready now?"

Maud studied her for a moment.

"Please. I don't want to be late," she said, the faintness in her voice betraying her.

*Quiet isn't good. Quiet is never good.*

"Mother?"

She crossed her arms slowly. "Alexandra. Why isn't Thomas coming here?"

"I—I already told you. We're going to meet there."

"I don't believe you."

*The dress. Remind her about the dress . . . the dress made her happy.*

"Fine. You don't have to. Where did you put my dress?"

"You lied to me," Maud said coolly, as if swiping away her detour.

"I . . . didn't lie. I'm going, aren't I?"

Her mother ran her fingernails into her palms, digging hard and then releasing them forcefully. "You think I'm a fool?" Her voice was low and steady.

"No—I don't. Mother, why do you always do this?" Knots began to tighten in her stomach.

"You think your own mother is some stupid . . . fool?"

"No." She shook her head hard and backed up to the bottom of the staircase.

Maud's jawline had hardened so much that the skin looked as though it would split.

"Your father thought I was some stupid fool. And now—my own daughter?"

"No, Mommy."

"'No, Mommy'?"

She stepped closer and closer to Alex. A stillness swept over them both.

"You . . . are not . . . to make me feel this way!" she screamed.

Alex scrambled up the steps. Her mother followed and grabbed her arm. She pulled her daughter into the bathroom.

"Clean yourself off."

"I'm sorry . . . I'm so sorry. I just wanted to make you happy," Alex pleaded.

"Do I look happy to you, Alex?"

She shook her head.

"Get in."

She stepped into the tub.

Maud turned the faucet on. Steam started to rise from the scalding water. She looked at Alex, as if to taunt her. Her hand reached out and adjusted the cold-water spigot.

"Don't come out until I tell you to." She left her to bathe.

As the water rained over her lashes and mouth, she spat it out. She didn't move. She let the hard streams pound the top of her head until it felt numb.

She wondered if somewhere in Rosemary Hills, there was another girl, this one laughing and smiling with her mother as they got ready for her first dance. This mother didn't care if her daughter lied. Or had bad thoughts. Or didn't know if she could take going to bed another night.

It was earlier that week that she'd seen the two of them. One was walking toward the cafeteria alone, the other with her group of popular friends. And for one moment, they all saw each other. A trio of locked eyes. There were no nods of acknowledgment; instead, that string that weaved between them yanked at each of their cores.

At once they were three little girls again. A memory they shared that stained them like black ink, seeping in through every layer—forever binding them with a history they could not erase.

The innocence was not lost on them.

# CHAPTER 21

## CLEO

**Summer 1995**

Ronnie flicked seven-year-old Cleo's ear.

"Ouch," she hissed, cupping it.

"Cheer up, Shorty. At least you don't have to go to math camp like me."

She swatted at him and pouted on the beige leather living room couch. Their mother had just explained to them both that Ronnie would no longer be joining her at summer camp. Rosemary Hills Elementary hosted an eight-week day camp for its students each year. Grades were often combined into groups. Ronnie had always been in Cleo's group until now.

It wasn't that she liked Ronnie being near her all summer. She *needed* Ronnie.

Everything came so easy for Ronnie. His natural coolness. Quick and funny comebacks. The ability to make everyone around him at ease was a deflection. No one teased Ronnie. No one made fun of him for being the only Asian boy in school. The other kids *worshipped* Ronnie. If Ronnie wasn't playing a game, then it wasn't fun. If Ronnie decided something was stupid, then it *was*. Ronnie had somehow become king of the third grade.

And so naturally, by association, Cleo was deemed "okay."

*"Her? That's Cleo. She's Ronnie's sister."*

*"Oh . . . that's cool."*

The best thing would happen then. They would leave her alone. She'd become invisible—a backdrop to all the chaos, her preferred status.

But *now* how would it work? Would the other kids still remember she was "Ronnie's little sister"? Did she need to wear a badge? *Don't forget! I'm with Ronnie!*

Her mother placed a bowl of cut pears and oranges on the coffee table. She picked up the remote and turned off the gigantic box-set television, on which *Mighty Morphin Power Rangers* was blaring. The rangers had started transforming into their alter egos.

"Hey! I was watching that, Omma!" Ronnie whined.

"Too much television bad for kids' brains," she replied in English. The rest that followed was in Korean.

"Cleo, you are old enough now where you don't always need your big brother. Ronnie has his life and you have yours. He needs to move on to something that will challenge him."

Cleo tapped her purple glitter jelly shoes together. *Click, click* went the buckles. Ronnie grabbed his basketball and began tossing it up and down.

"Are you listening, Cleo?" Her mother placed her hand gently on her daughter's feet, halting her tap dance. Cleo kept her head down. Her mother sighed.

"I worry about you, Cleo. Ronnie makes friends so naturally. Why can't you?"

Ronnie stopped tossing the ball. "Mom . . . she's only seven," he said gently.

"And you're only nine."

He rolled his eyes. "Whatever. I'm going outside."

Cleo watched as he cradled the ball and exited out the backyard sliding glass doors. Their mother didn't have to worry about him. Ronnie had always been so strong. So self-reliant. She had heard the stories over and over from their mother. Ronnie had surprised her from day one. He was the best eater and sleeper. Almost running by ten months. Practically taught himself to tie his own shoes. His teachers always raved about him at parent-teacher conferences. "Ronnie is simply a *joy* to have in class," they'd say. Her mother would nod politely, but Cleo was sure she was thrilled and boisterous inside. Athletic and gifted—that was Ronnie.

And then *she* was born—colicky and clingy. Apparently, all the old-school Korean baby tricks hadn't worked to soothe her. Running the faucet water so she could see it splash. Placing her piggyback style on her back and singing old folk songs. Cleo refused to nurse but then wailed because she was hungry. She was a late walker. Fussy eater. And everything had to be explained not once but three times to her.

Her mother turned back to her. "Omma can't always be right there next to you. You have to learn to be on your own." She leaned in closer and tucked a strand of her daughter's dark locks behind her ear. "Day camp will be fun. You'll see. You'll meet other little girls like you and have so much fun."

*Other little girls like me. Yes, so much fun.*

Her mother didn't get it. Every day would be like jumping into shark-infested waters. Ronnie had been her lifeline.

Now what would she do?

———

# ALEX

Alex watched as Maud tried on various dress suits. They lay neatly on the bed, organized by color and then style. The white ceiling fan whipped overhead, causing some of the skirts to ripple ever so slightly.

"Is it super fancy where you're going to work, Mother?"

Maud donned a maroon jacket and skirt set. Large brassy buttons ran up the front. She held up a delicate gold chain with three pearls and scanned her body in the full-length oval mirror.

"Why do you ask that?"

"Seems kind of fancy. Like you're going to church."

"Alexandra, dressing appropriately isn't reserved for church service. You should always look suitable." She continued to analyze the maroon skirt suit and smoothed the bottom out with approval.

"I don't get why I can't stay home. I stayed home when you worked at the drugstore," said Alex—constraining every possible note in her eight-year-old voice from sounding whiny.

Maud did not put up with whining.

"Well, your mother has a job now—the beginning of a *career*."

Alex played with the frayed end of the light-blue vanity rug. "Answering phones and getting coffee."

She froze, realizing what she had said out loud, afraid to look up.

Maud's face was far from pleasant. She bent down immediately to where Alex sat on the bedroom floor. "Who said that, Alexandra?"

"No . . . no one. No one said that."

"Then where did you hear that?"

"From nothing. I just thought that's what secretaries *did*, Mother."

Her face went from steely cold to determined. "That's not what my job is, Alexandra. I am an administrative assistant. And I plan to do much more after getting my sea legs."

"Your *what* legs?" Alex sat back up and continued to play with the rug.

"I'm lucky to have gotten this position—especially on short notice. Fortunately, Barb from the country club was able to put in a good word for me." She patted her hair and held up a seafoam shift dress and matching jacket with shoulder pads.

"Do I still get to go swimming at the country club? I mean . . . now that Daddy's gone."

Maud remained silent.

When her father had still been around, she had spent her days home in the summer, swimming at the country club's pool and eating ice cream bars under the umbrellas by the snack bar, her skin practically brown by the end. She would peel little layers off after her sunburns, rolling the white shed skin into little balls and throwing them behind her mother's vanity.

Instead, she would be stuck where all the other working parents sent their kids.

Summer day camp.

"Can I at least still go to the pool *after* camp?"

Maud ignored her and laid the seafoam dress down gently on the bed. She pulled off coral earrings and set them on the vanity.

Alex sighed. "Daddy would have let me."

She was suddenly there. It still surprised Alex how fast Maud could move for someone usually so deliberate and steadfast in her actions. Her hands gripped Alex's arms tightly.

"He is not in this house anymore. Which means he does not make the decisions anymore. Do you understand?"

Alex stiffened. Her arms didn't hurt. Not really—but Maud's grip was contracting.

"Do you *understand*, Alexandra?"

"Yes."

"Yes?"

"Yes, Mother."

———

# JEMMA

Even being just shy of nine, Jemma was well aware she and her mother lived on the "poorer" side of Rosemary Hills. And "poorer" meant single-car garage, smaller ranch-style home. The far-east end of town had a few blocks of these "shoebox" houses.

She never had a daddy like all the other girls in her grade. It was peculiar to her when she saw these dads pick them up after school. What was it like to have a male around all the time?

It had always been her and Mama. Mama worked during the day as a hairstylist and some nights at a bar around the corner.

This left Jemma with alone time. *A lot* of alone time.

Most afternoons were spent at the homes of these "other girls with daddies." Large homes where there were always freezers stocked with fruit icies. They all had the latest Barbies and accessories. One girl even had every single outfit and accessory for her American Girl doll. *And* she had a pool.

Befriending these girls wasn't hard for Jemma at all. She had learned early on that her appearance seemed to give her a pass. She was "the pretty one." It was never said out loud, but silently understood among the herd of third-grade girls.

She filled her empty hours after school being followed by them. But with school ending and almost all of them going to fancy summer camps up in Minnesota, she would be alone all over again.

The first day of Rosemary Hills Elementary Day Camp was a flurry of excitement. Kids running around everywhere in the gymnasium as parents quickly handed them off before rushing to work. The few teachers who had been stuck with the certainly non-coveted summer day camp positions attempted to organize the random mass of students into groups.

It was an unusually hot day in June. Jemma was placed at a table with two other girls. Due to the scorching temperatures, they were to remain indoors. Their task was to color the ocean-themed coloring sheets.

The smaller girl with dark hair on Jemma's right immediately went to work, coloring the beach ball with an orange crayon. She was quiet and barely said a word.

The other girl, seated to her left, seemed spacey and annoyed. Lazily drawing lines, she barely acknowledged Jemma.

This didn't really matter to her. She was too distracted to even lift a crayon, since one of the fifth-grade boys kept trying to reach over and pull her ponytail. She pretended to be mad at him. When he was finished, she turned to the spacey girl.

"You're Alex, right?"

Alex nodded drearily.

"My mama cuts your mom's hair. I think I saw you at the salon once."

"Probably. My mother gets her hair done all the time."

Jemma picked up a pink crayon and outlined a starfish. "And you?"

The smaller girl was furiously coloring, but she stopped when she realized two other sets of eyes were on her.

"Did you hear me?"

She placed the crayon down softly. "Yes. I heard you."

"Don't you want to say your name?"

"Cleo."

"Like Cleopatra?" Jemma smiled. Mama had let her watch one of those old Elizabeth Taylor movies the other night.

Cleo nodded.

"So your name is Cleopatra?"

"No. Just Cleo."

"I wish I had a name like that. 'Jemma' sounds like a jam brand." She shrugged and went back to tracing the starfish.

The same fifth-grade boy who had tugged at her ponytail leaned against their table.

"Jemma, you can't draw worth shit!" He grabbed her paper and started waving it around.

One of the teachers overheard the boy and immediately came over. "Nathan! That is your first warning. No swearing. Now go back to your seat." She moved on quickly to brother and sister twins fighting over crayons.

Nathan remained at their table. His ears grew red with embarrassment, and he immediately moved on to the nearest target.

"You over there."

Alex looked up. "Me?"

"No. Her." He pointed at Cleo.

Cleo sat motionless.

"What's your name?"

She opened her mouth to reply, but nothing came out.

"I know. It's Rice-A-Roni, isn't it? Don't you eat a lot of rice or something?"

Cleo froze, a horrified look on her face. Her hand clutched her crayon so hard that Jemma thought it was going to snap.

"Do you speak-a-dee English? Oh wait, maybe I should talk in ching-chong-Chinese. Then maybe you would understand me."

Alex furrowed her eyebrows. Jemma scowled.

*What a dick.* That was what Mama called her bar customers.

Jemma pushed his arm. "Back off, Nathan. She's not Chinese. She's Korean. Don't you know the difference? And she's Ronnie's little sister."

She had a thing for Ronnie Song. Besides the obvious of looking different from all the other boys in their grade, he had always been nice to her.

"Don't touch me," he said to Jemma.

"Believe me. I don't want to touch *you.*"

Alex threw her crayon across the desk. "Get lost!"

He angrily pouted before finally retreating to bother a different table of girls.

Cleo's hand that clutched the crayon released.

The small trauma of the morning seemed to bring their odd little table together. Throughout the month of June, they stuck together. Every snack and lunch was shared at that same table—even when they were not required to sit together anymore. On the playground, they would move jointly like some six-legged creature, Jemma and

Alex subconsciously protecting the youngest, most vulnerable of them against predators lurking around the giant asphalt blacktop.

Most days they would play mermaids at the top of the hill right outside the playground. A weeping willow perched at the highest point. It was perfect for pretending they were immersed in seaweed—an oceanic play they re-created every recess. Jemma was always Ariel. Cleo and Alex were her doting sister mermaids.

At the very end of the month, Cleo brought silk flower hair clips to put in their "mermaid hair." Jemma and Alex fawned over them, and Cleo beamed. They were in the middle of the scene in which Ariel meets Prince Eric when the flower on Alex's hair clip flew off in the hot summer wind. They chased it, giggling but also shrieking every time it flew farther away—until they realized they had gone far. Farther than any of the teachers would have let them go had they noticed. There were just too many kids that late-June day, and the three girls on the hill were overlooked in that moment.

The flower landed in a parking lot a block from the school. The lot belonged to a U-Haul rental office.

And in that lot, stood a man.

The man bent down to pick up the red silk flower. When he got back up, he examined it and then smiled when the three of them stumbled to a halt.

"Hello," he said.

Jemma felt her nose wrinkle. There was something commanding in his voice. Like he was used to giving orders. An aftertaste of dark notes, forceful and odd.

"Can I help you girls?"

She spoke first. "We want my friend's flower."

"Oh, this flower, huh?" He held it up, twirling the petals between his thumb and forefinger, the band he wore reflecting the light.

"That's mine," Alex said loudly before she shrank back.

"Yes. It's hers. It fell off her hair clip. Give it back, please." Jemma crossed her arms.

The man looked intrigued. "Broken, huh? I can easily fix that."

And then, it was his next words that burned in her memory. "I might have some glue in my car."

A net was cast around them, that net of an adult telling them what to do. Slowly, he was reeling them in.

"Really quick?" Jemma asked.

The man rubbed his hand over his mouth. "Sure, real quick."

He smiled—a wide and confident smile. A smile that showed he was a man accustomed to getting his way.

Jemma looked back at Alex and Cleo. She took a step forward. "Can we see the glue?"

"You have to come to my car first." He looked around at the empty parking lot and then down at her.

She anxiously clicked her feet together.

"I won't bite," the man said with a laugh.

*It's not like you're alone. He'll help fix the flower.*

She took a few more steps. Alex followed.

The man motioned as he opened the trunk of his hatchback. He leaned in headfirst, digging around for a while before pausing. He clamped his hands on the end of the car, shaking his head a few times. When he turned back to them, he smiled. But the outline of his mouth was twitchy—nervous.

"Well, sorry. No luck on the glue," he said with a shrug.

He twirled the flower again and stepped toward Alex.

"Pretty girl like you. You don't really need this."

The man examined her face for a long moment. He tucked the flower behind her ear, his hand trembling at first before lingering by her cheek and then tracing his finger down her nose and under her chin.

Alex stepped back. He took another forward. A noise pierced the air.

A loud, shrieking animal cry.

Cleo stood with her hands in little fists, her head tilted back and her mouth wide open.

The man stopped and drew his hand back. He looked at each of the girls, eyes widening and waking up with realization. He covered his mouth like he was going to be sick.

Jemma grabbed Alex's hand. They tugged at Cleo, who closed her mouth, then sprinted recklessly through the parking lot, across the field, and back to the top of the hill.

Recess was still going on, the teachers gossiping in the shade. Plastic jump ropes slapped the pavement. The swings creaked and balls bounced in games of four square on the blacktop.

It was as if nothing had happened.

But three little girls knew. Somewhere, there could have been a little girl in the back of that hatchback. The imaginary girl looked at them through the window of that trunk. Watched as her life shortened with each second the car drove away, banging her hands against the window as she vanished around the corner.

It could have been any one of them.

The weight of what happened in that parking lot did not go unnoticed. Each one carried a brick on her back from then on, each little girl never forgetting the others. Somehow, the burden of such a near tragedy sealed their mouths into silence. If they spoke of it, the weight of it all would be unbearable.

It remained their secret.

A secret that created a thread between them looping in and out of each other's eyes—invisible to everyone but them.

# CHAPTER 22

---

## JEMMA

*September 8, 2022*

The small café that served savory crepes and salads was nearly empty that afternoon. It had no name—it was simply known in Rosemary Hills as "the café." No signage anywhere, only a robin's-egg-blue awning to indicate the entrance.

Jemma arrived first. They had chosen to meet for lunch at 2:00—a late time. Of course, it really wasn't just lunch they were there to have. This was not a typical "ladies' luncheon."

Fresh from a Q and A at the senior center, Jemma was conservatively dressed for once in a tweed jacket and skirt. "More Jackie O and less Marilyn," Peter had advised her. "You don't want to scare a vulnerable class." Being on her best behavior at the senior center had taken a lot of energy—but now a new kind of energy was consuming her as she chose a table toward the back. A nervous one.

*What if they don't agree? What if it all comes out?*

She jolted her head up as if to cajole her senses back. Her early-morning campaign event in Des Moines had not gone "swimmingly," as Stevie had put it. She had not brought the best version of herself to "Breakfast with Jemma." Even after a double espresso, she hadn't been able to break through her fog of preoccupation as she gave her speech to a crowd of a hundred central Iowans.

The server handed her a menu. She ordered a green tea just as Alex entered the café.

Head down, buried in her phone, she furiously texted and then placed tortoiseshell sunglasses on top of her head. She spotted Jemma and gave a curt nod.

"Hi. Sorry, I know I hate it when people are stuck in their phone. Work duty calls, though."

Jemma raised her eyebrows as she watched Alex slide in across from her. She bounced once on the white wrought iron chair with Valencia swirl patterns.

"What the hell kind of chairs are these? They're hard and cold on my ass."

The server walked up.

"Coffee. One sugar," she said tersely.

Jemma gave an apologetic smile to the server. "We're going to have one more joining us."

Alex fanned herself and took off her jacket. "It's freaking hot in here."

They stared at each other, and for a second Jemma felt a stab of panic in her chest. What did she really know about Alex? Cleo, for that matter? Years had passed, each one a numbered dial spinning on a safe, changing each of them. She knew the years had changed her . . .

"I take it you received my text," she said without thinking. She studied Alex, waiting for a reaction.

Alex looked away and flipped her menu straight, her face not giving an inch. "Yes. Let's wait for Cleo."

*For God's sake, everything else seems to get a rise out of her.*

Jemma half shrugged and nodded slowly. A few sips into her green tea, Cleo arrived. She seemed out of breath, her cheeks rosy with a flush, her long dark mane windblown.

"I'm sorry I'm late. It's a bit of a drive from where I work. And those protesters today were blocking the road—again."

"It's fine. Sit," said Alex.

Jemma handed her a menu. "Hi, Cleo. It's no problem." She shot Alex a look. "Where is it that you work exactly?"

Cleo took the menu. "Oh . . . it's something temporary. I read to a patient who is—currently homebound."

"Oh?"

"The patient doesn't really communicate right now, so I'm there to help out. It's at a farmhouse out west."

"You just sit there and read to someone?" Alex asked. "How do I sign up for that?"

"It's only until I find something else."

"Honey, not judging. Seriously." Alex waved to the server. "Can we order? I haven't eaten since my nine-thirty deposition."

They each ordered a tomato and basil crepe. Jemma added a spinach salad. The lunch began with small pleasantries and exchanges, creating a protective shell over what they were *really* there to discuss. Updates on what each of them had been doing over the years—the perils of having a toddler or a teenager. A few college stories and then, of course, how the significant others were doing. They were millennials, independent women, mothers, wives, ex-wives, and a surplus more than such titles, but they'd each been brought up to respect Midwest pleasantries. It seemed no one wanted to even look at the elephant in the room.

Jemma felt unusually reserved. Normally, she would have blurted it out again, but something about Alex's flat response at her first attempt injected a fresh stream of apprehension in her.

It was Alex who finally said it.

"We got your text, Jemma."

Her words wrapped around all three of them, a lasso squeezing them together. Trapped and barely able to breathe.

Cleo pulled her chair in and sat up straighter. The metal screeching seemed to wake them all up.

"So that's it? You get to make the decision for all three of us?"

"No. That's not what I said," Jemma replied, her stomach dropping at the same time.

"You said you are not agreeing to submit your DNA." Alex dropped her voice midsentence, looking around.

"Yes."

"*That* makes the decision. All three of us must submit, remember?"

Jemma clenched her mouth closed. Words formed behind it, but they seemed to sputter to a halt. She wasn't used to this inability to express herself the second she meant to. She closed her eyes and saw Henry from last night, felt his warm head against her. She let it consume her.

She pushed her teacup to the side and looked at Cleo and then Alex. "There is no other choice. We can't submit," she answered, more firmly this time.

Alex threw her sunglasses off the top of her head, onto the table. "Okay . . . why not?"

Where does one begin when there are a million reasons?

Jemma glanced purposefully at each of them. "If we give in, what does that say? 'Yes. Please take our blood. Take our pasts. Take our *secrets* . . .'"

Cleo and Alex went silent.

"Am I right?" Jemma asked quietly.

"Spoken like a true politician," muttered Alex.

"Really? I was going to say 'lawyer,'" she shot back.

Alex smirked. "How about that night? Should we go back to that night?"

She shook her head slightly. "Let's not rehash that."

"Oh? Let's start with why not, Jemma. Let's—"

"You know why," Cleo said forcefully.

Jemma and Alex snapped their eyes to Cleo.

She lowered her head. "You both know why," she said, quietly this time.

Whatever Midwest pleasantries they had been able to feign—three mothers enjoying a late lunch in a café—were dissolved in an instant. The mass of her words was a tumbler full of heavy rocks spilling out onto their table. There was no room for banalities among them anymore.

———

# ALEX

The air suddenly felt different at their table. Alex wondered if anyone else could feel it, the thick tribulation they shared, how it reeked of rippled complications.

She turned her head to the front of the café. The server was busy rolling silverware in taupe linen napkins. The kitchen was mostly quiet, with the exception of a small clang or rumble here and there. The only other diners were a father and his toddler, finishing up as he hurriedly put her jacket on, a tantrum on her face ready to surface.

In the midst of it all, Alex found herself picturing Davis—sitting at lunch somewhere else, perhaps with *someone else*. Was he as troubled as she was? The thought of him eating, carefree and possibly even enjoying himself, swiftly filled her with resentment.

*Why should I have to waste energy on him? Especially now . . .*

Her irritation must have spread to her face, as Cleo gave her a sideways glance.

Cleo spread her hands out on the table and leaned in. "Are we ever going to talk about that night? It's like this—this ghost that floats around whenever I see either of you."

Alex, still lurched forward, withdrew as she noted Jemma's lower lip tremble—a few waves that were clipped immediately by her mouth clamping into a grimace.

"I don't know what more there is to talk about. We were all there," Jemma said softly.

"Were we, though?" Cleo raised an eyebrow.

"Yes . . . long enough," Alex broke in.

The silence that followed created a mutual understanding from one woman to the next, each one not ready to let anything from that night cross her lips. The cracks that had started to form would not give way just yet, as the echoes of what happened remained sealed somewhere behind them.

"Are we in agreement then? We won't submit," said Cleo, staring at the table glassily.

Alex rubbed her arms and felt herself slipping away. Anytime she had to bring herself back to that night, it was like a sedative was lulling her into submission. Her body's immune response to defend her from such memories.

"Nothing good will come from following Edie Parker's orders," she heard Jemma say and then watched her eyes lower and look away soberly.

*I'm not ready. I'm not ready to share our story.*

"Alex?"

"Agreed. We won't." She was back faster than she had slipped away.

"Then what about the widow? She's going to turn in our names to the police, and then what?" asked Cleo.

"Then we stop her before she gets to us," Alex said firmly.

"How?"

"The lottery. Without the lottery, there is nothing to submit DNA *for*."

Cleo shook her head. "Suppose we do stop it somehow. That doesn't end it completely with Edie."

"You're the lawyer," Jemma said, looking at Alex. "We don't know yet what this piece of evidence she has is. But how much weight do our names actually have?"

Alex smirked slightly. It always amused her when people assumed she had all the answers, being the lawyer. She bit her top lip in consideration. "Look, I'm not a criminal lawyer. But I know a few really good ones. I could set us up with one of them. Get a more definitive answer on that. But since you're asking me, I'll say this. I don't know what else Edie has in her back pocket, but our written names seem pretty weak."

"Weak enough to risk it?" asked Jemma.

"As I already said—we ask an expert and get some solid answers."

"What if they report us?"

"Attorney-client privilege," she stated flatly.

"And the lottery?" asked Cleo. "I know it wouldn't solve everything. But our chances are better with it out of the picture."

"I don't think that's going to be too much of a problem." Jemma raised her chin up slightly. "With all the protesting and bad press, there's talk of a special town hearing."

Cleo turned her face quickly. "Why didn't you bring this up earlier?"

"I was going to. Trust me."

"Hearing on what?" asked Alex.

"The validity of the DNA lottery. It's a hodgepodge of legal and ethical issues. Technicality of county gaming laws. Constitutional infringements. Not to mention it has most of this town in a frenzy. What did the news call her yesterday? 'Elitist Edie'? She's not the most popular figure these days. The media alone seems to have a case against her. Everyone likes seeing the top one percent get dinged now and then . . . even if it's from afar."

"So there's a chance we can knock her down?" Cleo looked hopeful.

Jemma tilted her head thoughtfully. "I don't like to use those words. But yes. I can work with my team on making a public statement against the DNA lottery. It's a little risky with my campaign, but that's already at stake now anyway . . ." She worriedly fiddled with the handle on her cup of green tea.

"If the decision is made that the DNA lottery is illegal or not in accordance with local laws, she has to abide by that, right?"

"Edie Parker may be richer than God, but she's not God," scoffed Jemma.

"Yeah, and neither is the government," Alex quipped and then leaned back in her chair to look out the café windows.

Cleo shook her head. "I still don't get why she's doing this. I mean, why does she have it out for us? Why the obsession with the Baby Ava case?"

"Maybe she knows more than we think," said Jemma with a grim expression.

Alex turned her head toward them. "Let's hope she doesn't."

# CHAPTER 23
## EDIE

*September 9, 2022*

Edie took her index finger and placed it on her bedroom window. The morning cast a vivid backdrop for the rolling hills. She traced them, up and down and then up again, her nose pressed against the cold morning glass. She imagined somewhere out there in those hills, she and Johnny were young again. Poor and without any comprehension of what was to happen to them. What was to become of them.

If she could face her younger self, she would shake her for ever having a worry. *Just stop, Edie. Stop and take a minute to live in this!*

She stepped away instead and got dressed. As she put on her rose-hued lipstick, she called for Belinda.

"Is he here yet?"

"He just arrived."

"Send him to the dining room. I'll be there shortly."

She found him standing next to his seat, waiting for her to arrive. Manners were one of Chief Lennox's strong suits.

"Soren." Edie always felt that going by a first-name basis eased any public figure. She put her hand out and he took it, giving it a few pats before pulling a chair out for her.

"Good to see you, Edie. Thanks for inviting me up again."

"I could use the company. Belinda is probably sick of me at this point," she said as Belinda poured coffee for each of them. She picked up the newspaper and glanced at the front page. The headline showed pictures of protesters near Rosemary House property lines.

*More garbage stories.*

"Juice?"

"No, thank you." He waved lightly. "Doc said I need to watch my blood sugar. It's creeping on borderline."

She set the carafe back down.

"What uh—brings me up here then, Edie?" He placed his napkin in his lap as Belinda set a plate of sunny-side-up eggs, bacon, and breakfast potatoes in front of him.

Edie sipped her coffee. "Let's have breakfast first." She folded the newspaper and tossed it to the side.

Chief Lennox hesitated and then took a knife and fork, cutting into the egg. The yolk oozed out. He seemed unsure whether to take a drippy bite or to forgo it altogether.

"Something the matter?"

"Oh . . . no. It's just I've known you for years, Edie. And we've never eaten together alone like this."

"That's because we used to have Johnny," she said bluntly.

"Yes, yes. And that's a shame. You know how I feel about that."

"Goes without saying." She raised her cup.

Chief Lennox rubbed his hand over his mouth.

"Edie. What's going on?"

She folded her hands near her chin, wiggled them a few times. "Soren. You and I go a long way back."

"Yes, Edie."

"And you know I admire all that you do for Rosemary Hills."

"It's my life."

"Now . . . it has come to my attention that you aren't cooperating as I asked."

"Cooperating? With who?" he asked suspiciously.

"You know."

His eyes widened with irritation. "That Ambrose? It's him, isn't it? How much do you know about this guy? I mean, really know about him? Look here, Edie—"

She held up a hand and shut her eyes briefly.

"First, do *not* speak at me like you have authority over me. I'm not one of your officers you can order around."

"Edie—" Chief Lennox exhaled loudly.

"Second, is it true? Are you making it difficult for Ambrose and his team to investigate?"

He put his fork and knife down and groaned. "I'm cooperating, Edie, believe me. It's just he comes barging into the station making demands. How do you think that makes me look in front of my department? These—these things have to be handled with discretion. Which brings me to something else. Where is Mr. Oliver in all this? I'm sure he would agree with me that this has gone too far. What does he have to say—"

"Mr. Oliver has nothing to do with this. I don't answer to him now, nor have I ever," she snapped.

"Yes . . . I know that, Edie."

"Soren," she said quietly.

"Yes."

"I want you to listen to me very carefully. Do not obstruct in any way what I am trying to do on behalf of Johnny . . . ever again."

His face flushed as his voice raised. "Do you really think this is what he would have wanted? *Truly?*"

"What did you say to me?" she asked with testiness.

"You need to drop all of this. Once and for all. I can't even imagine what Johnny would do if he was—"

Edie narrowed her eyes. "Why, Soren?"

"I'm sorry?"

She tilted her face ever so slightly.

"*Why?* Why do you want the DNA lottery to be dropped so badly?"

He began to shake his head but paused. "I already told you. Johnny—"

"I think you forget how good of a friend my Johnny was to you. But that doesn't mean I am as well."

His cheeks reddened with a mixture of embarrassment and anger.

"Johnny would never—"

"Johnny isn't here, is he?" she said coldly.

Belinda abruptly rushed into the dining room. "Edie. You need to turn the news on."

"What?"

"Turn it on."

"Turn *what* on?"

"The news conference."

"Where is my phone?"

She handed it to her hurriedly. Edie opened it and immediately went to a live stream. She turned the volume up. On the front steps of Rosemary Hills Town Hall, Jemma stood in a fire-engine-red suit, glowing in the morning light. It felt like a colorful flag of some sort, alerting her as if to say *Come and get me, Edie.* News cameras and boom mics peeked out on the edges of the screen.

"This isn't about rich versus poor, as many have suggested. This is about having rights and not having rights. And the people of Rosemary Hills have rights. After much prayer and reflection with my family, of course, I've come to the conclusion that I cannot support the DNA lottery."

She flashed a smile and nodded to a reporter.

"Senator Danowski, why the sudden stance? The lottery has been going on for a while now."

"As I mentioned, I needed time to reflect on this. Rosemary Hills is my hometown. I needed to really think long and hard about what this DNA lottery means for us. The people I grew up with. People I care about, family and friends. We know what's best for us. People like

Edie Parker do not. I will be on the committee at the hearing that is to be scheduled very soon."

Edie shut her phone off harshly, holding down the power button with such force that her hand shook.

Chief Lennox sat completely still.

"There's also this," Belinda whispered, sliding a letter across the table.

She stared down at the plain white envelope. She touched it with reluctance and flipped it over. It was addressed to her, with a return address from Alex Mitchell.

She tore it open and pulled out a note. Her eyes scanned its contents, each letter seeming to widen her eyes with increasing intensity. When she was finished, she set the note down.

"Get Robin for me. Now."

# CHAPTER 24

## CLEO

*September 10, 2022*

Cleo scrolled through the news article about Jemma (Senator Danowski) on her phone as she stepped out of the shower. The hearing was scheduled for September 14 at the town hall, just three days shy of the lottery drawing. Jemma was set to be on the committee. She had texted her and Alex with the news the same day Alex sent out the cease and desist letter to Edie. There was no comment from Edie Parker's camp.

*Yet.*

The silence on Edie's part did little to ease her nerves. It felt like the calm before the storm, and all they had accomplished was to make it angrier. She reached for a towel and heard the quick, pounding footsteps of Rocky running into the bathroom.

"Mommy?"

"Yes, Rocky." She pulled on her robe.

"Why do you have to go to work?"

She ruffled her wet hair with a towel. A drop of water landed on Rocky's cheek. He swiped at it with annoyance.

"Sorry, honey," she said, bending down to draw him into a hug. His face planted into the folds of her soft bathrobe.

"Can you stay home today?" He sounded muffled and then pulled back.

Her phone buzzed on the bathroom counter. It was Will.

Hey, I heard someone has been a stranger to the coffee shop lately . . .

She stared at the text as Rocky tugged on the belt of her robe.

"Listen, sweetie, it's just for the morning. You know Mommy will be back by lunch. And Grandma is going to show you how to plant seeds. Remember? Your first plant. Aren't you excited?"

Cleo responded to Will, who wrote back instantly.

I've been busy lately.

That happens.

Sorry . . .

You don't have to apologize to me. Listen, I really liked seeing you the other day.

Me too.

And I get you're busy. But I'm hoping not too busy for dinner this week?

"Only if it's not some dumb flower," Rocky whined.

"Hey. Who taught you to use that word?"

"It's not a bad word."

"It's a mean word, and I don't like you using it. I'm sure Grandma can help you plant something that isn't a flower."

I'll have to get back to you on that. Sorry, Rocky is getting pretty hungry for breakfast.

Oh no, is that another apology, Cleo Song?

She had enjoyed seeing Will . . . okay, *more* than enjoyed. But she wondered if he would see right through her. Would he know how messed up her life had become? How her uneasiness over the last few days had now rolled into being completely unnerved? The only thing keeping her afloat was the daily pattern of Rocky, work, Rocky, work.

What if she couldn't put up a "good front" for him? She wasn't sure if she would be able to hide it from Will. In fact, she didn't want to . . . hide herself from him.

She put her phone away and scooted Rocky downstairs with her to the kitchen, where she opened the refrigerator to get out some milk for their cereal.

"What kind of cereal do you want, Rocks? Same as yesterday?"

Ji-Yeon appeared behind her, shaking her head. "Cold cereal. Not good for Rocky. I'll make scrambled eggs."

Cleo rolled her eyes to the refrigerator door. "Mom. It's not necessary. I have to get to work." She poured the wheat flakes into a bowl as her mother brushed past her to retrieve the egg carton.

She silently fumed, eating her cereal as Ji-Yeon whipped up the eggs and slid them onto a plate for Rocky.

"That's too hot. Give it a minute," Cleo warned him.

"Not hot." Ji-Yeon touched a glob with her finger. "Eat, Rocky."

She tossed her spoon carelessly into her bowl of soggy flakes and milk, a large splash landing on her wrist. She groaned and grabbed a napkin, blotting at it as if this entire morning were the milk's fault.

"Why you so angry all the time? I just make eggs for Rocky." Ji-Yeon ran the pan under water, scrubbing at the remaining egg bits.

*I used to be nice. I used to be a decent human being. This is what you turn into when you try to be good all the time.*

"I'm not angry, Mom. I just don't need you to—ugh."

What was her mother doing that was so offensive? Cooking a proper breakfast for her child? Letting her grown daughter live with her? She felt herself soften a little, guilt trickling in, and she determined to chill.

Ji-Yeon remained silent. She began to wipe the counter. Slow, meaningless circles that cleaned the same spot over and over.

"I'm sorry. I'm going to be late if I don't leave now," Cleo said curtly, her tone shorter than she intended. She went upstairs to finish getting ready.

———

"What do you mean you saw the patient move?" Patricia looked up with alarm from taking notes on her laptop.

"There was definite movement."

"What kind?"

"Hand movement," Cleo said boldly. "I saw it at the last reading session."

Patricia forced a small smile and made a skeptical face. "Are you sure you weren't imagining it? Being alone in that room can probably play some tricks on a person."

Cleo raised her brow. "I'm not one to imagine things. And I wasn't alone."

*She could at least acknowledge they were a person.*

"Well, I'm afraid it's impossible," dismissed Patricia.

"And why would that be?"

"This doesn't really concern you, dear."

*Dear.* There was that word again.

"It does concern me. I read to the patient, don't I?" Cleo pressed.

Patricia seemed surprised by Cleo's boldness, tilting her head back.

"I thought I made it clear from the beginning. This is a very simple job. With very simple rules. I trust you will continue to follow them?"

"Haven't I been?"

Patricia tapped a finger on her laptop with a nervous energy.

"What is it you are asking for exactly? Because I'm not sure why this is such an issue."

Cleo shook her head. "I'm not asking for anything. I only thought perhaps your employer should be made aware of this? If it's improvement they are looking for in the condition—"

"That would be out of the question," she snapped. "The medical care of the patient is entirely out of the scope of your employment." She took off her glasses and carefully folded them with one hand while the other sealed the laptop shut. "Anything else you need from me, Cleo? Otherwise, I think you should get started." Her gaze dropped as if to close any further discussion.

"No. I guess not."

"Good. I'll leave you to it."

Cleo remained seated as Patricia swept up her belongings from the table and moved into the kitchen.

*What is it that bothers her so much? The fact that I noticed it? Or maybe I saw something I wasn't supposed to . . .*

She took a moment and then went up the staircase. The hallway was dark today. A morning thunderstorm had already rolled in, and a second front could be heard in the distance—an agitated rumbling that she could feel in the pit of her stomach.

She gradually opened the door.

Everything seemed to be in the same place she had left it since the last reading session, like an untouched room of relics. The book was still at the slanted angle she had placed it, her water glass half full. Patricia must not have deemed it worth her time to change out the water.

The outline of the patient blended in more with the shadows of the room.

"Good morning," Cleo began.

The patient showed no signs of acknowledging her.

She cleared her throat, sat in the chair, and began to read. After each paragraph, her eyes would dart to the patient and back, looking for any further signs of movement—of life.

She had seen it before and was determined to see it again.

There was something intoxicating to her about being the one to have witnessed what others had not, as though a light had shone on her, the one elected for such a rare display.

*Do you feel as lost as I do?*

At night, she would fall asleep thinking about the patient. Wondering if they had even been moved from that spot, their only seat in the world. The idea of it would suddenly make Cleo's chest feel heavy with the notion and she would shake it off, sometimes getting up to check on Rocky. Making sure he was safe—though safe from what, she wasn't sure.

She continued to read, finishing the chapter when the second front thundered in without any warning. Rain pelted against the windows and rattled the panes, the droplets so thick they were practically sheets of glass hitting the house.

She paused to look at the patient, as if all the noise would jolt them to life, and then kept reading, her voice rising with the onslaught of the thunderstorm. The smear of the water against the window created an unfocused picture. The lights flickered, dimmed, and then went out, the buzz of energy cutting off abruptly.

"Dammit." A muted complaint from Patricia on the floor below.

Without the electricity, the window glowed brighter as the only light source. She closed the book and placed it back on the table. Her long sundress fell to the floor as she stood. Clenching and unclenching her hands, she stepped forward.

*I'm not alone in this room. And neither are you.*

She took a few more steps, pausing when she heard rustling from below.

*What is it you are trying to say? Do you need my help?*

A hand moved out from the blanket, pale and eerie as it gripped the arm of the wheelchair. It shook, as if that single movement was almost too much to bear. The fingernails looked freshly cut. Despite its translucency, it was a well-groomed hand.

*I know what it's like to be unnoticed in a room.*

The lights flickered back on.

She saw the patient's hand retract, slithering away warm and back into the shadow.

# CHAPTER 25

## ALEX

*September 10, 2022*

Alex held Sasha's hand tightly as they looked for a bench in Avalon Park. Sasha's white silk ribbon whipped in a gust of wind. She had made painstaking efforts to present her as the little doll grandchild Maud expected. Hair curled and pulled back smoothly, dressed in a light marigold skirt and matching shirt. White tennis shoes that looked as if they had been soaking in bleach the night before—something she had actually considered doing.

The park was bustling on a dazzling fall Saturday afternoon, children crawling over the playground equipment like ants. It was warm enough to leave the jackets at home, despite the slightest hint of crispness in the air. No one was quite ready to declare summer really over, even though Labor Day had come and gone.

She set the double-chocolate Bundt cake on the ground, afraid it would somehow tip over if left on the bench. The wrapped gift she left on her lap. Sasha obediently sat next to her, wiggling a little at the sight of all the children squealing and jumping nearby. Their feet splashing in puddles formed from the rainstorm earlier that morning.

The rowdier the children became, the more guilt ridden Alex felt. She placed an arm around Sasha and gave her shoulder a squeeze.

"Sorry, honey. You can go play as soon as we chat with Grandma Maud a bit. Okay?"

"All right, Mommy."

Sasha tugged at her skirt and then wiggled up straighter.

"Mommy, why does Grandma Maud always look so dressed up?"

"Dressed up?"

"Yes. I've never seen her in jeans. Gigi at school says her grandma wears yoga pants and tank tops all summer."

"Well, Grandma just likes to look nice. Don't you like it when she looks nice?"

"I guess." She flexed and fluttered her legs out.

*Well, here she comes, the queen herself.*

Maud floated along toward them, her stride straight as an arrow. She was sporting an Italian wool coat, large buttons all down the front. She gave a taut smile and bent down to hug Sasha.

"Hello, Sasha. Do you have a kiss for Grandma Maud?"

Sasha became subdued. She returned the hug and kissed Maud on the cheek.

"You look adorable," said Maud, approvingly scanning Sasha. "And how are you?" she asked, turning to Alex.

"I'm well, Mother."

"Violet is late again, I see." Maud sat down next to Sasha and placed her stiff black tote purse on her lap. She wrinkled her nose. "This seat is still damp."

Alex glanced at the bench. She had wiped it dry knowing Maud would complain. "I thought you would come together?"

"She is hardly home these days. I can't keep track of all her school activities and social events. She never lets me do anything for her anymore."

Alex nodded, but inside she felt a pang of jealousy. Even though she knew how lucky Violet was with the version of Maud she'd gotten, how far better off she was because of it, she couldn't help but compare . . .

"Apparently, she wanted to see the sunrise with some friends this morning." Maud rolled her eyes and looked down at the ground. "What is that?"

"I brought a cake."

"I see that. I'm not sure what compelled you. She doesn't love sweets."

"It's her birthday."

Maud sniffed. "It will likely go to waste."

Sasha glanced sideways at Maud, her nose crinkled. Alex gave her arm a small poke.

"And I don't see why we decided to celebrate outdoors. Her actual birthday isn't until Monday," Maud said.

"The weather turned out nice, and you know Violet loves being outside."

"That she does . . . you are more thoughtful than me, I'll admit."

Alex peered over her shoulder with curiosity at this sudden display of softening from Maud.

"Oh yeah?"

"You get that from your father."

"I see."

"Alexandra . . ."

"Yes?"

Maud looked worn as she turned to place a hand on hers. "I sometimes wonder—" she began. Her chest went up, about to continue. She stopped and looked away quickly.

Violet appeared in the distance with a carefree gait. She smiled and waved rapidly, hair loose and blowing around wildly. Her dark jeans were skintight, and her peach blouse barely covered her midsection. She was probably taller than Alex by now.

"Happy birthday, Auntie Vi!" Sasha jumped down eagerly from the bench, abandoning her post of model grandchild for Maud to sprint across the park.

Alex felt a tug in her chest as she watched Violet ferociously hug Sasha and twirl her around.

"Sasha Bear. I've missed you." She kissed the top of her head.

"Look! Cake!"

"I see that."

"Can we have a piece now? Please, Auntie Vi?" Sasha asked, her hands pressed together with giddiness.

"I don't see why not?" Violet approached the bench, picked up the cake, and dug a chunk out with her hand, stuffing the entire moist chocolatey bite into her mouth. "Mmm! So good! Open your mouth, Sasha Bear." She dropped a piece in her mouth and laughed.

Maud sighed loudly, closing her eyes deliberately as if in mourning over the sight of this. "Honestly, Violet. You could use a fork."

"Who needs a fork for a cake this good? It's my birthday. I can forgo said *fork*."

"Really, Violet? I swear you do things like this just to embarrass me."

Alex quietly stood up. "Happy birthday, Violet." She picked up the silver-wrapped box and stepped toward her. Violet ignored the package and threw her arms around her neck, the wrapped present squished between them.

"I'm so glad we're doing this," she said in her ear. Her hair smelled washed, a plummy floral scent drawing over them.

"Your present." Alex stepped back hurriedly, pushing the shiny box toward her.

Violet nearly stumbled backward, a flicker of disappointment in her eyes.

"Oh. Thank you." She held the box and then brought it in close to her chest. "I can't wait to see what it is. Do you want me to open it now?"

"Whenever you'd like."

She immediately ripped into the wrapping to reveal a white box. Excitedly, she lifted the lid and pulled out a rose gold charm bracelet.

"Sasha picked it out," Alex said.

"I did! All the charms and everything," she chimed in proudly.

Violet held it up in the sunlight. She slipped it on and shook it, the tiny charms clinking against each other. "I love it. Seriously. Truly love it."

"There's a gift receipt in there somewhere. You can exchange it if—"

"No! Why would I do that?"

"You don't like it. Or get something completely different. I just thought, wow, eighteen is a big deal. You could get a ring instead, or earrings. Their exchange policy at the store is really great."

*Why am I talking so fast?*

"Alex."

"We don't mind. Do we, Sasha? If Auntie Violet wants something else?"

"Alex," she said evenly. "I really do love it."

She didn't reply. She nodded repeatedly, keeping in whatever had caught in her throat this time.

*If you only knew how I sometimes wish it wasn't me that got it so hard.*

Violet placed Sasha on her back and raced around the playground, Sasha laughing with each step, her eyes practically closed from smiling so hard.

How was she eighteen already? Even these last few months, she had changed so much. From lanky teenager at the beginning of summer to now a young woman so sure of herself.

She had always kept herself at a safe distance from this bright and shiny object that was her little sister. Never quite letting her get past a certain line. Even going away to college did nothing to stop Violet from yammering at her like a puppy that didn't know when to quit.

An unnerving sense of panic at having missed out seeped into her like cream soaking into a sponge cake.

She had told herself over the years that there would be another time. She was too busy, having just given birth to Sasha or landing another big divorce case. *Next time* she would be able to spend time with Violet.

It was a firm promise to herself but never to Violet. When it happened, she would ask her to lunch, just the two of them. Or perhaps a weekend trip, if Maud allowed it. And then of course Violet had become even more absent once she was old enough for boarding school—a posh all-girls school in Chicago. Away from Rosemary Hills, away from Alex. And the weeks would go by and then turn into months. Months into years, and the opportunity for the "next time" she had in her head had suddenly come and gone.

When she became pregnant with Sasha, a then eleven-year-old Violet was delighted at the news.

"An aunt! I'm going to be an aunt!"

As Alex's belly grew, Violet would ask to talk to and sing to *her*.

"How do you know it's a girl?"

"I just do."

Sasha was born a few days after Halloween. Alex couldn't believe how much love consumed her for the tiny, wrinkly pink body that rested on her chest. Davis was immediately smitten, but Violet . . . Violet was over the moon, gazing at her small hands that stretched out and closed reflexively, followed by a brief cry and then a satisfied yawn.

"She looks just like you."

Maud stood stiff in the corner, a bouquet of flowers in hand as though she were an acquaintance visiting her in the hospital.

She thought this newfound love would maybe open her up. Give her a willingness to let Violet in. But it only caused her to close the door even more. The more she loved Sasha, the more she could sense Violet floating away, as though a vast wind had come gushing in, pushing her into her own cosmos.

*At least you were spared. At least you didn't have to go through those nights like I did . . .*

"Are you going to put that cake away, or do I have to?" Maud asked her briskly.

Alex turned her attention to the Bundt cake with a large dent in it. She scooped it up and placed it back into the box.

Sasha came running back to the bench, hysterically giggling as Violet chased her.

"Sasha, a few more minutes. We need to head back."

"So soon?" Violet placed her hands on her waist, breathing in and out heavily.

"Why, Mommy?"

Alex looked at her lap and then up. "Sasha, please."

"It's just as well."

"Why is that?"

Violet squinted into the sun with one eye and looked back down at them. "Some of my friends who are eighteen are going to submit to the DNA lottery at the station."

Maud stood up. "Ridiculous notion. And you're not even eighteen yet. You still have a few days."

"I'm thinking about tagging along."

"You know exactly how I feel about that whole display of frenzy," Maud said fervently.

"I was just *thinking* about it. Anyway, it's too nice of an afternoon to spend in line anywhere. Right, Sasha Bear?" She gave her a wink.

Alex couldn't help but feel one side of her mouth tug up a little. A smirk spread across Violet's lips—one that made its appearance when she got any rise out of Maud. She took Sasha's hands and danced with her, rocking side to side.

After a little more coaxing, Alex managed to leave Avalon Park, with Sasha in tow. They arrived home to find an empty house, greeted by the cool air of a wandering husband. Davis was out on a Saturday. Again. She found herself putting away the dishes from dinner and still no sign of him. The idea of texting him seemed so pathetic that she put her phone deep in her purse to avoid the temptation.

Sasha said very little that evening and was even quieter as she tucked her in for bed.

"Something wrong, sweetie?"

She nodded.

"Do you want to tell me?"

She twirled her fingers together as if debating whether to say anything.

"Sasha, you can tell Mommy anything. Remember?" She pulled the blanket up higher and rested her hands on it. "Now, what is it?"

Her eyes got big as she asked, "Why don't you like Auntie Violet?"

"What—why would you think that, Sasha?"

"You don't want me to spend time with her."

Alex felt herself shaking her head hard. "That's not true. We were with her in the park today, weren't we?"

"Yes, but you made us leave early. And you never smile when she's around."

She gently swiped her little girl's hair back and leaned in. "I like your auntie Violet. I like her very much. You don't need to worry about such silly things. Now good night, my angel."

She brought her up in her arms, propped up like a doll as she held her and hummed. She could feel Sasha getting more relaxed as she sang. Her little shoulders sagged, and soon she went limp onto the pillow.

As she closed the bedroom door, she brought her hand up to her mouth. Her fist plugged in the heaves in her chest and wetness behind her eyes. Not once had she had such tenderness like that being put to bed as a girl. Not once had Maud eased her worries or held her with such maternal comfort and calm.

*No . . . you gave me a different sort of calm, didn't you?*

There were those nights, the ones where an object would slip out of Maud's pocket, one Alex had grown so accustomed to at bedtime. Her eyelids reacted with droopiness at the sight of it—her Pavlovian signal for quieter times. This was how mothers tucked their daughters in at night. This was how good night kisses were given. It was a song and dance she and Maud had created. She couldn't remember bedtime being any other way.

This was how it had always been.

A prisoner in her own body, her only company the shallow in and out of her breathing. While Maud enjoyed an entirely different sort of company for the evening.

And then the season came when Alex was no longer a little girl, and Maud did something she had never done before. She invited "one of them" over for dinner.

She would have done anything for this *dinner guest*.

She worshipped the ground he walked on. When he entered their home, he was Apollo—untouchable and to be revered. She was in disbelief that someone of his authority would ever give her a second glance, let alone attention. She held on to him with fingers dug in tightly for the ranking status she craved.

It seemed he craved more than just dinner when he came over.

The first time he joined them, her mother made sure Alex was her little doll. Sitting as well behaved as ever across the table. He hardly addressed Alex, only observed as she ate. Maud, in the meantime, would chatter nonstop, fawning over him—asking him the next time he would be in town for another dinner.

He requested Alex play the piano for him one evening. He stared at her over his plate, sipping his wine and rubbing Maud's shoulder. Maud proudly looked on as Alex played. Until she looked over at her dinner guest's eyes and then to Alex, a back-and-forth whiplash of dysfunction, a disturbed detection she muffled to silence. She buried it all with a stretched smile. Clapping alongside him when the sonata was over.

She put Alex to bed that night, and as Alex felt herself falling, dozing off to happy nightmares, she saw him lingering in her doorway as he passed by, watching her with a rub of his mouth. Maud whispered in his ear as they slipped away, and it wasn't until the last second that Alex realized it was not the first time she'd seen this man.

# CHAPTER 26

## JEMMA

*September 12, 2022*

"Jemma Danowski. I'm here to see Clifford Yates."

The receptionist with red-wire glasses blinked hard at her, and then recognition caused her to freeze. "Aren't you that state senator?"

*"That state senator." I'll just take that as a good thing for now.*

"Yes. And I am here to see Clifford Yates. A friend referred me to him."

"Right. I'll let him know you're here. Please wait over there." She kept her eyes on Jemma over her glasses as she took a seat in the waiting area.

A short man donning suspenders appeared almost instantly.

"Senator Danowski." He stuck his hand out and she took it.

"Clifford Yates?"

"That'd be me. I'm an old friend of Alex's. Please, please. Come with me."

He led her to a large office, glass windows on two sides. The law firm of Yates & Barnes, LLC, stood on the twelfth floor of a building in downtown Des Moines.

"Thank you for seeing me on short notice," Jemma said as she settled into a gray upholstered barrel chair.

"Of course, of course."

Clifford picked up a pen and jotted something quickly on his legal pad. He had a very childlike body, his legs barely reaching the ground.

Everything about him was slight in stature, even his fingers. Yet his face was covered in dark, burly hair. Alex had explained to her that he was the toughest criminal law attorney in the state. His record was impeccable, and he'd gotten some of the most impossible clients acquitted. Although, she had warned her, he had the skin of a jellyfish, and for the smallest slight, he would never let you forget. She had turned him down for a date, and it took years before he finally let it go.

"Alex had nothing but great things to say about you."

"She was a good, *good* friend of mine in law school."

"Oh?"

He chuckled. "Not like that." He waved his hands. "We had each other's backs is all. Law school can be pretty fierce at times."

"So can politics," she said with a brazen smile.

He shook a pen at her and laughed wryly.

Jemma laughed back but then crossed her legs and placed her hands on the desk. "Just to make sure. Everything we discuss today is confidential?"

Clifford nodded. "Yes. Attorney-client privilege does apply for this meeting."

"Good. Good. So exactly how much has Alex told you?"

His eyes widened as he whistled. "Let's just say enough."

"I'm going to get straight to it then. I'm here because I need to find out one thing: What can we do to stop Edie Parker?"

"Nothing," he answered rapidly.

*"Nothing?"*

He nodded and shrugged at the same time.

"Then why the hell am I here?" she nearly snapped.

"Look," he said calmly. "You can't with absolute certainty prevent her from releasing your names. That is entirely up to Edie Parker. She's not breaking any laws by doing so. There is nothing stopping an individual from disclosing information to authorities. *But.*"

He raised one finger as Jemma's eyes sparked with interest.

"What matters here is whether the police and prosecutors will deem it credible evidence."

She leaned forward. "Right—because anyone can write three names down."

"She will likely need more to get any of you subpoenaed. With your names alone, at least."

"So really, she could hand them over, and nothing would happen to us?"

Clifford cocked his head to the side. "In theory. However, I will caution you there are no guarantees how it will be construed by the police. But if I were a betting man, it would be a nonevent."

"But not for sure."

"Nothing is for sure in the legal world, Jemma. Otherwise, I would be a very poor man." He smiled grimly.

"Did Alex also tell you . . . ?"

"Tell me?"

"About the piece of evidence Edie claims to have. Where she supposedly found our names?"

He nodded. "Yes. It could be nothing and she's bluffing . . . *or* it could be everything. She holds the cards there, and she's holding them close for a reason."

Jemma bit her lip worriedly.

"Okay . . . and the hearing coming up? What grounds do we have to strike down the DNA lottery?"

He rubbed his eyes. "Oh man, if that isn't a can of worms. Listen. It's a Wild West can of worms, really. It's pretty unprecedented. This isn't the Supreme Court. We're not going to decide the constitutionality of it at a local hearing. However, there is one thing you can try."

Jemma perked up.

"Public persuasion is key here. And *you* can have a huge influence there."

"Great. Because that's been going so well lately," she moaned with sarcasm.

"You need to be prepared with everything you've got, Jemma. Tell the community why it isn't safe. Why it harms them. What's in it for *them*. This is what people care about."

"Yeah—becoming a millionaire will harm them."

Clifford shrugged. "Like I said, Senator. Wild West."

———

"What did that bitch Sylvia say this time?" Jemma spouted as she answered her phone.

Stevie sighed on the other end. "She's hitting you hard for your latest stance on the DNA lottery."

Jemma closed her car door. "What? She's pretty much on the same page as me for once, isn't she? Hasn't she been against it this whole time?"

"She's saying you're a flip-flopper and you can't be trusted now. I believe her exact words were, 'With a woman who can't take a stance, you can't take a chance.' Cute, huh?"

"Oh, so now she's a poet?"

"I'm going to be honest, Jemma. She has a point. You are going to get flak for this . . . Jemma?"

"Sorry. Just finishing an email."

Her hands flew over her phone, sending Alex and Cleo an update on the meeting with Clifford.

"Where are you, anyway?" asked Stevie.

"Lawyer's office. Downtown Des Moines."

"Lawyer? Anything you care to share with the class?"

"Not at the moment. Send me Sylvia's latest and greatest. I need to get home. Thanks, Stevie."

Later that night, as she waited for Finch to prepare her shot, she felt a surge of apprehension and then annoyance, followed by anger. She was already entirely on edge, not to mention lamenting over campaign woes. The hormones weren't doing her any favors.

*Why should I have to suffer anymore? Why should Finch?*

The giggles of Poppy floating down the hallway did nothing to calm her down.

"I need to double-check the dosage," Finch said as he flicked the needle a few times.

"Why are we doing this to ourselves?"

She sat on the toilet seat, her robe bunched up to her thighs.

More laughter from Poppy and loud whispers.

"Because we want a baby?" She posed the question as if it were absurd.

Finch put the needle down with exasperation as if to say, *Here we go again.*

"Does that mean we have to suffer to get one? Maybe this is it. We're starting over. All over again, Finch! I can't take it. It's like a gut punch, not just every round but every single aspect of it. Every email notification for an appointment. Text from you reminding me about shot night. The phone calls. It all goes to here."

She threw her fist against her abdomen.

"Jemma!"

"Right there. And I've had enough!" Her voice broke, but no tears came out.

The sound of Poppy talking in a low voice amplified in Jemma's ears. Murmurs that turned her grief into pure rage.

*That's it, Poppy. You've had your chance.*

She sprang up from the seat and dashed down the hall, her robe almost coming open. She indignantly tied it back up.

"What are you doing?" Finch called after her.

She threw Poppy's bedroom door open. A startled Poppy jumped up from the bed, her phone clattering to the floor.

"I thought I told you to do your homework?" Jemma nearly shouted.

"I was," Poppy answered defensively.

"You were on your phone. I definitely heard you on your phone," she accused with a pointed finger.

"All right. I'll start my homework now." She put her hands up and sat in her desk chair.

Her daughter's immediate obedience created nothing but suspicion in Jemma. She knelt down quickly and grabbed for the phone.

"Mom!" Poppy shrieked, reaching for it.

But it was too late. Jemma, wild eyed, opened it as she stuck her arm out to block Poppy like some college linebacker.

"What's going on?" Finch asked as he entered the room.

Jemma stared down at the photo that had just been sent to her daughter. Her heart pounded in sync with the throbbing in her head. She had always imagined the worst. But it was only to ease whatever Poppy was *actually* up to. She never imagined the worst being a reality.

She handed the phone silently to Finch, an alarming calm taking over her.

"Poppy. You tell me who sent this to you. Right *now*."

# CHAPTER 27

## ALEX

*Homecoming night: Eighteen years ago*

"Stand up straight, Alexandra."

Her hair, still wet from the shower, clung to her neck and wrapped around her like a snake. A single drop of water slid down her neck and stopped at her collarbone.

"Why are you still slouching? You know that irritates me."

Maud held up the maroon dress as though it were a prize deer she had shot. She shook it out and unzipped the sides.

"When I saw this dress at the department store, I knew it was the one." She sounded wistful . . . dreamy even. "Now—arms up."

Maud draped the skirt over her head, sliding it down and then adjusting it at the waist.

*I'm her doll. I'm her obedient doll, and it's dress-up time.*

"And these," her mother said.

Alex looked up to find an elbow-length glove in each hand. Black and glossy. Maud slipped them on, straightening the material and admiring them.

She looked in the bathroom mirror, half still foggy and the other half dripping. She was a drowned bride in a soaked dress.

"What's the matter? Don't you like it?"

She nodded.

"Then why the sulking? I had this dress tailored."

"I love it," she forced out.

"Lying won't get you out of this. You are *going* to that dance. You are going to let everyone see just how normal you are. Do you understand?" Maud took Alex's chin between her fingers and turned it straight. "Do you?"

"Yes."

She softened her grip as well as her voice. "You are a perfectly lovely young woman, Alexandra. You have every reason to succeed out there. So stop choosing to disappoint me. You are only disappointing yourself."

*I'm not choosing anything.*

She slapped her arms down. "Good. Now dry your hair. I'll be back to help you." She shut the bathroom door, leaving Alex alone in a damp homecoming dress.

She ran a finger across the sequins under her breasts, each one sharp and scratchy against her skin. She began brushing her hair with slow and methodical strokes until it was all flattened against her neck. The dress made her appear extra pale. She opened the drawer to the left of the sink and pulled out a compact. She dusted her face, but it only caused her skin to become ashen. She spotted a tube of lipstick—a brick red she had seen Maud sport many times. After twisting the block of color up, she applied it with absolute precision to her lower lip and then the top. She rubbed them together and watched the claylike substance smear and bleed outward.

*I'm bleeding, Mother. Look. Can't you see that?*

———

# JEMMA

The purple beaded bracelet shook on Jemma's wrist as she checked her hair one last time in the mirror.

"Come on, Jem!" Shaina called from her Jeep, honking a few times.

"Hold on a sec!"

She opened her purse to make sure her lip gloss and keys were in there and then made a dash for the back door. On the counter was a twenty Mama had left her before rushing off. She slid it into her purse but had trouble closing the clasp.

"Shit," she muttered, trying again. She looked up and halted.

He stood there, a tall figure behind the screen. The night was already getting chillier, and wind tapped the door open a few times.

"Hey, Jemma," he said.

"Eric—"

"Can I come in?"

"No . . . I mean. What are you doing here?"

He stayed behind the screen and studied her. "You look . . . wow. Beautiful."

She cocked her head. "Funny, that's what you said to me last time we went to a dance together."

He sighed. "That's why I'm here."

She hesitated. "I'm not letting you in."

"That's fine."

"They're waiting for me." She motioned toward the driveway.

"Yeah, they saw me walking up."

*Thanks for the warning, ladies.*

"What is it that you want, Eric?" she asked flatly.

He shoved his hands in his jean pockets. A little underdressed for the dance, but who would care? He was Eric Housley.

"I don't know why you just . . . cut me out like that."

She placed the purse over her waist, her arms crossed.

"You made me—" He lowered his voice. "You made me feel like I did something wrong. Did I?"

As he stared intently at her through the screen door, the net pattern casting a textured view of his face, she saw him for what he was. Not what she remembered from that night—nearly silent as he lay on top of her, unable to look her in the eye. His clammy hands holding on to her hands. He was a scared boy. And she was a scared girl.

It was neither of their faults.

She faintly shook her head back at him.

He looked relived, as if he were a child sprung from time-out. The depths of his understanding would never be enough for her to explain to him how that night had made her feel. It would be like diving head-first into a clearly marked shallow pool.

"Have fun at the dance, Eric."

"Yeah." His mouth formed a half grin, and he bounced off, the screen door tapping again from the wind—a weight clearly gone now, and he could go drink and do all the tawdry things a king of high school like him relished.

She envied him.

She envied the indulgence of it all. The choices he had laid out in front of him like a deck of cards, all winning ones, and all he had to do was fling one of them—any of them—onto the table.

Her airway filled with envy, and she thought it would suffocate her.

The Jeep honked again, and she breathed out.

———

## CLEO

Ronnie opened the car door for Cleo.

"You look . . . nice, Shorty. Didn't know you had it in you," he said as their mother watched from the front door with a worried expression.

"Gee, thanks, Ronnie."

The clip caught part of Cleo's rose-colored dress as she put on her seat belt.

"It's a compliment. I swear."

"Okay, Ronnie," said Cleo mockingly.

He paused holding the car key against the ignition. "You know you can walk if you want."

"Just drive." She half laughed.

The clunky gray Honda Civic sped down the street, Ronnie giving a few last honks to their mother. Cleo rolled her window down, lifting her chin to get some air.

"So . . . who's the guy, Shorty?"

"Huh?"

"Oh, c'mon. You're not going to meet friends. Who's the guy?"

He adjusted the rearview mirror and fluffed the front of his hair.

"There is no guy. I'm just going."

"Right. And I'm just going for the dancing."

She smiled and shrugged as he jabbed her with his elbow. It was a smile she had kept to herself since school started. The first day back, she had been completely terrified at the idea of Will pretending nothing happened—erasing Art 101 from the history books. And yet on the first day back, he'd sought her out.

"Cleo."

She loved the sound of her name when it came from his voice.

He sat next to her at lunch and told her about his summer, helping his uncle at his farm in Wisconsin. She told him about her job at the new clothing boutique on Main Street and how she never wanted to fold another T-shirt again.

They floated back together, as if two leaves had caught in the wind briefly and dropped right back in the stream. Sailing along seamlessly, their conversation gliding over the smooth surface of the water.

She would count the seconds until lunch period each day, eagerly sitting up in her desk, ready to take off as soon as her English teacher stopped droning on about the overuse of idioms.

He would be waiting for her, saving the same spot outside near the sycamore, and she thought there couldn't possibly be a greater thrill than seeing Will turn his head and grin at her.

The homecoming dance eventually came up.

"None of my buddies are going. They think it's a waste of money—having to buy all that stuff to take out a girl they aren't even dating."

Cleo had looked away quickly, too embarrassed to show any interest in her face.

"Do you think that too?" she asked carefully.

"Kind of . . . I mean, what's the point, right?"

"Right," she replied, nodding.

The bell rang. Lunch was over. She hurriedly picked up her tray. Maybe if she got out of there fast enough, he wouldn't notice her disappointment.

She was three steps away before Will called after her.

"Cleo, wait."

He towered over her, and she wondered if he had grown another inch overnight.

"I . . ." He stopped. His cheeks were flushed. Suddenly she realized he was nervous. *Will* nervous. She had never known him to be like this.

He snapped his fingers against his hand a few times. "I mean . . . I guess I wouldn't mind going. See what all the fuss is."

"I might too," she said softly.

"Maybe we could—I mean, if you're going. Maybe we could meet if we're both going to be there?"

She looked up at him, a true, unaffected smile. One that she saved for him. "That would be fun."

He reached out and moved a lock of hair that had flown against her cheek. His eyes appeared to concentrate intently on hers, and he smiled, his scar stretching with it.

"Okay then," he said.

She thought for sure he would never look away.

She soared on to her next class, trigonometry. It was short lived, though—she was met with more lingering eyes from Austin Blakesly.

She looked either at her worksheet or straight ahead most of the period, pretending not to notice.

Ronnie cranked the Civic into park. He opened his door and then lingered, shutting it. "Listen, Cleo. You going to be all right in there tonight?"

"Why wouldn't I be?"

"I know I said once we went in—"

"Ronnie. I'm sixteen. Not six. I'm fine."

He tapped the steering wheel a few times. "All right, all right. Let's go. And remember, I don't exist when we're in there."

The entrance to the gym was already full of couples making their way inside. Music vibrated in and out with the beat. Ronnie went inside, glancing over his shoulder once at her. She adjusted the top of her dress and waited to the side of the entrance, closest to the large sycamore. Just as she and Will had discussed.

Her heart raced, but not with nerves. She felt elation—a premonition of something great that was about to begin. The buildup in her head caused her to blush; each flush of color in her cheeks made her sensible side grow stronger.

*You are an idiot romantic, that's what you are, Cleo Song.*

She almost laughed out loud at this notion.

And she heard a voice calling her name.

"Cleo."

But the voice did nothing to stir her. This voice was not the one she was expecting.

# CHAPTER 28

## EDIE

*September 12, 2022*

There was no wind as she drove the Aston Martin down a country road she had never come across. One that went straight and then abruptly meandered left and then right. This was a place they had never traveled—all familiar markers ripped from their consciousness. She tried to search for the air, but she could not. The atmosphere was like that of being inside a tightly sealed mason jar. It was their world, and Edie was in the driver's seat.

"You watching the road, Edie?" Johnny tipped his coffee cup back.

Edie reached for hers, but there was nothing in the cupholder.

"Of course I'm watching," she snapped. Her hands went tense on the steering wheel.

"There, there, my girl. I know you are." He patted her shoulder and then smiled. He was loose with his words and his body, one arm hanging out of the side of the car.

*Johnny with no worries. Johnny with not a care.*

"Where are we going?"

"You'll see, Edie. Keep driving."

"But we're going to be late. We have to be somewhere else. I'm sure of it." She felt dazed, her sense of time slipping away in a disintegrating mist.

"Are you sure?" he asked.

"Yes. Now tell me. Tell me about when we first met," she said as she glanced at him through her cat-eye sunglasses.

Yet there was no sun today.

"Oh wow. How we met?" He held his chin. "Didn't I pick you up in a bar, Mrs. Parker?"

"Yes. I think that's exactly what happened. But come on, Mr. Parker. Romance it up for this old gal."

"All right. All right, I can do that."

She smiled, looking ahead down the road.

"You had on this dress. A yellow dress."

"It was green. Strike one."

"I knew that! It was green. A brilliant green. And I knew right then—"

"You knew, huh?"

"That I was going to marry the girl in the green dress."

"You are a liar. Strike two." She laughed.

"I did. I really did."

"Oh, horseshit, Johnny. Prove it."

A playful look came over him. She knew that one. It had been a while since it had come out. She could no longer tell if he was young or old. But she was still old—she could feel it behind her eyes.

"What are you up to now?"

"I'll prove it!"

She turned to him, but his face had been replaced.

Kane Oliver grinned wildly at her.

His hands darted out and grabbed the steering wheel, jerking it hard to the left.

"You got to watch out for those rocks!" Kane shouted over the noise—the noise that shrieked in Edie's ears, glass breaking, metal twisting and scraping against the ground. The car rolled like a marble, never stopping. She felt her head whip around, and then, in between the lashings, she could see Kane being thrown hard like a rag doll, his head going one way, his body the opposite. She heard a snap.

"Stop! Stop! Stop!" she cried.

They came to a halt, right side up, the car mangled. She could see her arms were twisted in unnatural angles. Her wrists had never flopped like that before.

She looked over at Kane. He sat up straight with an expressionless face. A ventriloquist dummy with no mouth.

"No! Johnny!"

Edie sat up in her bed. She felt absolutely cold, as though an ice bath had been poured over her in her sleep. She reached out to search for Johnny.

She placed her fingers along the pillow he'd once occupied for so many years.

Like tiny pixels coming together to form a picture, her realization that she was still alone, still Edie Parker, the widow, came to life. She felt foolish, even betrayed, that she had gotten sucked into such a facade of a dream for even one brief moment.

Duped.

It was the same way she'd felt when she received the letter from the women—a refusal to submit their DNA to the lottery. A flat-out no to getting any answers. Either they were calling her bluff, or they were trying to play games with her.

She would have none of that.

https://DNAlottery/tracker.com
Date: September 13, 2022
Number of Entries: 70,867
Days Until Drawing: 4

*The local hearing on the DNA lottery is scheduled for September 17 at the Rosemary Hills Town Hall. Due to limited seating capacity and fire code restrictions, attendance will be based on a first-come-first-served basis. The hearing will also be live streamed. More details to come.

Comments:

"There is no way in hell this lottery is going to be approved. Mark my words!!"

—B. T.

"Wow. B. T. seems to be the expert in local and state lottery laws. Does he not realize that Edie Parker has a team of attorneys behind her who would never let this happen if every T was not crossed and I dotted? Duh . . ."

—Maya V.

"Fuck Edie Parker and the whole Parker family corp. They can't and DON'T own this town and they aren't above the laws. This thing is going to be struck down."

—Anonymous

"What happens if the DNA lottery is considered illegal? Is that even the right term? I'm no lawyer, but what about all the promises made to those people who gave their blood?"

—H. Christian

"Blood money is what this is."

—Anonymous

"Senator Danowski is on the board—doesn't say much about it then. Can the woman wear anything that covers her ass? LOL!"

—Tina O.

# CHAPTER 29

## ALEX

*September 13, 2022*

"I want to laugh more, Davis. I want *us* to laugh more."

*Yes. That's it. That's what I would say if he walked through that door right now.*

The first line in an opening argument was always the most important in court. She knew it set the tone and theme for the jury members—planting a seed and preconceived notion they'd carry with them for the duration of the argument. No matter how skilled, beautifully articulate, and Shakespearean the rest of it was.

In the courtroom, she knew exactly how to put that first sentence together. All it took was puzzling together ten words to capture the jury's attention, like a Rubik's Cube of prose. She knew her craft, which gave her the gas each day to do it all over again.

But this wasn't the courtroom. This was her marriage.

*Let's hope this isn't actually the closing arguments.*

She and Davis had been drifting alongside each other for nearly a week, their discourse far too civil to be kind, Sasha the only saving grace for normalcy. Everything revolved around Sasha to keep it from going there. If Sasha opened her mouth for something, Alex practically pounced on her to address it—anything to avoid giving them enough space in the same room to tackle the chasm that was widening each day.

When Davis left his phone on the counter again on Sunday, she practically screamed at herself to keep her hands off. No good would come of looking through it. She didn't need to know.

But did she want to?

*He went out to eat for lunch. Maybe he really didn't want to eat with you. Sure, that hurts your feelings, but you're a big girl, right?*

She swiped her knife through an onion. The pan with oil on the gas stove was starting to smoke. She rushed over to turn the heat down. She was making his favorite—skirt steak tacos with grilled vegetables and extra jalapeños. Along with her favorite—red wine.

The glass was looking lonely, so she poured herself a little more. She tried hard not to think about the upcoming hearing. They weren't submitting their DNA. A cease and desist letter alleging harassment had spoken for them. Edie Parker was fully aware of this, yet so far, radio silence on her end. It was done now.

But somehow it didn't feel like it was over.

The day had not been kind to her. The morning had started with her burning Sasha's whole-grain toast. The stench of the charred bread filled the kitchen and remained on her clothes the rest of the morning. She had to roll her windows down the whole way to work to air out her suit. When she realized she'd forgotten her laptop, she had to drive all the way back home to retrieve it, and *she*, Alex Mitchell, was late.

Upon arriving at the office, she discovered Hattie had called in sick. Which meant she would be getting home late, when she had planned on beating Davis to the punch. She wouldn't feel prepared if she wasn't there first to present him with some kind of peace offering (hence the meal). Tonight, they would talk, no matter the cost. No matter how irritated or tired he seemed, they would get it over with. Even if the end product was not a good one.

Her 9:00 a.m. consult was a no-show, which only increased her irritation. She could still smell a hint of burnt toast, and every noseful of it upped the red on her meter bit by bit, until she reached her 10:00 a.m.—a first-time meeting with opposing counsel and her latest and greatest client, Deidre Halston. Heiress to a farm-machinery company, she was from a family worth millions, but her husband hoped to see at least a quarter of it after "years of supporting Deidre's passion in sculpture, both emotionally and financially." Both Halstons looked and talked like donkeys, with horselike faces but ambivalent attitudes to everything—although she believed just one of them was the ass.

"Mr. Halston? I can call you Richard, right?"

Griffin Alvarez raised his eyebrows. "I'd prefer you direct any questions to me, Alex."

"Wasn't it *Counselor* a week or two ago, Griffin?"

"Alex."

"C'mon, Griffin. This is simply an initial meeting. I'm sure Deidre doesn't mind you addressing her. Do you, Deidre?"

Deidre shrugged.

"See? Now where was I. Richard—right? Or can I call you Dick?"

Griffin abruptly stood up. "Alex, maybe you and I should step outside for a moment?"

"And leave these two here alone without a babysitter?" She pointed to the Halstons, then crossed her arms. "I think not."

Griffin eased back into his chair, cautiously watching Alex.

"All right. I think we can continue then."

"Yes, let's continue," Alex said, nodding with exaggeration.

Deidre looked down at her nails and swiveled her chair.

"Alex, I'll let you have the floor again. What is it that you wanted to address first?"

She turned toward Richard and smiled. "I think I'll address Richard here."

"Again, Alex, I would advise you not to speak directly to my client."

"Bullshit, Griffin."

He tossed his pen down and placed his hands up in the air, rubbing his brow.

"As I was saying, Richard. I'd like to address you first."

Richard, slumped over with droopy eyes, shrugged. "All right."

"Is it true that you ran up a credit card bill of nearly fourteen thousand dollars the month of December?"

Griffin stood up. "What is going on here? This isn't a deposition, Alex. We're here for a preliminary meeting."

"Yes, thank you, Griffin."

"Don't answer the question, Richard."

"I guess I did," he drawled.

Griffin groaned.

"And that this bill contained many charges for hotel stays in Des Moines? Expensive dinners? Flights to Chicago and stays at suites there?"

"Yeah."

"Quiet, Richard."

"Did you cheat on your wife, Richard?"

He shrugged. "She knew about it."

Deidre nodded. "I did know."

The indifference of them both only further heated the hot plate that was plugged in to Alex's already overly full outlet. She glared at them separately—a full five seconds for each of molten eye contact.

"So that's it. You were wining and dining and *screwing* some other woman."

Richard acknowledged it as if the accusation were going through the McDonald's drive-through.

"And you. You knew about it and didn't give a crap? Does that even make any sense? As a woman, you would think you'd have some pride to confront your completely aloof and adulterous husband. But you chose to stay silent. You chose to be the coward."

"Yeah . . . so I thought you were on my side? Like—as my lawyer and everything?"

Alex slapped her hands on the table and turned to her. "I am on your side, Deidre!"

Griffin stood up without hesitation this time, took Alex by the arm, and dragged her out of the conference room.

"Excuse us," he said gruffly.

Out in the hallway, he put his head down as if to take a breather. He finally lifted it.

"Alex. What the—I don't even know what happened in there!"

Alex crossed her arms, a teen refusing to admit any wrongdoing to a scolding parent. She scoffed and tapped her foot.

"Nothing."

"Nothing? *Nothing?* You verbally badgered not only my client but your own! I've never known you to be so unprofessional."

"That makes two of us," she muttered.

"So then please explain to me what is wrong or how I can freaking help you, Alex. I've known you a long time and I respect you, so I will ignore—no, pretend this never happened. But you can't go on like this. Got it?"

She pressed her lips together and nodded.

"Alex . . . I'm being serious."

"Yes."

Deidre Halston texted her ten minutes after the conclusion of the meeting, firing her as counsel.

The kitchen reeked of burned food as Alex sucked down the rest of her wine. Her front teeth felt puckered. The steak had sizzled down to a dry heap of jerky. The vegetables were blackened. Still no sign of Davis or even a text saying he was going to be late.

Sasha had called from Nala's house, begging to stay there for dinner.

"Mommy, they're having pizza. On a weeknight! And the kind with stuffed crust."

"Okay. Just be sure to thank Nala's mommy. And remember your manners."

*Better to have her out of the house.*

Alex poured the rest of the wine into the glass. She began clearing the cold dinner from the counter. She was closing a Tupperware lid when the garage suddenly opened.

He looked surprised to see her still in the kitchen, then nodded and started to retreat upstairs.

"Davis. Wait."

He didn't have to turn around for her to see the rigidness in his face.

"Alex . . . let's not do this tonight."

"Please. I don't want to go on any longer like this."

He heaved a big sigh, and his shoulders dropped. "This isn't the time."

"But it *is*."

She wiped her hands on a rag and went around the counter. His eyes grew more wary the closer she got to him.

"Davis—we can't keep acting as if nothing has happened."

"And what exactly is it that you think has happened?"

"Do you truly think Sasha doesn't notice? She may not say anything explicitly, but she knows something is up between us."

His lips snarled. "Do *not* bring Sasha into this."

"Bring her in? She's already in the thick of it. That's what I'm trying to tell you. Let's at least have this out for her sake, if not for mine."

She stepped closer to him. Somehow, she felt the need to touch him. To let him know she was still here. Still his wife. The woman he'd chosen to marry.

*What kind of woman are you if you let your husband cheat? If you see him go in the restaurant and drive away?*

"What is it exactly that you want to discuss then?"

She moved even closer to him and placed her hands on his. They went rigid as if he were in pain. She held on.

"I want . . . I want to discuss us."

*There goes your opening line, Counselor.*

"Us."

"Yes, us."

"Alex, there is no us. There hasn't been for a while now. Why do you make me say these things out loud?"

She pulled her hands away.

"You don't care that I already know?"

He stepped backward, alarm spread all over his face. He peered at her as though he didn't recognize her.

"You . . . you know?"

"I think you wanted me to know," she said quietly, lowering her eyes.

He put his hands by his ears. "I don't believe this . . . how could you know?"

"It doesn't matter now."

"But how—was it someone at your firm? I don't understand how this could have happened. I thought there were rules against—"

"Davis, you were out late most nights. Avoiding me on the weekends. Missing the Labor Day parade and carnival. You never miss out on anything . . . with Sasha anyway."

He swallowed hard, the vein in his neck practically pulsating out through the skin.

"That doesn't mean anything. I—"

"The texts, Davis. I saw them on your phone."

"You snooped through my phone?" he asked indignantly.

She threw her arms up. "As if that compares to all the lying you've done. I can't count how many times you lied to my face. But listen, it doesn't matter. I don't care about any of it. I really don't . . . I don't—*I don't* want to be a repeat!"

The haze of wine was now making her mouth spill open.

"Repeat?"

"Never mind."

"What?"

She shook her head. "Davis."

She grabbed his hands this time—clenching his fingers as his entire body stiffened. The repulsion practically leaped off him like an electric current into her hands. She felt as though he had slapped her in the face.

He suddenly looked sad—maybe even sorry for her. "If you know the truth, then why are you doing this?" He pulled his hands away and put them in his pockets. "Please stop this, Alex. Don't make it worse."

"I already told you. I don't care . . . unless—was it only the one time? After the lunch?"

"Only the one time?" Davis craned his neck with utter confusion.

"You were meeting her. For lunch that day instead of me. Look, I left before I saw her. I didn't even catch a glimpse. I left as soon as I saw your car. I just assumed you were fucking her, I guess."

His lips parted. "Alex."

*Maybe I can't do this. Maybe I don't want to hear how he had his hands all over some other woman.*

"I want to know what you did with her . . . we can start there."

*Some woman who probably orgasmed on command like a Yorkie being asked to sit for kibble.*

"Alex, I didn't sleep with anyone else."

His voice was shaky. She had never seen him so emotional. Where was this emotion the last five years? Even before then? On their wedding day?

"I wasn't meeting that woman for the reasons you think."

He pinched his mouth together and looked down.

*More lying. Lies, lies, lies. Go on, Davis, I can take it.*

"I was meeting that woman because she's a divorce attorney. I'm filing for divorce."

# CHAPTER 30

## CLEO

*September 13, 2022*

"I don't like my new school," Rocky announced at the dinner table.

"Eat more bean sprouts," Ji-Yeon said, glazing over his statement and poking her chopsticks at his bowl of steaming rice.

Cleo paused midbite. "What? Why is that, sweetie?"

Her heart rate picked up as though she had started sprinting across the room. A sense of mama-bear rage swelled up. Who had picked on him? School had only started, and they were already going after him? Immediately, she could see herself in Rocky. The quiet kid who didn't look quite like everyone else. And he was the new kid, on top of it all—what had she been thinking bringing him here?

"They don't have Pizza Fridays like they did at my school in Chicago," he answered glumly.

She almost laughed at his response. But she bottled up her relief by placing a piece of kimchi in her mouth.

He shrugged. "Oh well. At least they have better snacks."

*Maybe he will have it better. Maybe things are different now.*

She swallowed her food hard, a lump blocking it from going down with ease. The carefree nature of her son was all that she had ever wanted for him. But she was always prepared, holding her breath in anticipation of something that would knock that easygoing spirit loose and cause it to tumble away forever.

"Rocky, I think you will be okay without Pizza Friday," she said with as much seriousness as she could muster.

Ji-Yeon picked at her bowl, her chopsticks clinking.

"Mom. Why aren't you eating?"

She looked up with a blank face. "I'm eating. Why asking?"

"You're acting funny."

"Funny?"

"You know what I mean."

Her mother slowly chewed what little food she was eating, refusing to respond.

"Please. You've been silently sulking around me the last few days. I know something is up."

She continued to ignore her and turned to implore Rocky to place more bulgogi in his bowl.

And then, like a sniper attack coming out of thin air, her mother had to ask.

"You talk to Michael?"

Cleo looked over at Rocky and widened her eyes. "Mom . . . *no*. Not right now."

Ji-Yeon shrugged. "He's still his father."

"Mom!"

Rocky stopped chewing. He glanced at Cleo and then his grandmother, back and forth. Cleo felt biting words ready to tumble out of her mouth but stopped herself.

"Rocky, are you finished? Or do you want to watch some cartoons?"

He stared at the plate, as if weighing the options.

"I'm finished."

He bounded away into the living room faster than Cleo could respond.

"You talk to Michael. Maybe things will get better," her mother continued.

"There is no talking to Michael. Michael is no longer my husband. I don't know if you noticed, but we're divorced."

"Then talk to me," Ji-Yeon said suddenly, turning to her.

"I *am* talking to you."

She shook her head. "You don't. Not like Ronnie."

*Jesus, just what I need. A Ronnie Fest.*

"Then go talk to Ronnie. I'm sure he'd be happy to tell you all about his latest adventures with Miss Sailor Moon."

"Sailor who?"

"Nothing."

"He let me in. That's the difference, Cleo."

"Ronnie isn't as perfect as you think, Mom."

"I know Ronnie not perfect. But Ronnie is honest with me," she said, touching her chest once.

"So now I'm a liar?"

"That's not what I said."

Cleo held her palms up with frustration. "What is it that you want to believe? That I'm a failure? That I failed at a career? Failed at being a wife? And now my failed marriage, you decide to pick on?"

Her mother sighed. "Not pick. I'm trying to help."

"I'm okay, Omma. I really am. You need to let me move on. Move on with Rocky. That's why we're here."

Ji-Yeon sighed and continued to eat in small bites, ending the discussion.

Later, after Cleo had put Rocky to bed, she noticed her face felt wet and hot and she rubbed at it. She needed some air. Space. She needed to get out of the house.

She pulled her phone out and sent a text. I'll take you up on that dinner. But only if it's drinks.

She put her head back and closed her eyes. A few minutes later, her phone buzzed.

Big Blue Bar in twenty?

Make it ten.

———

A smattering of patrons were at Big Blue Bar when she entered. A cozy little wine bar on the east end of town, it smelled of chargrilled meats and orange zest being twisted by the bartender. Will had not yet arrived, so she sat on a stool at the bar and ordered an old-fashioned.

She could see her reflection in the mirrored wall, which held shelves of colorful liquor bottles, giving the appearance of a modern apothecary. Her hair looked flat, and what little makeup she had thrown on earlier in the day was now smudged from tears.

*Dear God, Cleo. You could have at least put on some ChapStick.*

There would be no time to fix the mess that she was. He looked even taller for some reason, standing in the entryway with a strikingly secure presence. When he spotted her, his grin seemed excited and then shy.

"Hi there. I hope I didn't keep you waiting."

He reached for a greeting hug. She let him scoop her in from the barstool, and she felt foolish in an instant at the notion forming in her head to sink into his arms and stay there. They felt like a bed that finally would give her the comfort and sleep she had needed all this time.

She pulled away before the urge took over.

"No. Not at all."

Will pointed to the bartender and then to her drink. They mutually nodded.

"When did you get so slick?" she ribbed.

He feigned confusion. "Are you kidding? I pulled moves like that in our high school days. You just never witnessed them."

"Ha."

"I will not take a pity 'ha.' Un-uh." His drink arrived, and he took a sip. "So what changed your mind?"

She swiped at the condensation on the side of her tumbler. "I changed my mind?"

"C'mon, Cleo." He tilted his head playfully at her. "Your last texts weren't exactly—inviting, should I say?"

"Truth?" She glanced at him and then back to her glass.

"Always prefer it."

"I needed to get out of the house."

"Ah. So now it has come to pity drinks."

She elbowed him gently. "Stop. I enjoy your company too."

"Thatta girl." He patted her head.

"Quit." She smiled.

He reached down and fixed a stray strand that had flopped in front of her eyes. She was sixteen again and felt an embarrassment of nostalgic emotion. She sat up straighter and shook it out along with her hair.

"I'm a mess tonight."

"Messy can be good."

She picked the maraschino out of her glass and bit into it. "Oh yeah?"

"Sure."

"Were all your past girlfriends messy then?"

He gave her a half grin. "All of them. Every single one turned out to be a mess. I say 'mess,' not 'messy.' That's key."

"Anyone serious?"

His brow twitched upward. "One. Maybe two."

"And now?"

"Now I find myself wondering where the last nearly twenty years of my dating life have gone."

She poked his arm. "Hey. Don't lump me into that. I refuse to admit it has been that long."

He put his hands up as if to surrender.

She twisted the cherry stem between her thumb and forefinger. "Really, though. I'm a little confused here. Nice-looking young officer in town. Known to be an all-around good guy. I'm really the only prospect? C'mon, *Will*."

He set his drink down and leaned on his elbow.

"You're not some prospect, Cleo."

"Hmm?" Ice slid into her mouth, and she crunched it. "Ah. So who's being pitied now?"

She laughed, but he just smiled gently, his expression forming a thoughtful glow.

"You know what you are. You've always known."

She could feel her smile vanish but not out of unhappiness. His words cut into her in a good way—like a slit releasing pressure from a bulging wound.

They remained at the bar for a little while longer, Will cracking jokes, Cleo laughing freely. She sensed just a slight warmth from the drinks but nothing that created a heaviness on their words. She felt like, in some ways, Will had been by her side ever since that homecoming night. With each story, each look, they were flipping the pages of a book unwritten but told so many times in their minds. Shape-shifters from being young and beguiled to a period of knowing so much while knowing very little.

He suggested a walk, and she found their hands twisted together. The evening was warm, summer's last grasp at straws to remain lingering in the air. Each street they walked down was another memory, another layer of the past they had to let the other catch up on. She soaked it in with such pleasure, noticing how his eyes lingered on every expression she made. They came upon the playground at Rosemary Hills Elementary. The equipment was colorful and new, likely the second replacement of what they had grown up on. A square trampoline marked the center of it all. The black tarp was cold as Cleo sat on it. Will dared her to jump.

"Only if you do too," she said.

He hopped on, sending her flying and then down. She couldn't stop laughing.

The absurdness of them bouncing into each other left her breathless against the mat. He suddenly drew her in and held her with such closeness.

"Princess Peach's secret slide," he said, softly chuckling.

"Secret," she whispered.

He looked at her as she had never been looked at before. His hands, though touching just her arm and back, spread a warmth throughout her entire being. She wanted him to know her. She wanted him to know everything there was about her so that she could maybe someday get the same in return.

"Can I tell you a secret?" Cleo asked as they lay flat on their backs.

"That depends."

"On what?"

"What kind of secret?" asked Will.

"Oh—so for you, there are species of secrets."

"Exactly. You read my mind." He turned on his side, toward her. "You see, there are those secrets that do no harm. And then there are those that just settle in and don't go anywhere."

"Any others?"

"Oh yes. There's the kind that can hurt. Cause some real hurt."

"Huh." She flipped toward him.

"Still the kind you want to tell?" he asked quietly.

*Yes. Because if I don't, then I will have to keep pretending. Pretending that you know all of me, when you can't. Not if I don't tell you this.*

"It is."

She lay back again and told him—never looking at him but sensing his intensity as she went on, talking about the night of the carnival and the car that pulled up. The widow's demands and the paper with their names on it. How she had been hired to read to a patient who seemed to be silently asking for her help. Her constant worry whether she was doing the right thing for Rocky. And how she didn't feel alone when she was near him.

He took her hand when she was finished.

"I suppose that was more than one. Sorry."

"Don't apologize anymore, Cleo Song. Not to me anyway."

She felt her eyes get wet, and he drew her in again. But this time he placed his hands under her chin—a slow draw toward her mouth. There was no longer any sense in her body. She fell into him. Her finger traced the scar, smooth and silvery.

A fiber of their past innocence wrapped around them. She fell asleep somehow, his soft voice in her ear. He must have, too, because when she woke up, she felt the rise and fall of his chest—a rhythm that succeeded in keeping her calm. Yet she had every reason not to be.

Her dream had not been pleasant.

The baby was there again. Wet in her arms. She cried out, and the truck doors slammed shut.

# CHAPTER 31

## JEMMA

*September 13, 2022*

"I'm heading into the lion's den," Jemma whispered into her phone. "I'll call you when it's over."

"Let's not make too big a drama out of this," said Finch. "It wasn't that bad—"

"Not that bad . . . not that bad?" Her voice immediately rose three octaves. "Finch, a pervert sent our daughter a lewd photo of himself."

"I don't know if it was *lewd*."

She bent over and looked into the phone, as if he could see her.

"Please tell me you're doing that thing where you are only joking to annoy me. Which is bad enough because I don't need to be provoked right before meeting with Tweedledee and Tweedledum," she griped as she yanked on the front doors of the school.

"I'm assuming you're referring to the school principal and superintendent and not Disney characters?"

"Same thing."

"Jemma . . ."

"Okay—that made no sense. The point is I feel like you aren't taking this seriously. And if you aren't, then who's to say they will?"

"They scheduled this meeting with you right away. A response has been made," he tried to assure her.

She stopped in front of the office, popping her head in the window and then back like some wired meerkat.

"Yes. But only after three rounds of emails and one irate phone call emphasizing that I am a state senator—which is a card I do not like pulling."

"Ha! You pulled it on me this morning, when you said you were too tired for sex."

"I did no such thing."

He chuckled and then sighed through the phone. "Please don't go all wild woman on this, Jemma. Your energy needs to be focused on the reelection. I know that's what's important to you."

"And Poppy isn't?"

"I didn't say that."

"You implied it."

"I've been married long enough to know this is a no-win conversation. I am here if you need me. Of course Poppy is important to you; otherwise you wouldn't be there right now. And I may or may not have eaten the last of the brownies you baked. Good luck!"

"Finch, don't think you can sweet-talk—"

"Love you!" he called out speedily.

"Finch!"

*Damn, I must have trained him too well.*

A small smirk formed on Jemma's lips. It was what she loved the most about him. As dark as it had been with the IVF the last few weeks, he always lightened things—elevated them to a place where nothing could touch them. It had been a slow warm-up at first, but he had been such a solid tree to lean on after discovering the photo on Poppy's phone that it shoved them back into place. It was nothing short of a miracle that Jemma hadn't burst through the doors of the principal's house that very night.

Poppy had been "mostly" cooperative under questioning in her room the night of the discovery. At first, she'd answered all Jemma's questions like a witness on the stand under oath.

"Who is this from, Poppy?" Jemma had demanded.

"A boy."

"Yes, I can see that, thank you. How do you know him?"

"From school."

"Is he in any of your classes?"

She hesitated, biting her lip.

"Poppy," she warned, her eyes so wide she was sure one would roll out onto the pink shag rug she had gotten her at Target last week.

"Sort of."

"*Sort* of? That's not a straight answer. I said straight answers, Poppy!"

"No." She put her hands together as if to seal the deal.

"No, he's not in any of your classes?"

"No."

"Does he go to another school?"

"Yes. But he hasn't started just yet . . ."

"Which school?"

Poppy grimaced. "Drake."

"Drake . . . as in Drake University? So he's in college?"

"He will be," she said hurriedly "He's taking a year off. 'Deferred' is what he called it. But he's going to be a biology major. And run track. He's so smart, Mom. Like, super smart."

Jemma closed her eyes in an attempt to calm down. "Spare me the details . . . actually no. I want all the details. Why is a college boy sending you pictures like this?"

"We like each other."

"Poppy, that doesn't matter. You are only fifteen. Fifteen!" She paused to collect herself. "Okay, okay. So how did you even meet him?"

Poppy raised her eyebrows. "I told you. From school."

"No talking in circles. You said that already. How?"

"He helps out with track."

Jemma spread her hands out by her sides, like a mother hen flapping her wings in sheer shock and surprise. "You—you mean—he is a school *coach*."

She nodded. "Uh-huh. Assistant track coach."

"Poppy!" Jemma screeched.

From that point on, the screechier Jemma became, the more withdrawn Poppy grew, until Finch had to physically remove Jemma from the room.

She didn't feel the slightest bit of reassurance about the whole thing until the meeting was scheduled and in place the very next day.

She took a breath and entered the office.

Principal Pascal Reardon stood waiting in front of his door.

"Senator Danowski. Please, come on in. We're all ready for you."

He was the human equivalent of a praying mantis. Long limbs and eyes too far apart behind dark glasses. His long arm extended to her, and she nodded.

"Thank you."

Superintendent Geneva Harris sat waiting. She uncrossed her legs and stood up.

"Good to see you, Senator Danowski."

"Yes, thank you for agreeing to meet with me."

The three of them sat around Pascal's desk, no one sitting directly behind it. She wondered if this was a strategic seating arrangement, determined before she got there. No one in a complete position of power—level the playing field.

Geneva spoke first in her smoky, deep voice.

"We received your emails and are obviously as concerned as you are, Senator."

Jemma broke in immediately. "I would hope there is more than just concern. Where is the action on your part? The second I alerted you of what happened to my daughter, you should have had that pervert arrested."

"Senator—"

"You don't have to call me that. Jemma is fine."

She lifted her brow. "Right. Jemma. We did some investigating on our end and brought in Mr. Tinsdale this morning to get his side of the story."

Jemma stiffened. "His side? There are no sides. This is as clear as can be. The assistant track coach hired by your school district sent an inappropriate picture to my underage daughter."

Geneva glanced apprehensively at Pascal, who had to fold his long legs awkwardly, as there was very little room for them in his corner.

"That's the thing, Jemma. Unfortunately, this may not be as dark—"

"'Illegal.' 'Pedophile.' I believe those are more appropriate words to describe this than just 'dark.'"

Pascal nodded. "We take such allegations *extremely* seriously, Jemma. Believe me. It's a very serious matter. When you alerted us last night, we took immediate steps mandated by our school district's protocols. However—"

"I don't need to be hearing words like that. Where is the district attorney's office? The Rosemary Hills Police Department? I expected to have them very much involved in this case already."

"But there may not actually be a case."

Jemma felt like her ears had suddenly closed off. Was she hearing them right? Yet it couldn't have been any clearer. Were these two fools even on the same planet as her?

"Excuse me? Did you see the photo?"

Both Pascal and Geneva nodded awkwardly.

"He was naked," she reminded them at a loud volume.

"Technically he was shirtless."

"Shirtless? You could almost see his—what do you call it?" She snapped her fingers a few times. "Penis ravine! It was practically in the picture."

Pascal's face grew red.

"But it wasn't," Geneva corrected.

"I'm not here to argue about what's in the photo. The assistant track coach that you are responsible for engaged in highly inappropriate, illegal behavior with my underage daughter—"

"If you would please let us finish, Jemma."

"Finish what?"

239

Pascal rubbed under his nose and looked at Geneva as if to take the ball from her.

"Bowen Tinsdale is not an adult."

*"What?"* Jemma's chin dipped down toward her neck.

"Legally speaking, he is still a minor. He finished high school early. He is technically still seventeen. His birthday is in October. Which means he is a seventeen-year-old engaging with a fifteen-year-old."

Her mouth dropped open. "But—"

"And yes. His actions are still completely inappropriate, being in the position of assistant track coach and engaging with one of his students. Absolutely no contest there. He will be suspended until further notice."

Geneva leaned in. "But it is not illegal. Do you understand that, Jemma?"

*So he's getting off easy.*

"This predator went after my daughter. And all he's getting is a slap on the wrist?"

"Well, he will not be receiving pay while under suspension by the school district," said Pascal.

"As an assistant track coach. It doesn't mean anything to him—it was just a pit stop on the way to college," she argued.

Geneva placed her hands in prayer position as if to gather herself. "Look, Jemma. From a mother to another mother, I get it. I would be absolutely outraged if this were my daughter."

"But it *isn't* your daughter."

*Why does my voice sound like I'm going to cry?*

"Right . . . but I can still empathize with how outraged you're feeling. But we have done everything we can from our side. We will continue to work with Mr. Tinsdale and discuss his actions with him. There is no other legal action we can take."

"There have to be further consequences," she said firmly.

"What exactly is it that you propose then, Jemma?"

———

"You got him fired!" Poppy shouted.

Jemma placed her purse on the kitchen table, weary from the meeting. She wasn't sure if she was ready to engage in round two with Poppy.

"First of all, of course he's fired. He was your coach! Believe me, I wanted more to happen to that pedophile. But that was apparently all they could do. And second of all, how do you even know that?"

Poppy's face grew red. "He texted me. Okay? Happy now?"

There was no gas left in Jemma—fumes were floating around her. She rubbed the space between her eyebrows, almost laughing from mental exhaustion.

"Poppy. Why are you still talking to him? I thought I made it clear. You are never to have any communication with him again. If I find out you have, I am taking away your phone. Understood?"

Her sudden calmness created a perplexed expression on Poppy's face.

"He really cares about me, you know."

"They all say that, sweetie." She turned to open the refrigerator and grabbed the nearest cold can to place on her forehead.

Poppy slapped her hand on the table. "Why are you always such a witch?"

Jemma rushed forward instantly, her nose almost touching Poppy's.

"Listen closely. You get one pass this time for saying that to me. Just one. And only because I know this has been hard for you. And I am not going to blame you for what he did to you."

"What he did to me?"

"Yes."

"He didn't *do* anything to me, Mom."

"Well, honey, I hate to break it to you, but that was pretty much all he was after." She placed the can back on her face.

Poppy clenched her jaw, her fingers rubbing against her palms—an explosion at the surface, rearing its ugly head. But she suddenly stopped, her body lax. She looked almost triumphant in whatever real-ization she had just come to.

"What happened to you?" she asked.

Jemma shook her head. "I don't know what you mean."

"What did he do to you?"

"Who?"

"Whatever screwed-up shit happened to you in high school, Mom, does not mean it's going to happen to me."

"I beg your pardon?"

Her cheeks flushed. "I'm not going to let your issues screw up my life. And you can thank me for saving you a therapy session with that little nugget."

"Poppy, I'm warning you—"

"And you'll do what? Take my phone? Go ahead. Here."

She tossed it on the table. It spun and skidded to a stop against Jemma's purse as Poppy fled to her room. The door slammed and cre-ated vibrations throughout the house. She put the can back on her forehead, waited a few minutes, and returned it to the refrigerator. She made her way upstairs, paused at Poppy's door to hear music playing, and then peeked into Henry's.

He stirred and she stepped back. When he seemed to settle back to sleep, she slipped in quietly. Parenting had given Jemma army combat skills at being stealthy and soundless.

She found Henry lying on his back, one arm above his head, his little chest expanding so softly that she couldn't help but pat it gently as she sat next to him. The contrast between her youngest and oldest was never more startling—she felt as though she was suffering from parent-ing whiplash. She wanted to wake him up. Ask him about his day and whether he'd finally dug up the worms in the backyard.

Instead, she leaned forward and kissed his tender cheek.

"I love you, Henry."

She stood up to leave.

"I love you too," he mumbled in his sleep and then turned to his side.

She was closing the door as her phone buzzed. A text from Stevie reminding her of the town hall appearance she needed to make that night, and last-minute updates.

**I changed the last paragraph, second sentence in your speech.**

She didn't remember getting ready for the event. Or driving to the high school auditorium and forgetting the printed copy of her speech in the car. She vaguely recalled the town hall coordinator whispering excitedly to her backstage, thanking her for coming and informing her that she would be on in a minute.

All she was aware of moments before getting onstage to speak was her hand reaching down again for her phone. She was slightly irritated that Stevie was texting her right then. But it wasn't Stevie. It was an urgent message from Peter.

**Turn on the news. Now.**

She proceeded to do so on her phone. A minute later, she dropped it. She felt as though what she had started to watch was choking her. The bright lights from the auditorium reached through to her back-stage, flashing into her already-blinded eyes.

# CHAPTER 32

*September 13, 2022*

*Click. Click. Click. Flash!*

The lobby of the Renaissance Hotel Savery in Des Moines was packed with reporters and camera operators from every news outlet, both local and national. A few international members of the press had managed to fly in on time for the press conference. Elbowing and jostling for the prime spot had created a near brawl-like atmosphere. The general manager of the hotel, the closest one to being considered luxury in the city, looked panicked at the sudden onslaught of media and borderline chaos. He flitted about like a cricket, hopping from one area to the other, trying to create order, but he only added to the pandemonium with his nervousness.

Edie Parker was going to address the public for the first time.

The press conference was scheduled to begin at 7:00 pm CST. It was 7:16, and still no sign of her.

More test shots by cameras fluttered and echoed in the lobby. When someone came out and adjusted one of the lights, murmurs and a ripple of whispers ran through the mob of bodies pressed tightly together.

Edie Parker had arrived. Following closely behind her was the Rosemary Hills police chief and a woman with dark hair.

Dressed in a dark-green suit, Edie stepped up and looked out. The flashes and camera shutters intensified as she turned to the others at her side and whispered something in their ears. They both nodded, and she leaned forward toward the mic.

"Good evening. I'd like to thank you all for coming."

She looked down at a printed-out statement likely crafted by her attorney. Her hands spread out on top of the paper, trembling. She closed them hard into fists.

"It has been a little over two weeks since I announced the commencement of the DNA lottery. What was meant to bring positivity in light of the passing of my dear husband, the great Mr. Jonathan Parker, founder of Parker Inc., has turned into something far from that. There has been much questioning of the origins and even the validity of the lottery. I would be a fool to ignore the public outcry and demands for answers as to why such a lottery would be created. Today, I am here to tell you the truth in hopes of more accord and cooperation."

She paused. Her hands had grown wet, dampening the paper.

"The rumors are true. Yes, I am trying to solve the nearly two-decade-old case of Baby Ava. It was a quest of my late husband's that I wish to fulfill. The injustice of the unsolved case in the very community he was born and raised in had always been close to his heart. There has been very little progress since the remains of this innocent victim were found. In hopes of furthering the case, we are looking for a DNA match to that of the remains of Baby Ava."

An audible gasp went through the media mob. Outbursts of questions were immediately cast upon Edie. She held her head up higher.

"Please. I respectfully ask for no questions until my statement is finished."

She looked down for the next line and forged ahead.

"The circumstances of Baby Ava's death are a mystery. We hope to solve this mystery and put that poor soul to rest at last. In an effort to increase our chances of this, I am officially *doubling* the lottery amount, on the caveat that a match is actually found and made."

Like insects storming a fertile field of crops, questions covered the space between the podium and the mass of reporters. Each one came in like a dart, one layered over the other, to the point where she held her hand up as if to deflect them.

Her voice grew stronger.

"Due to the cooperation of the Rosemary Hills Police Department, I am about to release a finding that was kept undisclosed to the public for investigative purposes. Baby Ava was not a female, as many assumed, but in fact a male."

Another tidal wave of flashes and murmurs. She talked even louder and pressed on without hesitation.

"We have been working with a private team of the nation's top forensics investigators. Technology has advanced and continues to advance."

She stopped, giving the crowd a moment to digest each salacious word, their buzzing growing louder as they salivated.

"There is more. And this is evidence that I have not released yet. Not even to the police."

The chief of police rocked on his heels and looked up with surprise, his face somber and edgy.

"Three names were found written down. Due to the circumstances in which these names were discovered, it is believed they are connected to the death of Baby Ava."

Her eyes looked triumphant, burning with resolve.

"The three names are as follows . . ."

# CHAPTER 33

## CLEO

*Homecoming night: Eighteen years ago*

She had been expecting a different sort of voice.

One that caused no trepidation in her heart. The nervousness that embarrassed her on a daily basis dissipated with this voice—a welcoming call of her name.

But she was met with something hostile in its place—masked by a forged pleasant greeting.

"Cleo. What are you doing out here by yourself?"

He was everything that being handsome required in that moment. No one had probably ever looked more like a Greek god, albeit one donning a blue button-down shirt. Tan skin, a muscular build, and an innocent face—he was high school Adonis incarnate. Piercing eyes you felt that if you were to look away from them, you'd be missing out.

Yet Cleo felt none of this as he stood in front of her.

Austin Blakesly reached out and touched the shoulder of her dress. "You look really nice."

"Thank you," she said automatically.

She looked around him to see if anyone else was coming. But there was a sudden lull in people entering the gym.

"Trigonometry class, right?"

"Right."

"Pretty sure I'm failing. Maybe you could help me out sometime?"

She tried walking around him. But he kept moving closer to her, pushing her to the side of the building. Her hand felt for the brick wall.

"You okay?" he asked softly.

*He's just trying to be nice. Maybe he actually is nice. Not everyone is out to get you.*

"Mm-hmm. But I'm looking for someone."

"Really? That's funny. I was looking for someone too." He scratched his head and cocked it to the side, followed by a smile that disarmed her for just a second.

"Oh. Who? Maybe I can help you?" she suggested politely, masking her concern.

*Something doesn't feel right here.*

"You."

The whites of his eyes appeared bloodshot.

"What?"

*Go inside now. You can look for Will in there.*

"Yes, you. I can't stop thinking about you, Cleo."

"I have no idea what you're talking about." Her back scraped against the brick as she tried to move along and around it.

He tilted his head up and grinned. "Yes, you do."

"Really. I don't. You're starting to freak me out. I'm going to go—"

His hand was suddenly on her shoulder, and he fell against her, a heavy weight she had never felt before on her body, only made worse by the fact that a brick wall was on the other side. He may have looked the part of Adonis, but his smell was far from it. The sickly-sweet smell of alcohol on his breath wrapped around her nose. He put his mouth to her cheek, holding her arms down. The shock of it all happening so rapidly made it feel as though it weren't happening at all. Or in its place, it was happening to a different Cleo.

*Weren't you supposed to be inside by now? Oh, Cleo, now look what's happened.*

"Can I kiss you, Cleo?"

She couldn't shake her head or speak.

"You know you want it, Cleo. You looking at me in class all the time with those chinky eyes of yours."

His words were hot and sticky, and she stood completely straight, arms to her sides—rigid and unable to move. The moment he touched her, she became paralyzed.

"Don't pretend to not like it. I've always wanted to see what this would be like."

There was suddenly something wet in her mouth, fleshy and slimy. The alcohol odor seemed to take over her face, and she wanted to spit it out. He felt around her mouth with a harshness, his saliva bubbling, and she felt a pool of it.

He jerked back and started to laugh, his hand over his mouth, muffling huge waves of uproarious laughter.

"I'm sorry," he said, holding up his hand, followed by more muffled laughs.

Around the corner she saw Olivia Lockman and some of her friends. Each of them looked impossibly beautiful and impossibly ugly all at once, with their sneers and eye rolls, their snickering and pointing balled into one bolt of revulsion aimed at her.

"I told you I could do it," he said to them. "Sorry, Cleo. They told me I couldn't . . . with you I mean. And I just had to prove them wrong. No hard feelings, right?"

He punched her arm lightly as if she were a teammate on the JV squad.

"Have a good time in there," he said as he hitched both thumbs toward the gym.

The girls waved at her as though simply saying hello—as if they had not accosted and violated her out of sheer callousness.

She slid down the wall and sat in a heap. There was a ringing in her ears that would not stop.

———

# JEMMA

Shaina threw both arms up in the middle of the dance floor, beckoning for Jemma to come over to her as Nelly's "Hot in Herre" blasted over the speakers. The gym was starting to flood with students like ants crawling in for the crumb cake, the DJ booth the epicenter. The pulsating was already starting to hurt Jemma's head. Her tongue felt dry, but she smiled through it as she moved to the beat with Shaina.

"We didn't get our picture taken yet," Ashley said as she bounded in behind them.

"Do we have to?" Shaina whined. "It's so pathetic when girls take those formal pictures together without dates."

"So we're pathetic?" Ashley crossed her arms. "Jemma? Are you game?"

Her face was hot, and she steadied herself on Shaina's arm. She had forgotten to eat something before they left. She looked over Ashley's shoulder and saw Eric entering the gym with his entourage around him, already looking half-wasted.

"Jemma?"

Ashley's mouth moved, but she could barely hear her over the music. Each pound and thump increased the feverish sensation in her head.

She shook her head.

"*See.* Jemma doesn't think it's a good idea." Shaina put her head down and got into the music, looking over her shoulder to see who might be watching her.

"Um, okay. No need to get all huffy." Ashley raised her hands up.

Eric and his followers were getting closer to them, making Jemma's head feel like it was going to explode from the growing throbbing. She gripped Shaina's arm once more and then put a hand on Ashley's shoulder midbop.

"Bathroom. Let's go to the bathroom. I can barely hear you." She motioned to her ear and then outward.

They nodded and followed her.

She was hoping for relief from the noise and headache once in the girls' restroom. But the overly bright lights made things worse.

*What is wrong with me?*

Sweat formed on her forehead.

A girl from her economics class entered and immediately complimented her on her baby doll–style dress.

"So, so cute," she said.

*Everything is a fricking echo. I need air.*

"Thanks," she managed to get out. She held her hand over the skirt of her dress, smoothing it out carefully.

The girl looked at her funny.

"Huh?" Jemma asked, confused.

"I asked where you got it."

"Oh."

Shaina put her arm around her. "Okay, enough primping. Let's get back to the dance floor, whoo!" She swept her out of the bathroom with her arm still draped over her, a welcome gesture as Jemma leaned into it.

"Shaina," she said in her ear. "I think I want to go outside."

The music once again drowned her out. Ashley wiggled close behind, pushing her farther on to the floor. She felt as though she were spinning in circles. She looked up, and the metal beams of the gym looked scattered, as though they were going to fall on her any second. The room was a cyclone of kids shouting and gyrating, the bass pulsating louder and louder, the gym growing with more circling energy, taking her further away.

*I need to get out. I need to get out of here fast.*

———

# ALEX

Alex leaned against the wall by the vending machines. Both the humming of the machines and the music drowned out any thoughts in her head. She was grateful for it, as it allowed her to simply look the part of "teenage girl at homecoming dance." If there was ever a description for a movie extra, she was it. Hair pulled back into a curled updo, each tendril shiny and cascading—smooth and perfectly laid out on the crown of her head. Maud had pierced a thousand bobby pins into her scalp, each one a purposeful jab. Draped on her neck was a beaded black Y-shaped necklace and matching earrings. She kept touching the black beads, feeling an urge to yank the necklace off altogether.

An overweight kid in a white dress shirt, his striped tie hanging on by a thread, bumped into her.

"Watch it, fatty! You're taking up too much space!" he yelled.

His friends laughed behind him as though it was the funniest joke of the century.

*Ha. Ha.*

"Ask her to dance," one of them said.

The look she gave them was all the answer he needed.

"Jesus, chill out," he said, and they left for the dance floor.

She closed her eyes slowly, hoping that when she opened them she wouldn't feel the need to scream. Instead, she was met with the sight of *her*.

Holding her hand against the wall on the opposite end of the gym, she looked like she was catching her breath. She straightened up and looked around, as if searching for the closest way out. She spotted her escape and rushed for the gym's side exit door, practically stumbling out.

It was like being drawn to a light she couldn't see. But Alex knew she had to chase it. Motion entered her body, and she ran across the gym floor, bumping into a few people, followed by hisses to "Watch it!" She burst through the exit door, the cool air enveloping her.

She looked down to the right, the brick wall an optical illusion leading toward two figures huddled together on the ground, barely visible in the shadow the building cast down on them. They did not seem to notice her at first until she said their names out loud.

Their faces shone with awe and fear, pleading with her to shut the door and join them.

# CHAPTER 34

## EDIE

*September 14, 2022*

"Are you going to attend—"

"I'm not going to the hearing, Robin."

Edie set her teacup down forcefully. The white porcelain saucer shifted, and a splash of green tea stained the tablecloth.

"It might help for the public to see you again. The media attention has been mostly positive since the press conference. I think—"

"They don't need a visual of what they're against. Not in this town," she said, swiping vigorously at the stain with a few fingers.

"Belinda can take care of that," Robin said to her quietly.

She could see pity in Robin's eyes, and it only irritated her further.

"Robin, I may be considered a *senior*, but you do not need to talk to me like I'm someone who needs my mouth wiped for me."

Robin sighed. "That's not what I'm saying, Edie."

Edie stood up from the table. "You have been most helpful, Robin. Especially with the press conference, preparing the statement and the legalities, but—"

"But you want to be alone," Robin interjected. She pushed her chair back. "I understand."

As she walked out, she passed Belinda, giving "looks" that Edie didn't need to see for herself to know were being exchanged.

"Is everything all right, Edie?" Belinda asked. She poured more tea and placed a fresh napkin over the stain.

"No. Nothing is all right," Edie answered without looking up, staring in her lap.

Belinda cleared her throat. "Well . . . will that be all then?"

"Yes. You can go too."

After she heard the door shut, the sound echoing in the dining hall, Edie had never felt more alone in her life.

She ached so much for Johnny right then that she thought her bones would fracture. The pain she could feel invaded every pore, fiber, and tendon. She clenched her hands, her teeth, and every part of her, willing Johnny to be back. To be here with her, the man who had been at her side for decades. All she was left with was pure regret. Unwanted rage.

*Suffering.*

The sheer torment she had been feeling in waves over the last month was now beginning to eat away at her, like acid dripping on her tongue. And now she wanted to share it, out of the goodness of her heart; she wanted to share this suffering.

She was not one to be greedy.

Her hand reached down into her pocket and pulled out the photo. She had not let the photo leave her physically since the moment she had set eyes on it in the lockbox. Her other free hand dialed on her phone.

"Ambrose," she said flatly.

"Yes," he answered.

"Make the call."

Silence.

"Are you sure, Edie?"

Her fingers pressed tighter into the photo.

"Edie . . . there's no going back if you do this. Are you certain? This is what you want to do?"

She moved the napkin and uncovered the tea stain, then ran her hand over the mess.

"Yes . . . I'm sure."

# CHAPTER 35

## The Hearing

*September 14, 2022*

"Standing room only left!" shouted a reporter.

The throng of press had been camped outside Rosemary Hills Town Hall since midnight. The inside of the hall was filled to capacity, people flooding out in lines like tentacles reaching down the steps of the building.

Someone had set up a makeshift viewing area using an expansive projection screen. A secondary crowd had gathered around it, dozens of heads bent over their phones, only to glance up now and then for air. The live stream showed a packed hall and the long podium still unoccupied.

"Do you know if *those* three women are here yet?" a burly-looking man, arms crossed and smug, asked to his right.

"I heard they already snuck in through the back. Senator Danowski I'm sure will be here," answered his wife as one of their three small children tried to crawl up her leg.

"I wouldn't show up if I were her. All that extra scrutiny."

"Or any of them, really. Can you imagine?"

"Shhh!" someone nearby said, hushing her.

"Seriously? Not one council member is seated yet, and you're shushing me?" The woman rolled her eyes but stopped short as a dark car pulled up front.

"It's them! It's them!"

Cleo Song ducked out first, followed by Jemma Danowski and Alex Mitchell. They ran with their heads low, the crowd of people merging in on them. Reporters shoved hot mics into their faces, camera shutters went berserk, and boom operators hit a few people as they rushed forward. Police officers standing guard pushed them back as the women darted inside.

Moments later, the live stream panned to Cleo and Alex taking seats in the front row. The council filed in, Mayor Janet Vogel leading the way, followed by council members Rhett Hull (hog farmer), Ida Truhorst (high school teacher), Bill Conrad (family physician), and Senator Jemma Danowski (added on to the city council as special adviser).

The live stream camera zoomed in on the council members.

**Mayor Vogel:** This emergency public hearing is officially called to order. Anyone move to commence the hearing?

**Council Member Hull:** I move to commence.

**Council Member Conrad:** I second the motion.

**Mayor Vogel:** The hearing shall commence.

**Council Member Truhorst:** I then move to cancel the hearing.

**Mayor Vogel:** On what grounds?

**Council Member Truhorst:** That the hearing is moot and the DNA lottery is valid.

**Mayor Vogel:** Anyone second that? [Brief pause.] Well, I move, then, to strike that due to the fact the very issue of validity is why we are gathered here today.

**Council Member Conrad:** I second that.

**Mayor Vogel:** Then let's begin. The purpose of this emergency hearing by the City Council of Rosemary Hills is to determine the validity of the DNA lottery commissioned by city resident Mrs. Edie Parker. At issue are local gaming laws and policies. The constitutionality of the lottery is a judicial matter. At this time, I would like to invite Senator Jemma Danowski, who is here as special adviser, to speak. Senator?

**Senator Danowski:** Thank you, Mayor Vogel. I appreciate everyone coming out today and taking the time to discuss this very important issue. I believe that as your local district state senator, it is my duty to oversee that this is handled with legitimacy. But first, I'd like to address something else—I'm not going to sit here and pretend it isn't already on everyone's minds. With your permission, of course, Mayor Vogel.

**Mayor Vogel:** Uh—why, yes. You may proceed, Senator.

The camera panned to Cleo Song and Alex Mitchell, who both looked on stoically.

The crowd outside town hall took a collective breath together and grew silent as a few whispers faded. Camera shutters stopped. All eyes were on the projector. Cleo sat with her hands folded in her lap, while Alex remained completely rigid—only her eyes would roam back and forth to each member as they spoke.

**Senator Danowski:** Last night, Edie Parker made further revelations about the DNA lottery. In fact, it was the first time she had publicly addressed the lottery that she herself had created. Details were finally revealed. Among those details were how the lottery is being utilized for the purpose of solving a nearly two-decade-old case. My name and those of my friends were brought up in an alleged connection to the case.

Jemma paused to look out at Alex and Cleo. Alex responded by raising her chin up high, Cleo with a slight nod and subdued smile. Not one of them was alone in this. They would not hide. The whole world was there to see that.

**Senator Danowski:** I will publicly state this once and only once. My friends and I had nothing to do with the Baby Ava case. And that is the only comment I have regarding Edie Parker's accusatory statement.

A mixture of boos and cheers came from the hall as well as from outside, blending into one collective undecipherable noise. Above the fray came shouts full of both venom and vigor.

"She's a liar!"

"They all are!"

"Why aren't we talking about the lottery?"

**Mayor Vogel:** Order! I call this hearing back to order. Please, can we get someone to shut the doors. [Clamoring; doors are shut.] Thank you.

**Council Member Conrad:** Mayor Vogel, if I may, I think we should move on to the main issue at hand.

**Council Member Hull:** Yes, I move for that as well.

**Mayor Vogel:** Any opening statements from council members?

**Council Member Truhorst:** I would ask to please address the council first.

**Mayor Vogel:** Proceed.

**Council Member Truhorst:** The DNA lottery has not violated a single local gaming law. I have a memorandum from Gaming Commissioner Foles, confirming this finding. Furthermore, the ability to provide one of our residents with serious financial gain should not be seen as anything but positive. Some proceeds will go to charity, and we have even learned of the possibility of solving a case that has been a thorn in the heart of this community for decades.

**Council Member Hull:** With all due respect, I strongly disagree with Council Member Truhorst. This has been a blight on Rosemary Hills since the day the lottery was announced. We have had nothing but a media circus and protests overrunning our town ever since. I would like to take a look at the memorandum by the gaming commissioner, as I myself was on that committee for ten years. And I do question the analysis.

**Council Member Conrad:** I think we are all forgetting about what's most important here. Gaming laws, memorandums, financial gain, charity—we can all talk about these in the same breath. But what about what matters? We are asking for people's blood.

**Council Member Truhorst:** This isn't the Supreme Court, Bill. Come on, let's be real here. And no one is forcing anybody to do anything.

**Mayor Vogel:** Council Member Truhorst, may I remind you to address your fellow members accordingly.

**Council Member Conrad:** But is that honestly the case here? Money is not a coercion? Respectfully, I am being real. Just because we aren't deciding that issue today does not mean it has no merit or weight in whether this DNA lottery is right or wrong. Does it violate the rights of people of this town? Can this town trust those who govern? I would add that I doubt Senator Danowski is truly looking out for their best interests over her own.

**Council Member Hull:** You bring up a good point. We should hear from our own residents before we make any further declarations. That's why we're here, isn't it?

**Mayor Vogel:** Yes. Please, let's move forward with that. [Waves to first resident in line to speak.]

**Senator Danowski:** Excuse me. I have to stop you right there. I believe I should be given the opportunity to respond. My name was brought up, was it not?

**Mayor Vogel:** Yes . . . but please make it brief. We need to hear from the people of this town.

The live stream camera focused on Jemma's face.

There were some jeers in the viewing crowd as reporters stood on a variety of boxes and crates in front of their cameras, giving quiet live updates.

**Senator Danowski:** Council Member Conrad is correct. I am a senator. And yes, that does come with its own interests. But I'm not just a senator. I am also someone who grew up in this town—I know every road and street like the back of my hand. Every hill and turn of a cornfield. The DNA lottery has *not* been good for us. It has been divisive. It has caused hurt. And above all it has lacked any transparency as far as its true intentions. We can't trust someone who has been lying to us from day one. Why are we letting one person dictate how this town is run? Because of wealth? Power? That is not what Rosemary Hills is about, nor what it stands for. Do you really want anyone else having any say about your own body? Your *blood*? [Doors burst open loudly.]

**Mayor Vogel:** What is the meaning of this? [Chief of Police Soren Lennox walks in, flanked by three officers.] This hearing is in session, Chief Lennox.

**Chief Lennox:** Mayor Vogel—I apologize. But in light of new evidence that was just brought to our attention, the hearing has to be interrupted.

**Mayor Vogel:** On what grounds?

**Chief Lennox:** [Motions for officers to move forward.] Senator Jemma Danowski, Cleo Song, and Alexandra Mitchell: you are all to be taken into police custody immediately.

> https://DNAlottery/tracker.com
> Date: September 14, 2022
> Number of Entries: 186,861
> Days Until Drawing: 3

> *The lottery drawing is still scheduled to take place on September 17. Details for the event will be released after the pending outcome of the local hearing is resolved.

Comments:

"All politicians lie. Why did anyone think Senator Jemma would be any different? She lies about what she's going to do for the district and of course she's lying about her past. This is why I'm voting for Sylvia Motts."

—H. Stine

"News flash, H. Stine! It's not 'Senator Jemma.' It's Senator Danowski. Would you address her that way if she were a man? And we don't know anything yet about if or how she is even connected to Baby Ava."

—K. J. Whittaker

"I still can't believe Baby Ava is actually a boy. After all this time!"

—Penny V.

"Look, there's a reason why those women were taken into custody. And there's definitely a reason their names were found in evidence."

—Mara J.

"Anyone know what this new evidence is? The whole thing is super sketch."

—E. Q.

"Edie Parker does not come off as someone to be trusted. Did you see how cold she was in that press conference? She's a stiff just like her dead husband. I say let's get on with this lottery and win some money!"

—Anonymous

"I heard they were all in high school around the time Baby Ava could have been born. That's too much of a freaking coincidence for me, I'm sorry. One if not all three of those women were involved in the killing of that poor baby. Why haven't they been officially arrested yet? That's the real question!"

—Joshua I.

# CHAPTER 36

## CLEO

*September 14, 2022*

"Cleo—did you have anything to do with the death of Baby Ava?"

A petite female reporter thrust a mic into her face, almost striking her in the mouth.

"Why didn't you come forward earlier?" another reporter shouted, jumping up to get a view of her.

Cleo bowed her head and raced out the front entrance of the police station. A crowd of cameras and members of the press closed in around her, a spindle of moving mouths and flinging hands. Every step she took seemed to only increase the intensity of the shouts.

"Why did the police let you go? Tell us what happened in there, Cleo!"

*How the hell do I get out of here?*

"Excuse me, excuse me," she kept saying futilely.

She turned around to see if Alex or maybe even Jemma could be behind her. Instead, she was met with another mic jabbed straight into her cheek.

"Hey, hey, hey! Back off!" a familiar male voice shouted.

A hand reached out through what seemed like a pile of tangled arms and limbs to grab on to her shoulder.

"You okay?" he asked quickly, his face half-covered by a camera.

Will broke through and placed both hands on her arms, shielding her from the crowd and pushing them through to his squad car.

The yelling grew even louder as she slammed her door shut, Will sliding against the patrol car front and then forcing his way into the driver's side. His door sealed off the rest of the world like a vacuum, muting it down to muffled calls.

They stared straight ahead, taking a moment. There was something so deranged about the mass of people still hanging on to the front of the car, as if the longer they stayed, the more likely Cleo would be to give them answers.

He turned to her as he shifted the car into drive. "Cleo. Look at me."

She shook her head, trying to take two seconds to process the last two hours.

"It's okay. I'll get you out of here."

The patrol car crawled forward, parting the mob like a curtain drawing open to let in the light. As soon as it was clear, Will stepped on the accelerator.

"Where should I take you?"

She looked out the window. "Anywhere. Just drive."

He drove out past the city limits and then onto the county highway. The leaves were just starting to turn—barely there hints of gold and red, as if the edges had been carefully dipped in paint. She rolled her window down and let the air stream away all the noise still trapped in her ears. There was that soothing melody of the hills in the distance she was fond of, rolling up and down. It was like being rocked to sleep.

And in that moment, she was able to fool herself into thinking nothing had changed. She was on a fall drive with Will, and nothing else mattered.

They drove on until he finally pulled off the road in front of a clearing.

"Cleo . . ."

"Please don't," she said.

He turned to look at her quickly at the sudden sharpness in her voice. "Don't?"

"Don't say my name."

*I can't hear it coming from you. It used to be everything.*

"I don't understand." He put his hand delicately on her shoulder. "Did you not want me to—"

"No. I mean—yes. I can't thank you enough for getting me out of there."

"You don't need to thank me. I was never going to leave you like that. It's beside the point; that's not what I'm asking."

She stared forward out the windshield. "Then what are you asking?"

"Did I do something wrong?"

*Wrong. Everything about this is wrong, and you know why.*

She folded her arms harshly and suddenly felt a rush of guilt. "You don't need to do this. I'm okay, really. Can you please take me home now?"

"Cleo, what . . . where is all of this coming from?"

All at once his face was full of confusion and sadness, and she wanted to reach out and touch the side of his head. But she held her hand firm against her side.

"Where is what coming from?"

"This . . . this anger."

"I need to get home. Can you do that for me?"

"Hold on now—"

She got out of the car. The skyline looked as though someone had dimmed the lights just enough to create a pink haze off the horizon. She leaned against the hood and inhaled deeply.

*I wish I never told you. This isn't your fault, Will. It's mine.*

"Cleo," he said, getting out.

She whipped her head toward him.

"Why did you do it?"

He looked confused. Or at least pretended to.

"Do what?"

"Why did you do it? It's a simple question."

He stepped forward and reached his hands out toward hers. "Cleo, look. I care about you. I really do. I would say more, but I don't want to scare—"

She pulled away, more afraid that if she didn't act fast enough, she wouldn't be able to let go.

"I trusted you, Will. I really did." The backs of her eyes stung, and she blinked the tears away.

"You still can. But you have to tell me what it is you think I did . . . Cleo, please."

Her face grew hard.

"You told them, didn't you?"

"What?"

His eyes went wide.

"The chief of police. The investigators. You told them everything I shared with you. Why else would we be suddenly taken in like that? No one else knows about any of this. *No one.* Except you!"

He shook his head hard. "That is insane. No. I would never, Cleo. I *swear.*"

"And you just happen to be on the police force? The day after I tell you some of the most—"

*I can't even say it again.*

She felt like a spout had turned off, her feelings gone dry. There was nothing else to say. Maybe he was telling her the truth. Maybe she was the one who wasn't being truthful—that this was all a safe way to withdraw. To go back to being where it was easiest—to be the Cleo everyone was used to, that *she* was used to.

Maybe it was better this way.

"Cleo, I promise you. It wasn't me," he said steadily.

She opened her mouth to speak, but he drew her in close before she could utter another word. She let him hold her. Only for a second. Until she had to rip away before his warmth could take over all the injury and confusion. Feelings she wished had nothing to do with him. But was this what she wanted? Was she sure of it?

She wasn't sure of anything. Nothing was certain anymore.

He put his head down.

"I don't know what else to say."

"Then take me home," she said softly. "I need to be with my son."

# CHAPTER 37

## ALEX

*September 14, 2022*

The house seemed so much smaller than she had ever remembered it to be.

For years, it had been this larger-than-life force, Maud's domain where she ruled over everything inside it—including Alex. The looming frame of a family that looked so normal—the bones of a home created for the care of a little girl. Her bedroom window a tiny porthole that one only had to look through to really see the darkness.

She got out of her car and walked up the front yard, her steps slow and deliberate. A caravan of news crews had followed her from the police station. She ignored their shouts for a statement, their arms extending over the edge of the property line, feeble attempts to connect with her in some way.

She found her, sitting in the darkened living room. The piano was unceremoniously shut. The stillness now belonged to her.

"Oh. I see you've brought some of those vulture reporters home with you," she said.

Alex stayed near the entryway to take in the view. She wanted to keep a mental picture of Maud this way—alone in the shadowy room, an outline of something from the past.

"Are you staying for dinner?"

She shook her head.

"You've completely embarrassed us by publicly showing up to that nonsense of a hearing. An absolute nightmare is what this is. Why did you have to go in front of all those cameras? And this hearing is over what? As if those idiots would be able to decide anything."

She walked closer to her mother and remained muted.

"Alexandra. Are you listening?"

Her mother's voice was demanding. But her eyes told a different story. There was a flash of fear in them. Every time she blinked, the fear revealed itself like a lighthouse casting out its beam.

"This will not be tolerated. You will cease any further communication with those other two women and drop all of this. It is a *spectacle*, Alexandra! Do you hear me?"

Alex bent down and placed her hands over Maud's knees. Her fingers dug into the knobby outline of each bone.

"Yes. I'm listening. I've always listened, Mother."

The bridge of Maud's nose crinkled. "What are you doing? Take your hands off me at once."

"No," Alex said, digging in harder.

"Excuse me?"

"Not until you tell me."

"Tell you what?"

"How you could do that to me."

Maud rolled her shoulders back, trying to release herself from Alex's grip.

"What has gotten into you?" Her eyes flashed.

"I was your daughter. I still am your daughter."

"Alexandra, I haven't the slightest clue what you are talking about. Now let me go. I have to get dinner started." Her voice faltered on the last word.

Alex threw her hands off. "I was just a child."

"Yes. And now you are an adult acting like a child."

Maud shot up and walked briskly to the kitchen, Alex on her heels. She threw the cabinet open.

"Every time I look at Sasha, I wonder how you could do it? How does a mother do that to a child that she loves? Or maybe that's the answer. Maybe there was no love?" Her voice had risen higher and sturdier.

Maud paused from filling a large stockpot with water.

"Yes. That's *right*, Alexandra. I did not love you. Is that what you want to hear?" She threw the pot in the sink. "Who are you to say such things to me? I am your mother."

"Yes, you are," Alex spat out harshly.

Maud laughed. "I can't believe how immature you are acting—a grown woman. And I thought I had done something right with you. What do you want? Do you want me to tuck you in? Is that it? Tell you that the world will always embrace you with warm, open arms, ready to hand you everything at a whim?"

Alex nodded feverishly. "Yes—yes. Anything. *Anything* but what you did to me!"

"No!" Maud shouted. She raised a hand and jabbed a finger toward her. "I refused to. Because that is not how it works. I never waited around for opportunity. I went out and *seized* it. I did whatever it took to better my position. I did *not* let my circumstances control *me*. In this world, if you're a woman, that is a fatal mistake . . . believe me. I did you a favor."

Her voice cracked on the last word. *Favor.* She returned to the pot, now toppled over, and stood it right side up.

Alex felt tremors forming throughout her body—like an allergic reaction to her mother's answers.

"Is that what you call it now? A favor?"

And there Maud was. She was still quick, her face directly in front of Alex, like two mirrors ready to smash into each other.

"You will stop talking about this nonsense. And I know you will. Would you like to know why, Alexandra?"

She felt an answer come to the back of her lips. Yet it stayed there, orphaned words that never saw the light of day.

A shuffle and a shifting sound brought them backward, separating them as quickly as they had clashed, their heads down like two dogs caught in a fight by their owner.

Violet stood in the kitchen entrance, a strange smile creeping up on her lips.

"They've upheld it. The news just came in. The DNA lottery has been upheld."

# CHAPTER 38

―――

## JEMMA

*September 14, 2022*

Jemma watched as Finch drove up hurriedly to the rear entrance of the police station, tires squealing. An officer held the door open as she ran outside, flanked by Clifford Yates. She practically threw herself into the back, Clifford following suit. A rogue group of reporters spotted her and sprinted after the car like a pack of hyenas as Finch pulled away.

She looked over her shoulder through the back window until they were out of sight and proceeded to collapse against the seat.

"I didn't know you could run that fast, Yates," she quipped.

He half chuckled, half scolded her. "This is no time to joke, Jemma."

"It's not?"

"Jemma, really," Finch said with a warning tone, looking at her through the rearview mirror. The car radio blared. "Hold on. Listen." He turned the volume up even louder as he sharply turned the corner.

"And at the top of the hour, we have some breaking news. Senator Jemma Danowski, along with the two other women recently named by Edie Parker, have been taken into custody by the Rosemary Hills Police Department. All happening right in the middle of a special hearing for the DNA lottery—which, of course, unless you live under a rock, has been the hot topic not just around these parts but also across the nation. What a twist in developments, folks! No word yet on whether she's been charged, but boy—the Baby Ava case has certainly lit up this town."

With worried eyes, Finch looked in the mirror again, this time toward Clifford. "Is she in serious trouble?"

"If I had a dollar for every time I got asked that question . . ."

"I'm sure I could spare one for you," said Jemma. "Finch, did you hear anything from Peter? Stevie? What's the damage yet on the campaign? I haven't had a chance to look at my Twitter feed ever since Chief Lennox decided to crash the hearing."

"C'mon . . ." Finch shook his head.

"Okay, okay. I'm listening. He's the best lawyer. Aren't you, Yates? And he was able to get me and the other ladies out of there."

Clifford blew out a hard sigh. "Yes, for now. I bought all three of you some time. But you will need to cooperate further."

"I *have* been cooperating."

"That includes going in for questioning. It's better to get ahead of the game in these situations. We don't want to be reacting to everything the police and prosecutors throw at us."

Jemma sat up straighter. "Prosecutors? We're already at that point?"

He put his hands up as if he were stopping her from coming at him. "I don't know anything for sure. That's why I think you should go in for questioning. That'll give you time to collect yourself and you and I some time to chat."

"I had nothing to do with Baby Ava."

Clifford looked at her hard.

"I swear. Absolutely nothing," she said with firmness.

"I believe you. I'm your defense lawyer, Jemma. I'm paid to believe you, whether I like it or not. I'm not the one who needs convincing."

"Wouldn't they have charged me already if they had anything on me?"

He shrugged. "Prosecutors don't usually make their move unless they're armed with everything. It's like pulling the trigger without any bullets loaded. Just because you have the gun doesn't mean you're ready to hunt. As of now, we should assume they have something."

"But what? I have nothing to do with the case."

"You don't know what they could pull out of their hats. It seems like Edie Parker is one step ahead of us all."

"Don't get me started on that woman. I can't believe—well, it doesn't matter. I have nothing to hide. Let's do this questioning thing and get it over with. When can we get it done?" she asked urgently.

Clifford pulled his phone out. "I will be in contact with Chief Lennox to schedule that. Which reminds me . . . have you been in contact with any of the other women?"

"Since the hearing? No," she answered, wide-eyed.

"Good. Do not talk to them under any circumstances. You don't want to incriminate yourself by being around the two other people whose names were released in connection with the case. I can't stress this enough."

———

"Sorry I'm late. I got held up putting Rocky down. He's been acting up lately—it's like he knows what's going on."

Cleo closed the sliding glass door behind her as she entered Alex's kitchen.

"Did you park a few blocks away and walk?" asked Alex immediately.

"Yes."

"And he knows more than you think. Kids are smart—they pick up on when we're upset. Even when we try to hide it," she added.

Jemma started to hand Cleo a very full glass of wine. She was already a glass and a half in herself. Before leaving, she had grabbed the nicest red she could find in their stash, Finch watching with a slight look of protest.

"Don't even," she had said, waving it in his face as she brushed by.

"But that's the best one from our Napa trip—"

"Finch, honey. This is not the time. Vino emergency."

She practically had it uncorked as she walked through the door, Alex then silently handing her a glass. The smooth unspoken language between them nearly made them laugh aloud at the insanity of their lives right then.

"No—no thanks. I need to be clearheaded." Cleo waved it away.

"Suit yourself," she said, about to take a sip.

"Screw it." Cleo wrapped her hands around the stem and took a large gulp. "Nectar of the mommies," she sang, then poured herself a bit more and raised it in the air.

"Is it safe for us to talk here? I mean—could anyone else be listening?"

Alex nodded. "Sasha was out an hour ago. I think she's aware, like Rocky. Getting worked up makes her tired."

"And Davis?" Cleo asked, scanning the kitchen.

Jemma quickly glanced down at her glass to avoid answering this question herself.

"He's . . . he moved out," Alex finished bluntly.

"Oh. I'm sorry, Alex. I didn't know . . ."

"You couldn't have. I basically didn't know either," she said, her shoulders sagging.

Cleo took another large drink as she stood against the counter. There was a moment of silence as they all collected themselves.

Alex waved her arms down. "All right. Everyone sit."

It was as though they were the Witches of Rosemary Hills. A trio of outcasts at this point, assembled around the table to determine their next move. It didn't matter what choices they had made since that night eighteen years ago to catapult them away from it. It was a game of chess they could never win, carrying them back together, no matter what. This was their bond. This was the inevitable cost of what they'd done.

"Here we are then," Cleo said quietly. "The DNA lottery was upheld, as I'm sure you all know."

Jemma scooted her chair in. "I'm sorry. I tried. But even if I had stayed to vote, I would've been outnumbered. Money always wins." She raised her glass again. "I guess everyone decided to lawyer up, huh?"

"We took Clifford's recommendations."

"That's good . . . he told me not to talk to any of you. To stop all communication. Something like that. But he doesn't know the half of it."

Cleo sharply turned to her. "Do we?"

"What?"

"Even know the half of it?"

Jemma narrowed her eyes.

"You were there, Cleo. And so was Alex. You both know we didn't do anything wrong."

*Why do I feel like this is two against one?*

"Or did we?" Alex cut in, staring with intensity but not really focused on either her or Cleo.

Jemma pushed hard away from the table. Her face felt heated, and she knew it wasn't from the wine. "You really think that I—"

"We left after—after it happened. You made us, remember?"

"He was alive then." The words caught in her throat. She swallowed and let more wine drown them away.

"Yes, but did he stay alive?" Cleo demanded.

She stood up angrily. "I can't believe you both—after all this time. If you ever suspected such a thing, why didn't you go to the police then?"

Alex put her hand on her wrist steadily. "We wouldn't do that to you."

Jemma jerked her hand back. "You mean to yourselves?" She bit her lip in bitterness and disappointment. "The one thing that has been keeping us together is staying together."

"We still are," said Alex.

Cleo shook her head. "Baby Ava was a boy." She stared back with grave eyes. "That changes everything."

"In what way exactly?" Jemma hit back.

"It was the only thing that kept me from really questioning if—"

"If what? Go ahead! Accuse all you want. I didn't—we didn't have anything to do with Baby Ava," Jemma nearly shouted, face flushed and hands balled into fists.

*I won't do this. I won't defend myself. Not to them. They know the truth.*

Alex remained expressionless—she gazed down into her glass as if it were a bonfire, burning bright and hypnotic. Suddenly, her eyes snapped up.

"We never spoke about it. I don't know if it was out of fear or to protect you from having to—protect ourselves. Maybe it's all of that. But we need . . . we deserve to know the whole truth."

"The truth," Jemma murmured.

"Yes. The truth about what happened after we left you."

# CHAPTER 39

## ALEX

*Homecoming night: Eighteen years ago*

When she looked down at the two figures huddled together, she saw two little girls. Two friends from a time when she had a simpler heart. The same scared faces from that parking lot before their innocence was frayed—a questioning look that said *What now?*

She blinked and she was back again.

"Alex?" one of them asked faintly.

"I'm here," she replied, her answer gaining strength. "I'm here."

Cleo rose from the ground, using the brick wall to support her. "Something isn't right."

She pointed down toward Jemma, who was breathing hard, her high-heeled sandals kicked off, bare feet wiggling in the grass.

"I can't explain it. I just know something is off. It's too soon, though," Jemma said through hard breaths.

"Too soon?"

She pulled her dress up, cautiously, as if it hurt to move.

The aqua material glimmered, and Alex would always think of this moment later whenever she saw a similar shade. Underneath she bared a nude material of some sort stretched taut against her midsection. She released its grip by pulling at the small of her back—the rise of flesh so smooth and curved. The skin surrounding her navel was a swirl of softness, jutting out.

"I counted the weeks. I kept careful count—it's too soon."

Alex gazed at her roundness, unsure if she should be the one to ask, to say it out loud. She stared at Cleo and then Jemma. The minutes, months, and years since they had last shared such a moment together flashed away quickly—as if they had been transported straight here from little girls to young women.

They still needed each other.

Carried in their insides for years, like a parasite burrowed in and dormant, was the sensation they would need each other again one day. Waiting for when it would come alive to warn them all.

"It's not—not *time?*" Cleo asked.

Alex knelt and pulled the skirt back to cover her up. A vast need to protect and nurture her friend came over her, masking the shock waves that had rattled them all.

"No. Not for another month or so." Jemma squinted her eyes hard. "Please. Please help me. There's no one else. Please."

"What do you want us to do? Are you sure that it's—" She paused.

*Is it wrong to say it?*

Alex found her nerve again. "A baby. It's coming?"

Jemma nodded.

"Why us?"

"Why wouldn't it be?"

She suddenly clamped her hands against her belly and seemed to squeeze her whole body together. Her knees pulled up and clanked against each other a few times before flopping back to a straight position. Her mouth formed a tight frown, and she gave a low moan, followed by a tension that even Alex could feel. She took her hand instinctively, letting her transfer some of the pain.

Jemma abruptly gasped in surprise. Her hands moved down quickly, catching something. They gripped the skirt material, gathering it upward to form a ball.

The gush of wetness that seeped down her dress left a dark shape. Streams rolled down the inside of her thighs. She scrambled upward as though something horrifying had exited her body.

"I can't do this here . . . not here," she said, sounding panicked. "I need to get away. Far away from here. It can't happen anywhere near here."

Cleo tried to calm her. "Jemma. It's going to be okay. We need to take you to a hospital, where they can—"

"No. I'm not doing it here. Whatever happens, I will always know it happened here. And I will be reminded of that forever."

"Jemma . . ."

"You have to understand. It's the only thing I have left!" She lifted her head toward Alex, as if looking to her for permission.

Every part of her knew they should do as Cleo said. Yet the desperate ringing in her plea found its way down to her very core.

Cleo shook her head. "What if something happens?"

*Enough has already happened.*

"I can't keep it. I can't let anyone know this happened."

"I don't think you have a choice."

Jemma's eyes stretched big and furious.

"Yes, I do. There is—there's always a choice. I am choosing to not let this define me." She gripped her midsection. "Help me. Please? Help me. Otherwise, I will always be the girl who screwed up. Don't you see? It will be a mark I carry forever. That's not what I intended—that's not who I want to be! This can't happen, not to me. I'm going to be someone different. This baby will have a life—but not with me . . ."

It was the first time she'd heard her call it a baby. Another contraction seemed to hit her as she stopped to dig her hands into the grass.

"I still don't—" Cleo began.

"Enough. She wants our help. So let's help her," Alex broke in.

Jemma nodded, a flash of relief in her eyes. "Please."

Alex stood up and looked around. "We can't stay here regardless. Where would you even want us to take you?"

"I know where to go," said Jemma.

—

# Cleo

Cleo regarded the side of Alex's face, silently wondering if inside she was ready to bolt, or if she felt a similar compulsive obligation. If it had been one of them, would they have wanted the same thing—would they be making the same choice as her?

*You aren't that kind of girl, Cleo.*

"Safe-surrender laws," Jemma said flatly.

She paused to take a deep gulp of air. "I looked it up at the library when I first found out. If we take the baby somewhere like that—it wouldn't be wrong. The baby would be taken care of . . ."

Her face had grown pale, her eyes less focused.

"And it will be like it never happened."

"But Jemma—it *is* happening. This is dangerous. What if something went wrong or with the baby? What if—" Cleo started again.

"Then leave!"

Cleo sat back, the grass cold and startling.

"If you don't want to help me, then don't. Leave. That goes for you too."

Jemma looked up with an unbreakable stare at each of them—daring them to object.

"I'm doing this with or without you," she said through clenched teeth and then started to rise. Her dress was soaked with fluid, her hair limp and clinging to her neck.

Alex reached out with one of her gloved hands, helping Jemma up. The two of them began to make their way down the side of the building as Cleo watched, frozen.

*What kind of girl are you then?*

She was the same girl she had always been. Sitting back and letting it all pass by. The girl who went unnoticed.

The girl who followed the rules.

A girl who let him violate and humiliate her.

Cleo pulled herself up. The screaming in her head telling her to leave shut off. Like a rogue wave, she felt an urge rumble through. Her lips were the first to act.

"We can use my mother's truck."

They stopped, turning back toward her.

"I want to help."

Jemma weakly nodded her head with gratefulness.

Alex remained with her while Cleo ran back home. Her lungs burned with a need to stop, but she couldn't. The churning of her legs was a windmill of resolve, her dress wrapping around her ankles. When she felt his burning mouth on her face, she ran even harder. The farther she ran, the lighter she felt, as though each step was shedding an unwanted part of her.

Her house was not far from the school. There were no lights on as she sneaked quietly into the garage through the service door. The keys were in the cupholder, where her mother usually left them. The truck was used for loading and delivering flowers from the shop. She was sure her mother had never imagined it would be used for such a different purpose.

She turned the truck on, waiting for her mother to burst through and demand to know what was going on. But all she could hear was the low hum of the motor. It was an older truck, a light-blue model that her mother had bought cheap for the shop. She reversed and felt the need to drive far and fast. Her foot pushed harder on the gas.

*Hurry, hurry, hurry.*

The headlights beamed on a struggling Jemma, Alex holding her up and making their way toward the truck. The faint beats of the gymnasium music called out to them just as a patrol car rolled by. They huddled together in the front, holding their breaths until it had passed. Jemma grabbed on to the door handle as another wave of pain passed over her face.

"Joliet," she sputtered.

Cleo nodded.

A town more than an hour away.

They passed the last of the streetlamps as she merged onto the county highway. The truck remained in the dark as Jemma's groans turned into screams. Cleo, eyes half on the road and half on the rearview mirror, urged her to keep breathing.

It was the longest ride of their lives, a tumble of reassurances and cursing, hand-clutching, and pulling over at least three times. Each time, they thought for sure this was it—they couldn't possibly go on, and they'd surely turn around. But Jemma, with her newly gained warrior attitude, would resist.

The lights of Joliet glowed like a beacon as they approached. But the light also revealed the blood, smeared on the seat into a rusty hue. The sight of it halted any relief at reaching their target.

"What's in Joliet?" Alex asked, holding Jemma's hand hard as she yelled with her head back.

She pressed her lips together. *Mmm.* Hard panting before she could open her mouth.

"Cathedral . . . the little cathedral."

Cleo parked a block away from the small brick chapel. The light box sign spelled out in black block letters: HOLY TRINITY, ALL ARE WELCOME.

———

# JEMMA

She had aged a decade in the last few hours of her life. The Jemma at the dance was gone and replaced with a much harder soul, one who was clinging fast and hard to a life that could still be.

*It will be like it never happened.*

She was the homecoming queen on her way to a much-altered coronation. Somewhere in another universe, she was being crowned and dancing in the arms of an Eric who didn't drink. Smiling at a future of college parties, a jet-setting career, and all the things her mother never had or gave her.

She was not going to be another casualty of the flawed maternal cycle she had fallen into.

The convex shape of her belly was not a large one. She was fortunate to be showing so little, considering how far along she was. She secretly believed it had been her own sheer will exerted daily that it not reveal itself any sooner than it had to. Somehow, she'd gotten her wish.

It made it easier to deny its existence.

Two lines. Two stripes she didn't want to earn. When she'd seen them appear, faint at first and then growing darker by the second, she'd thrown it away immediately. An automatic reflex of her wrist: the test stick hit the trash with a sharp ping, and she tried to wipe it all from her memory.

Weeks went by, and she continued to be in denial. To refuse what was starting to split and multiply inside her. The denial would eventually cost her.

If she just told herself that it wasn't true, that she would carry what was inside her forever—*could* carry it forever—that nothing would change . . .

When her belly began to rise, she did everything to make it go away. Pushing it down, closing her eyes, and willing it to be gone as she wrapped it tight like a wound that needed to be buried.

*It would be like it never happened . . . but what about when it does?*

The more she grew, the more frequent the panicked reality would lurch up her throat, and she would shake it away, floating back into her chosen delusion.

But now it seemed the dance was already over for her.

The truck's rumbling engine shut off. Cleo took the keys out and clutched them in her hand. The strands on Jemma's forehead had formed a clammy web. Alex smoothed her hair back, her satin gloves stained with blood. For a moment, the cab brought itself to complete silence.

She used it to gather herself.

As if she had been holding on until she was sure it was safe, she began to push. They ripped fabric from their dresses. Cleo feverishly searched the back of the truck as Alex yanked off and discarded her bloodied gloves to help. They found a single burlap seed bag, empty and rough.

Jemma's screaming ended, replaced instead with suppressed moans from behind her lips. She kept some of the most guttural yelps inside so that the energy could be used to push. Each time they wondered if it had all become too much. But she wanted it done—she wanted it *over*. She would bow her head down and continue, her jaw trembling with force. They were in awe of her strength.

The baby came out pink.

They could see very little except that there was life. The tiniest of cries and smallest of hands reaching up. She let the baby hold on to her finger, the cord still attached. They wrapped the burlap cloth around the baby, and she asked for something sharp. They handed her a pocketknife from the glove compartment, and she sliced through, separating herself from her child forever.

She didn't hesitate. She slid out of the truck, dizzy at first. The two others rushed out to steady her. She shook her head.

"No. Just me now."

They refused. She looked down at the tiny face and then back up. Her eyes sparkled brilliantly with tears.

"I'll see you at the end of the road."

She was gifting them with blindness. They had come this far with her, and for that she would be forever grateful—but this was only for her eyes.

Hesitation permeated the air until they got into the truck and drove away, watching her as she steadily made her way to the cathedral steps.

The town was at an hour of desertion—as if all had fled in anticipation of what was to come that night. A few sprinkles of rain cooled her forehead. She tucked him—she'd seen that it was a him under the first streetlamp—farther into the cloth. Something from him came forth and latched on to her, an anchor that dug deep into her chest. Her body shook with a cavernous anguish. This was the moment that would surely slaughter her if the ones before had not.

She looked up at the top of the steeple, a point so sharp and precise it pacified her for the shortest of moments. He was so very small, but so very full of life right then.

She drew the crisscrossed fabric over his face.

When it was over, she trudged back to the truck, waiting at the end of the road as promised. She climbed in, her head becoming the third in a row of minds that could not take another thought. Another whisper would have tipped the scale. In silence they rode back, three figures in a truck that drove on and on into the night—a ride they would never get off.

# CHAPTER 40

## CLEO

*September 16, 2022*

Cleo was the first to be questioned.

Her lawyer, a friend of Alex's at her firm, had advised her not to go in for questioning at all. But she ignored her—delaying the inevitable was like holding a hot pot of water over her head. She wasn't going to let it be some intolerable slow burn—she was ready.

Chief Lennox sat across from her, giving her all the usual niceties, offering a drink of water or coffee. She politely declined and turned her attention to the detective brought in from Des Moines to investigate the case. Detective Laila Reyes was not the angular, sharp-edged detective Cleo had somehow expected. She was robust and curvy in every possible way, a mother hen in a dark-gray pantsuit.

"Thank you for coming in voluntarily, Ms. Song."

"You can call me Cleo."

"Great," she responded briskly.

She tapped her pen a few times and proceeded.

"How long have you been friends with Jemma Danowski and Alex Mitchell?"

"We've known each other since we were little girls."

"That's a long time."

"Yes. But I wouldn't say we were friends the entire time," Cleo added quickly.

Reyes tilted her head. "Why is that?"

"You know how it can be with girls. We were friends when we were little. We were all in different grades, though. It was sort of off and on."

"'Off and on'? Let me ask this. Were you ladies 'on' during your high school years?"

Cleo shrugged. "Not particularly."

"Do you mean that in a negative way?"

"No. Not at all. We were just different back then. People tend to change when they get to high school. And we still are three very different women. But what links us is that we are all mothers now."

"Interesting you bring that up. It seems people in town spotted the three of you having lunch a little over a week ago . . . let me check my notes." She ran a finger down her folder. "Ah yes. September eighth. A place you folks refer to as 'the café.' Is this correct?"

"Yes. We had lunch."

"When was the last time you had lunch together before that occasion? A few weeks? Months?"

"Years," Cleo answered.

"Two?"

"More than that."

"Ten?" Reyes became louder.

"I moved to Chicago after college. I'd just moved back. You can see why it'd been so long."

"Did you keep in touch with the other women over the years?"

"Not really."

Reyes held the folder above the table. "Not really or not at all?" She let it drop.

"Not at all." She felt her throat tighten. "Chief, I think I'll take a little water, please."

His chair creaked as he rose to pour her a glass.

Reyes leaned forward. "You doing all right, Cleo?"

"Yes. I've just never been questioned before. Up until two days ago, I'd never even been in a police station before."

She flashed a smile. "I can understand how it would be a little unnerving. But please. It's just some questions."

*Yes, just some questions. A few that I do not care to ever answer.*

Chief Lennox placed the water in front of her. She nodded at him and drank a few sips, holding the cup with both hands.

"Are you okay to continue, Cleo?"

"Mmm. Yes." She wiped at her lips carefully.

"I'm going to review what I was getting at. You did not keep in touch with the other women. But then you all decided to meet suddenly. After the DNA lottery was announced."

She frowned. "Is that a question?"

"Why the sudden meeting?"

"I had moved back."

Reyes stared at her. "I know. You already mentioned that. Who set up the lunch?"

"We all kind of did."

"Was this before or after you all convened at Mrs. Edie Parker's estate?" She motioned with her hand back and forth.

Chief Lennox cleared his throat and shifted in his chair.

"After."

"Why did Mrs. Parker have all three of you over?"

Cleo folded her arms across her lap. "I'm sure you already know the answer to that, Detective Reyes. That's why I'm here, isn't it?"

Reyes dropped her head down, then brought it back up with a small grin.

"I need to know why she had you over at her home. Her very private home—she is not known to have just anyone over."

"She had the names. If you were her, you would want to know more, wouldn't you?"

"And that was it? To tell you the names?"

"She demanded that we submit our DNA to the lottery."

Reyes nodded, urging her on. "And if you didn't?"

"She would release our names to the authorities. But it doesn't matter anymore now—she clearly already went ahead with it."

"Then why—why not simply submit?"

"We agreed we wouldn't."

"All three of you?"

"Yes."

"What was keeping you from submitting?"

"We didn't think it was her right to force us into it."

"Is that so?"

She wasn't buying it. Her mother-hen demeanor had morphed during the last few questions into that of a hunter, sniffing out a scent.

"You can see why that seems odd, Cleo. One would wonder what the holdout's all about. Unless there is something to hide?"

"I didn't say that . . ."

"You didn't have to, Cleo. You know I have to ask it. Did you have anything at all to do with the death of Baby Ava?"

---

# ALEX

Alex was far less . . . cordial than Cleo.

Having spent some time working for an assistant DA during her third year of law school, she knew that she didn't really have to say much.

And the know-it-all smugness of Detective Reyes did nothing to improve her mood. Clifford had warned her about Reyes and her reputation for being a bit of a wolf in sheep's clothing. Her response to this: *Great, I can be too.*

"I'd love for you to get straight to the point, Detective." She took a sip of the coffee she had made Chief Lennox go warm up for her. He had been less than thrilled at her request.

"Do you have somewhere else to be?" Reyes asked, her mouth forming a bemused pout.

"Yes. There are plenty of other places I would rather be. But unfortunately, Mrs. Edie Parker seems to have put my friends and me in this predicament."

"Oh . . . so you blame all of this on Mrs. Parker?"

"Of course. She claims to have a piece of evidence implicating us. Threatened us, really, if you think about it."

Alex's mouth formed a small smile.

"She turned in the evidence, didn't she?"

Reyes shifted uncomfortably. "I'm sorry?"

"Edie Parker. Whatever it is, she turned it over to you guys. That's why you brought us into custody in the first place. We all know names alone aren't enough."

"And *we* both know I'm not going to disclose anything about evidence, right?" Reyes answered, grinning.

She blew lightly over her cup. "Your card to play."

Reyes paused, examining Alex as she rubbed her fingers together.

"Okay, then. Why didn't you report it to the police? If you felt so threatened by Edie Parker, as you say."

"I admit, it was a mistake on my part—especially being an attorney. But I'm a divorce attorney, and I went with what I know best. We tried to cooperate with Mrs. Parker until we could figure something out."

"Figure something out?" Reyes questioned mockingly.

"You do realize that Jemma is up for reelection? She doesn't need crazy attention like that. As her friends, we tried to keep this under wraps. In my opinion, Mrs. Parker has been a bit unhinged since the unfortunate death of her husband."

"Why would she select your names then?"

"Your guess is as good as mine. She could have randomly picked them from the yearbook—which is a public record. Anyone can check that out at the Rosemary Hills Library."

Reyes smirked. "That doesn't explain why you didn't submit your DNA. Make it all go away, right?"

Alex laughed dryly. "Why would we do something so ridiculous? Just give in to the whim of a widow on some crazy witch hunt? Our blood, our bodies. Isn't that what they've been chanting outside this very building the last few weeks?"

"Purely on principle?" Reyes raised her eyebrows incredulously.

"Look—" Alex sipped her coffee. "I'm not saying we, or really *I*, am some constitutional martyr. But the line has to be drawn somewhere. We were protecting our friend, who has her political career on the line. It was all a bit jarring."

"Jarring? Hmm, doesn't seem like you get rattled easily, Alex." It was Reyes's turn to scoff back.

"Okay. Since you pointed that out, go ahead. Get on with it, Detective. We know why you brought all of us in here—actually, we didn't *have* to come in. We came in completely of our own volition. So did I have anything to do with Baby Ava? Absolutely not."

Reyes opened her mouth but paused, glancing over at Chief Lennox.

"The real question is this—do *you* have anything on any of us other than our names?"

— — —

## JEMMA

Reyes perched herself on the table and made steady eye contact with Jemma.

"Did your political career have any impact on whether or not to comply with Mrs. Parker's demand?" she asked, sweeping away stray strands that had loosened from her bun.

Jemma looked up almost scornfully.

"Are you kidding? Of course. I'm not ashamed to admit that. I put blood, sweat, tears, and time away from my family into my career—not to mention it's reelection season. I hope you remember to vote, Reyes."

Reyes did not look amused. She stood up and drank the last bit of coffee from her mug.

"There was no other reason that you refused to submit your DNA?"

"No."

"The threat of exposure had nothing to do with it?"

"Exposure to what?"

"Being a match."

She shook her head. "That's a ridiculous notion. No, that was not why."

"Then please tell us why."

"I already did."

"Uh-uh—" Reyes tossed her head to the side. "I'm not taking that as an answer."

Jemma put her palms and shoulders up. "Uh—you're kind of going to have to."

"You wouldn't want to prove us wrong then?" She narrowed her eyes with intense focus.

"Are you telling me I have to submit my DNA?"

Reyes remained silent.

Jemma pointed to the door. "I could get Yates in here real quick, you know. I know my rights."

"I'm not going to answer that. But I will say this. All of this could go away if you just submitted."

Jemma stared back with a hint of loathing. "I'm sure it would."

Reyes sat back on the table and propped open the folder on her lap. "What does your husband think of all this?"

"Leave them out of it," Jemma snapped.

"Who?"

"My family."

"It's simply a question. And your daughter . . . Poppy? Does she know about your involvement?"

"What involvement? I told you to leave them out of this."

"Perhaps that's on *you*, Senator," Reyes shot back.

"They're off limits. Especially Henry."

Reyes paused. She put her feet back on the floor. "Who?"

"Henry. My son. He's only four."

She gave her a blank stare. "I'm sorry?"

Jemma leaned closer.

"What is wrong with you? I have a son. He is four. And his name is Henry." She threw her arms up in disbelief, making eye contact with Chief Lennox.

"I didn't see anything—" Reyes flipped open the folder again. "I must have missed—"

"Of course you did. I have a son."

*Why doesn't she believe me?*

Chief Lennox stood up from his corner. "You have a daughter, Poppy."

There was something in the tone of his voice . . . something that caused Jemma's heart to race, releasing a surge of alarm through her limbs.

She shook her head indignantly. "I don't need you to tell me that. Yes, I have a daughter, Poppy. She's a teenager, which is a lot of fun right now, believe me—and then there is my youngest, *Henry*."

Chief Lennox exchanged glances with Reyes. His thin face seemed to get thinner, and worried eyes looked back at her.

She sat up straight, and then her jaw went slack—as if the curtain had suddenly been pulled. *He's here. He has always been here with me.*

"I had a son," she whispered.

# CHAPTER 41

## JEMMA

*Homecoming night: Eighteen years ago*

She had tried not to look down at him. If she had, she would have had to memorize his face. She would have to stroke his cheek and then hold him close against her chest.

"I'm doing this for you," she said, peeling back the burlap cloth and letting his arms reach out, one hand curled tight around a strand of her hair. The intoxicating scent coming from his body was going to overtake any reasoning left in her mind.

The doors of the cathedral had seemed so far away only a second ago. How had they suddenly appeared like that?

She wasn't ready.

She would never be.

"Please hear me, baby boy. Remember me. Please . . . remember my voice," she said shakily.

The first time she had felt him kick in her belly, she'd tried to ignore it. But it became stronger—each one a defiant tap against her gut, letting her know, *I'm here.* She didn't allow herself to even think it until one day she looked up the memory capability of newborns. She learned about their capacity to never forget their mother's voice.

She read the single line of text over and over again, scanning hope into her brain.

*He will remember me. Even if he forgets it.*

The steps seemed so cold as she began to lay him down. For a second, she looked back and thought about running. Cradling him and taking him back to the truck. She could hear the hum of the engine—a timer waiting for her return.

"You will be loved. You already are. That is my promise."

She tucked him up as tight as she could.

"Goodbye . . . Henry."

She knew with certainty a piece of her heart was left on the steps of the cathedral that night. The rest of it was bruised and beaten.

In the days and weeks that followed, she waited for a knock at the door—someone coming back to return him, to shame her for doing such a thing. With the noise of each car that drove by the house, she would jump up and stare with anticipation. Another few months passed by, and nothing. She had gotten what she asked for. It was as if it had never happened.

She would wake up from nightmares of police officers storming in to take her away. But they never came. There was not one story in the paper or local news about a baby being found. Had it even been real? Had she dreamed the whole night?

But it had to be real.

As real as the hole inside her. The one that had formed the moment she left him. The blank page that remained in her heart, that she could only fill with her own visions to placate. A version of him that she more than imagined; she believed in him with every part of her. Her Henry who never left her . . . whom *she* never left. But it was never enough, could never quite restore the aching trauma in her chest.

The *unknowing*.

---

## ALEX

When she returned home that night, she slipped off her dress in the kitchen, a ring of torn and bloodied fabric circling her feet.

She was looking down at her hands, which she realized were bare, when a noise stopped her. Muted. Measured. A dull knife that would cut if she wasn't more careful. Silent and swift, she stuffed the dress down into the trash, crossing her arms across her naked body as she trod lightly upstairs.

Her body halted like a soldier. She paused.

She thought she saw movement out of the corner of her eye but turned to find nothing. She sighed with relief, everything in her aching for rest as she reached her bedroom.

She had made it. Undetected and unseen.

*No one will ever know. This stays between the three of us forever.*

She opened the door and froze.

Something had been waiting for her. Something that made the lining of her throat constrict and sting with horror.

There it was on her bed. Laid out as if it had always been there. A single satin glove. The blood dried around the fingers like lace.

She picked it up, her hand shaking, her mouth crumpling into fear.

———

## CLEO

The leather seats of the truck were spotless. The keys placed back just as they had been in the cupholder. The pocketknife wiped down and nestled in the glove compartment.

Everything was back in its place. All was clean again. No one suspected anything of the quiet girl in trigonometry on Monday.

But she had never felt more unclean.

*We can't undo it. We can't undo what happened Saturday night.*

She stared hard and straight ahead in class. She wanted to pretend the boy who'd violated her didn't exist. She wanted to pretend that she didn't exist.

When the class was over, she thought she would be relieved, but it only made her more anxious. The realization she would have to do this all over again tomorrow. The day after that and the next.

She didn't hear him at first as she kept her head down in the hallway. Calling her name. If only he had been the one to call her name that night. If only she had walked straight inside to the dance.

*If only she could erase everything from that night.*

"Cleo!" Will shouted after her.

She kept going and burst out the side-entrance doors.

"Cleo," he said breathlessly as he caught up with her at the bottom step.

She stopped, keeping her eyes on the concrete stairs.

"Why are you ignoring me?" he asked.

She glanced at his face to see the confusion and hurt in his eyes.

"I guess I didn't hear you," she said.

Her answer only increased his concerned expression. "What happened at the dance? I looked for you."

He looked down after he said this, almost embarrassed.

"Sorry. I—I got into it with my mom. She didn't want me to go. So . . ." Her voice trailed off with this lie.

"Oh," he said quietly. "Sure, I get it."

She couldn't tell if he bought it or not. But it didn't matter. She wasn't the same girl anymore. She wasn't the Cleo Song whom Will Hart had gotten to know.

She was someone else now . . . someone who now more than ever couldn't share all of herself with anyone.

"I guess I thought . . . ," he began to say.

She could see the hopefulness in his eyes, and it hurt her more than anything had before. The searing pain of hurting someone she cared about.

"I did too," she said as she took his hand and squeezed it once.

"Cleo—"

"I'm sorry, Will," she said. "Really . . . I'm so sorry."

She left him on the last step as she turned away. If she looked at him one more time, the tears in her eyes would spill out. But she kept them in, forcing them back. They could never come out.

None of it could ever come out.

# CHAPTER 42

## EDIE

*September 17, 2022*

Before she opened her eyes, she knew. It was the morning of the drawing. Today was the last day to find a match. Even with all the money in the world, an obscene amount that tasted so green and rich, enough to not only change someone's life but to redirect it to another stratosphere of possibilities—

It was not enough.

She had no more answers than she'd had at the beginning. The waste of it, the fruitless result after casting a golden net on the town, was more than she could handle. Her mood became a pot of water set carefully on a burner, the temperature rising gradually—a few bubbles forming before slowly coming to the surface, popping up with more intensity.

By noon, she was ready to burst with aggravation.

Ambrose arrived unexpectedly before dinner, just as she had retreated to her bedroom. He knocked tepidly on her door as she sat at her vanity, brushing her hair, even though she had already brushed it an hour ago. She was a woman with no tasks, no agenda. This was her torment. All she could do was sit on her hands and wait. Wait for the possibility of an answer before the timer went off and a winner had to be chosen.

"I'm not going, Ambrose. I already told Robin my decision."

He nodded from the doorway.

"That's not why I'm here, Edie."

"Then what?"

She placed the brush down with force, staring at him in the mirror. "I wanted to make sure you were okay."

"That *I'm* okay?" She placed her hand on her chest. "Or do you mean if I'm okay with the fact we have gained nothing from all of this?"

"You knew the chance of that happening." There was a slight agitation in his voice.

She stood up and turned to face him. "That doesn't make it any easier."

He let out a low sigh. "Edie, it's time to let it all go. It's out of your hands now. This hasn't been . . . healthy for you."

"I don't give a damn about how it's *been* for me, Ambrose. Johnny Parker . . . my Johnny, is gone. *Gone.* And the only thing I have left is to solve this case. Because maybe, just *maybe*, it will give me some peace."

"Edie . . . there's nothing else you can do now. I know you hate to hear that, but Johnny would have wanted you to move on with your life. We all do."

"Move on," she said quietly.

"Yes," he answered with relief in his eyes. "It's time to finally move on."

Her eyes flashed. "How much time until the lottery drawing?"

Ambrose looked down at his watch. "Less than an hour."

She grabbed her purse from the vanity.

"Edie, what are you doing? I thought you weren't going to the drawing—"

She stood in front of him. "I should have done this sooner."

"What? Done what sooner?"

"Get answers."

Ambrose narrowed his eyes with worry. "Edie, I don't think it's a good idea to go—"

"You're in my way," she said haughtily.

He grabbed her arm as she tried to walk past him.

"Ambrose," she said, looking down at his grip with surprise.

"Don't, Edie," he said in a low, dark voice. "I'm warning you. Don't. Do. Anything foolish."

# CHAPTER 43

## CLEO

*September 17, 2022*

Cleo silently ate dinner as Rocky chatted next to her. The more he buzzed on, the more she felt herself floating away.

She could still hear Reyes and her voice, the endless questions hammered at her in that small room. One after the other, like pellets that filled her mouth, choking her answers.

*What is your relationship like with your son?*

*How was your marriage with your ex-husband? Did it end amicably, Cleo?*

Rocky held up his empty glass and then asked for more milk. When she didn't respond, Ji-Yeon got up and went to the refrigerator, glancing once at her as she poured the carton.

*What did you see at the Parker estate? I mean—was there anything unusual?*

She slipped a bite of rice in her mouth.

*Can you tell us what you saw there?*

She heard her mother's voice calling her Korean name through the fog.

"Da-Eun."

Her mother's mouth moved, and Cleo nodded as if she understood her. She said something else, but she couldn't quite make it out.

Cleo rubbed one side of her face. "I'm sorry, Omma. What did you say?"

Ji-Yeon reached out and tapped her arm gently.

"We should go soon. The lottery drawing."

*Answer the question, Cleo.*

"Yes. We should," she answered, her voice trailing.

Rocky stopped chewing, staring at her with a confused expression. "Mommy?"

"Da-Eun. You . . . okay?"

She looked across the table at her mother, expression worried, twisting the ring on her finger. Her eyes focused on her mother's hands, turning the gold metal round and round with rhythmic clarity.

It shone in the light, and she saw it.

*What did you see, Cleo?*

She could see it now. How had she not seen it before? The jewel that shone so brightly on the band.

She had seen that same band exactly one other time.

———

"What are you doing here? This isn't appropriate. You aren't scheduled to work today."

Patricia braced her body in front of the doorway.

"I need to see the patient," Cleo demanded.

"I'm afraid that's impossible at the moment. He is not well."

She tried closing the door, but Cleo moved her foot forward. She couldn't care less about being polite. She couldn't care less if she was fired on the spot.

She was going to get through.

"He."

Patricia's face froze.

"You said *he*."

"I didn't—I mean . . . ," she stammered.

"That's what I thought," Cleo said. "Excuse me."

She ran up the stairs and heard a voice. The door was already open.

# CHAPTER 44

## EDIE

*September 17, 2022*

The slow burn of disgrace angrily rippled like a chord inside Edie's chest.

*Who is he to tell me what to do?*

"Remove your hand, Ambrose," she ordered indignantly.

"Edie," he said gruffly.

She tore her arm away from his grasp. "Don't *ever* touch me again."

He said nothing more and stood motionless as she ran out to the garage.

Her fingers fumbled against the board of key hooks, grabbing the first one that dropped into her hand. After unlocking the white Buick, she climbed behind the wheel.

*You can't hide it anymore. No more games.*

The road was barely lit, but she knew the way. The Buick ripped down the dirt road, grinding everything in its path. The rocks pelted the sides of the car, and she fishtailed once—her foot hit the gas even harder in response.

The lights of the driveway glowed as she pulled in, then barely got the car into park before she stumbled out. The keys were still in the ignition, and the car beeped to alarm her. She paused in front of the door, her chest heaving, and then pounded with both fists.

A woman answered, eyes squinting in alarm, arms folded over her chest.

"Mrs. Parker? What are you doing—"

"Where is he?"

"He's upstairs . . . but is something the matter? You—"

She pushed the woman aside, scrambled up the staircase, and flung the door open. Her eyes adjusted to the darkness, a sliver of light from the window casting the outline of his head in a glow. His back to her already seemed to scream defiance.

"Tell me," she said.

He did not move.

"Did you hear me?" she asked loudly.

The scorn she had for this man, the disdain that rumbled inside her. She lurched toward the window, stumbling once and then getting up with a wildness she didn't know she had in her.

"Tell me." She bent her head down, shaking, then pulled out the photo and thrust it up to him. "*Tell me*. What do you know? What happened to those girls?"

# CHAPTER 45

---

## ALEX

*September 17, 2022: The lottery drawing*

Alex was the first of the women to arrive.

The entire town of Rosemary Hills had assembled, it seemed, a hive of bees bustling and crawling over Avalon Park. She could hardly make out any of the white picnic tables lined up, the crowd thick with bodies and expectations. A low hum hung over them all like a veil.

*Ten more minutes.*

*Ten more minutes and this will have ended.*

She had contemplated whether to bring Sasha, but then thought it would be nice to have her at her side when it was all finally over. When the winner was called, and all attention would go there. The spotlight would be willingly sucked away from them like a vacuum, and she could take Sasha in hand and leave, knowing it was all behind them.

Davis had called early that morning, his voice less than pleased.

"You are not dragging my daughter to that."

"We're in the midst of a divorce, and suddenly you're opposed to the lottery?"

"Alex. Please. Don't."

"Don't what?" She felt hands of anger trying to crawl up her throat and out toward Davis.

"Oh God, this feels like such a cliché . . . we've become that divorce cliché, but I'll say it anyway. We promised we would keep it civil for Sasha's sake."

"I am being civil. I can't say the same for you."

"Dammit, Alex!"

There they were again. The little hands strangling her throat, only now caught with tears.

"Where was this?" she asked hoarsely.

"Where was what?"

"This emotion. Where was this earlier? All those years?"

He remained silent before finally breathing out hard. "It doesn't really matter anymore now . . . does it."

Ultimately, Davis agreed to let Sasha go so long as she didn't stay out too late.

"Look, Mommy! There's Rocky." Sasha waved at him wildly. "Can we sit by him, please? Did you know he's in my class? Please?"

She nodded and let her lead the way to a table not in the very back but far enough from the podium that she felt comfortable.

Ji-Yeon smiled politely and said hello as Sasha nearly jumped on Rocky before sitting next to him.

"Hi, I hope you don't mind," she said apologetically.

"No. Please sit," Ji-Yeon replied.

There was a sudden rise in the low murmurs, the pitch higher and louder but still below crazed. Alex looked over her shoulder to see Jemma with Finch. She held her head with pride, unfazed by the mocking whispers and stares.

She paused and seemed to be looking for someone, a slightly worried expression on her face, before pointing toward Poppy with her friends and giving a quick wave. She and Finch held hands tightly as she scanned the crowd again and made eye contact with Alex.

They scooted down the bench to make room, bobbing up and down like gophers.

"Senator," Alex said, leaning over. "Are you ready for this to be over?"

"I already have a bottle of rosé in the chiller waiting at home," Jemma replied through clenched teeth, keeping a serene smile and nodding to those who walked by and greeted her.

"I don't know if I'll be reveling like that, but I never want to talk or think about this again," Alex said resolutely.

"Yates told me he heard through the grapevine that you were a real killer yesterday."

"Yeah, well, I guess it pays to be the bitch attorney after all," she said, shrugging. A creep of a smile followed.

Jemma turned to her. "Well . . . thank you."

"Eh. Don't thank me. I don't take well to that kind of thing. And where the hell is Cleo?" She straightened her back to glance around.

"Didn't you see her text?"

"No." Alex pulled her phone out.

The crowd began to clap. Chief Lennox stepped up on the podium, flanked by four other officers. Mayor Vogel followed, looking jittery as she stepped up to the mic.

"Welcome, residents and former residents of Rosemary Hills!" she exclaimed.

The crowd came to life even more, cheering and calling out. The atmosphere had shifted from uneasy anticipation to a celebration.

"She said she was going to be late. But that she'll be here," Jemma said into Alex's ear, over the whistles and whoops.

"How can she be late to this?"

Mayor Vogel pressed on. "I can see that most if not everyone in this great town of ours has shown up for this historic and unprecedented event. And for those former residents viewing from their homes via live streaming or television, we welcome you back!"

Alex opened her mouth but suddenly caught sight of a figure in the back. She turned her neck to get a closer view, feeling like she was seeing a ghost.

"What is she doing here?"

"Who?"

"My mother . . ."

Maud strode around stealthily in the back row of picnic tables, scanning back and forth. It seemed everyone was looking for someone tonight.

——

# CLEO

Cleo rushed past the line of journalists and cameras, breathless from running. She peered out, trying to see Rocky's head. She could always spot him before anyone else in a crowd. She would recognize him from a single movement.

She'd started to make her way toward the last row when a hand lightly touched her shoulder.

"Cleo."

Will looked at her, eyes glossy with pain.

A strong swell of both uneasiness and longing poured into her. Part of her doubted things between them could ever be the same again. And yet the other part, the hopeful part, wondered if maybe they had fragmented necessarily—like the shell of an egg before the yolk, golden and rich, could be exposed.

But her words came out cold. "What is it you want, Will?"

"I want to say that I'm sorry."

She searched his face. "Sorry for what?"

"That somehow I hurt you."

"It's done. We can't go back—"

"You still don't believe me then," he said with disappointment.

"Will . . ." She reached out and put her hand in his.

They had done this before. Eighteen years ago, he had looked at her in the same way. She'd chosen to turn away from him on that last step. Maybe this time she could choose something different. Maybe this time she could be honest.

Except time wasn't going to change anything.

She let go of his hand.

"Too much has happened, Will."

"What if I could prove it wasn't me?"

*What if. What if I never doubted and hurt you? What if I had met you at the dance? What if I had never left Rosemary Hills? What if . . .*

The town roared with applause as Mayor Vogel concluded her speech.

"I have to . . . I have to get to my family, Will," she said, slipping away.

She ran with her head down, wishing that somehow all her what-ifs had been different with Will. She slipped in next to her mother and Rocky, the bench cold and hard.

"I'm sorry I'm late," she said quietly.

"Mommy, what took you so long?" asked Rocky.

"They are about to announce," Ji-Yeon said, shushing them and looking forward at the podium.

She took a breath, trying to collect herself. The crowd was growing hot and hostile with each passing second. There was no going back now: a lottery winner was to be named.

*There's a reason you rushed to get here. You have to tell them.*

Jemma reached over and tapped her knee. "Where were you?" she hissed. "I can't believe—"

"Listen," she said.

Alex started to stand up, craning her neck. "Excuse me. I'm just going to see—"

"I have to tell you both something," she broke in urgently.

"Hold on. I thought I—"

"No. This can't wait," said Cleo harshly, pulling her down.

Jemma and Alex, both startled, sat still with alarm.

"I saw him."

"Saw who?" Jemma asked with impatience.

"The patient. She was there with him. Edie Parker. She's kept it a secret this whole time."

Jemma shook her head. "You're not making any sense. Kept what a secret?"

"The patient. I know who the patient is."

She leaned forward and whispered. Her lips pushed each syllable of a name, cool and hushed, into their ears.

# CHAPTER 46

---

## ALEX

*September 17, 2022*

Years ago, when she was deep into studying her criminal law book, Alex had come across the psychological response of those convicted of serious crimes: when a defendant rose at the sight of a jury, as the bailiff handed the verdict to the judge, the tension as it was read out loud and finally given. It was their demeanor at this precise moment that received much scrutiny. What were they thinking? How would they react to such a fate?

There were those who were emotionless and cold. And then there were those with immediate passionate reactions.

She had pondered right then: Which category would she fit into?

She never thought it would be her turn to find out.

Somewhere between blank emptiness and utter terror, all at once she felt like buckling to her knees. She managed to hang on to each of them, her fingers clawing onto Cleo's blouse, her other hand gripping Jemma's arm.

"I thought he was gone," she said.

"What do you mean?" asked Cleo.

She rocked her head. "I'm sorry. You have to know I'm so sorry," she stammered, turning to Cleo and then Jemma.

"Sorry . . . sorry for what?"

"I had to protect her. It didn't matter what else happened or who else took the fall. I was going to protect her."

"Protect who?" Jemma urged.

"My sister."

They spun around, searching for Violet, to find her tossing her head back, laughing with a group of her friends a few rows up, her hair shaking and wild.

"Violet? She's okay, Alex. Look. She's right over there . . . she's safe," Cleo said gently.

Alex's shoulders shuddered, and the ironclad presence she had always tried to present to the world melted in front of them.

"No. She's not. She's far from it."

———

She thought she'd gotten rid of him for good that night. Away from Maud, away from her. For a while she felt she had won. For a while she believed she was safe. She had beaten the monster and, maybe through all of it, somehow driven the monster out of Maud.

But some monsters can never go away.

Maud would do anything for him, after all.

When she'd started the new job all those years ago, she'd been just another office admin. *Secretary* was what they called it back then.

She watched him for years from afar, always apprising Alex, who listened with stone ears, of any encounters with him. She was another face he passed by on his way into his office as she carefully bided her time. He was a man who embodied everything she thought a powerful man should be. He was nothing like all the others. This one . . . surely this one would be different. This one could provide beyond anything in her wildest dreams and more.

This one would never abandon her.

And then one day, he walked by her desk and stopped, staring at a picture of her daughter. When she told him about her, he seemed engaged. Interested.

He asked to come over for dinner.

He had his eye on Alex from that first night on, like a pet she could bring out and dangle in front of him to keep his attention. It wasn't long before he would stay longer into the evenings and then into Maud's bedroom.

But eventually he grew restless with dinner. With piano playing. *With Maud.* He wanted more. By the time Alex started her senior year, he was all but agitated. *On edge.*

And Alex saw it, too, his eyes turning into something else—black and tar-like.

She woke up that night to see him standing in her doorway.

She closed her eyes, not wanting to look. She heard him enter and shut the door. Her body was trapped in a tomb, her limbs lead, but her mind still raced. He said nothing as he knelt. She kept her eyes shut tight. If she did this hard enough, maybe he wouldn't really be there. She felt his fingers stroke her hair and then down her face. The same pattern, a treacherous familiarity.

This wasn't the first time he had done this to her face.

The first time it happened, she was a little girl who had lost her hair clip in the wind. She wasn't alone then. Two other little girls made sure of it.

They had saved her.

His breath entered her ear, and words slid in like something from the gutter.

"I remember you and your friends," he said to her.

Her eyes flew open.

A voice inside her could not be silenced any longer. It was a deep-rooted seed filled with a power she suddenly possessed.

He stopped, startled by her glare.

She flashed her eyes at him with everything she had, wide and potent. She wasn't going to look away. Not anymore. Every muscle in her face was weak, her lips barely able to move. But she forced it once.

A small rasping call.

"No."

The door flew open against the frame and bounced. Maud blearily looked at them, asking what was going on as he stumbled up from the floor.

Coward that he was, he didn't look her in the face as he fled the room. She watched them in the hallway, their feet casting shadows as they danced.

Her mother's pleas with him to stay. His angry answers to her, muffled and then louder before going quiet. Hurried footsteps down the stairs, which had never sounded sweeter to Alex's ears, a symphony of an exodus. Her mother's wailing, begging him to come back—begging him to never leave her.

There was silence in their house after that. For months Maud never spoke of him. Her subdued reaction haunted Alex. Where was the anger? Had it disappeared along with him? Every day that passed by without incident increased her wariness, a tsunami collecting its waves before striking.

But she would be leaving for college soon. She would be far away from all that had happened, and for once, she found herself smiling at the future.

*Just a little longer. A little longer and you'll be free.*

She remembered eating her breakfast as the coffeepot gurgled that winter morning. Sunshine pierced through the frosted windowpanes—she lifted her chin to catch some of it. Yet something was not quite right. A beat was off in the daily rhythm of the morning. A sound she wasn't used to hearing.

Maud hummed as she moved around the kitchen, a novelty of carefreeness that made the hairs rise on her arms.

She looked up to see Maud turn to the side, the bright morning light casting a spotlight on the outline of her profile.

She heard her fork clatter on her plate. She felt vomit come up and then release back inside her.

A round belly. Small but full of dark promise.

Her mother smiled, running her hand over its shape. She handed her something. A photo. Angrily cut out, the edges jagged and uneven. The black-and-white design, swirling into shapes showing early signs of life.

An ultrasound.

She had an expectant mother's glow full of all the rage in the world, seething and ready to cause pain back onto him. Grinding constantly under the surface, she would wait to make her move to inflict the most precise blow of retribution.

"He can never fully know the truth," she said to Alex. "And that is the greatest punishment."

She watched as her mother rubbed her midsection again, a content smirk at this thought. This was her consolation prize. *This* was her power she would forever hold over him.

"How can you . . . it isn't right," she stuttered.

"Right?" Maud demanded. "And you think what you did with your friends that night was *right?*"

There it was. What she had been dreading. What she hoped she had escaped.

Her heart pounded in her ears.

She should have known better. She should have known Maud was only waiting to strike.

"You thought I would let it go?" Maud clenched her hands. Her voice darkly composed. "That I wouldn't know? I am your mother. I know. Even before you think another thought, I know. *I know* everything about you."

*How silly of you, Alex. How silly to think you'd gotten away safe.*

"Do you want to hurt your friends?"

*She's never going to let you forget about that night.*

She shook her head.

"Then ask yourself this . . . what are you willing to do for my silence?"

*She's never going to let you go.*

She nodded. Wet drops rolled onto her upper lip, but she refused to taste them.

"Good girl," Maud said. She smiled at her with satisfaction.

There was something in her snideness that made her feel ill. A disgust that broke through and forced her to spit out her next words.

"You don't know the whole truth," she said.

"What did you say?" Her eyes peered at her with suspicion.

"I said," Alex said, her voice growing louder, "you don't know the whole truth."

She leaned closer, holding her belly with one hand, the other extending out. "Then what is the truth, Alexandra?" She raised her brows, humoring her, taunting her.

She felt her entire body tremble with both fear and anger. "He knew who I was."

"What?"

"Before you brought him into our house." She slowed down. "He already knew who I was."

"That's impossible." Maud faltered. "How?"

"When we were little girls . . ."

Her eyes shimmered.

"He tried to hurt me and my friends."

"No." She shook her head. "You're lying." Her chest heaved up and down, panicked heaves of someone who had willingly ignored the truth.

"Don't you see, Mother? He never wanted you." She felt her mouth twist into a smile. "He only wanted us."

She placed her hand over Maud's.

"You let a monster into our house. And now you're having his baby."

Her mother caught her breath. Her head shuddered as she slowly looked up. Her eyes met Alex's as if she'd suddenly realized she was there. Something unnatural shifted in them.

She moved so quickly that Alex didn't have time to react. She shoved her chair in, flipped the photo over onto the table, grabbed her hand, and forced a pen into her fingers. Whiplash stung her neck.

"Write them."

"What?" Alex cried.

The grip on her hand tightened, and she winced, bending forward with resistance. She could barely see through the strands in her eyes.

"Your names," Maud said with clenched teeth.

"Why . . . why are you making me—"

"A secret for a secret, dear," she said, moving the hair out of her face. "He has to be reminded of what he did," she said with threatening eyes. "Isn't that what you want?"

"I can't. I can't do that to them—" She shook her head back and forth.

Her mother clutched Alex's face in her hands and spoke slowly.

"When the time is right, I will deliver this to him. He will always wonder if he had a child. And he will always be reminded that we know of his darkest desires."

She released her face hastily and took her place behind, leaning over as she waited for her to complete her task.

Alex held the pen against the photo, watching the ink start to bleed into a black dot. Her hand stiffened. She stopped.

She felt the roundness of Maud's midsection rub against her. Warm, growing flesh that held life beating inside, waiting to get out. An innocence she knew all too well would be taken away by a mother who only inflicted pain upon pain. Whatever was growing in there stood no chance. Whatever was in there was also a part of her.

"No," she said quietly.

Maud narrowed her eyes. "No?"

"You want the names? Then promise."

"I don't owe you any promises—"

*"Promise,"* she said with strength. "Promise this baby will never suffer like I suffered. Do that and you can have them."

"Or *what?*" she snapped.

"The truth comes out. *All* of it. I don't care anymore."

"I highly doubt that," she said with a coarse saltiness.

Alex raised her head. "Your move, Mother."

She could see it, the uncertainty beginning to seep into every pore of Maud's face.

Alex spoke steadily. "You can be different this time. Different than how you were with me . . ."

Her mother's fingers slid over her belly. She looked down at it, her hands tightening as she stared back up with watery eyes.

Alex's hand clutched the pen, her mouth quivering. "You never could bring yourself to be that with me . . . could you?"

Maud shook her head once, a twitch.

"Okay," she breathed out. "Write them."

With each stroke of ink, Alex stitched her own mouth shut. She dropped the pen as the last letter was written.

As the weeks went by, she began to wonder if any of it was real.

Weeks swiftly changed to months. She tried to ignore her mother's figure, which grew along with the dread knotted in her own midsection.

Her ghost of a high school senior year was coming to an end, and she counted the days until she could escape to college. But nothing would allow her to escape what was next.

She came home one night late summer to find spots of blood on the kitchen floor, so bright she wished it were paint. She followed it up the stairs, like some sick scavenger hunt laid out for her, and into the bedroom. Her heart pounded with deafening fear as she pushed the door open.

Maud lay in bed with an infant in her arms, her face drained of any color. A tiny hand reached up and curled back inward.

"There were two of them," Maud announced.

*Them. The babies.*

"He didn't survive," she said matter-of-factly. "But she did." She stared down with triumph at her new daughter.

She didn't have to ask—she knew what her mother had done with him.

But the worst part was yet to come.

She never fathomed the sweet bitterness of this baby. Her arrival brought with it a dark chain forever linking them to a past she thought conquered.

Every moment spent with this new family member of theirs was a reminder of who the father was. She could never escape him. She would always be there, forever a reminder of *him*. Of what they had done. Despite all she had surrendered to protect this baby. To give her a chance before she was ever born. To never know the same pain her older sister had endured.

She felt the resentment.

This baby girl was not a miracle to Alex. This baby girl was only the beginning of her nightmare.

A baby girl who became known as a sister, named Violet.

A sister who was the daughter of Jonathan Parker.

———

A large glass case was wheeled out on the podium by two of the police officers. Mayor Vogel beamed, rubbing her hands together with exaggerated excitement.

"It's time, everyone!"

She began to turn the handle on the case, thousands of white papers fluttering in a cyclone, falling all over one another and then tumbling back down as she continued to spin it.

The crowd whistled and cheered, giving a few calls to "Hurry up!" and "Pick one already!"

Maud had hunted down Violet, who was sitting with her friends in the middle row. She proceeded to grab her by the arm and drag her to the back. A red-faced and bewildered Violet reluctantly followed.

"No," Alex whispered.

A surge of energy coursed through her. "No!" She shot up. "Don't touch her!"

She ran quickly toward them, reaching out and taking Violet's hand.

"What are you doing?" Maud demanded.

"Let her go."

"Alex? What's wrong?" Violet held on, looking at her with confused eyes.

"We're leaving. Both of you. I told you not to come here, Violet!" Maud snatched Violet's wrist, and she twisted away angrily.

"No. I'm staying."

"I forbid it!"

The cheers of the crowd nearly drowned them out, piercing whistles cutting the air as Mayor Vogel reached into the glass case, her fingers grazing the flutters of white paper.

There was a yell from the back.

"Stop!"

Liam Ambrose bolted down the aisle, charging at Chief Lennox. He whispered something in his ear and handed him an envelope. Chief Lennox gripped it in his hand and nodded, immediately motioning to

Mayor Vogel. She looked out at the crowd, keeping an uncomfortable smile as she sidestepped to him. She leaned down, her mouth collapsing into disbelief as he spoke into her ear.

"I'm not leaving, Mother. I want to see if I win," Violet blurted out. Maud's face went white.

"I submitted my blood to enter the lottery. I'm eighteen, after all." She turned back to Alex. "*You* understand, right, Sissy?"

Alex gripped her hand, tears falling down, her heart both dropping and rising at the same time. "Yes. Always."

Mayor Vogel returned to the podium. "We have a match. A DNA match."

# CHAPTER 47

Edie Parker pulled the plug on the DNA lottery.

She finally got her answer. But at a cost she would never be able to repay.

The people of Rosemary Hills, distraught and confused at the bottom dropping out, focused instead on doing what people do when they become unsure and scared—they lashed out. Lawsuits were filed immediately; class action lawyers had a field day over civil liberties and the promises of a windfall. No one had gotten their dream of becoming rich overnight for just a little bit of blood. Someone had to pay.

The protesting, of course, raged onward to a fiery level, turning directly to Parker Inc., their stock plummeting overnight at the news of the lottery being canceled. Talking heads on late-night shows swooped down to make their statements and jokes at the expense of Edie Parker and even the town of Rosemary Hills.

"It was never going to work. This was doomed from the beginning."

"This just goes to show—wealth and privilege really can buy anything. She literally bought the answer to a nearly twenty-year-old mystery."

"Yeah, but she never really paid out, did she?"

"Did you see the mother who was arrested? She seems like a piece of work."

The police and prosecutor had agreed to keep the identity of the DNA match result anonymous, to protect Violet for as long as possible. Quietly, in the night, they'd brought in Violet, Maud, and Alex. Violet was surprisingly calm, while Maud refused to say a single word. Alex released decades of pain and truth to Chief Lennox and Reyes. Neither of them spoke or breathed another question once she began to tell her story. When it was all over, Reyes stood up and excused herself. She then proceeded to go to the restroom and sob silently in one of the stalls.

Alex, on the advice of Clifford Yates, agreed to a plea deal of probation and community service. It was argued that she was a minor at the time and under severe psychological distress by her mother.

Maud was charged with murder and abuse of a corpse. Her defense team argued the infant was already deceased, while prosecutors painted her as a scorned lover and cold-blooded killer. The trial drew the media's attention like a magnet—the newer, shinier object to come out of the entire DNA lottery debacle. Her ice-cold demeanor made her a tabloid and media darling—speculation and hype took over like a storm, pushing Parker Inc. out of the picture.

For Edie, this was the only break she was to get.

Ambrose broke the news that his team had finally located Kane Oliver. He had been hiding in Costa Rica, avoiding questions from the board about accusations of years of embezzlement and fraud. He told her he would spare her all the details of how much he had been screwing over Parker Inc. But she didn't want to be spared anymore.

She wanted the whole truth . . . no matter what the damage.

As she sat across from Chief Lennox the evening after Maud's arrest, he told her the story of Baby Ava, the *real* story, and what her husband had tried to do to a young girl. Ambrose and Robin could barely look at her. They braced themselves for her reaction.

But she had none.

# CHAPTER 48

## EDIE

*September 21, 2022*

She was a hollow woman—the truth had made sure of that.

She did not immediately go to him. For three nights, she kept the television off, refused to let anyone in her room, and kept herself closed off from any noise. She could only hear a buzzing echo in her ears and snippets of Chief Lennox's words. When she emerged, she was impeccably dressed and groomed. She drove out to the farmhouse where he was still being kept.

Patricia held the door for her as she entered the front, a cold gust pushing her in.

"Is she here?"

"Yes. She's in there," she replied, motioning toward the fireplace.

Cleo Song sat looking into the fire. Edie had invited her to the farmhouse. At first, she had not replied to her request. But the previous evening, Edie had received a last-minute "Yes" via Robin.

She looked slightly alarmed but then emboldened, raising her head high as Edie sat across from her.

"Thank you. For coming over, that is."

Cleo nodded. "I don't trust you. You should know that."

"I know."

Neither of them spoke for a few moments. The crackling flames seemed so ill fitting to Edie, their warmth and promise.

She turned her head to Cleo, closing her eyes first as if it was too painful to look at her and form words at the same time.

"I want you to know something. You can believe me or not, but . . . I didn't know about all that he did. I know you and your friends don't believe me. But it's the truth. I can honestly say I knew something was wrong. That something dark had happened, and he came upon it . . . but never. Never that *he* . . ." Her voice caught like an insect trapped in a web, curdling with torment. She held her hand up to her mouth in a fist.

Cleo looked at her face directly for the first time.

"I have to know something."

She pulled her fist down from her face. "Why did I hire you?"

"Yes. It didn't occur to me right away. But when it did, I couldn't make sense of it. You had to have known who I was when you hired me?"

"That is correct. I did."

"And yet—"

"It seems crazy, I know. When I was alerted by Ambrose that you had applied, I felt strangely . . . relieved in some way. That somehow, in all the chaos and unanswered questions I had for my husband, this had fallen into place. That it was not simply by chance you had applied for the job."

Cleo pressed her lips together. "And now? Knowing what was to come? Would you have still done it?"

Edie stared back.

*Knowing what was to come . . . what my Johnny did.*

"Yes."

Cleo narrowed her eyes. "Why fake his death? Was it because of his . . . condition? Did he not want anyone—"

"Money," Edie said, cutting her off.

"I'm sorry?"

"Money. That's always why, isn't it?"

She shrugged with confusion.

"Stocks don't like uncertainty. *Death* is certain," Edie answered as she smiled wearily.

Cleo nodded and began to stand up. "Is there anything else you wish to discuss?"

"Yes. There's one other thing."

"Oh."

"Did you ask her for me? Alex, I mean. Has she given it any consideration?"

"You mean about Violet?"

Edie bowed her head with anticipation. She had relayed through Robin what she had realized even in the thick of it all: that Violet, *Violet*, was next in line for Parker Inc. She could be the answer to the future of the company, a future that was shaky after all that had been revealed. Her offer had been more than generous in what Violet would inherit. Surely, she was what could bring them out of the ashes.

Cleo bit her lip and then grinned with disdain. "Yes. I did . . . I believe she told me to tell you and Jonathan to go fuck yourselves. And to never mention her sister's name again."

She remained in front of the fire after Cleo left—entirely still, a statue letting all the pigeons peck at her, afraid that a single movement would cause her to crack.

She finally rose and made her way up the stairs.

He faced the door in his wheelchair. His mouth frozen in a gaping hole.

She saw all that was left of him. As if a fist had been thrust through the center, clung on with an unimaginable force, and the flesh ripped out. The arbitrary fissures and scarring created a scene so incongruous that even to her it was beyond startling. A concave canyon of scarred flesh. Two holes served as his nose, and a creased fold of skin formed his mouth. Shiny bits of pink mixed among patches of his old roughness.

The shape of it all random in its outline, no longer the familiar form she had run her finger against for so many years. The only recognition he was still alive were the two roving eyes that refused to reveal anything to her.

He tilted his head slightly toward her.

One look from her, and he knew she had discovered the truth. His scars seemed to wither at this, his ugliness magnified by what he had done. She felt something come up in the back of her throat, the revulsion ready to pour out, but she contained it. She leaned against the doorway, the only thing keeping her weary body from falling.

"I lied for you." She stepped into the room. "I did exactly what you and the board asked of me."

He looked away.

"Look at me, Johnny," she said sharply.

He stared back.

"I lied to the whole world for you. Do you know what they told me? That it was better you were dead than in this condition. For the sake of the company, I lied. *For the company.* I had to pretend to grieve you, all while hating you for leaving me. Hating you for leaving me with this secret of yours."

She stood next to him, staring out the window.

"When she gave you that photo . . . that's when this all must have started. You must have gone mad. Wondering if it was yours, wondering if it was Baby Ava? And the names of those girls . . . those girls you tried to—"

She clenched her fists and tried not to scream.

"How many? How many others, Johnny?"

She knelt next to him and grabbed his finger, tearing off the ring. She squeezed it in her palm so hard she hoped the emerald would crack.

She moved her face in front of the shrieking chaos that was his.

"Why did you keep the photo? Did you want some souvenir of your sickness?" She placed a hand on his face and pressed hard into it. "I never knew you, did I."

He turned his head away.

"Ask me, Johnny," she said.

His gaping hole of a mouth shook—she could not tell if it was from sorrow or anger. She didn't care anymore. She placed her mouth over his ear.

"Ask me if I still tolerate you."

He seemed to shiver as she closed the door.

# CHAPTER 49
## JEMMA

*March 3, 2023*

"You okay doing this by yourself?"

Finch held the door open and looked around the room, as if it would close in on them.

Jemma nodded.

"You sure?"

"Dr. Sibian said it would be good to try something on my own. It might help bring more closure."

He took her hand and kissed it. "Hey. I'm right down the hall if you need me. Okay?"

"Okay."

She smiled back and leaned in to kiss his cheek. This man. This lovely man of hers—she had realized how many ways she was blessed after therapy sessions with Dr. Sibian.

He had gained even more admiration from her, if that were possible. After the drawing, he immediately buried himself in finding out what had really happened to her "Henry." A month later, a priest at the cathedral where he was left came forward with answers. Not wanting to draw unwanted attention, he quietly took the infant to an order in Missouri, where he'd been newly assigned. It was there the baby boy was adopted by a couple in a closed adoption.

When she found out the truth, she wasn't sure if she wanted to pursue anything further. While it gave her comfort in finally knowing what had happened to him, it also left her wondering what was ultimately best for her family—the one she already had right in front of her.

There was still so much for her to understand and sift through, but she was at the very least ready. Ready and willing to push on through all the rubble she had buried herself under.

"'Trauma.' It's okay to use that word, Jemma. 'Trauma.' You went through it," Dr. Sibian had said in their latest session.

"Did I? Am I through it?"

"You will be."

"I will."

"And, Jemma?"

"Yes?"

"I think it's time. You're ready."

She looked around the nursery she had started to put together over the last few years. Bare wood floors, a white crib, and a few boxes of newborn items. Three white frames with woodland creatures hung on one of the walls. She touched the one with the fox, tracing its outline over the glass. Dr. Sibian was right. It was time to put all of this away.

She reached into one of the boxes and pulled out a soft yellow onesie. This was where she had gone to when she thought of him. The room had been her secret shrine to Henry. It was okay to say his name. He existed.

Just not with her.

"Mommy?"

She hadn't heard from him since the interrogation. *I had a son.* The words had been the incantation to make him disappear.

But here he was again.

"Where have you been? I wanted you to tuck me in."

*Sweet angel voice.* She felt her heart wrap around itself tight, and she thought she wouldn't be able to breathe again.

She turned around and reached for him. "Henry."

He was there in her arms, the unmistakable smell of his skin, his hair—all wrapped up in an innocence that she would soak in forever if she could. She buried her face in his shoulder and rocked him.

"What's wrong, Mommy?"

"Nothing. Nothing, my sweet Henry."

She pulled back to look at him, stroking his face and hair. "I never left. I am so sorry that you thought I left."

He forgave her in an instant, so quick to smile and shine back at her.

"Can you tuck me in then?"

She nodded.

There they were again, mother and son, as she leaned over him, propping his head on the pillow and drawing the blanket close under his chin. She sang to him, watching him gaze up at her with admiring eyes—the eyes of a boy who loved his mother and who was loved back an infinite amount. His face was so comforted in knowing she was right there—nothing could harm him as long as she was there. She kissed him and whispered over and over again how she was so glad he had been born into this world. That he was always part of her.

His eyelids began to flutter. He struggled to keep them open—as if he knew that would be it, closing a window to their world, the one only the two of them could exist in.

"Don't stop singing, Mommy," he said breathily.

"Okay. But listen to me first, my Henry."

He sighed and shifted his head. "I'm listening."

"I have to go now."

"Don't go." He put his hand on her arm, sleepily patting it.

"Not that kind. Not the forever kind." She drew in a shaky breath, and the loss of it all rained down on her so hard she paused to get her words out. She closed her eyes and imagined all the moments she had missed, would continue to miss. But they were not hers to have. She needed to let him go.

"You were supposed to keep singing," he said.

She stroked his head and began to hum before pausing once more.

"I'm always here, baby boy. Always, always. But you need to go on so that I can go on."

"Oh, Mommy." He sighed.

"You will always be a part of me. And I will always be a part of you, Henry."

"I like that," he said, eyes half-shut.

"You do?"

"Yes."

"That's good, Henry." She kissed his hand and then held it to her lips, holding it so close she realized the tears had wet both their hands.

"Good night, Mommy."

"Good night, Henry."

# CHAPTER 50

___

## CLEO

*April 17, 2023*

Two months after the lottery drawing, she'd bought a small house of her own.

A week later, Whittner's went up for sale. The owner wanted to retire and move someplace warmer—Sedona was what she'd heard.

"I think I might go for it," she said to Ji-Yeon as she placed some of Rocky's clothes into a box as they packed.

"For?" she asked without looking up from folding.

"The coffee shop."

Ji-Yeon nodded. "So brave."

"Is it?"

She smiled. "Best kind of brave."

Rocky immediately took to the little two-bedroom bungalow they moved into. Mainly because Cleo decorated his "big boy room" with an explosion of dinosaur decor.

"Whoa, Mommy. Way cool," he said before throwing his arms around her neck.

She felt her insides melt and clamped her mouth shut to keep her tears in. The home was theirs now to build memories in, and it was one that she had needed no one else's help with.

Winter passed, and there were still no buyers for the coffee shop. She pulled in a business loan and made an offer that left her breathless—she officially became the owner just as the snow was starting to melt.

She had somehow found a rhythm as not only the new owner but a brand-new entrepreneur. All those years of pent-up boldness had somehow released and now served her well as she navigated an entirely different season of her life.

One that was absent of Will. An absence she wasn't sure she wanted to live with or not.

It was about a month after reopening Whittner's when she discovered the answer. A bag of coffee beans had broken open behind the counter. As she straightened up from sweeping the last of them into a dustpan, she found herself staring into a gentle face.

Her eyes moved to his scar, which melded into the small smile he gave her.

"I heard the new owner kept the cinnamon rolls on the menu," Will said.

"She did," she said softly.

"Maybe this new owner might want to get a coffee sometime?"

Cleo couldn't help but laugh. "She owns all the coffee."

It was his turn to laugh. "That's a problem then." His cheerful eyes were mixed with a seriousness she didn't want to think over.

There was nothing to think over. She didn't owe that sort of sensibility to anyone.

"No . . . not anymore," she said.

He smiled with a puzzled expression.

She knew the woman she was and could be, not just for Will, Ji-Yeon, Rocky, or anyone else. She claimed a wholeness that was for her.

She was that kind of woman, after all.

# EPILOGUE

## ALEX

*September 10, 2023*

A monument dedicated to Baby Ava would be erected in a few months in the center of Avalon Park. Alex, however, would not be around to see it. There had been much debate over whether to change the reference to the infant, but it represented more than the one lost soul to Rosemary Hills. The name remained as it always had.

She sat on the bench with Cleo to her right and Jemma to her left. The three women watched as workers finished leveling out fresh wet cement, the beginnings of a base for the memorial.

"You sure you can't stay for the ceremony?" Cleo asked.

"I don't know if I want to see it. It would be too . . ."

"Yeah. I know."

Jemma handed each of them a half sandwich. "When is your flight?"

"Tomorrow at six in the morning. Sasha has had her Minnie Mouse suitcase packed for weeks. She asks me every day if today is the day."

"And Violet?"

"Thrilled to be getting up that early."

Jemma elbowed her playfully. "Nothing we can do to convince you to stay?"

Alex smiled serenely, knowing her answer was what she needed. "No. It's time for us to move on."

Her probation had not yet ended, but she had been granted permission to move with Sasha. Davis, surprisingly, did not put up a huge fight, wanting only what was best for Sasha. His concern for her and even Alex in the aftermath outweighed most of any contention.

Violet, now being of age, was going with them of her own volition. Yet the intense sessions with her court-appointed psychologist had done nothing to alter her sudden coldness toward Alex. She was disinterested and aloof, perhaps punishing her instead for what Maud had done.

It was late spring as she was drying off Sasha from a bath one night, Violet lingering in the doorway watching them together, when the dam seemed to crack a bit.

"Violet? Do you want to read my bedtime story?" Sasha had requested.

She nodded and sank into the bed, letting Sasha lay against her. Alex sat next to her and reached out slowly, placing her arm around both of them.

Violet turned to her then, eyes welling. She blinked the tears away. It was a glimmer of what was to come. It was enough for Alex.

The bench creaked now as she settled into her seat, turning her attention to the sandwich. She took a bite and proceeded to scrunch her nose. "What the *hell* is in this?"

"Chicken curry and cucumber," Jemma said. "Poppy made it. Please. I beg you, just eat it. She ditched her latest food blog. She's now starting what she calls her 'boho food blog.' I don't even know what that means. All I know is it's keeping her out of trouble and talking to me again. Take another half."

"I'm good," she said, waving her hand away with a smirk.

"Cleo?"

"Sure. Will loves anything with curry."

"Ohhh. Things are heating up with your boy toy cop?"

She raised her eyebrows. "Please don't ever use those three words together again. And yes. But we're taking things one day at a time."

Jemma winked. "I'm sure you are."

Her face seemed to glow.

The workers had finished smoothing out the cement, and one of them propped up a few caution signs as they left the park.

"Maybe you should give them some of your sandwiches, Jemma," Alex joked.

Jemma laughed. "It's funny but it's not. You have no idea the weird food I've had to ingest lately." She patted her midsection. "And Finch has a sensitive stomach. You should see the supply of antacids he has stashed away."

Cleo turned to her. "And when do you and Finch go? Jesus, I feel like you're all leaving me."

She leaned over and squeezed her shoulder. "A few days from now. And I'm not *leaving* leaving, like this one over here."

Alex flicked a piece of crust in her mouth in response and chewed it with satisfaction.

They had received the call two weeks ago.

Jemma had answered it at their weekly lunch. In the middle of showing Poppy's latest food-blog pictures, the phone rang. The three of them stared at it—she had been anticipating a call for months. When she hung up, she looked as though she had been electrocuted.

She told them the news, and they all screamed and hugged each other, crying and laughing. A child was ready to come home to her from Haiti.

"We're on standby until then. I have too much free time. My nesting is getting out of control. You should see the room—Finch thinks it's going to bust any second with all the toys and books I brought out from storage."

"I love it," said Cleo.

"They sent us his picture yesterday."

"His?"

"Yes." Her smile was so wide, it stretched out to them both. Wisps of contentment surrounded them all as this was their fortune. This was what heartache waited on.

# ACKNOWLEDGMENTS

To say having my first book published is a dream come true is an understatement. I am beyond thankful for this chance to have shared this story. And now for all the other immeasurable thank-yous to some wonderful people.

Thank you to my agent, Rachel Beck, for believing in me and being such a steadfast champion over the years. Your advice, wisdom, and kindness have truly changed my life, and I am so grateful to have gained a friend in you along the way.

Thank you to my editor, Alicia Clancy, for taking a chance on this dark story and seeing exactly how to make it even stronger. Your sharp eye, creativity, and insight have been invaluable, and I am forever grateful to you as well as the entire team at Lake Union.

Thank you to the writing community and author friends who have been generous and supportive behind the scenes. A special shout-out to Sara Goodman Confino, who has been the most selfless, genuine, and witty mentor to me.

Thank you to all my friends and family—you have been such incredible cheerleaders on this writing journey of mine. To my sister, Jennifer Grilli. Thank you for being a constant support, an early reader, and a confidante who never let me give up.

To my parents, Jung and Kyung Won. I would not be who I am today without you. Your sacrifice and unconditional love for your daughters is the real story here. Thank you.

To A. J. You have always believed in me. I love you always.

And to my beautiful boys, Preston and Archer. My hope is I've inspired you to never give up on your own dreams someday. You two make up my heart.

# ABOUT THE AUTHOR

*Photo © 2022 Caitlin Bielefeldt*

Ellen Won Steil grew up in Iowa in a Korean American family. She earned her BA in journalism from Drake University and a law degree from William Mitchell College of Law. She lives in Minnesota with her husband and two young sons. She believes most good stories have at least a hint of darkness in them. For more information, visit www.ewsteil.com.